BLOOD ON MY NAME

K. ELLE MORRISON

Copyright

Editing by Caroline Acebo

Proofreading by Norma's Nook Proofreading

Cover Designed by Designs By Charly

Interior page design by Ayden Perry

Kellemorrison.com

DEAR

READERS

This book contains material that would be considered inappropriate for readers under the age of 18.

These materials cover:
Graphic sex between consenting adults. Blood, gore, fear, and mention of death. There's also a touch of manipulation here and there.

This is not a clean and fluffy romance, but there is a happy ending without a cliffhanger. This is a completed novel, but many of the characters appear in the Princes Of Sin series which is now complete.
If you enjoy asshole angels, and demons that make you question everything, then this book is for you! Please leave a review :)

This book is dedicated to anyone who simped
for the morally grey "big bad" in
early 2000s TV shows and movies.

DEDICATION

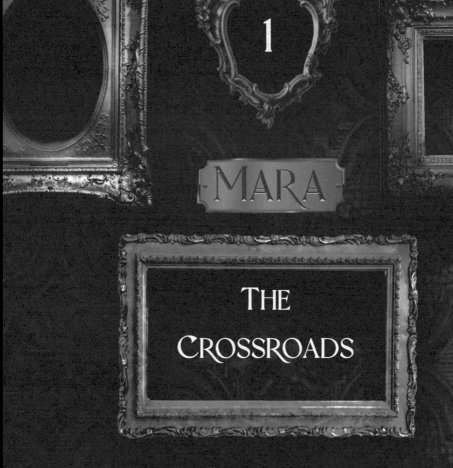

1

MARA

THE CROSSROADS

It was the last-ditch effort for my salvation.

I drove to the outskirts of town and found the old dusty crossroads between two farm fields. I'd been to several closer to the city with no luck… or misfortune.

"Far from home, aren't we?" His voice was filled with smoke.

"Are you going to help me or not?"

He'd been sizing me up for several minutes since he'd appeared. The demon prowled around me one last time, his golden eyes tracing my outline against the night. The only light came from the overhead of my car. I had left the driver's side door wide open for a quick getaway if things went terribly wrong.

Bargaining my soul to a demon wasn't how I'd expected to resolve my issue, but I had nowhere else to turn. Curt would find me and kill

me as slowly as possible. He loved doing that.

The demon's cunning smirk pulled at the mushroom-like skin around his bruised mouth. He dipped his chin into his chest then tilted his eyes to mine again. The pale gray of his skin blurred my vision. It was as if he vibrated in and out of focus as he moved. The mutilated brand at his neck oozed black tar and identified him as Vepar. A duke of Hell. One of dozens from what I had been told by the *bruja* who'd given me the summoning spell.

"I could help you. For a price," he coughed out, his voice hoarse against the dry summer air.

I shifted from one hip to the other. It was the point of no return, and I was at the edge of a cliff.

"Name it." I took in a deep breath and held it as I waited.

"Hmm. Desperate, are we?" he hissed and licked at his gruesome teeth. "Have you gotten yourself into some trouble?"

"I would have to be to come here and summon you, wouldn't I?" I crossed my arms against a sudden wind that kicked up dust from the field behind him.

I squinted and raised an arm to shield myself and was met a moment later with the smell of burning flesh and sulfur. We stood face to horrific face, and the stale breath from his decaying nose crept into my nostrils. He had moved so quickly, inhumanly.

"I love the smell of the foolhardy." He grinned, showing blackened teeth. Foul, hot breath rushed against my cheek.

"One favor for one soul. You get to choose which one," he said into the shell of my ear.

My lungs ached from deprivation. I only dared take small, shallow breaths as my stomach churned at his putrid smell. He took a step back, then another before starting to pace in front of me like a predator trapped in a cage.

"You don't want my soul?" I squinted at him, straining my eyes to keep him in focus.

"Is that what you're offering?" His eagerness tipped the tail of his question.

"That's how this works, isn't it? I ask for a favor, and in return you get my soul?"

"I'm not picky. Any sinner will do as penance for my services." He stopped pacing and faced me, eyes gleaming with anticipation.

He waited for my next move. The next words to fall from my mouth.

"Curt. Walsh," I managed to choke out. "Curt Walsh."

"Curt Walsh," he repeated, bringing two long, dirty fingers to his chin. He tapped against the wiry hair there.

"He's a drug dealer in Los Angeles." I took a step forward but regretted it instantly.

He watched my foot hit the dusty road and answered the bit of bravery with a dark smile.

"Do you owe him money? Humans do love their money."

"Does it matter what I owe him?"

I owed Curt more than money. He wanted me dead after I'd messed up a drug drop a week ago. I'd lost several pounds of his best product when the buyer decided to take his share and not give me Curt's cut. When I'd called to tell him, Curt told me to get his money or the drugs within the day or he'd kill me. That was several days ago, and I didn't want to find out what he had planned for me when he did catch up. I'd been couch surfing and sleeping in my car, trying to stay one step ahead of him, but I was running out of time and places to hide. I might be a coward, but I'd seen him skin men alive for less.

Vepar slinked closer again, hunger in his grin. "If you don't want to discuss what you owe him, then what is it you would like to happen to him? Choose wisely."

"I don't care what you do to him, as long as he forgets I exist and doesn't come looking for me."

"As you wish. And your name, miss?"

"Why do you need my name?"

"How else will I know which name to erase from his memory?"

"Mara."

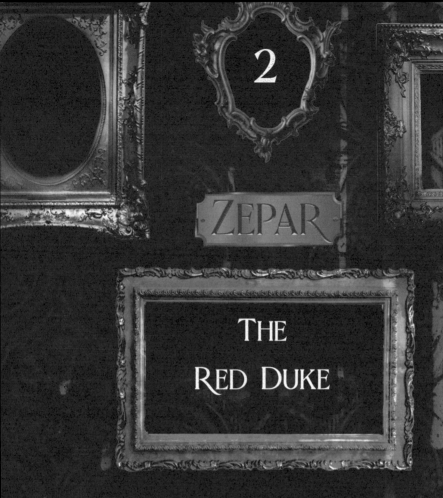

2

ZEPAR

THE RED DUKE

When Vepar returned from being summoned, he sauntered into my office with a shit-eating grin. He'd been called away during our annual progress meeting, and you would have thought he'd won the soul-sucking lottery.

"What did I miss, brother?" He dropped down on the leather couch across from me then propped his feet up on the edge of my desk.

I glanced down at the building expansion contracts I'd been going over before shuffling them and bringing my attention back to my brother. He raked his hands through his long dark hair before gathering up the length and tying it on the crown of his head. A few rebellious locks fell to the sides of his face. With his hair clear of his neck, his tattooed sigil was on full display: the heavy black outline of a round-bellied ship with three crossed masts. The crude sea serpent laid across

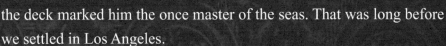

the deck marked him the once master of the seas. That was long before
we settled in Los Angeles.

The brands we received in our creation had denighted with our
descent into Hell. What was once a holy etching into our souls and
skin was now the appellation of the damned. And we wore them with
sullen pride. Most of us, anyway.

Vepar had a similar hairstyle through the centuries, typically longer
than my own, which was one of the few features my twin and I didn't
share.

The cosmic joke of twins who'd never shared a womb. No egg
to split, yet our cheekbones curved the same way, and the angles of
our jaws tapered to a similar point. Though I preferred the clean-
shaven look, Vepar often donned longer, groomed stubble. We hadn't
been mistaken for each other in centuries, but our eyes were a dead
giveaway. Earthen gold. Human women loved to comment on their
unusual glint.

"Focalor stopped the meeting shortly after you left," I said. "Didn't
like the direction the conversations were going."

He scoffed. "Not in her favor… again?"

I couldn't help but chuckle along with him. Focalor had a way of
using our gatherings to find a reason to bring up her plan to take us
home. We'd been roaming the Earth for as long as humans. We had
weaved our way into the lives of humans comfortably, but she wanted
more than anything to return to the Father's promised lands. Being
of the Fallen had never sat right with her. She claimed to be the true
neutral between the dark and the holy, but when the hammer drove us
down, she'd been among us.

Vepar gave a miffed sigh and dropped his head back. "It's all fun and games until she brings Daddy Dearest's wrath down on us for conspiring to move back home."

"Sitri would love that. I think he's tired of the squabbling."

I stretched and shuffled my documents into a neat pile. Maddie, my secretary, would pick them up in the morning and get them delivered to the right places.

"Sitri is a spoiled brat."

I laughed deeply at that. Vepar had never been Prince Sitri's biggest fan, but Sitri was one of Lucifer's favorites and the head of our ranks here on the West Coast.

"You haven't been summoned in ages. Anything interesting?" I asked and leaned back in my chair, also propping my feet up on the desk.

"A human woman looking for an easy out. Cute. They always are. That's how they always find themselves in trouble."

"Let me guess. Trouble with an ex-lover?"

"Good guess, and a sleazy drug lord at that!" he answered with a sly tone. He enjoyed being the bringer of pain to wicked humans. Making deals for the price of a soul for a quick solution to any human problem was an added bonus.

We'd chosen the side of Lucifer and had been cast out of Heaven thousands of years ago for it. Humanity's free will and our Father's favoritism toward the beings He created after us were only catalysts to the war. There had always been a clear line between dark and light. The Fallen who resided on Earth and in Hell would never be allowed to enter Heaven and were monitored by the angels who had been assigned to uphold the laws we were forced to abide by.

Our punishment for choosing to support Lucifer over the Father was to be rejected from His kingdom, but we'd quickly found our place in the fabric of the universe, becoming the tempters of fate and human morality. And those who welcomed us as their solution and salvation became property of the dark and unholy.

By being the hands and tendrils of Lucifer's reach over the influence of the mortal beings, we were the masters of our own immortal lives. Lucifer, King of Hell, watched from his throne and relished in the iniquity we inspired.

As those who dealt in souls of the sinful, we enjoyed our time on Earth. Gambling. Lust. Greed. All the deadly sins ran rampant in the streets and were embodied in every demon who walked them.

"Care for a drink? Thinking of hitting The Red Room. Nice little dive I passed on the way to fulfill my end of that deal."

"I have to be up early. Stockholder meetings." I stood and gathered my things to head out of the office.

"One drink, brother."

"Alright. Just one."

It didn't take much for me to give in. Vepar had a way of finding good trouble, and after Focalor's rant today, I could use some fun.

He smiled and held out his hand, ready for me to take it.

I filed a few contracts in my messenger bag and pulled the strap over my head before giving him a nod.

Snap.

A moment of darkness, the sound of rushing wind, and we were standing in front of a bar entrance illuminated by a red neon sign. The windows were blackened by cheap paint. It wasn't just a dive bar. It was a strip club.

Vepar's hand clapped my shoulder, and a wide grin hung on his face. I shook my head and rolled my eyes at his presumed cleverness.

He gave a knowing nod to the bouncer at the door, who promptly let us cut the line. I glanced down the row of human men who were waiting to get into the club. Several grimaced at our fortune. We moved deeper into the dark main room. The only lights pointed toward the stage that cut down the middle of the open space. Stools lined the raised platform, which we'd bypassed to sit at one of the small round tables with seats coupled to them.

Vepar slunk toward center stage and pulled out two chairs for us. A young topless woman appeared at his side with a tray in her hand. She smiled and bent down low to his ear to speak to him, her voice drowned out by the loud music pumping through the speakers. Her warm, brown eyes followed my movements as I sat next to him.

He turned toward me. "Whiskey?"

I nodded and met her eye to confirm my order. The harsh stage lights reflected off her glitter eyeshadow and gem-studded thong. She winked and spun around to the bar to fetch our drinks. Vepar looked after her as her hips weaved through the men waiting for the next dance set.

"It'll never get old," Vepar said above the noise. "The curves of a woman will always be tantalizing."

I chuckled and hung my bag over my chair and leaned back to get a better angle of the room. The lights dimmed, and two bodies stepped out from behind the curtain: one a woman in a light blue and lace-lined bodysuit, the other a man in a tight pair of shorts that hugged his package and bottom. Both moved down the stage and began whirling their hips to the beat of the base thrumming through the air.

The waitress returned and held out a glass for me to take then passed Vepar his. He downed the liquor in one gulp and watched as the male dancer mounted the pole to spin around with his back arched and his head dangling close to the ground.

The other dancer got to her hands and knees to crawl seductively down the length of the walkway. The front of my slacks tightened, and the whiskey down my throat burned. Both dancers fixed their sights on Vepar and me. They gave each other a quick glance of recognition then headed to the section of stage before us.

Vepar pulled out a stack of cash from the inside pocket of his jacket and placed it on his thigh. Neither dancer missed the action. The strobe lights flashed, and the music beat against my ear drums. I looked at Vepar, who was watching the woman as she slid her hands up her body and tangled her fingers through her hair, all the while bouncing her ass up and down slowly. The male dancer snaked his body over the stage, twisting and undulating to the tempo.

When the music dulled to signal to the dancers that the set was over, Vepar split the stack of money and handed each dancer hundreds of dollars. They smiled politely and mouthed, "Thank you," before heading back down the stage and behind the curtain.

"Care for a private booth, gentleman?" A voice came from behind us.

We turned to the waitress who had reappeared with two more drinks and a broad smile on her face.

"The dancers sent these over." She lowered the tray for us as an offering.

Vepar took the drink nearest him and replaced it with another stack of cash from his pocket.

"Thank you, lovely, but we have to get going. Half of that is for you. Half for the dancers as a rain check." He winked and downed the drink.

I mimicked his action with a slightly larger stack of cash and smirked at him. He scoffed at my hubris. But the waitress thanked us both and walked away with a swish of her hips.

Vepar waited for me as I downed my own drink and stood to grab my bag to leave. I turned toward the door to see a familiar face standing in the shadows of the entryway. One that always brought trouble.

"What's that twat doing here?" Vepar said close to my ear.

I shrugged my response.

Vepar walked toward the exit and stopped in front of Mikael, who opened the door expectantly and gestured for us to join him outside.

When we stepped out onto the walkway, the city-lit night dulled the noise from inside the club, but the base hummed against the windows. Mikael stood regally next to a parking meter. A group of women passed by and giggled to themselves as they looked from him to my brother and me. Mikael gave a smug grin and watched after them.

"What do you want, Mikael?" Vepar spat, unamused by Mikael's prowess with humans.

"I was just checking in. It's been a long time since you've made a personal deal with a human, Vepar. Wasn't sure if you needed reminding of the Soul Armistice?"

"She called upon me, Mikael. Summoned me. Out of the dark." Vepar casually slid his hands in his pockets with an innocent shrug.

"I bet she did," Mikael chortled, looking my twin in the eye and not blinking.

"You're overstepping your bounds, angel," I said, attempting to sound bored of his presence. "I suggest you leave before you get in trouble for breaking curfew."

"Annoyed with me already, Zepar?" Mikael said, turning his attention to me. "Or are you disappointed it wasn't you the girl summoned to save the day? I know how much you love to play the dark hero."

I didn't answer.

Mikael's eyes flicked between me and my brother, sizing us up. Likely deciding whether to push Vepar further in his display of petty manipulation. I glanced at Vepar, who was practically dripping with anticipation of a fight. He hated Mikael, always had. They'd always played off each other's emotions, but since the Fall, any visit from Mikael turned into a pissing contest.

"I suggest you collect on that agreement as soon as possible, Vepar. Or I will do the honors myself and deliver her soul to you personally."

"Is that so?"

"Her request would violate our agreement. You wouldn't want to have to take the long time-out in Hell, would you?"

"How would taking care of one drug leader interfere with the humans' grand design?" Vepar darted back. "You've never cared about humans' spoiled love affairs before. What makes this one so special?"

My brother shifted his weight from the heels of his feet to stand up straighter. Something had struck a chord and piqued his interest. This didn't go unnoticed by Mikael. Not much did when it came to his encounters with demons. He was vulnerable Earthside, especially on his own. I flashed him a dark smile, a small glimpse of a threat to remind him that he wasn't the one in charge down here.

"She offered you what she did not have a right to give. That act alone calls for my intervention," Mikael recited from a rarely enforced rule.

The Soul Armistice had been made to end the Great War between angels and demons but came down to three basic guidelines: The being to make first contact owns the soul. The collection of souls cannot alter the universe or the existence of the human race or this state of reality. And lastly, humans who make deals with demons can only offer their own souls.

This last rule had been blurred for as long as it had been in use. Humans had been offering their first-born children to demons as payment for the means of community survival since the Black Plague and most recently the Spanish flu. This didn't absolve the human who'd come to call of their responsibility. They would still be marked for Hell when their lives came to an end. Their souls would be collected by the demon who had made first contact. We thought of it as a two-for-one deal, a sly loophole that worked in the demon's favor when so little else did.

After all, whoever was willing to sell another soul to demons in place of their own was damned to pay for their wicked deeds.

Whoever Vepar had taken as payment was no more important than a child. Meaning, Mikael's enforcement was more about tugging at Vepar's leash than the deal he had agreed to.

"How is the cleverness of humans a fault worthy of an early collection of her soul?" Vepar prodded further, the pleasure of cornering Mikael playing on his face.

"Theirs is a web we shouldn't weave ourselves into. She does not know who she was getting in bed with." Mikael shifted in his stance defensively. "Surely, you understand the ramifications of your actions if you let this agreement proceed."

"I don't think we do, Mikael," I teased. "Why don't you explain it in great detail. Don't miss a single bit of information."

I crossed my arms, waiting for his next effort to throw us off this intriguing development.

Mikael stood as still as stone. As still as the many statues around the world of him portrayed as one of the great and mighty angels who'd saved mankind from Lucifer and his evil comrades. The angels who'd cast the dragon to Hell, a purgatory to rot in for all eternity. A punishment for all who'd disobeyed the all-powerful Creator. Good and light personified now stood before two dukes of Hell, cowering like a rabbit before two wolves.

I could see the thoughts pass before his eyes, the choices he could make next.

"I suggest you take flight, dear one." Vepar spat venom. "The night is full of terrors, and I'm sure you're late for your bedtime story."

Mikael didn't respond. In one blink, he was gone without a trace of ever being there.

I looked at Vepar, who grinned darkly. He turned, and we fell into step together down the sidewalk. Several steps later, Vepar dissipated into the night. I assumed to fulfill his promise to his newly found tool to get under Mikael's skin. I couldn't help but wonder what Mikael had meant by this human being different, that her circumstance would violate the Soul Armistice.

That damned treaty. When it had come about after the Fall, it was meant to keep both sides in check. To keep some semblance of neutrality for the creatures our Father had loved so dearly.

Dukes and princes along with lower-ranked demons and spirits were given free rein of the human world on the condition that Lucifer himself could not directly manipulate the delicate balance. His power was too great for this plane.

Those of us who lived to collect the souls of humans, including Vepar and me, spent most of our time building empires just to bring them down. Many souls were collected during corporate mergers and the downfall of the rich. Desperate humans were willing to do anything to keep the money they had swindled from the destitute.

You could say that my fellow demons were doing the Lord's work by punishing those who deserved it.

You could say that.

But taking Father's greatest accomplishment and turning them against Him then keeping the souls for ourselves in Hell for all time? That was sweet revenge. A fine, aged wine of spite with notes of petty that could keep a demon content for as long as the human race kept itself alive.

It had been the work of the angels to keep humans on the righteous path, but even they had abandoned their posts as of late, their faith in humanity wavering after thousands of years of war and hatred aimed at each other. Mikael and a few others remained connected to the humans, but their authority only ran so deep. If Mikael was to make good on his threat to force Vepar's hand, whatever his reasons were, he would have to call upon the archangel Raphael, his commander. Mikael would have to be desperate to disturb Raphael over the squabble that had happened here in the streets outside of a strip club. Now it was just a waiting game to see if the human was worth the risk

3

·MARA·

HOME
FOR THE
NIGHT

I didn't wait around to see if Vepar would be back to tell me the deed was done. When he vanished from my sight with only my and Curt's names, I'd taken it as an invitation to leave.

Curt would be at his apartment or at the warehouse at this time of night—just after eight o'clock—and he would be binging on liquor and barking demands to his underlings.

What would Vepar do to him? How would he erase every memory of me like I hoped, or would he merely erase my name from Curt's tongue?

Demons were tricky and unpredictable. The witch who'd sold me the spell box to plant at the crossroads told me to heed her warning: "Vepar is most cunning. He will be eager to make a trade, but be careful what you offer in exchange for a favor. He may just deliver."

I wished she would have warned me about his stench. I don't know if I'll ever be able to not recall the putrid, sour smell of death on his breath. Or the mushroom texture of his rotting skin. A gross inkling crawled up my neck, causing me to shimmy my shoulders to rid myself of the imaginary feeling of his presence.

A chill wrapped around me, and I checked my rearview mirror. He wasn't there. No one was. But still the sinking feeling of eyes on me encouraged me to push the gas pedal closer to the floor.

If Vepar had worked fast, then maybe I could go back to my apartment and finally sleep a full night. If Vepar had upheld his end of the bargain, maybe Curt had put up a fight and ended up bleeding out on the floor. It was what Curt would have done to me. It was what he'd done countless times to others who had angered him or turned against him.

The Los Angeles city lights finally made their way back into my view and lit up the back seat of the car.

Empty.

I took a deep breath through my mouth and dragged an exhale out my nose to calm my nerves. I let myself sink into autopilot as I drove the last few miles back to my apartment. I hadn't been home in days. I knew Curt had people checking to see if I was there. About a block away, I slowed my speed and cased the area. I drove around the entry three times but didn't see anyone familiar. No one waited in a car or on the corner.

I parked my car several buildings away from the front of my own and tried to stay in the shadows as I strode the sidewalk. When I got to the entry gate and punched in my pin to unlock it, I heard a sound behind me. Lighter than a footstep, almost like the sound of a bird's wing against the wind.

I turned to see nothing. Only an empty street, parked cars, and trees lining the walk.

I held my breath and pushed the gate open.

The first step I took inside the courtyard of the complex, I heard a slight crunch under my boot. I lifted my foot and assumed I'd see a snail or dry leaf, but instead it was a necklace. I picked up the silver chain to examine it further. The dangling hammered circle pendant was about as big as my thumb and imprinted with an M. Three small stones were encrusted in the last line of the letter. Next to it, on another small loop, was a coin with what looked like a carving of a boat, or maybe a large-bellied sea dragon with three crosses coming from its back. Overtaking waves and a V were etched onto the hull. It was familiar, but I couldn't place where I had seen it before.

I looked around the courtyard for any sign of who could have dropped it, but it had likely been lying there for hours. I clutched it in my hand until I got into the door of my apartment and turned on all the lights in the small studio. Nothing seemed amiss. If Curt had sent people to my place to watch for me, they hadn't broken in to trash it. A small kindness, considering what he wanted to do to my neck.

I tossed my keys and the necklace into the wooden bowl in my entryway, where they blended in with the loose coins and a package of mints already taking up residence in the catch-all vessel.

I wouldn't have much to eat in the fridge; I hadn't been to a proper grocery store for months. Takeout would have to do. I pulled out my phone and turned it on for the first time in days. Missed calls and texts sprang to life the instant it booted up. Twenty-seven missed calls were from Eric, Curt's brother. He wasn't as deep as I had been in Curt's business. He reaped the rewards and laundered the money through several of his businesses around L.A. Curt split the cut with Eric at a small percentage, but even that was more than I made in a month working odd shifts at the coffee shop.

I took a deep breath and dared to listen to the newest voicemail he had left earlier today.

"Hey, Mara. I don't know if you'll get this. Or if you've gotten the million other messages I've left, but please call me back. I can help you if you let me."

No, he couldn't. His version of helping would be smoking weed with me just to get my mind off his brother or letting me crash with him for a couple days before he realized how much shit he would be in if Curt came knocking and I was there.

"Check your account. I sent you a little something to help get on your feet wherever you are. Just let me know you're okay."

He had left the message hours before I had gone to summon Vepar. If the deal had been fulfilled already, I would have had to guess Eric would have called again to tell me. I couldn't breathe deeply just yet, and I couldn't leave the apartment again until I knew for sure that Curt had been taken care of in whatever way Vepar had seen fit.

I pulled up the pizza menu from the delivery place several miles away. Not my usual place because they knew me there. They knew Curt. The stone of paranoia in my chest was warding me off from doing anything too familiar. Anyone could have been threatened to look out for me, or they could have been convinced I was in some sort of trouble that Curt would have been able to help me through. He had the face of an angel but was a vindictive bastard to anyone who came to know him too well.

After putting in an online order, I went to the bathroom to take a quick shower and change. I had been wearing the same clothing for days, and there was the stale film of filth over my skin. I locked and chained the door and then turned off the lights in the living area. The idea to place a chair under the doorknob of the bathroom door crossed my mind, but the illusion that the place was empty would be enough for anyone who might pass by at this late hour.

4

ZEPAR

LONG AWAITED REUNIONS

With Vepar out doing whatever it was that he felt he needed to do in the middle of the night, I decided to head back to my office in the city, though I would much rather have gone to my home out in Big Bear. The quiet of the mountains reminded me of many places I had lived over the years before they had been touched and tainted by human hands and capitalism. Every beautiful place in every corner of the world had been put in travel magazines for wealthy tourists or on social media.

I couldn't be too critical. Capitalism had lined my pockets and the pits of Hell, as had the millionaires and billionaires who thought that if they collected enough wealth, they'd live longer, more fulfilled lives. But no matter how they created their wealth—through a deal with me or by exploiting their fellow man—they all wound up in Hell.

Universal justice at its finest.

The office was dark when I arrived from a blink through the void. Cleaning staff had long since gone, not knowing I would be returning late. I made my way down the hall from the entryway, flicking on a light or two. I had several items to look over before dragging myself through the void home to sleep, but my thoughts wandered back to Mikael. As Vepar's consecrated keeper, Mikael had been tapped to solve whatever problem the human was before it started. My own containing angel wasn't as unwelcome as Mikael, but a visit from her would further pique my interest in the matter.

It had been a long while since Mikael made such an appearance: out in the open and unguarded by lesser angels. Whatever warning he had been carrying, he didn't want anyone else to know about it just yet. Or perhaps he had been sent by someone higher up in the food chain and hadn't been aware of the can of worms he'd delivered. By the look on his face before running away with his tail between his legs, I would guess his visit wouldn't be the only attempt to persuade Vepar to give up his claim over his new toy.

If it were me, I would be on my way to seal the deal and collect the girl's soul before one of the holy, winged rays of sun could come and sweep her away into the light. But it wasn't me, and I was lucky for it. Divine attention never came without concern from Hell. Not from Lucifer himself. No, he was far too comfortable with his position to give a second glance at an angel like Mikael. Even before the Fall, Mikael had been beneath Lucifer's line of deserved sight. It would be the other dukes in the region or our Prince Sitri who would stick their noses where they didn't belong.

I set down my bag on my desk and crossed to the liquor cart. With any luck, I would get an evening of peace before Vepar brought Heaven and Hell to their knees with the deal he had made with a simple human running from a spoiled love affair.

A gust of wind shook the window behind my office chair, and then a subtle pop of air behind me told me who had come to call. Sooner than I had expected, but a smile spread over my face nonetheless.

"I was wondering when Mikael would bring you into this." I poured another glass of scotch and turned to find the hands of my old friend. "Hello, Hakamiah."

"Zep." Kami took my offering and dipped her chin in greeting.

She ran her long fingers through her raven hair, dragging the length over her shoulder before moving to lounge on the leather sofa.

"It's been a while. Been keeping yourself busy with righteousness?" I perked my brow.

The coy comment brought a slight smile to her lips. "Actually, it's been rather dull since the hellions became more interested in the collection of sinners than finding their way back into His good graces."

"What can I say?" I smiled into my glass. "We enjoy the simpler life."

I strode across the office and sank down in the plush cushion next to her. The force of my larger body caused her to slip down into the frame of my arm and torso. She huffed in amusement and laid her head back onto my shoulder. Calm, peace, and light warmed my skin beneath her touch. A reminder of what the Fallen used to call home.

She took a long pull from her drink and savored it on her tongue before swallowing. She gave a satisfied sigh before taking another sip.

"Tell me about the human?" she asked as if wanting me to tell her a fairytale.

I took a swig from my own glass before answering, "There isn't anything to tell. Vep made a deal with her, and Mikael threw a hissy fit. Then he seems to have called in the cavalry."

I laid my cheek on the top of her head. We hadn't been this close in ages. I wanted her to seep into my every pore, to keep me company in the long decades it would be until I saw her again.

Long before the humans had built the massive cities of Egypt and Greece, she'd held the power to compel and constrain me. A weapon sent by Raphael to keep me in line. I was once seen as a whirlwind of fire. I'd demolished legions of lesser angels when my rage had gotten the better of me. Before my fellow Fallen had banded together to live among the humans and resist the inherent need to be welcomed back into the Kingdom we had been tossed from.

"If that were true, he wouldn't have called me down here. We both know that. What did she trade her soul for? Riches? Did greed get the best of her?" She tilted her head up to meet my eyes.

"No, not greed this time. Some mishap with a lover. She called on Vepar to save her from his wrath."

Kami watched me carefully, waiting for me to reveal the evil Vepar had delivered. "He hasn't made a deal in ages. Why answer her call?"

"Boredom?" I shrugged and emptied my glass. "Why does Vepar do anything?"

"Has he fulfilled his promise already?" She pulled away, taking with her the sense of nostalgia from my skin.

"I believe he has. Why?"

She turned to face me, worry replacing the playful smile that had been there when she first appeared. "This isn't good, Zep. Father is going to be furious."

"If He would like to rectify it, He could." I stood from the couch and crossed back to the liquor cart to fill my glass once more. I turned and offered to fill hers as well, but she silently declined.

"Why would He have so much concern for this agreement? None of Vepar's past trades have elicited so many feathers to ruffle." I perked my brow and waited.

She crossed her arms over her chest, her empty glass clutched in her hand. I cocked my head down to meet her far-off gaze. My fingers witched to touch her. Tuck the black strands of hair from her cheek behind her ear. Hold her face in my hands and bring her into me. But I refrained. She would deny my affection and leave me here with more questions than I had when Mikael had appeared.

"We both know I am not high enough in the chain of command to know why there has been a call of concern. Nonetheless, here I am to interrogate my charge. But it is never a wasted trip. With any luck, the issue will be rectified swiftly and Father will be none the wiser." Back from her worried thoughts, she found my gaze. "Thanks for the drink. You always have the best liquor."

She winked and outstretched her hand to give me the glass.

I took a step closer. "You won't stay for one more? For old time's sake?" I offered the bottle one more time.

She looked me over, letting her eyes wander over the expensive bottle of scotch and up my arm to the cunning grin I couldn't suppress.

I bargained with myself.

If I could get her to have one more drink, she'll stay for a third. If she stays for a third, she'll stay for another hour. If she stays another hour... she'll stay for the night. If only she had one more drink.

A cocky smile lit her face, and she rolled her eyes with a nod. "One more."

The leap of my heart in my chest gave relief to my lungs. For at least one more drink, I had her all to myself. I poured her a generous dose then another for myself before handing it back to her. I sat first, allowing her to make herself comfortable in whatever position suited her. She sat with her back to the arm of the small couch and kicked off the white high heels she had been wearing. Then she propped her feet onto my leg. Her skirt slipped up her thigh to reveal her Heavenly sigil above her knee. I smoothed my thumb around the edges of the geometric angles leading to a cross. There had been many nights when I'd traced those lines with my tongue, back when my outbursts would lead to passion.

When was the last time Mikael had sent her down to wrangle me? One hundred? Two hundred years? I took lovers often, but she would always be a conquest. Each and every time she allowed me close enough.

I watched her bring her glass to her lips and part them to allow the bitter liquor to breach her luscious mouth. I couldn't imagine being jealous of a liquid before this evening.

"You're staring." Her voice did little to shake me from my trance.

I took a deep breath, letting the air slowly pass over my tongue as I replied, "Can you blame me? You are a rare event to behold. A comet. A blood moon. An emblazoned galaxy. I would gaze upon you for hours if you let me."

"Ever more the devilish charmer." She jokingly nudged me with the heel of her bare foot.

I took a deep pull from my drink, set the glass down on the side table, and turned back to catch her eyes trained on my face. The way light danced behind her irises from within, the purity of her being ready to burst forth and drench me in sunbeams and starlight. She took another drink, her eyes not leaving mine. I slid my hand up her calf and raised her ankle to my lips. One short kiss, and a mischievous smile found its way onto her gorgeous features. Another caress of my lips to the side of her calf caused her eyelids to close and her head to fall back. She opened herself up to me as my mouth trekked farther up the length of her leg to her knee.

My tongue etched over her carved hallmark. Her flushed skin awakened at my touch and brought with it an anticipatory intake of breath. Kami's fingers weaved through my hair, pulling me toward her thighs. The folds of her skirt parted for my hand to reach her sex. I pressed the pad of my thumb over her nerves in circles. Her chest rose and fell with each pass of my finger.

"Zepar...," she breathed, her sweet voice full of longing.

I wanted to draw out that pleasure, have her begging for release, but

I wouldn't get what I wanted. I never did with Kami.

She picked herself up and dropped into my lap in one powerful movement. Her hands pulled my head back by my hair, and her teeth latched onto my bottom lip. I groaned at the heat of her over me, the warmth between her thighs now pressing down onto my engorged cock tightly constrained by my slacks.

The sting of her bite only lasted a moment before she released the pressure to glide her tongue over the small bead of blood she'd drawn. A playful grin pulled at her cheek.

"Did you miss me?" She spoke into my open mouth, her lips plump and sweet.

"You have no idea." I wrapped my arms around her waist, pinned her down harder against me. Kissing her fiercely. Starving for every bit of her to dance on my tongue.

I could will myself anywhere in the world and Hell, but she wouldn't be transported with me; I didn't have that kind of power. No demon did. Not to move Heaven incarnate.

I needed more than anything to be deep inside of her. A thirst that was never quenched by the flesh of humans or fellow evil. The question still remained if she would take pity on my black hole of a heart and give me solace in her depths.

Her hips bored down, grinding back and forth against me. I fingered the hem of her dress and pulled it up over her head. Her lips only left mine long enough for the fabric to pass between us. She went for the buttons of my shirt then pulled it down my shoulders and off my arms. Her bare skin was a breath of fresh air against mine. Her breasts were stiff to the chill of the room, brushing the top of my chest as she circled her perfect pussy over me. I could feel her moist excitement when she brushed over my lower stomach, the dusting of hair there wet.

She pulled away breathlessly with determination and need in her bright eyes. I gripped her hips and stood, allowing her body to drift down my torso, and led her to sit before me on the couch. Her hands darted to my belt and unleashed my throbbing cock. She took it in her hands and rolled her eyes up to me and didn't leave my gaze when her lips dropped open to take me. The confines of her tongue and her soft palate brought another groan from my chest. She pulsed her lips over my tip. A teasing I wouldn't be able to handle much longer.

The amusement in her eyes burned brighter than before. Her mouth opened wide and took as much of me as she could, her throat closing around the head of my cock. My hips shuttered and my jaw clenched, a hiss of enjoyment passing through my teeth. She pushed and pulled over me, bringing me closer to climax, but I wasn't ready for it to be over. Not like this. I looked down to see her beautiful mouth full and her fingers massaging her wet clit. The sight sent a shiver down my spine.

I took a step back and sank to my knees before her, and she spread her legs wide for me. I basked in the glory she presented to me, the glistening lips. I watched her face over the curves of her stomach and breasts as my tongue slipped between them and found her clit. Each light flick of my tongue drew a sensual gasp from her chest. A gentle tug of my teeth against the nerves caused her legs to clench and threaten to pull away, but a soft kiss to replace the pain brought her back.

I alternated between broad strokes with my tongue and suction from my lips until her hips began to buck against me. I slipped two fingers inside of her and focused my tongue on her clit until she was writhing and cursing my name. I devoured her until her cunt spasmed around my fingers and her thighs squeezed my temples.

I stood up and she got to her knees and faced the wall, spreading her legs wide for me to enter her from behind. My chest pressed down onto her back, the warmth from her orgasm and the leather still clinging to her skin. I kissed the pink-hued spots on her shoulder blades where it had rubbed her delicate skin while she'd ridden my face to climax moments before.

I fisted my cock and lined up the tip with her center. I guided myself inside slowly, and she whimpered at every inch that filled her. Her hips pulsed back and forth onto me, a tantalizing ebb that had my cock twitching inside of her. I gripped her ample hips, my fingers dimpling her soft curves.

She adjusted her knees to a solid stance to prepare herself for my first full thrust. I held her still and drew my hips back then ricocheted forward, waiting for her reaction. My thighs slapped against her ass, the sound freeing something inside of me. Unleashing the beast that had been locked away for decades. With Kami, I didn't have to hold back. I could deliver each punishing blow of my hips and she would not be torn to shreds by my strength or brutality.

She pushed back, driving me deeper inside of her, then pulled away, a silent invitation to give in to my own desires. I thrust deeper and slower than before, still cautious that she would rescind her consenting motions. Without any protest from her, I drove into her again.

This time, she let out a gasp then a curse. "Fuck, Zep! You feel so good."

A flash of white light burst through me, and I became fully immersed in the moment. I plowed into her cunt relentlessly. Every draw of breath or moan from her throat an encore until she crashed around me once again. Her arms gave out against the back of the couch, and she slumped over the edge and held on to it as her thighs shook.

I wrapped my arm around her waist and brought her down to the floor. I grabbed a throw pillow and placed it under her hips before laying over her. She pulled her legs around my hips as I drove down into her once again. This time, I slid my arms up her back and hooked my hands at the tops of her shoulders. I pulled and thrust. Her thighs tightened and released with my rhythmic movements.

Her fingernails dug into my lower back, encouraging me to fuck her harder and deeper, and I obliged. Her screams of pleasure rang in my ears and around the sparse office. Her celestial voice bounced off the glass panes that separated my office from the reception area. The dull vibration increased as she came closer and closer to another orgasm until it ripped through her and the glass shattered. Shards of glass rained down over my back as I thrusted and filled her until I burst through ecstasy of my own, spilling into her.

I grunted out one last pump with a curse. Kami panted beneath me, struggling to fill her lungs quick enough with fresh air to cool her body. Her skin hummed, and a low, golden glow radiated from her damp pores. I sat back on my heels and propped my hands on the tops of my thighs. The proof of my release slowly seeped out of her pussy in a stream down to the pillow under her hips. A sight that filled me with more lust and fire than anything I had ever seen.

I glanced around at the shattered windows and the scattered slivers of glass that circled us. A satisfied smile brought my attention back to Kami's beautiful face. She scooted her legs up and around me to stretch. I reached over and handed her my shirt to clean herself up with, knowing the remnants of our time together would last a few hours longer once she left.

"That was…" She smiled broadly, a shiver running over her still-bare skin.

"Too short," I finished for her.

"I have somewhere to be, and it seems you need to find someone to replace your windows." She stood and pulled her dress over her head after tossing my shirt to my chest.

I grinned down at the damp fabric then back to the jagged window panes. "I really thought bulletproof glass would hold up better."

She shook her head with a light-as-air laugh and slipped her feet into her heels. I pulled on my briefs and walked over to my drink, which still sat on the side table. It had survived with only a few cracks to the thick crystal walls.

I perked a brow over my shoulder. "Are you sure you can't stay?"

"I probably could. But I shouldn't." Her smile faded into a look of somber regret. A look I had received from her before on similar occasions.

"Right." I downed my drink and set the chipped glass down on the table. "I suppose I'll see you in the next few hundred years?"

"If you're lucky." She threw me a playful wink, but it was stale in mood.

I dipped my chin and gathered the rest of my clothes, turning to find her putting her mussed hair up into a bun only a step away from me. She reached up and held my face in her hands then lifted onto the tips of her toes. She gave me a short kiss to my cheek, one of her more intimate gestures to pacify me through her goodbye.

"Keep Vepar out of trouble, okay?"

I rolled my eyes at the request, both of us knowing that Vepar knew trouble more intimately than any other pastime.

"Goodbye, Kami." I took one last, long gaze into her soft hazel eyes and committed every line of her smile to memory once again.

"Goodbye, Zep. Be good for me."

And she was gone.

The pressure of her body released and dissipated into the void between this plane and all others. The ghost of her ever being here lay in glass shrapnel and in the stain on my dress shirt.

"Always."

5

MARA

OUTLIER

When the delivery guy came by a half hour later, he had said I was their last stop before calling it quits for the night. A pang of anxiety at being memorable shot through me. I locked the door and took several deep breaths after he left, but I decided that if he had someone to tell, he wouldn't have come alone.

After eating my fourth slice of pizza and watching the credits roll on the movie I had been comfort watching, I wiped my hands on my stained sweatpants and tossed the pizza box in the garbage. Then I loaded up another movie on my computer. I wouldn't be able to sleep until I knew if Curt was alive or dead. A rom-com had just started when my phone buzzed next to me on the couch. Eric's name flashed on the screen.

My heart dropped into my stomach as I answered, "Hey, Eric."

"You're alive!" Eric's voice came through the phone, airy and slightly muffled.

I heard the clicking sound of a turn signal and realized he was in his car and had me on speaker.

"Yeah, well, Curt won't be happy to hear it," I said with a roll of my eyes.

"He won't know." His end of the call cracked and faded in and out.

"You should probably stay out of it, Eric."

"Where are you? Do you need a place to stay?" He seemed distracted, his turn signal echoing behind his winded voice once again.

"No. I'll be fine for the night." I sighed, holding on to any remnant of a cool persona I could muster.

"Mara, you don't have to lie to me. I know you've been crashing at Steve and Alisha's place the last couple of nights."

Which meant that Curt likely knew as well.

A bundle of knots formed in my stomach at the thought of what Curt would have done to Steve and Alisha for hiding me. They hardly knew Curt. I had met Alisha while working part-time at the coffee shop, and she'd thought I'd run from Curt because he had hit me. Which wasn't a lie, but I didn't tell her why he thought he had the right to put his hands on me. Steve was her husband and had been kind enough to drive me to my place the first night to grab a couple of things while I figured out my next move.

"When I went by the coffee shop to look for you, Alisha said you hadn't called her back tonight. So where are you?" His tone wasn't harsh or punishing but held annoyance, like he had been driving around for hours trying to find me.

I hadn't called her back after I left this evening to find a crossroads out in the middle of nowhere. Now, I couldn't until I knew for sure Curt wouldn't show up at their house looking for me. It was better that they hadn't heard from me or knew where I could be. It was easier to lie if it was partially truth.

"Did Curt ask you to track me down?" I finally asked the question that I had been biting back since the phone rang.

"Yes. But that's not why I've been looking for you. I'm not going to narc on you. I just want to be sure you're safe. Something's happened. Curt is…" He paused, his voice deeper than before. "Curt's hurt. I know you don't care but he was in a car accident tonight, and he's in the hospital. The doctor said his skull was crushed when he was ejected from the car."

He sniffed. I heard the jam of the gear shift, and the rush of background noise halted on his end.

"I'm sorry, Eric."

I felt for him, but I couldn't say that I was at all upset that my wish had been fulfilled.

I didn't know what to expect from my deal with Vepar, but I had several theories, and many included Curt's death or him developing some rare brain tumor that gave him amnesia. But I guessed a car crash was just as good.

"I'm at the hospital but I'd like to see you afterwards." He sounded tired, already exhausted in his grief.

"Sure. Text me when you're done."

I hung up then glanced at the time. It was well past midnight now, and I was stuck between feeling energized from my relief and guilt for my part in hurting Eric.

Around two o'clock in the morning, Eric's text came through as expected. I told him I was home but held my breath until he showed up alone. Years of Curt's lies and gaslighting had me questioning everything I hadn't seen happen with my own eyes. But Eric was always the more reliable of the two. Aside from his part in Curt's illegal business, he held his own outside the drug game. He stayed clean, and there were many nights when Curt would leave me at a bar alone and I would have to call Eric to come pick me up.

It was one of the many reasons I'd found my own apartment about a year ago: I had been left high and dry by Curt too often. I scraped together rent on an apartment that I couldn't afford with whatever I could manage to keep from odd jobs and part-time shifts at the coffee shop. When Curt went on binges, I'd go through his pockets and hide away any loose change or bills in case he decided to run off to Vegas for the weekend and gamble away every cent.

Having my own place was freeing in a way I had never experienced. I came and went freely, but every responsibility was my own as well. I'd never had the luxury of choosing where my money went. Even if the only accomplishment I had that month was that my rent was paid, it was enough. When I started taking on drops for Curt, he promised to pay me more than his usual runners.

But what he was really doing was setting me up for failure.

I had embarrassed him by moving out. Plus, his underlings often told me I was too good for him and that I deserved the kind of man they claimed to be, which set Curt off.

I was almost positive that the drop I had botched was a setup. The buyer had no intention of paying for the product and had laughed in my face before driving off with the van.

Eric knocked on the door a half hour after he sent the text. The shadowed, heavy bags under his eyes and scruff of his chin mirrored the heavy slump of his shoulders. He sank down on the couch with a sigh and laid his head back against the cushion. Though he and Curt were siblings, they hardly looked alike. Curt was tall and lanky, with a long mop of dirty-blond hair, his skin pale between the tattoos that covered his arms, torso, and legs. Eric spent more time out in the sun and at the gym. He was bulkier and tanner, and his smattering of skin art stopped at his wrists and knees. His sun-bleached hair was teased up, and the sides were closely cropped to his head. He was the more handsome of the two but was terribly shy when it came to women.

I folded a leg under my bottom, my arm propped against the back of the couch for my fingers to linger at the tips of his unruly blond hair. "Are you okay?"

A stupid question, but I was never good in these situations. The right words escaped me the moment someone was beyond any sadness a taco couldn't cure. My mother would have said that she would pray for him, but I had done that already, hadn't I?

Eric turned his face to me and gave a weak smile. "It's really good to see you."

"You too," I somberly returned and twisted a lock of his hair between my fingers.

The guilt that should have been rattling my nerves was absent. Curt was laid up in a hospital somewhere, broken and bloodied, but my chest was coming unclenched as I got used to the idea that he wouldn't be ruling over my every move. I wouldn't have to look around every corner or fear any noise I couldn't explain coming from outside my door.

Eric leaned forward to untie his shoes. "Do you mind if I stay here tonight?"

"Oh…umm. Stay?"

"I mean, it's late and I can barely see straight. I'm so exhausted."

I got up and moved toward my bed, which was tucked away in the corner, to grab him pillows and an extra blanket.

"No, of course you can stay. You've just never stayed the night before." I held the pillow out to him. "Here."

"You don't trust me to sleep in your bed with you?" he teased, the attempted grin falling flat.

"Eric. You're sad and Curt is hurt." I pulled the pillow to my chest and sighed, but more relief escaped without being replaced with grief or remorse.

"Curt…" His voice cracked under the weight of tears springing to his lashes. "He died."

He hung his head. The broken sight of him doubled over was a punch to my gut. Sharp stabs of guilt plunged into my lungs all at once.

Curt was dead because of me.

I had guessed it would be the solution Vepar would have seen fit, but the reality of it coming to fruition…

Abuelita Carmen had warned me. She had handed me that spell and said Vepar was the demon for the job, but what had I really been expecting? Of course he would have killed Curt.

Ice flooded my veins and filled my belly. The earth could open up under my feet and swallow me whole and I would not have been surprised. I had killed Curt. My soul was tarnished and headed to Hell, for sure. It would have been a welcomed reprieve from this moment with tears streaming down Eric's face and my conscience catching up to my actions.

Eric came to stand in front of me and wrapped his arms around my shoulders. His head dipped and nestled into the crook of my neck. His heavy sobs racked his breathing. I pulled the pillow out from between our bodies and brought him closer and patted his back, the only form of consoling I could muster in my shock.

"He was a bastard, but he was my brother. He's gone," he said between choked-back tears.

"I'm so sorry, Eric." My voice should have been filled with sorrow, but it sounded hollow and far away.

"Mara." He pulled away and held me at arm's length. "I really need a friend tonight."

I nodded, and he led me to my bed then waited for me to scoot to the far side before lifting his hoodie over his head and removing his pants. The click of the lamp threw darkness to the corners of my apartment. He came to lie down on his back next to me, staring blankly at the popcorn shadows on the ceiling.

"Are you okay?" His voice was thick with sadness and closer than it had been a moment before.

The mattress shifted, and the sound of my old bed springs squeaked with his body tucking into my side.

"I think we will both be more level-headed in the morning." I turned into the wall and brought my knees up to my aching stomach.

"Can I…hold you?" He placed a hand to the rise of my hip over the covers.

I looked back at him. His face was full of pain and loss, searching mine for comfort.

"Yeah. That's okay."

I shimmied back into the curve of his body. He still had his shirt on and his boxers, but his bare legs tangled through mine, the hair there brushing over my skin like sandpaper. His muscular frame wasn't unfamiliar; we had spent many nights hanging out together at Curt's place. I'd often found myself curled into Eric's side while we watched movies long after Curt had passed out from drinking, but it had never come to lying down in a bed. Now, there wasn't slow breathing from another person in the room to stave off any wandering hands.

Eric nuzzled the hair behind my ear and took a deep breath, and his hips wiggled against me on his exhale. The thick arm at my waist pulled me closer until I felt him getting hard against my ass. I pulled away and turned to face him.

"Eric," I warned.

"I'm sorry, Mara. You just smell so good and I missed you so much. You have no idea what it was like thinking he had hurt you or worse when I couldn't find you at Alisha's." He sat up and looked down at me, his face unreadable in the dark.

"I missed you too. But—"

"Please. Don't finish that sentence." His warm palm met my shoulder. "I just need to feel you next to me. We're both going through so much together; I think you need me too."

I flinched at the kindness in his tone. Even through all his pain, he was trying to be a good friend. I sat up, and he became clearer at the shift of light coming from the closed blinds.

"Curt wasn't always the kindest or most present person," he said, "but he brought you to me. You're one of my best friends."

His fingers caressed my arm, and a flash of goosebumps rose over the spot. Though his affections were screaming more than just friendship, he was one of my only friends in L.A. and likely the only person who'd kept Curt's goons from raiding my apartment while I was on the run.

"Thank you for letting me stay with you. For being here for me. I know it can't be easy." He leaned in and kissed my cheek. His warm lips pulled away but not far.

His eyes hovered near mine, his pupils blown from the blackened room around us. I reached up to the spot and found it damp; both of my cheeks were wet from my tears. I was crying, but I couldn't reach for the feeling they had sprouted from. Curt's death brought me relief for my safety but also the loss of the person who had brought me into my current life. He had been the one to introduce me to so many things I didn't have in Oklahoma. The first for so many things for so many years.

First trip to the beach. First cigarette. The first person I had given my body to.

In a way, I hated him for all the firsts, but without them, I wouldn't have the freedoms I had come to love more than anything. More than the value of his life. More than my sanity and morality.

He had stolen experiences from me as well.

Places that should have held happy memories were scarred with the remnants of late-night fights, bruises, and busted lips: the ice cream stand at the pier where he'd screamed at me in a paranoid rage, or the carousel at the amusement park where he'd thrown up from drinking too many beers then forced me to share a horse with him.

For one kind thought of our time together, Curt had tarnished it tenfold with heartbreak and embarrassment. And now he was dead by an extension of my hand.

The last words he had said to me rang truer than I could have imagined when they had passed his lips: *I'm going to be the death of you. No matter where you run or hide, I will find you.*

His memory still found me in the late hours of the night with the company of a friend.

Eric's lips brushed over mine, and he watched me closely for my response. A small flame licked up in my stomach, thawing the fear that had taken a harsh hold over all other senses. With another pass of his lips over mine, he moved his hand up my arm to the base of my neck. He got to his knees and brought another hand to my chin when I didn't stop him.

I placed my hands over his and held him still. The pump of blood behind my eardrums matched his rapid breathing. He took my bottom lip between his briefly and pulled away to search my face for the answer to his silent question. I didn't move. The thoughts racing through my mind were too knotted to connect feeling to a coherent response. He closed his eyes with his next kiss.

This time, he held my mouth against his, longer and deeper. His tongue darted through my lips and slipped between my teeth. He sucked and tasted at me, no longer waiting for me to reciprocate. But when I finally did, he moaned my name and lay down over me, the awkward angle of our limbs in my small bed doing little to change his mind. I fisted the back of his shirt and held him close, coaxing his excitement. His hands traveled over my thighs and spread my legs so he could settle his hips between them.

"I need you, Mara," he said in a husky voice.

His hard cock ground down onto my pelvis harshly while his hand traveled over my chest then under my shirt. He cupped and flicked my hardened nipple with the pad of his thumb, but when I didn't moan with intense pleasure, he continued the path down over my shorts. The loose fabric parted to one side and gave his fingers access to my pussy. Without warning, he thrust two dry fingers inside and groped in and out without any sort of rhythm.

I gave a squeak, and his mouth finally left mine. He hovered over me with his lips agape with a drowsy, lust-filled look.

"Does that feel good, baby?" he asked as his fingers gouged my labia in rough circles. "You're so wet for me."

When I had imagined sleeping with Eric, I thought he would be sweet and tender. That he would know what he was doing with his hands and tongue. But those hopes were quickly being dashed away as fantasy.

His last girlfriend had gushed over how great he was in bed during double dates, but she was much younger than I was and had craved his validation while eye-fucking Curt when she thought I wasn't looking.

Curt wasn't going to be the best I'd ever have in bed. I didn't know who would ever take that title, but I knew how to get it over with quickly so we could move on with this failed experiment of lust and grief. So, I did what I always did when it came to lackluster sex. I faked it.

"Do you have a condom?" I said in a breathy and eager voice.

He stopped and looked down between us then back to my face, his dumbfounded smile visible in the low light.

"Yeah. Hold on."

He scurried off the bed, took the rest of his clothes off, and dove for his pants to pull out his wallet. He set out three foil packets and ripped the first open then frantically pulled it over his head and down his shaft. When he got back between my legs, I had taken off my shorts but didn't do much else. He would be done within moments, judging by the way he was so desperate to get started, and though I wasn't turned on, I wanted to feel something other than the melancholy burrowing its way through my guts. He was blind to my indifference, like Curt usually was, and why would he bother to notice when he was about to get off?

His cock was lined up with my entrance when he stopped and looked down at me. "Are you sure? I don't want to do this if you're not okay."

He didn't mean it.

He wouldn't have kissed me if he didn't think he could convince me to sleep with him, but he was doing what men did when they thought they had hit the point of no return: checking to see if they had crossed the line between convinced consent and rape.

"I'm fine." I reached up and pulled his mouth to mine.

When he eased inside of me, I gave a whimper. The sound unleashed a round of hard jackhammer poundings from his hips and grunts of pleasure from his chest. The smell of warming latex filled my nostrils with every pump of his hips. I wrapped my arms around his torso under his arms, the sweat from his armpits slick against my skin. With each grunt of my name, he sounded more grateful. The dragging of each syllable through his lips and teeth chorused his thrusts.

The insinuation that he would sleep with me anytime and anywhere had been tossed around playfully for years. Curt had on occasion put Eric in his place when alcohol had made them both too bold, but toward the end of our on-again-off-again relationship, Curt would toss out threats like I was weak like his brother and that I should be with Eric instead. Sometimes, he left me stranded in the middle of nowhere between Mexico and L.A. and told me to call my knight in shining armor for a ride home. He would drive up the road several miles and wait for me to catch up on foot then love bomb me with candy and junk food at the next rest stop.

Eric sat up. The glistening sheen of sweat clung to his forehead, and a bead streamed down the side of his face. He gripped my hips firmly and plowed into me over and over, all sensation lost to the wrinkled condom.

"You like that, don't you?" he grunted. "You love my big, fat cock, don't you."

The bounce of my torso up and down the sheet as he pumped caused my words to shudder just right for his encouragement.

"Oh, that's so good," I lied but screwed my face up just the same. He was getting close, judging by the intensity of his hips.

"Say my name."

"Eric, oh, Eric. Fuck me." I moaned for him.

He cursed out into the room. The echo of his orgasm bounced up to the ceiling then the walls. He collapsed and panted in my ear as he worked his hips to his full completion before rolling over to his back. I reached down into the mess of blankets and sheets to find my shorts, and he pulled off the used condom to tie and dispose of in the bathroom. The moonlight coming from the slits in the blinds set his ass aglow and revealed his dark surf-shorts tan line.

I rolled over onto my side and pulled the blankets up to my chin. When he got back from the bathroom, he slid into the bed next to me. He leaned over and kissed my cheek before draping an arm over my waist again.

"That was so amazing," he whispered.

He gave a sigh of satisfaction, then sleep overtook him.

His steady breathing kept me company for the next few hours as I stared at the wall and waited for the sun to rise in the morning, bringing with it the shame of sleeping with my dead ex's brother and the first day of a new life without being under anyone else's control.

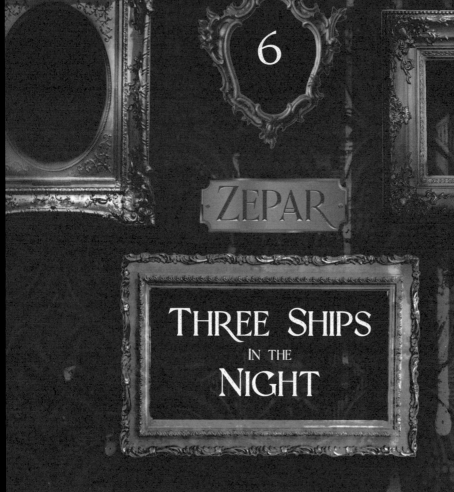

6

ZEPAR

THREE SHIPS IN THE NIGHT

It had been late when I dissipated back to my home just outside of San Bernardino to shower and drown the rest of my night in whiskey. Kami's visit hadn't come without its own concerns. Mikael sending her to me was a show of his hand. He had major concerns for the deal Vepar had made with the human.

Vepar had sent me a text mid-afternoon when the liquor had made its way out of my system and the sun had filled my bedroom. He had been asking around about what had been going on in Heaven that would make Mikael poke around. If there was a gathering of forces that we had been unaware of, that could have triggered an alarm.

What Mikael said was true. Vepar hadn't taken a crossroads deal in many years, but that had more to do with humans than with Vepar. There had been a large movement away from the dark arts

in human witchcraft. Many witches practiced garden and crystal magic, communing with their ancestors or spirits of light. If Lucifer was called upon, others went in his place. Humans never knew the difference. But a good ol' crossroads contract hadn't come through in ages.

Though I had showered when I got home in the wee hours of the morning, I needed to go back to the office soon and didn't need my receptionist to question the smell of booze while the windows were being replaced. I would imagine a story about me throwing a drunken, raging tantrum over a sour deal would be more believable than the truth: an angel's orgasm had shattered them.

I was getting dressed when Vepar pounded on my bedroom door.

"I need your help." Vepar barged in and flung himself across the foot of my bed.

I slipped my feet into my shoes and began tying them without bothering to look at him. The annoyance in his voice told me all I needed to know. Mikael had gotten under his skin. He had a way of burrowing into Vepar's brain and making himself at home until Vepar spiraled.

"What sort of trouble have you gotten into this time?"

I went to my closet and got a tie. *Black or maroon?* I held them up to my neck, comparing them against my black shirt.

"Mikael Golden-Child sent Kami to you last night, didn't he?"

The maroon tie it is.

"How would you know about Kami's visit?" I watched him through the mirror as I knotted my tie.

"You woke half of Hell with your oh-so-subtle encounter," he teased with a wiggle of his brow.

She had been loud, but I hadn't bothered to worry that we'd been heard. I needed to get my office soundproofed.

"What does Kami's visit have to do with you storming into my house in the middle of the day and going on about Mikael?" I moved to my dresser and shuffled through bottles of cologne. I chose one and spritzed it over my chest and arms.

"He is far too invested in this human: Mara. Whatever it is he's up to, I need to be two steps ahead of him. The selfish prat deserves to fall flat for once in a millennium." Vepar was fired up, more than usual when it came to our God-fearing brother.

"What do you intend to do about it then?" I finished readying myself for the day and turned my full attention to where he was now standing with his arms crossed over his chest.

"I have to strike before Mikael gets to her or someone else catches wind of his interest and kills her before we find out why she's important enough to warrant a visit Earthside."

His plan lacked practicality, but he'd threaded the conclusion together with determination and more curiosity than he likely should have. For all he knew, Mikael was causing a stir for fun. To get a rise out of him by making him chase his tail over a human who meant nothing more than another soul for Lucifer's collection.

"What would you do with her once you take her? Hold her captive until she's old, gray, and shriveled? A doll in your house until she dies?" I checked the time before slipping my hands into my pockets. I needed him to wrap this up; I had meetings scheduled for the rest of the day and late into the evening with greedy businessmen on the brink of handing over their company holdings or their souls to keep them afloat.

Vepar paced the floor and ruffled his hair, the wavy locks falling back to his cheeks.

"I don't know, which is why I need you to come with me, brother. Who better to rein me in than my cool and level-headed twin? My shadow." He stopped his relentless pacing and held my shoulders at arm's length.

His shadow.

He hadn't called me that in ages. He was desperate.

I rolled my eyes and slacked my shoulders. "Can't you take Eli? He loves a foolhardy errand with no real direction." I clapped my palm to the base of his neck and pushed him away gently, breaking from his hold.

"Eli, dear twin, would get too carried away. He hasn't been a part of a move against Mikael in so long, he'd take actions too far."

"Alright. Make it quick, and we're bringing her back here." I ran my fingers through my hair, the gel clinging to the ends giving it a slight curl.

Vepar perked a brow. "Why would I bring her here?"

I smirked back. "Your house isn't suitable for a human. Too many endless hallways and pits of hellfire. She would perish before you had the chance to finish this puzzle you're determined Mikael has presented."

"We don't all crave to assimilate so easily to human life, Zep." He glanced around the room and paused on my bed. "She likely would be more comfortable here with your Egyptian cotton sheets and imported sparkling water in the mini fridge."

What he meant to be a dig at my home wasn't far from the truth. Human luxuries and technology never escaped my wonder. The comfort of soft linens or the ease of a remote-controlled coffee pot were small conveniences that weren't available in Hell.

"Slip into your Sunday best, brother dear."

His appearance shifted and took on the gray decay of death and perceived evil. I rolled my eyes and did as he requested. The CEOs of one of the largest corporate law firms in L.A. couldn't be seen kidnapping a young woman from her home, but it would take me hours to get the stench out of my clothes.

We passed through the void and appeared a moment later in front of an older, pale-orange apartment building. Mara had picked up Vepar's parting gift as he'd hoped, a little reminder of him to carry with her. When she put it on, he'd be able to find her no matter where she ran. The poor girl would likely have thrown the token in the ocean if she had known.

The rustle of leaves on the ground and the distant sound of car alarms and police sirens were all that met us. The common space in the middle of the complex was abandoned save for a broken bench and rather sad date palm.

Vepar led the way up a flight of stairs then stopped at a door. He held his hand over the doorknob, sensing he had the right place. He dipped his chin to me in confirmation that Mara was inside. His hand gingerly gripped the knob and turned one way, then the other, persuading the pins in the lock to trigger and the deadbolt to slide over. The door eased open without as much as a creak.

The dark entry room was small, sparse, and well lived in. She had the typical Southern Californian decor: photos of the sunset over the ocean, warm-toned tapestries, seashells and weathered wood from strolling the nearby beaches.

I moved into the middle of the living area while Vepar stalked into the kitchen. The only light was coming from under the bathroom door and the sunlight through the slats of the window blinds. I sat down on the couch and watched Vepar lean against the counter. The shower turned off, and then the curtain rungs were cast aside. There was a soft thud, perhaps a cabinet door closing, then the bathroom door opened, spilling light over the stained carpeted floor. Her eyes widened and her flesh bleached at the sight of me.

Mara's terror-stricken expression quickly turned to that of a mouse trapped in a corner. Her eyes darted around the room looking for an exit and then lit up when she thought she had found one.

Vepar stepped into the strip of light. His voice was callous and deep in this form. "Hello, Mara."

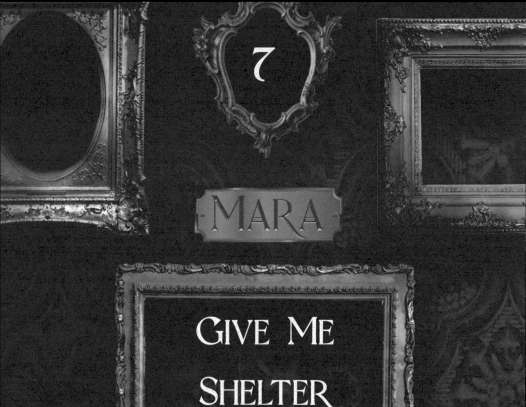

7

· MARA ·

GIVE ME SHELTER

How did two hideous demons get into my apartment so quietly?

I stilled in horror. Their fuzzy edges gave lumps and grooves to their bodies and faces. I looked between them as panic chilled me to the bone.

Run? Scream?

Do something, Mara!

My feet moved before my brain knew which way to run, and blood pounded against my ears. My hands reached out to the doorknob, but solid muscle met my fingers. Vepar's rotten, cold glare rained down on me. The stench of his flesh and black teeth churned my stomach.

"I do love it when they scurry," he said to his companion.

"Quit playing with your prey and let's go. I have a meeting to get to," the other replied.

A meeting? Is that what they would call a possession?

I stepped back, but Vepar towered over me at his full height. He raised his hand and held out the necklace I had found on the ground from his skeletal fingers. The charms dangled and clinked together like bodies from a noose.

"Time to go, little lamb." His wicked breath hit my senses and forced my throat shut.

Pure and utter darkness enclosed me. Silken black wind rushed past my ears as my body and brain scrambled to find which was up and where in space my body was being dropped, flown, or suspended.

Before I could decide, my hands and knees pressed against cool, smooth flooring.

I'd shut my eyes at some point and was having a hard time convincing my eyelids to crack open again.

"Take her to one of the guest rooms on the second floor. I don't care which one."

The deep and sultry voice encouraged me to peel my lids back.

Two tall, well-dressed men stood a few feet away from where I was still hunched on the floor. One was wearing a maroon suit and holding a cell phone. His thumb scrolled and tapped at the screen as he walked out of the room, leaving me and the other man alone. This one was more casual in his dark clothing, but he didn't look like he was off to conquer a corporate merger. One hand slid into his jeans pocket, and the other swung the necklace around his slim fingers.

My mind searched for any logical reason why a demon would transport me somewhere and hand me and the trinket off to another set of strangers.

Little lamb?

"Let's get you settled in upstairs." The man extended a hand to me and gestured out of the room with his chin. At his neck was a tattoo which sealed my suspicions.

"Vepar?" I asked, fumbling over my words as thoughts were sluggishly forming conclusions and words on my tongue.

He winked. "Quick as a whip, you are."

This version of him was jarring. His rot and decay cleaned away to warm brown skin. His bald and patchy head was now full of thick, long, brown hair. The scrawny, gaunt limbs were now swollen with muscle and girth.

I could also see him clearly.

The adjustment gave every feature more definition than any other man I'd ever seen. Where once-smudged edging took residence was a crisp and etched jaw and sharp cheekbones.

"Where are we? Why did you bring me here?" I scrambled back, my common sense finally returning.

He shook his head and tsked. "I will answer all the questions you need on the way upstairs. Come now."

He took a step toward the door the other man had used, turning his back on me. I took the opportunity to get to my feet and turned around, searching for another exit. I found none and turned back to find Vepar gone. I blinked and spun again, searching every corner of the large room. I bolted to the door, catching my fingers on the door frame to round the corner, but Vepar appeared out of thin air in front of me.

I shrieked and jumped back, landing on my ass. "You didn't say anything about kidnapping me during our deal."

"Our agreement had unforeseen repercussions," he mused, once again extending his hand down to me to assist me from the floor. "So, for your own good, I have imposed your relocation for the foreseeable future."

"What are you talking about? Take me home, now!" I got to my feet and balled up my fist, letting adrenaline rush up my spine and through my arm.

My knuckle grazed his smug chin but didn't make a full impact. He laughed as my feet tripped over themselves, and I fell to the ground yet again. I felt a blush bruise my cheeks, and frustration bubbled up in my chest. Embarrassed and vulnerable wasn't how I should have felt after making a deal with a devil. Regret was more comfortable.

I got to my feet again and stood firmly. I screwed up my face and looked him dead in the eye. "Take me home."

His expression shifted from amused to confused then back to amusement, bringing with it a furious heat to the back of my neck.

"No. I don't think I will, and you should thank me for it. The asshole looking for you would make Curt look like a saint." He rolled his eyes at the last words.

What could be so bad that a demon would fear for my safety? Why would it be after me?

It didn't look like I was going to get any answers. Vepar turned on his heel and headed down a dark hallway.

"This way, little lamb," he threw over his shoulder.

I was beginning to hate this pet name he had adopted.

There were no windows in the hallway, and the sconces on the walls were dimmed. It was safe to assume I was in a house of some sort, but where was it located?

Another question to ask when I caught up to Vepar, who had almost disappeared at the end of the long hall. I trotted up behind him and let my eyes wander around at the many paintings on the walls. Some of the frames looked like they were made of real gold, shined and polished to gleam from the minimal light surrounding them.

We walked for several more yards until we reached a large open entryway. To the right was a set of double doors and to the left a wide staircase leading to a second floor. My heart fluttered in my chest as I eyed the brass knobs.

"You'll be wandering the grounds for hours. That is, unless the hellhounds find you first." Vepar stood a few steps above me and grinned. "And they haven't had a good chase for ages."

The pit that had been opening up in my stomach sank about several feet at the thought of being chased and devoured by demonic dogs. Reluctantly, my feet followed Vepar up the stairs to the second-floor landing. He waited for me to join him in the hall before taking a left and escorting me further. There was a row of windows on one side of the hall that looked out onto what he had described as the grounds. It seemed like miles of dark forest that cut jaggedly through the sky above. Where the fuck did they take me?

On the other side of the hall was another wall filled with art. We only passed two other doors before reaching the end of the hall, and Vepar turned to open the door for me. I didn't step inside the room. I was holding on to as much of my sanity as I could.

"Where are my manners?" He leaned in and turned on the light before taking a step back.

I tilted my head and looked deeper into the room. From what I could see, the walls were papered a two-toned gray. The dark furniture was arranged to have a large open space between a reading chair and the large bed. Dungeon chic, if there were such a thing.

"Bland, isn't it?" Vepar mused just behind me. "But it'll do."

His hand flattened to the middle of my spine, encouraging me to move inside. I shot him a fiery glance, and he removed his hand and held it up in a silent cease-fire.

When my feet reluctantly breached the threshold, I got a full view of the interior.

The black and gray theme blanketed the bed, rug, armchair, and linens. The black-stained wood bedframe and headboard contrasted with the almost cozy monotones of everything else.

Vepar stepped in behind me then crossed to the cold fireplace in front of the chair. He moved around a few pieces of wood then waved his hand out in front of the logs, which ignited instantly.

I blinked at him as he stood.

"The bathroom is through that door." He gestured to the door off to the side of the bed. "Knowing my brother, there is an assortment of ungodly expensive flesh-cleaning products in the cabinets."

I remained quiet as he continued his tour.

"The towels are fresh, and there is a chef on staff. He sold his soul to Zepar ages ago to become some kind of celebrity. Whatever that means for someone who overcooks fish. But in exchange for several TV shows and dozens of restaurants around the world, he is at Zepar's every beck and call. Don't hesitate to summon him. Instructions are on the fridge downstairs. You should have no problem summoning someone." He gave a cocky grin.

My stomach was still full with rocks and terror. I wasn't sure I would ever eat again.

"There is a television here above the fireplace; you only need to open the wall." He demonstrated by giving the area above the fireplace a light tap to open a hidden cabinet.

"You said you'd answer my questions." I finally spoke up, my voice sounding hollow and small.

"Right, well, as for where you are, you are now in the guest room at one of my brother's homes in San Bernardino, of all places. I already told you why I brought you here and for how long. I will not be taking you back to that hole-in-the-wall in Los Angeles. Did I miss anything?"

I reached through my racing thoughts to pull out anything more, but nothing formed clearly enough to leave my tongue.

"I have some business to attend to, but I'll be back tonight. It may not feel as such, but you are safe here. In this room. I suggest you stay within it." He slid his hand into his pocket and held out the necklace once again.

His fingers worked the clasp and pulled the two ends apart between his fingers. He held it out in front of him expectantly and jutted his chin toward it.

"You'll want to keep this close to your heart," he said in a tone that suggested it was a gift from him all along.

"Why?" I took a defensive step back and brought my hand to my bare throat.

"If you were to go missing, I would be able to find you as long as you were wearing it," he said matter-of-factly.

"Why would I want you to find me?" I countered.

His dark expression twisted his lips into a menacing smile. "Let's just say that there are places where you would be screaming my name and I would not be able to hear you. No one would."

I hesitated a moment but gave in and stepped into the chain, allowing him to clasp it. He leaned back to admire his handiwork with a content nod. I moved my hair out of the way, and the cool length slipped to rest at the back of my neck, and the charms nestled at the swell of my breasts.

"Haniel would approve of this piece's new mantle." He thumbed the coin then let it fall back to my skin.

"Who's Haniel?"

"Haniel is a fascinating being, if we are being fully honest. One of the first and only true alchemy teachers. But in most recent centuries, he has transitioned to creating enchanted jewelry for…practical purposes," he explained freely and then disappeared before my eyes.

I had to have been dreaming. That was what it was.

I spun around but didn't see him hiding in any of the corners.

I went to the bathroom door and pulled it open, but only the tub and shower met my eye.

Vepar had left me alone and at least a hundred miles away from my apartment. Eric was supposed to stop by after dealing with the release forms and funeral arrangements for Curt. The awkward morning we had shared was brief. He had stayed only long enough to give me a quick peck on the cheek and promised we would talk when he came back. He would find my apartment empty, but for how long?

I flung myself onto the middle of the bed. The mattress was much softer than mine and puffs of air from the duvet jutted out from my weight. I looked around the room, still hoping I was dreaming; this had to be a nightmare. Like the ones I would get for months after moving to L.A. I would be stuck in my parents' house with no money or car to get back home. Trapped in the dusty small town forever.

That's what this was. A new manifestation of my fear. I was so desperate to be rid of Curt that I'd called upon a demon to take care of the situation for me.

I pulled my legs up to my chest and turned onto my side to watch the fire light dance on the headboard. That was when I noticed what looked to be claw marks shallowly dug into it. I reached my fingers out and traced the closest set. The pads of my fingertips dipped into the grooves, and my eyes followed them higher and higher to the top of the wooden fixture. They stopped at the brimmed lip of the thick headboard. The line drew my sight to the bedpost and snagged on a metal ring bolted to it.

My breath caught in my chest. I sat straight up to inspect it. I lifted it and then let it fall with a metallic thud. I looked over to the post on the other side to find this one's twin. I slid to the end of the bed, and at the footboard, as I suspected, there was another set of rings bolted to the side posts.

Whoever had been in this room before me had had either a very good time…or very bad one.

8

·ZEPAR·

PRINCE
OF
PESTILENCE

Vepar took Mara upstairs, and I retreated to my office to retrieve my bag and laptop before heading to the office in L.A. I would deal with her presence later. We were miles from any other residence, and Vepar would likely scare her away from any idea of escape while he went and dealt with Mikael.

I could have taken the Hong Kong call from home; I didn't need to leave in the dead of night to the downtown office. But I didn't want to be witness to Mara's realization she was marked for death. Either by angel or demon, she wasn't going to survive the choice she had made to call upon Vepar. She didn't know the domino effect she had caused, but now that it was in motion, it was too late. By the time Vepar caught up to whomever Mikael had tipped off after speaking with us, there would be several bounties on her head.

Mikael's previously relaxed watch on Vepar's comings and goings had their physical boundaries. Like Kami, Mikael could sense where Vepar was and would be able to find him easily unless the area was warded against angels. Demons, including myself, warded their homes for privacy but higher-ranking angels could easily penetrate the boundaries without an issue. It would be anyone's guess who would find Vepar's new deal worth their time.

I stepped through the void to the office in a matter of seconds. The phone would ring any moment for the merger call and the whining from middle-aged men about the profit-sharing and stocks plummeting would start immediately. I had been working on his deal for almost a year, and it was sure to reap the benefits of close to a thousand souls at the promise for an abundance of profit for the next quarter. Humans were simple. Politics. Power. It all boiled down to money and sex.

The phone rang, and I punched the loudspeaker. Mr. Sheung's greeting came through. He proceeded to rattle off of numbers and projections for the coming week.

This was a going to be a long night.

The sun rose several hours later, the rays spilling onto the floor of my office as about the tenth or twelfth call was ending. Through the merger, I had secured over twelve hundred souls, sneaking the verbiage into the contracts I was having faxed over by my assistant, Maddie.

I stood and stretched. The ache from my too expensive office chair reminded me that I needed to hit the gym before heading home this afternoon. I grabbed a bottle of water from the small fridge next to my filing cabinet when a buzz came over the intercom.

"Sir," Maddie's voice sang, "Mr. S is here to see you."

What does that little shit want?

My finger hovered over the call button on the machine on the corner of my desk. Tension brewed behind my eyes at the thought of hearing Sitri's voice rambling on and on for however long he felt his rant permitted.

"I'm unavailable—" I began, but Sitri had already opened my office door and sauntered past the guest chairs to lounge in my desk chair.

The prince of my own personal hell for the morning.

"Zepar, how good of you to make time for your prince."

He began shuffling through the files I had laid out, already testing my patience.

"What do you need, Sitri?" I took a swig of water from the bottle and waited.

"It would seem there is a rumor going around upstairs that you and Vepar kidnapped a human last night. Care to explain why you took the woman and why Mikael wanted the human's head mounted on a pike?"

He ran his hand through his white-blond hair and leaned further into the cradle of the chair's backrest cushion. I supposed he was handsome to those who didn't have to hear him string together coherent thoughts. The product of nepotism at its finest.

Lucifer had chosen him to rule over us in this part of Earth because Sitri had been one of his most favorite generals in the war following the Fall. Sitri's position allowed him to rule over demons like Vepar and myself. We were just dukes under his feet to kick around when he had ideas on how to tempt more humans into abandoning their path to Heaven.

The Prince of Lust—the grand title he had been given upon the Fall—usually sat at his throne, barking orders at lesser demons at The

Deacon, a posh nightclub in Hollywood where only the most exclusive celebrities mingled with his own legion of demons. The deals he made there were credits to his success as a ruler, but most of the souls collected at The Deacon were a product of blackmail or secrets he procured from its patrons.

"Vepar has found an attraction to her. Nothing more." I slid a hand in my pocket, a show of boredom and to hide my white lie. "Mikael is creating issues where there aren't any. He has nothing better to do."

"Is that so?" he challenged with a narrowing of his eyes.

Vepar was attracted to Mara, but not in the physical sense. Her utility had intrigued him into action the moment Mikael had warned him to stay away. Unfortunately for Mara, that was enough for Vepar to stake his claim over her human life.

"Mikael is merely stoking the fires to rile you up. A practice he has mastered, as it would seem." I lifted my brow to him, mocking his authority.

I didn't have to make time for him, but he would have gone to Lucifer if I hadn't taken this meeting. Claiming my disobedience would have been enough to get Lucifer's attention, and it would have been a toss-up if Lucifer would call next. His interest could be piqued enough to elicit his involvement.

Until Vepar could find the reason Mikael was so interested in Mara, it would be best to not involve our fearsome leader. If he felt his time had been wasted, he could revoke my and Vepar's privileges to walk this plane and assign us back to Hell for a few centuries to teach us a lesson on time management.

"I would like to see why Vepar is putting his freedom on the line by pursuing this human for myself. Tonight. Bring her to The Deacon. Eleven o'clock." Sitri stood, rounded my desk, and met me in the middle of the room.

"I don't think that is for the best. She's still getting used to being Vepar's new pet. Wouldn't want his new plaything to run off or cause any commotion among other humans, now would we?" I countered, but he returned with a laugh.

"Then I suppose I will have to stop by your home this evening. I'll be having dinner with Lucifer before heading to the club. I'm sure he will want to hear all about Vepar's new obsession and how you're keeping her locked up in your house."

He was calling my bluff with his own, and the deck was stacked against me.

"We'll see you at eleven o'clock." I sighed.

"Perfect. Don't be late, and don't overdress." He patted my lapel and was out the door.

9

· MARA ·

SAY MY NAME

I had fallen asleep hours after Vepar had left me in his brother's house unattended. The thought of running out the door and over the driveway as fast as I could crossed my mind hundreds of times. But I was barefoot and had no clue where I was or how far the nearest human would be. I had gotten the courage to leave my room once, but a death rattling howl climbed up the hall from the direction of the stairs.

Vepar had said he would be back later, but I wasn't taking much comfort in his promise. The last one he had made caused a bigger problem than my original one. I hadn't heard anyone else in the house, including the owner. My quick glimpse of them before they'd left for their meeting had been fleeting. The only detail I could remember was that they had dark hair and they were much too busy to worry about a

stranger being dropped in the middle of their living room.

The sun had risen, and the light filled my room with its orange glow. The glinting reflections off the metal restraints on the bed frame renewed the dull panic that had taken up residence in my chest. My pulse started to race as my feet hit the cool floor. I needed to try. I needed to run. I had spent too many years of my life scared to fail or feeling stuck, though leaving my parents' house had been much less worrisome than trying to outrun a pack of hellhounds.

Before the fear could freeze my nerves, I was pulling open the door to my room and stepping out into the hall. The line of windows faced a tree-lined driveway, and there was no sign of prowling demon creatures ready to rip my throat out.

I bolted to the top of the stairs then bounded down two at a time, my heavy footsteps be damned. The front door came into sight, and without pause, I skidded across the slick floor and reached out for the doorknob. My body came to a crashing halt when I plowed into a mass of muscle in a designer suit.

"I wouldn't do that if I were you." A tall, handsome man looked down at me, his golden-brown irises aglow in the sunlight. Or maybe that was what demon eyes did when they sensed fear?

My eyes darted around him to the door, and every instinct was screaming for me to run. I moved around him, and he didn't try to stop me.

"They can smell your bravery." He turned and watched me as I made my next choice. "I wouldn't be surprised if they were waiting a few yards away. They do love a good chase."

An amused smile spread across his face.

I looked down to my hand on the knob then back to him. His dark, wavy hair was slicked back loosely. A thin lock dropped down the side of his sculpted face that was familiar, but I wasn't sure why. I'd never met a man so gorgeous before. He brought his thumb up to his chin and roughed at the shadow of a beard. I swallowed against the dry knot in my throat and tightened my grip on my only way out.

His eyes flicked down to my wrist then to my face once more. He didn't move toward me, didn't look angry that I was trying to escape. In fact, he almost looked surprised. Impressed that I would look into the faces of two demons and go against their warnings.

My heart stopped as I made the final decision. It was now or never. He wasn't going to stop me. I tensed my fingers to twist when his voice met my ear again.

"Are you hungry?"

I blinked and looked to see his back to me as he began walking down the hall where Vepar had indicated the kitchen had been.

Was he serious?

The sound of cabinets opening and closing then liquid being poured told me he was. I glanced down to my hand once more, waiting for my previous gusto to return from being shocked by the offer of food instead of a forceful escort to my room. I cursed myself for even thinking of following a demon into his kitchen. I didn't know whether to blame curiosity or fear of what was lurking outside for my foolishness, but it didn't matter. I was already trailing behind him.

When the dark hallway opened up into the large kitchen, I had to squint. The black, polished countertops and forest-green cabinets set the steel appliances in shocking contrast. Dark-stained wood beams framed the white-washed ceiling, and the tall windows brought in the late-morning light to warm the whole space.

Whoever decorated the house had used the natural lighting to carry the elegance of simplicity, and they had done it with ease. Every item in his kitchen seemed to have a purpose and a place where it belonged. My gaze traveled over the deep-set sink, the large iron stove, then more countertops, until my sight snagged on the crisp white shirt of the stranger. His jacket hung discarded on the back of a stool at the island.

He turned around holding a small glass mug. "Do you drink coffee?"

I nodded and took the small cup in my hands. A foam leaf design peered up at me. I brought the rim to my lips and took a sip. The hot latte tasted bitter and sweet, and hazelnut undertones washed over my tongue when I swallowed.

"I'm starving," he said, going to the fridge and looking inside. "Eggs?"

"Wh-what?" I stumbled over the question into my drink, splashing foam over my top lip.

He pulled out a carton and held them up for me to confirm that they were, in fact, eggs. "Do you want eggs? I typically take them sunny-side up, but if you prefer them scrambled?"

"Sunny-side up is fine." I wiped the mess from around my mouth on my wrist.

He pulled out a pan from under the counter and placed it on the stove and lit the flame beneath it. He twisted around, spatula in hand, and pointed to me. "The bread is in that cupboard. Toaster is over there."

I set my coffee down and rounded the large island that sat in the middle of the kitchen and pressed my back to it as I passed him. After setting a couple slices of bread into the toaster, I sat down at the stool and cradled my cup again to watch a demon cook me breakfast.

From behind, I couldn't see his hands at work, but the motions of his arms moved his torso, and the muscles under his shirt shifted with the slight shuffling of his spatula in the frying pan. Lines of a simple black tattoo peeked through his rolled cuff with each twist of his wrists but didn't give way to the image fully. There was a crack of fresh pepper then salt and splash of water to steam the egg under a lid.

He reached up after a few minutes and grabbed two porcelain plates and placed two slices of toast on each. Clicking off the stove knobs then taking up both plates in his hands, he walked around the island and set my plate down in front of me, then his own. He went to the fridge one last time and took out a bottle of hot chili sauce and a sliced avocado.

"Here." He handed me a butter knife and finally sat down next to me.

I took the plate of sliced avocado and scooped up a couple slices to lay over my egg-topped toast. Wordlessly, I took a bite. Warm yolk leaked over the crust of my bread and dripped onto the toast below it. He hadn't reinvented brunch, but it had been so long since someone cooked for me.

I glanced over to see him bite into his, and a dribble of rich orange trailed down the corner of his lips to his chin. He dabbed it away with a napkin and continued. A dull buzz from his phone in his pocket pulled him away from his third or fourth bite, and he sighed with indignation. His thumbs thudded against the screen and then he set it down next to his plate.

He sat up and stretched then looked at me. "I will have to take a call in a few minutes, but afterward, I'll give you the full tour. That is, unless you've built up your courage again to face the dogs?"

He winked and crammed another bite of food into his mouth.

"I'm sorry, but what is your name?" I braved.

"My name?" He looked bemused at my question, making me feel small for waiting until he had fed me to ask at all.

"Or…what should I call you?"

He smirked. The pull of his wickedly handsome lips to his cheeks had my stomach in new knots that tightened further as his dark eyes pinned me to my chair.

"I could think of many appropriate things you could call me." He gave me his full attention. "So many names suit me when they're strung together by moans and gasps."

I blushed from head to toe, suddenly aware at how quickly and deeply I was breathing.

"I-I just thought it would be polite to ask." The words thudded out.

"And what is it you would do with my name?" he volleyed. "You'd be hard pressed to find a demon so willing to give a perfect stranger their name. They can be quite dangerous on the wrong lips."

I didn't know what to say to that. Abuelita Carmen had said that knowing Vepar by name would work in my favor when I called upon him, but he didn't seem to give me a second glance when I'd used it to summon him.

"I wanted to be respectful and address you by your name," I explained, but the social etiquette was now lost on me and subsequently him.

"Names are one of the most important monikers we carry, Mara. For a demon, our names hold power. We don't give that sort of domination over so willingly." He sat back and allowed the back of the stool to hold his weight.

But he knew my name.

And Vepar had asked for my name. For Curt's. Would that mean anything now that Curt was dead?

"You don't have—" I started, but his phone buzzed and rang next to him.

He answered it, speaking Italian to the caller, and picked up his plate to take with him to some unknown fortress for foreign business to be handled discreetly.

I sheepishly nudged the corner of my toast. I should have asked Carmen about what would happen after a demon answered my call when she'd offered me that spell.

The demon stopped in the archway leading out of the kitchen and turned back to me.

"Zepar," he said, his phone pressed into his chest to muffle it.

"Zepar?" I repeated.

His lips parted in a foxy grin. "My name. For when you need it later."

"Why would I need it later?" I asked, my brows knitting together.

He winked, brought the phone to his ear once again, and left me with a fresh burst of butterflies in my stomach.

10

ZEPAR

A CASUAL HAUNTING

My business associate in Milan quickly rattled off the soul count in a recent merger they conducted then reminded me of the trip I would be taking there in a few weeks. The itinerary had been emailed last week and the tickets bought to keep up appearances. I'd much rather dissipate than travel over twenty-four hours for three days, but I had to keep a low profile in Europe. L.A. was crawling with evil monsters, most of them selfish humans who didn't take their eyes away from their phones long enough to notice a speeding bus barreling toward them in the street. But in France, England, and especially Italy, there were those who were still aware that demons roamed among them. And they had found ways to trap, banish, and even eliminate us entirely.

Preparing Mara for The Deacon was next on my schedule for the

day. I called Vepar, who answered within three rings.

"Is she driving you crazy?" His amused voice came through the line.

"I've only just fed her breakfast. She is surprisingly content in her new confines." I glanced at my office door as if she would be standing in the doorway.

"I'll be by in a bit to drop off some things to make her more comfortable. Eli has no idea why Mikael would be interested in her but said to ask Leo. I'm on my way to their house now."

Leo would know nothing about the titters from angels. Eli was sending Vepar on a wild-goose chase. I'd have to talk to Eli later, but for now, Vepar chasing his own tail would keep him out of trouble.

"Sitri came to the office this morning. He wants to see Mara tonight at The Deacon. Eleven o'clock."

Vepar gave a heavy sigh of frustration. "Fuck. I should have taken her to Godiel. He could have concealed her a little longer."

"He would have come with his own can of worms," I reminded him.

Godiel could have used his magic to hide Mara away, but not for long. The Emperor of the West, Cabariel, would have been the first he would tell. Although Cabariel was a shut-in on his tiny island in Puget Sound out in Washington, he would come out of hiding for a good scandal. The last time he had been disturbed from his solitude, a cult was erected in Yelm, Washington, in his honor.

I sat at my desk and flicked at the remaining corner of my toast on my plate. My thoughts drifted to Mara, who lingered somewhere in my house. I hadn't given her any directions or any idea about what to expect while staying here, but I could already feel the tension in my neck from the storm of questions she was going to rain down on me.

"Who told Sitri about Mara? Maybe I need to remind them of where their loyalties should lie."

Vepar was becoming annoyed and stupid.

"We'll worry about that later. Right now, you should finish your errands and come prepare Mara for her first outing under your ownership." He had a responsibility to the human he'd kidnapped. No matter the reasons, he had to take ownership and show the others that she belonged to him.

"That isn't what's happening. You know I don't take humans as companions."

"Too late, brother. You've already done so, and if you want that story to be spun so you don't lose her, you're going to have to be the domineering, cutthroat bastard to keep her."

"Humans are exhausting," he said before hanging up.

I chuckled and pocketed my phone then picked up my plate to take back to the kitchen.

Mara wasn't there, not that I expected her to be. I deposited my scraps in the trash and laid the plate in the sink before heading out to track her down. It didn't take long. She was sitting in the downstairs lounge, her feet tucked up close and her arms wrapped around her knees.

Her eyes snapped to me as I approached, but she didn't flinch when I sat on the cushion next to her. I draped my arm over the back of the couch and turned to face her fully, opening myself up to her. I wasn't here to hurt her, but she didn't know that. To her, Vepar and I were the big, bad wolves. She wasn't wrong, but she wasn't the prey we typically fed upon. Though the thought of her skin on my tongue didn't sound like a curse.

"Would you like a tour before or after you ask your questions?" I asked, and her shoulders tensed for a moment.

She relaxed a bit and took a deep breath. "Are you going to kill me?"

"Hmm. No. I don't believe I will." Her eyes bulged at my response. "Killing humans is messy and brings too much unwanted attention."

"Are you going to hurt me?" She tightened her hold on her limbs.

I gave her a cocky smile and wet my lips. "Do you want me to?"

Nothing like sexual tension to alleviate the threat of pain and sorrow. She pulled her lips between her teeth, but her cheeks pulled at the corners of her mouth pleasantly before she caught herself.

"Why did Vepar say I was safer here than at home? Safe from whom?" She was opening up, letting go of one of her knees and leaning toward me to hear the answer.

"When you summoned Vepar at the crossroads, he held up his end of the bargain. He took care of your problem in exchange for two names. Unfortunately for you, that act placed a mark on your soul and branded you as his property."

Vepar hadn't told her these conditions; any normal summoning wouldn't have needed any further contact between them until it was the end of her life and he had come to collect her soul.

Mikael's interest had changed those circumstances.

"He is still tracking down why the angels are so interested in you and the deal you made, but one thing I can guarantee is that you have their attention for the wrong reasons."

I had no reason to lie or withhold this information from her. I didn't know much else, but she would be more complacent in her situation if she knew that our intentions weren't malicious.

"Angels want to hurt me?"

"Angels likely want to kill you."

She pulled her bottom lip back into her teeth and held it there tightly, the flesh bleaching at the pressure. After several moments of thought on my answer, she took a deep breath and spoke again.

"Why would two demons want to protect me?"

"One." I held up a finger. "One demon wants to protect you, albeit for his own reasons. And I want to protect my brother from doing anything foolish that would backfire onto me and the rest of us living among the human race."

"Then why let him bring me here?"

"Vepar's home resides in Purgatory. It's a pit of desperate and lost souls, the walls lined with weapons he's saved through the ages and lovely beasts he collects each one more terrible and deadly than the last. You wouldn't be comfortable there."

She shivered, the imagery creeping down her spine like the slimy snakes that roamed Vepar's home. I took a look around my sitting room. Francisco Goya, William Waterhouse, and Asensio Julià canvases were mounted to the walls. Lesser-known works, but each artist had gladly accepted mountains of money for them in exchange for their artistic souls.

"Our tastes in home decor are very different."

She let her gaze wander about. A small sign of relief was evident in the relaxing wrinkles of her forehead. She wasn't tensing her shoulders as much, and her breathing had steadied.

I stood and offered her my hand. "Vepar will be back in a little while with items to make your stay here more comfortable. Until then, I'll show you around a bit."

She stared down at my palm and then rolled her sight up to meet mine, her big, brown eyes a conflict of what to do next. The thoughts practically spelled themselves out across her vision like a news broadcast. She blinked, making up her mind, and placed her hand in mine.

A bit surprised that she'd made the choice so quickly, I braced her as she pulled herself off the couch to her bare feet.

"You've already seen the kitchen. The chef's summons is on the fridge. He's rather mouthy but has a devilish way with food." I winked and moved to the entrance of the foyer, Mara at my heels.

"Upstairs to the left is my wing. I'd prefer you only enter if invited." I looked her up and down and lifted my brow. "And freshly showered."

Her face screwed up into a scowl, but she didn't say a word as we moved up the staircase.

"Your quarters are to the right. It is warded against all things that go bump in the night." I led her up to the third floor, which held the library and entertainment rooms.

"The theater room is right there." I pointed to a soundproof door then swung to the left. "The game room is there." Another shift to the left to a set of double doors. "And that is the library. There is an espresso machine and coffee bar in there as well, but I would ask that you take your mug to the kitchen when you are finished."

I turned to Mara, whose mouth was slightly open as she gaped at the third-floor accommodations. Vepar wasn't wrong when he said I had the taste of most humans. I enjoyed the luxuries that came with power and wealth.

"What's behind that door?" She pointed to the red door just beyond the theater.

The edge of my mouth perked up. She eyed me uneasily, likely expecting the room to be filled with horrors. And to some, perhaps it was, but for others it would be a treasure trove of pleasure and adventure.

I moved toward the door and placed my hand on the knob. It clicked under my touch and unlocked.

"I reserve this room for those who give themselves over to me fully. Soul, mind, and body."

Her eyes widened to saucers. I tensed my grip and waited for her to back away, or for the scream she had been holding in since the moment her eyes caught sight of Vepar and me in her apartment last night to erupt from her throat. But she stood her ground and watched me carefully.

"Would you like to see?" I gave her one last attempt to turn her curiosity off before plunging her into the darker aspects of residing in a demon's home.

She swallowed hard and nodded. I opened the door and stepped aside to give her access to the place where I fulfilled my darkest urges.

The room had a large bed bolted to the middle of the floor. Four posts adorned with restraints were what she saw first. A sex swing was tucked in the corner, an impulse buy, if I was being honest. The walls were lined with a variety of pain- and pleasure-play implements.

"The bed in my room." Her fingers reached for the closest bedpost.

I answered the question she was too timid to ask: "It has been used for more casual affairs."

"Casual?" Her eyes snapped to mine, and a renewed surge of curiosity bubbled behind them.

"Not everyone has a taste for what I could provide in this room." I moved to a cabinet and opened the door to reveal more pleasure toys. "Not everyone wants to be driven to the brink of pain and pleasure to experience how truly breathtaking life can be."

Mara considered the room, a blush of something that looked like a mix of panic and depravity lingering on her face, but I could feel the slight tremor of excitement. Her pulse quickened, igniting her pheromones. An intoxicating collision of feelings and senses pulsated off her golden-brown skin.

She turned her back to me, and I took a few steps closer to her. "The experience can be both punishingly painful and exquisitely erotic. But it isn't for everyone."

She took a step back, hitting my chest. The tension of her every muscle that brushed against me stoked the flames at the back of her neck. Goosebumps dashed across her skin as she turned her head and looked up to me.

"I think I'm ready to go back to my room." Her voice was as light as air—or lack thereof.

"Lead the way, Mara."

I couldn't help but curse the timid nature of humans and their reluctance to ask for what they wanted in the moment and not care about the social protocols that had been so ingrained in their societies.

82 | BLOOD ON MY NAME

She turned into me, a hand to my bare forearm as she left the room. The small pressure of her fingers to my skin dug through me and fed a dimmed flame.

The evening with Kami had scratched an itch but had really only provoked the beast that lay dormant for years. Lovemaking with Kami had always been like that. Every encounter had been farther from the last. Every time she came to call was memorable down to the smell of her hair, but she was gone like a puff of smoke—and just as fast.

Like a meal at a fine-dining restaurant, the smaller portions were more divine than you could imagine but left you starving and craving something else hours later. I could feast on Mara. Have her begging for me to allow her to come. Drive her to the very edge of a climax and deny her the ecstasy until she was speaking in tongues. But not today. Not tonight when I had to help prepare her for Sitri and The Deacon.

11

·MARA·

CRUSHED
BENEATH
THE HEEL

Of course the mild-mannered demon holding me hostage had a *Fifty Shades of Grey*-style sex dungeon. I should have known the avocado toast was a facade. He followed me out of the room of his wildest desires and into the hallway. He took the lead as we made our way back toward the stairs and to my room.

"Have you always lived in California?" Zepar asked from over his shoulder, the small talk catching me off guard.

I shook it off. "No. I'm from Oklahoma; my parents have a farm there. I've only lived here a few years."

He paused and I caught up with him. He considered my answer a moment but didn't say a word. The way his eyes trailed over me felt as if he were looking for something deeper, but he wouldn't find it. He wasn't the first to ask how I'd ended up in L.A. from the Southwest.

I never blended in with the locals, and I wasn't as fond of the sun as they were. But I loved the ocean and being able to escape into the waves when my mind needed a break from Curt or being stuck in dead-end jobs that would never make me comfortable.

"What brought you here?" He slid his hands into his pockets.

"Curt. We met in an online forum and he promised me the world. But I didn't need much encouragement to pick up and leave." I was well aware I was oversharing, but he was looking at me with all his attention, and something inside of me wanted to keep it as long as I could.

"He was good for something then."

I shrugged. Curt was abusive, careless, and a scam artist. I would have found my way out of that dusty town one way or another, and I wasn't going to give Curt's memory any sort of gratitude.

Zepar stood quietly, taking me in.

Several questions came to me, but one finally found its way to the tip of my tongue.

"How long have you been here?"

A wide smile overtook his curious expression. "You are very bold for someone who wasn't raised in Los Angeles."

"You've answered all my questions thus far. You don't seem shy about any of this. May as well ask while I'm still alive."

"No one is going to kill you, Mara." His features darkened. "You have my word."

I swallowed hard. That wasn't the response I had been expecting. The severity in his tone hollowed out my stomach. He turned and put out his hand, an indication for me to keep walking. When my feet started moving, he took up pace right behind me.

"My fellow Fallen and I have roamed Earth for thousands of years. But I was granted a portion of California's territory about a hundred years ago. I built my company knowing that desperate humans would do anything to hold on to their money during bouts of war and the Great Depression."

We reached the stairway, and he followed me downstairs to the second floor, where my room was.

"My brothers and I have done well for ourselves, as you can see," he continued. "Offering humans short-term solutions for what they see as life-or-death problems is lucrative in the form of currency and the soul count."

"Did Vepar collect my soul?" I blurted out.

I hadn't felt any different since making the deal, but I hadn't felt much of anything since hearing that Curt had died as a result of my wish.

Zepar stepped in front of me, both our feet coming to a halt. "He has taken ownership of your soul." He touched the necklace at my throat. "But no, your soul is still intact until your life comes to an end. Then you will become another strike on his tally."

I looked down at the charm hanging from my neck. The weight seared into my chest where it sat.

"Will he be able to take me back home after he finds out why an angel cares about our deal?" I didn't want to know the answer to my question, but it came tumbling out nonetheless.

"I'll let you ask him yourself." He stepped out of my view, and waiting outside my bedroom door was Vepar, his hands full of bags and boxes.

"Perfect timing, brother," Vepar said to Zepar. Then he stood back for the door to be opened.

Vepar looked down to me as I approached, then to the pile of garments he held in his arms. "My dear little lamb, I have gifts for your favor," he said in a mocking tone.

I squinted my eyes at him, and Zepar ushered us both through the door of my room. The curtains had been opened, I wasn't sure by who, but the light from the tall window welcomed us inside.

Vepar went to the bed, laid out all he had been carrying, then began opening bags and boxes to arrange the items into outfits.

Zepar pressed his hand to my lower back to pass me then sat in the chair near the fireplace. He watched his brother rifle through the dresses and accessories for a moment before huffing his growing boredom.

"You don't have to stay if you're going to be impatient." Vepar didn't raise his eyes from his work.

"I think it would be in Mara's best interests if I stay so you don't dress her as Sitri's evening meal," Zepar replied, bringing his ankle over his knee.

"Who is Sitri?" I asked to the room, not caring at all who answered.

"Prince Sitri is a stubborn pox who can't allow anyone to have their own toys," Vepar answered, holding up an almost translucent dress with a pair of black heels.

"That dress is exactly why I stayed," Zepar said, questioning his brother's taste. "Please tell me you've brought something that at least covers her ass."

"Sitri is coming here? For me?" I turned to face Zepar fully. "You said I was safe here."

"Unfortunately, bureaucracy doesn't end with humans. Sitri needs to see that you are a run-of-the-mill human and that Vepar has formed a bit of an attachment to you. Nothing more."

His answer didn't bring me comfort.

"What if I don't want to see him?" I threatened.

"Little lamb, no one wants to see him. Our wrists are tied on this matter, but you will look the part of my new favorite plaything and he will be none the wiser."

Vepar held up a black dress. The long slits up the sides would meet my hips. The deep V plunged dangerously close to my pelvis but stopped at the only solid portion of the dress which may have been the only thing keeping it together.

"Come now, darling. Give us a show." Zepar's voice brought my eyes to where he sat, a playful grin on his dark features.

"I'm not going to undress in front of you!"

"The bathroom is right through there." Zepar wet his lips and lifted his chin toward the door behind Vepar.

Vepar held up the dress on its hook, letting it drape down and pool on the floor. In his other hand he held the shoes, black matte with cherry-red bottoms and gorgeous, if I was being honest. I snatched them out of his hand as I passed by and caught a hungry look in his eyes as I slammed the bathroom door behind me. Out of habit, I locked it but knew it was likely useless. They were able to take me from my locked apartment. A flimsy lock on a bathroom door would do nothing.

I dressed quickly and looked in the mirror. The curves of my waist and hips filled the dress out, but the top felt a bit loose, and the length was a black puddle at my feet. I slipped on the shoes, and they helped a little, but unless I could maneuver myself so that the slits up the thighs parted just right, I would trip easily.

When I opened the door with my arm over my chest to hold the dress in place, Zepar's jaw tensed. His brows darkened his eyes, and he wet his lips.

"No," Vepar blurted, "that won't work, will it?"

The wolfish expression on Zepar's face vanished.

Vepar turned back to the bed and grabbed another dress to hold out to me. "The shoes will be fine but we don't have time to fix the dress."

"I-I'm sorry." I didn't know why I said it. I had no reason to be polite or apologetic to two demons who'd kidnapped me then insisted I be paraded in front of more demons.

Vepar took my chin between his thumb and forefinger. He lifted my eyes away from Zepar, who still held a look somewhere between murderous and predatory.

"Don't ever apologize to one of our kind. It shows weakness, and from this day forward, you have none." His pupils dilated, a storm of severity affronting my vision.

I swallowed down another set of shameful words, and in their place I nodded my understanding.

He released my face gently then laid the new dress on my arm. "Good girl."

His breathy tone sent a heat up my spine, and I couldn't get away fast enough. I turned back to the bathroom and caught a glimpse of Zepar scrubbing his hand over the scruff on his jaw. The dangerous expression was gone, but the ghost of a thought still clung to his brow.

I retreated behind the closed bathroom door and changed into the next dress, a cocktail style with another plunging neckline. At the back there was a curtain of sheer, glistening black fabric that trailed down to my heels.

There came a knock on the door and a call from Vepar after I had been fussing with the hem for longer than he liked. When I opened it, he took a step back to admire his keen eye for women's fashion. He nodded and looked me up and down before calling over his shoulder to Zepar.

Zepar stood and slipped his hands into his pockets while waiting for me to step into the light of the room. The shawl of the dress licked at the backs of my calves as I walked. He turned his head to one side then the other before twirling his finger, encouraging me to do a spin for him. I rolled my eyes but did as he silently requested.

They both seemed satisfied with the living doll they'd created, giving each other a nod of approval before Zepar returned to the chair near the fireplace.

"Sitri isn't coming here," Zepar said, marking the look of confusion on my face. "We will be going to him. He is expecting us at his nightclub tonight, and he will likely be flanked by several of our kin to determine whether you are worth stealing away from Vepar."

I shot a look to Vepar, who was putting the rest of the clothing in a closet. "And I would stand to bet that he will make a grand show of it," he tossed out from inside the hollow room.

He came back out empty-handed and stood next to me in the middle of the room. "Don't worry your darling brain, little lamb. He will be disinterested the moment you open your gorgeous lips."

"I…" I was halted by the mix of insult and compliment. Was I really that offended that some demon prince wouldn't be interested in taking me from my current kidnappers?

No. If being a doe-eyed dimwit meant I'd be left alone after whatever mess Vepar had caused was cleaned up, then so be it. I looked at Zepar, whose shoulders were quaking in silent laughter.

"Best to not open your mouth at all, actually." Vepar winked to finish his slew of insults.

I blushed, the sudden rush of vulnerability of my situation catching up to me now that the little fashion show was over.

"Am I supposed to stay dressed like this until we leave?" I looked down at the outfit then back up between them both.

Zepar shrugged his shoulders coyly. "Would it be so terrible if you did?"

"If you need me to walk anywhere, I'll at least need more comfortable shoes." I kicked off the heels and tossed them onto the bed.

Standing in only the dress felt incomplete and out of place. I turned to Vepar and crossed my arms, waiting for his next witty retaliation.

It was his turn to roll his eyes. He held out a brown shopping bag on a long finger.

"Here." He didn't sound annoyed, more disappointed that I wasn't fawning over the fine cocktail dress.

When my hand entered the handle loops, he let it fall to my palm and proceeded to walk toward the bedroom door.

"I have one last errand to run, and I'll be back for dinner." He addressed us both but then finished his statement to Zepar. "Beef Wellington?"

"I'll be sure to pass along the request." Zepar chuckled back, remaining in the room after Vepar left.

For a demon who wanted to keep a watchful eye on me, he was gone more often than not.

I looked down into the bag to see a new pair of jeans, a wooly sweater, and a white T-shirt. It was fairly heavy, so I assumed there was a pair of shoes at the bottom. I set it down on the bed and looked over to Zepar, my arms barricading my chest out of instinct.

"Your parents." He adjusted in his seat but did not look at all like he was ready to stand and leave. "You said they have a farm in Oklahoma?"

I blinked at the question, and an icy sensation flooded my veins. Would my family be in danger too?

"Yes. Well. My father does. My mom passed away last year from ovarian cancer. Why do you ask?" My heart pounded in my ears while I waited for him to respond.

Moments ticked by as he watched me silently, surveying something I couldn't see.

"And they were both human?"

"As far as I know. My grandparents didn't breathe fire or smell like boiled eggs," I countered, placing my hands on my hips.

He smiled at that. I wasn't sure where he was coming from. Would being some type of mix of human and demon make me appealing to angels?

"I had a theory, but if you are sure your family is only human, then the reason for Mikael's attention isn't about your blood."

"The archangel?" I asked, recalling Sunday school tales of Michael being God's right-hand man.

"No, darling. That is the all-precious and pretentious Michael."

He quirked a smile and emphasized the slight differences in the pronunciations. "Originality with names wasn't Father's strongest attribute, if you haven't realized by my and my twin brother's names."

"What was your theory, then?" I asked, not sure I wanted his smile to fade, but it did as my question ended.

"A very long time ago, a group of angels descended upon the Earth and human women. The Grigori, as we called them, spread their seed at every reach of the world, producing giants among humans. Many women died attempting to give birth to the Nephilim."

Sometime between his sultry voice dipping into a storytelling tone and his explanation, I had sat on the edge of my bed and tucked a pillow onto my lap.

"Many of Nephilim claimed to be of our Father's grace themselves, holding power over communities and taking up positions as the heads of states until the Great Flood washed most of them out of history."

"You thought I could have been part Nephilim?" I clarified.

"There is something about you. But that isn't it."

He considered me for a moment, looking into my skin to see something lurking beneath. My cheeks heated as his pupils swept from my feet to the top of my head then met my gaze. The stillness of his frame being washed over by sunlight from the window was like staring at a living painting. Too beautiful to be real. Too fragile to touch. His existence in this room was both terrifying and peaceful.

"What is it then?" I wasn't sure my timid voice would travel across the distance to meet his ears, but he parted his lips to answer.

"We shall find out soon, won't we?" He didn't break the hold his eyes had on mine.

All the breath in my lungs turned stale and my stomach dropped as he stood, towering over me. I swallowed hard at the eruption of butterflies in my stomach as his fingers brushed over my cheek. He leaned down to bring his face closer to mine. The deep and unholy abyss of his pupils shrank his honey-brown irises to thin threads. His palm cushioned my face, and his fingers fanned out against the base of my head. A slight pressure from his wrist persuaded my chin up, leaving my throat open to him.

"Please don't hurt me." The words came out subconsciously and sounded more like a question than a plea for mercy. An instinctual defense that my present senses disassociated from the moment his eyes locked on mine.

"I assure you, I will not bring you pain until you are begging for it. And even then, I would deny you until you were on the cusp of madness without it just to witness the gratitude wash over your body at the impact."

My heart skipped a beat. Blood froze in my veins. The deep tone of his promise sent me plunging into cosmic ice. My mind had no quick remarks to volley back. His words had stunned my tongue beyond forming language. My thoughts drifted back to the room with his many whips, paddles, and ropes. I'd be out of my mind to allow a demon to tie me up and torture me for his own pleasure. But the heady smell of his cologne and the way his eyes seemed to glow as he looked down through my soul were causing me to flirt with the idea of insanity.

I cleared my throat and backed away, and he didn't protest. In fact, he looked pleased by the action. A cocky grin perked the tips of his lips and produced a set of dimples in his cheeks. How had I not noticed them before?

"I'll leave you to dress. My office is downstairs beyond the kitchen if you need anything. I have a guest on—"

"Zepar!" A furious feminine voice snaked up through the house, chasing away the dimples from Zepar's face.

"Ah. They've arrived." He slipped his hands into his pockets and tilted his head toward the open door. "Coming, sister dear."

I looked between him and the hallway, hoping his sister's anger wouldn't find its way up here. An angry demon who sounded as if she could rip my throat out with a cut of her tongue was terrifying.

"You look beautiful, but I believe there is one more dress that would suit the occasion much better. In the closet." He pointed toward the closed door, taking my gaze with him.

The startling feel of full lips to the arch of my cheek caused me to gasp, but he was gone as quickly as his skin had left mine. My fingertips shot to the spot and held the sensation as long as they could, but it cooled from my senses. A shiver ran down my spine followed by liquid fire.

Voices somewhere deep in the house traveled through my bedroom door. The murmurs drew me closer, but the slamming of a door hurled me back. I closed and locked the door quickly, knowing full well that the lock wouldn't have given me a moment more of time to run or hide. Shaking off the fear, I went to the closet and pulled out the last garment bag.

12

ZEPAR

BRING ME PEACE

The sound of Mara's distant surprise momentarily diverted my attention from Focalor's pacing. It was not an unfamiliar sight. Focalor often brought her frustrations about our brothers and sisters to me.

"Mikael warns Vepar to stay away from the human, and your first reaction is to accompany him to kidnap her? What were you thinking?" She threw her arms in the air, wide gestures of anger and disbelief as she scolded me.

"And what's worse, you told Sitri! The arrogant dung beetle is going to demand you hand her over to him. Never mind what he would do to her, but Mikael is going to be furious and every angel is going to have a vendetta against us all."

She slowed her pacing, but her eyes darted about, her rapid thoughts veering in her mind's eye. I had the suspicion that I didn't have to

be present for the conversation she'd come to have. I had no defense that would cool her anger or ease her worries. Sitri would request we relinquish Mara to him, and he would throw a fit if we refused. But at the moment, I wasn't sure if Mara would be safer with Sitri or with us. Without knowing exactly why Mikael thought she was special, there was no telling the consequences of either option.

"I couldn't let him go alone. He wasn't going to rest until he found out why Mikael was so interested in Mara. What was I to do then, sister?"

She rested her hands on her hips and took a deep breath. Not wanting to admit defeat, she remained quiet. I rounded the corner of my desk and placed a hand on her lean shoulder.

"Who has been speaking through these grapevines that you've been so preoccupied with?" I narrowed my eyes to her. The news had been spreading faster than I had expected, and that was growing tiresome.

"Mikael himself told me. The curse of being the last of the Fallen he can still trust," she admitted.

I thought on that a moment. Mikael reaching out to Focalor for information was more to induct her into the situation rather than him thinking she actually had any knowledge of Vepar's intentions. The web he was weaving was getting denser by the hour, it would seem.

"Focalor. I saw Kami the night before we extracted Mara," I confessed. The slight heat of shame rose up my neck when she looked at me with surprise in her cool blue eyes.

"Hakamiah came to you?" Her breathy words of confirmation didn't need a reply.

"Several times, actually." I smiled wolfishly.

Focalor scowled then gave me a look of disgust. Then she turned and plopped down on the couch. She tossed her long blonde hair over her shoulder.

"This is bad, Zep." She leaned forward and framed her face in her hands. "What is it about Mara that has everyone so flighty?"

Her words fell to the floor below.

I couldn't find the answers yet. There was something about Mara that I wanted to explore more. The calm stillness within her soul was deep and crystalline. A infinite pool in the clearest ocean. Unexplored and unexploited by human grime. She wasn't without wrong or sin. Mara was far from clean or saintly, but beyond her mortal ways, there was a siren's call to me. Enticing me to look into her depths and find the meaning to every mystery that had ever plagued me.

"Mikael is going to come for her. He has requested the help from Raphael." Worry weighed heavily on her face when she looked up to see my reaction to her warning.

"Let them come," I answered.

Shock stained her cheeks. "Rattling that cage will bring wrath raining down onto all of us. Not just you and Vepar."

She stood before me. A head shorter than I was, she still held more power than I did. Her coveted angelic powers were cloaked in her demonic soul. She hadn't Fallen like the rest of us. She had been cast out for remaining neutral all those centuries ago. When the battle had been at its bloodiest, she'd soothed the wounds of both sides. Allied with anyone who'd wanted to see the war end.

Focalor, the peacemaker.

I took another contemplating breath, and our eyes locked. Her pleading stare waited for me to bend to her will and call for the mercy she desperately wanted. She'd always believed that the Fallen would be welcomed back into the Seven Kingdoms.

Vepar appeared in the doorway of my office, back sooner than I had anticipated him to be, a cheeky grin on his face. Focalor's saturnine demeanor weighed on her shoulders as she rolled her eyes at him as he dropped down onto the couch.

"I hope your trollop is worth risking us all being condemned for a few centuries," she snapped, crossing her arms over her chest.

"Jealous that I'd choose a human as a bedmate over you, Focalor?" If he pushed too much further, she would put him in his place. But this was a dance they took anytime they were put in a room together.

"Festering swine," she mumbled beneath her breath.

Vepar cocked his head to her with a devious glint in his eye. Focalor had favored Vepar many years ago, but Hell hath no fury like a woman passed over for lesser beings.

"Is my little lamb ready for dinner?" Vepar addressed me, but he did not take his eyes off Focalor, prodding her for retaliation.

"Once she smells food from the kitchen, I imagine she'll be down." I took up my phone and sent a message to my chef.

The cranky bastard would huff and curse the entire time, but when you sold your soul for three Michelin stars, you were summoned on a whim.

"Will you stay for dinner, Focalor?" I asked.

She looked over at Vepar. "No, I'd rather not be further implicated in whatever malfeasance the two of you are concocting."

She walked toward the doorway but turned to me one last time. "Please consider others with your next moves. Vepar has made his choices clear, but you can still pry yourself from the speeding train before it crashes."

"Always with the dramatics, Focalor." Vepar threw his arms up, obviously done with the amount of discourse he had brought on himself. "There is nothing disastrous about this human. Mikael has been itching for a confrontation for half a millennium and has found one to hold on to. You can meet her for yourself and see there is nothing to fear."

"I don't wish to meet her," Focalor rebuked.

"If you are going to come here and try to turn my twin brother against me, then you will be confronted with the reason." Vepar dissipated from the cushion, and footsteps upstairs came quickly after a screech of surprise.

Focalor took a step back into the office, her face steely with frustration. She shifted on her heels. I half expected her to dissipate from the house before Vepar could make it downstairs with Mara, but Focalor stayed glued in place. Curiosity seemed to be getting the best of her.

Vepar swooped into the room with Mara at his heels, his hand firmly clamped on her upper arm. She had changed into her casual jeans and T-shirt but was still barefoot. Terror-stricken, she tossed glances to Vepar, Focalor, then me.

"Mara, this brooding viper is Focalor," Vepar proclaimed and released Mara, causing her to stumble toward Focalor. "She would have me throw you to the hounds to be rid of the inconvenience of your existence."

Focalor stepped back several paces as if she were avoiding sludge on the street. Offended at the comment but not enough to hide her discontent, Mara got back to her feet and wrapped her arms around herself.

"You see—" Vepar's voice dropped, vengeful pride seeping into his tone as he defended his own honor. "—there is nothing dangerous about her. She is nothing but human. No divine creature hidden away in the skin of a martyr as His son was. Not a drop of Nephilim blood to be had. May Raphael or any other of the highest order of angels try and pass down their judgments upon her head. She would be tossed to Hell for mortal sins regardless."

His cold words had Mara cowering and tossing her gaze between the two. I took a short step toward her before stopping myself. This wasn't my fight. Focalor needed to see that Vepar was the one calling the shots and that I was merely supporting him.

"Then why take her plea? Why kidnap her from her bed and bring her here to be hidden from Mikael?" Focalor protested, her eyes passing over Mara for a third time, trying desperately to see what would make the angels and our demon prince so interested.

"Spite!" Vepar countered. "The opportunity to creep beneath Mikael's skin and rot his wits was too great to pass up. For whatever reason, he has chosen to take favor on this human, which was enough to perk my interest. For too long has he had me on a short leash, and the chance to snap his wrist presented itself in my deal with Mara."

Mara's eyes volleyed between Vepar and Focalor as they spoke about her. She was the unknowing pawn of the children of Heaven and Hell. The fear in her eyes became overwhelming, and a gloss of panic passed over her. She shot a glance to the door behind Vepar once. Twice. She took one step before I reached out and placed my hand on her shoulder. Her face snapped to me, and I gave her a subtle squeeze then stepped closer to shield her from the argument unfolding.

"He will punish you—"

"And I will be smiling through every lashing." Vepar cut Focalor off in a sharpened low timbre. "Knowing that for one moment Mikael was not the one to prevail. The golden child ripped from his stature for a blink of his existence is worth the continued damnation."

Focalor's jaw fell, and her brow knitted at Vepar's confession.

"No amount of bootlicking will bring you back into His good graces, Focalor. You sit upon a notion that you have risen above us, but you have lived amongst dogs for thousands of years. If you have not earned your wings and adornment back by now, you never will, and I pity your reluctance to accept that."

He had cut her deep. Anger and a wounded expression flushed her face. It had been her campaign to bring Heaven and Hell back together for as long as I could remember. She had been the common ground. She had always held her faith that our Father would someday welcome us back with open arms and a place in His kingdom. But there had been no trace of Him to be found within the last several hundred years.

Focalor's face contorted with her rage, the light behind her eyes brightening as the well of unearthly power filled her small frame and readied to deliver a blast of unholy energy.

Vepar gave her a mocking, twisted grin.

"You're cruel and blinded by your own selfishness to see the effect your foolishness has caused," she replied, the air in the room electrifying as she spoke.

I turned to face Mara, bringing her into my chest, and waited for Focalor to retaliate. From behind me, I could feel Vepar wielding his own abilities to build a shield. The palpable presence of it filled the room and thickened the already agitated oxygen.

"Do your worst, Focalor. Because you will not want to bear the consequences if you don't kill me. I will not give you the same mercy of walking away," Vepar warned, but it was a bluff on both of their parts.

Mara brought her arms up to her chest, allowing me to fully conceal her. A punishing blow of heat and a flash of light lit the room behind me, followed by a curse from Vepar. Focalor hadn't smote him in decades, but he'd never earned it so heavily as he just had.

The room dimmed again, and a thud sounded behind me. I turned my head to check the room was still intact only to see Vepar gripping his chest and splayed out on the floor. Focalor was nowhere to be seen.

When I turned back to Mara, I opened my mouth to speak, but the look of gratitude in her eyes dried my mouth instantly. The brown and green flecks of her irises danced as she looked over my face. My sight dropped to her pouty lips, and a stitch to my chest screamed at me to take one between my teeth and devour her whole. She pulled away from my hold and looked beyond me, bringing me out of the moment with her.

Vepar groaned in pain and held his hand to his singed shirt, dark blood seeping into the halo of charred fabric. I got to my brother's side and bent low to assess the damage. The torn flesh began sewing itself back together and slowing the bleeding. He would heal in a matter of hours, but the first stone to his glass house had been thrown, and it would be followed by boulders once Focalor decided who she was going to run to. The list of possible angels or demons that would come knocking next was miles long, but I had an idea of who to talk into being on our side.

I extended my hand to Vepar and hoisted him to his feet. He let out another grunt of pain and coughed against the impact of the unholy power Focalor had hit him with. He'd likely crushed a few ribs and was lucky to not rely on his mortal form to survive.

"I think it's time to start gathering contingencies."

Vepar rolled his eyes and stretched his arms over his head, releasing tension. "There will be no living with him after I call upon him."

"Better than not living on this plane at all, wouldn't you agree?"

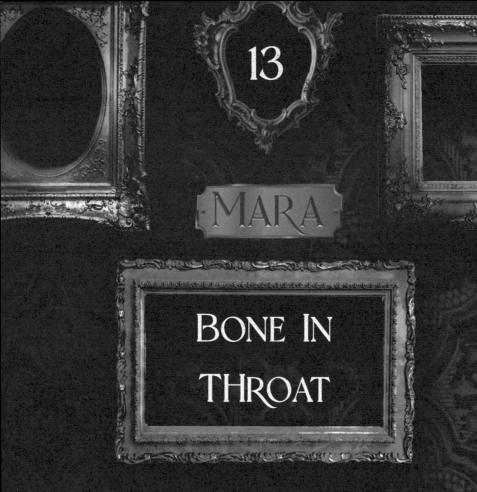

13

MARA

BONE IN THROAT

My hands were still shaking from the argument between Vepar and Focalor. I hadn't been sure if she was an angel or demon when Vepar brought me downstairs, but the blast she'd inflicted on Vepar had sizzled through the room. Behind the fear of being hit myself, the radiation of her power had sucked all hope from my body. It felt like I had been plunged into a deep abyss within myself and I'd never be able to claw my way back out. I had clung to Zepar, but something in the way he looked at me caused my skin to crawl, and it felt like something inside of me was trying to tear through my flesh to escape him.

That would be the natural reaction, wouldn't it?

I shouldn't feel comforted or protected by a demon. Especially not one whom I hadn't given a soul to so there was no reason for him to

harbor me from danger within or outside the walls of his home.

After he had helped Vepar to his feet, they spoke in whispers before Vepar vanished once again. I began to wonder why he bothered coming back at all if he left every few minutes.

Zepar looked back to me from the doorway, but his gaze didn't linger. "I'm going to go check that the chef has everything he needs. Dinner will be ready soon. Then I have someone I'd like for you to meet before we head to The Deacon to see Sitri."

"The Deacon? You're kidding, right?"

"If only I were. The pestilential river snake owns the club and building."

Only the most glamorous and wealthy were welcome at The Deacon. I'd been to a few clubs around it, and there was never a line to enter, but it was known that if you didn't have a direct invitation, you were not getting in.

Zepar's silhouette had disappeared before I could choke out my concerns and insecurities on not being ready or feeling presentable. I trailed my way back upstairs but didn't go to my room. Zepar had said that I was welcome to wander and use his amenities, but I hadn't dared to think about actually doing so.

When I ventured into the game room, I dragged my fingers over the line of movies, games, and consoles arranged near the overtly massive television screen. I moved into the library next, where the walls of shelves were lined with books by popular authors I'd heard of and many more older volumes by unknown names. Some looked as if they would crumble at my touch, their dingy yellow pages worn and sticking out every which way, and many sticky notes flagged passages by whoever had read them.

At the end of the row of aged tomes was a small, pristine Bible. The black leather and tissue thin paper were like any I had seen at the town church when I was growing up. I pulled it from its spot to see it was less cared for than its shelf mates. Pages were dog-eared, ink and highlighter fluid marred passages, and thick black blockings bled through several leaves. I thumbed through a section and found some pages to be torn or missing.

I placed it back in its previous resting place and looked through the titles neighboring it. They were all religious texts from all over the world. Some in other languages and some so old that the titles were barely legible. Just gold flecks where the letters had been worn to dust. Searching for the sturdiest, I pulled one that seemed to be written in Latin. The brown, fibrous sheets were stiff to my touch. Zepar, or someone else, had made notes on slips of paper and stuck them within the chapters. Some notes looked to be translations of passages, while others were comments on the author's interpretation of the text.

Being around for the events written about and watching from the opposite side of the righteous gave the commenter a unique perspective, but the notes weren't overly critical or vicious. Some corrected who had been present or added the actual location to clarify vague textual references to "the East."

The sound of clanging pots and pans brought my nose up from the text. My mind wandered down to the kitchen and the only other human around for miles. Closing and returning the book, I headed to the kitchen on quick bare feet. Maybe the chef could help me leave or get a message to the police. Zepar had said the chef had been indebted to serve him, but that didn't mean he wouldn't be able to help liberate me.

I jogged into the kitchen, and my jaw flopped open at the sight. One of the most famous chefs in the world was cursing every pan and utensil he was using. His starched blond hair and crisp white chef's coat gave the illusion that he was performing on one of the many shows he starred in.

"Blasted demon nutter! He always forgets to refill the bloody salt!" he spouted to the empty kitchen.

The smell of seared meat and sautéed vegetables wafted from the stove behind him. A large bowl of mixed salad greens was teetering on the edge of the counter, and his head was popping in and out of cupboards, searching for the assumed missing salt. I cleared my throat, and he lifted his head to meet the sound.

"You there. Where has the bloody devil hidden the damned salt?"

"There?" My voice cracked at being put on the spot.

I pointed to the cabinet off to the side of the stove Zepar had been rummaging through while making eggs and toast earlier. The chef turned around and pulled the salt grinder from the shelf and gave another brandishing curse to our captor.

"I-I mean, you're—" I stammered foolishly.

"Yes. Yes. I am. And I would implore you to keep your mouth shut about who I am and the bastard whose oven I'm chained to." He slammed another frying pan onto the cast-iron burners.

He murmured under his breath about how fame wasn't worth being a knife jockey for a pack of demons then went to the fridge to retrieve more ingredients.

"What are you? His new contracted housekeeper?" He raised his voice, implying he wanted Zepar to hear his frustrations. "He finally found someone foolish enough to do his every bidding?"

He lowered his voice once again, pointing the head of a radish at me. "Do you know he had me washing dishes for three hours last time he dragged me here? In the middle of the night, no less!"

With a slam, he brought a large chopping knife down onto the root veggie, made impossibly thin slices of it, then tossed them haphazardly onto the salad.

"I'm Mara." I looked around and lowered my voice to a dull whisper. "Do you have a phone I could use?"

"Oh, love. You won't get a ring out before he finds you." He looked up at me kindly, like I'd seen him do with various cooking co-hosts. "Best just to sit tight and work off your sentence. I have about five more years until I'm rid of him."

I didn't want to think of what would happen if I was caught trying to call for help. Zepar seemed to be rather indifferent of my existence for the most part, but Vepar would find me quickly. I hadn't found a way to take the necklace off and knew it would only be moments before he caught my trail.

"Pathetic," the chef scoffed at the chopping block in front of him. "Here. Make yourself useful."

He pointed to a strainer of potatoes next to the board and a sharp chef's knife. An empty pot sat on the other side. I rounded the counter and picked up the knife to begin cubing potatoes.

"Very good." He passed behind me with a large cut of meat, and the short words of encouragement brought a smile to my face.

My mother taught me to cook when I was a child. She'd wanted me to know how to feed my husband and many children if I ever got married. I was the only hope for the continuation of the family farm's legacy. After I was born, my mother began to experience ovarian cysts then suffered several miscarriages, making me her only living child. In a town and community that thrived on the labor from large families to balance the household economy, my mother felt ashamed of her infertility, and in turn, I took on the weight of all my would-be siblings. After several surgeries, the doctors discovered a larger cancerous mass that had been hidden by other symptoms.

Every time I picked up a wooden spoon or cast-iron pan, flashes of my mother baking bread or making large pots of stew for the church potluck came to mind. I felt a clutch to my heart at the thought of her knowing that I had put myself in the hands of demons after her years and years of praying for my salvation; that my rebellious ways would someday bring me home so I could help my father as he aged. The stain of disappointment had kept me away when she had been at her sickest, and my father hadn't bothered to invite me to her funeral.

In a way, I felt like he'd always blamed me for being his only offspring. That I was somehow engrained with evil and my being born had stopped all other prospects of additional children to our family. The way that Vepar and Zepar looked at me didn't do much to convince me that my father hadn't been right on some level. That somewhere deep inside of me lived a true evil that poisoned all it touched.

"Ouch!" I yelped when I brought the sharp blade down on the edge of my finger.

The blond and sassy chef whipped around with a towel and snatched my hand to wrap it.

"Hold it above your head," he snapped, dumping the cutting board and knife into the sink. "And sit down."

Only a few drops of blood had escaped, but it was enough to cause a mighty stinging sensation to my whole hand. I held the towel firmly and felt my pulse through the layers of cloth. It had been years since I'd cut myself while cooking, but it had also been years since I'd had the pressure of someone else in the kitchen while I cooked. Curt had usually been drunk and hadn't known his way around the kitchen or hadn't cared to learn. Not that it had made a difference. He had hated everything I had ever made. He'd complain about the flavor being off or that my food tasted like sewage water, never admitting that the years of cocaine use had rotted his senses.

The chef bustled over with a small first-aid kit and sat on the stool next to me at the kitchen island. Silent and calm, he unwrapped the towel and went to work bandaging my wound.

"You won't need stitches, but you need to keep your wits about you here." He looked to the kitchen entryway then back to my hand.

"You sound as if they threaten your life every time you're here."

"I don't pretend to be brave enough to think they wouldn't," he said in a low tone.

He was right. Just because they had said they wouldn't kill me didn't mean they wouldn't realize that it might be in their best interests to be done with me and shake off the attention I had brought on to them.

"There. A bit bodged, but it'll do for now," he announced and went back to cooking.

I inspected the bright-pink bandage wrapped around my forefinger. A small ring of blood showed through the layer of gauze and plastic.

"Thank you," I squeaked out.

"Happens all the time. Have to be quicker than the pointy end." He winked as he rubbed herbs and butter over meat on a rack.

"Can I ask you a question?" I watched his hands expertly dress the roast before sliding it into the oven.

"Have at it, then," he answered but didn't slow his business.

"Why did you call on Zepar?"

"I thought that might be your question." He smiled. "Back when I was a much younger man, my wife was pregnant with our first child and I was busting my arse to put a roof over our heads. We hadn't seen enough of each other, and I knew that most chefs ended up divorced once they hit a certain level of notoriety. I couldn't let that happen. I wanted to watch my child grow up, and I wanted to be there to support my wife. I did it for her. For our family."

It was known he and his family were very close, but I never imagined that he had given his soul to create what seemed to be a perfect life.

"How did you know how to call on him? Did you also know a witch?"

He scoffed and met my eyes. "Daft girl, no! He came to me. I had received top rating in my London restaurant, and one night a rather handsome gentleman and two of his brothers came in during the dinner set. They ate and drank the most expensive items on the menu then requested to compliment me personally for the 'meal of the century.'

That was when Zepar offered to fulfill every dream I had ever had: restaurants around the world, the highest esteem amongst my peers, my name going down in history as one of the most prolific chefs of all time."

The chef's eyes lit up at the memories. He wasn't exaggerating either. He was one of the most well-known chefs in the world. I doubted he could walk down the street without being recognized.

"All he asked for in return was my soul." His face fell. "I thought he was joking. A play on words. But the moment I signed that contract and every door began to open for me, I knew what I had done."

"Do you regret it?"

"I regret not reading the bloody fine print! Thirty years of servitude whenever he calls. Do you know, once he called me in the middle of an acceptance speech at one of the highest-honors ceremonies in Europe. Yeah. The press suggested I had food poisoning. Mental."

He gave a vague frustrated gesture to the kitchen and slammed the pot of potatoes in the sink to fill with water.

I couldn't help but giggle at his circumstances. He'd gotten everything he had wished for in his deal with Zepar but had no clue Zepar was a demon who wasn't only interested in his cooking skills or investing in his brand. I wondered if that was how Zepar had built the wealth around us—buying souls and investing money into powerful humans in exchange for their aspirations to be realized.

"Sorry to barge into the party." Zepar appeared in the kitchen entryway.

"I highly doubt that," the chef shot back and turned to the stove.

Zepar smirked at the chef's disdain before addressing me. "I just heard from Vepar; he'll be back soon. He took a detour and will be bringing you more gifts that you likely won't want or need."

He had removed his tie and suit jacket. His sleeves had been rolled up to mid-forearm, and a smattering of hair peeked through the window of two undone buttons. He casually leaned against the frame and crossed his arms. He was deadly handsome. A visualization of sinful fantasies contained in what looked to be a human body. A flex in his fingers and arm enticed my memory back upstairs to the claw markings on my bed's headboard. A pull of his lips dipped my stomach low and released a hoard of butterflies. How could something so beautiful be so evil?

"Mara?" His voice shook me from my thoughts. "Are you alright?"

His smile didn't hold concern for my well-being at all. In fact, it looked as if he were relishing my eyes wandering over every inch of him they could.

I cleared my throat. "Yeah. Yes. I'm fine."

I looked down to my injured hand and flicked at a loose corner of bandage.

"What's this?" He pushed off the wall and came to stand next to me, taking my hand in his larger palm.

"I cut myself while chopping potatoes. It's fine," I explained sheepishly, suddenly embarrassed.

"For being so skilled with your hands, chef, you're terrible at dressing wounds," Zepar said, but he didn't take his eyes away from the fluorescent-pink wrapping.

"She's not a bloody chicken to be trussed, now is she?" the chef barked. "Bloody well do it yourself, you mad bastard."

His harsh words didn't match his distracted tone. He clearly didn't care for Zepar, but he held a level of respect for his own life when addressing the demon.

"Very cheeky today." Zepar spoke down toward my hand still, unbothered by the tongue lashing he was getting from his personal cook. He raised his eyes to mine, brushing his thumb over my fingers gently. "Come with me, I'll fix you up."

I blinked in place of actual words. Sounds and syllables were lost once again in my throat when his golden-honey eyes connected with mine. I hopped down from the stool at the slight pull of his hand and walked with him to a bathroom off the sitting room. I stared at his fingers clasped over mine as he led me through the door and flicked on the light. He released me and slapped the counter, indicating for me to sit while he rummaged through the linen closet.

I sat where demanded and waited with my feet dangling over the edge, my heels bumping against the cabinet door. The soft thud did little to calm my nerves. Zepar came back with a larger first-aid kit than the chef had had and opened the lid. He practically had a pharmacy stashed away. Small packets of pills, bandages of all sizes, bottles of rubbing alcohol, and healing balms were all set snuggly inside.

After picking out what he needed, he took my hand in his again to remove the chef's handiwork. The cut filled with blood and beaded on the surface of my broken skin as he manipulated the appendage. Thin lines of blood spread through the grooved details of my fingers then down to create rivers and streams in my palm.

Zepar placed a sheet of gauze around the source and squeezed. He pulled my wrist down, exposing the mess covering my skin. The silence of the room pushed in on me, but every word that tiptoed on my vocal cords fell short of my tongue. His hip pressed against my knee, and an itch in my spine begged me to move. But to lean into him or to scoot away? Neither felt like the right answer.

His hand wrapped around my wrist, and a finger softly circled at the sensitive notch over my pulse. "Once the bleeding stops, I'll put some ointment on it. Can't have your death attributed to infection while staying here. Doesn't do right by my reputation."

He looked up and winked. A small relief to the tension.

"Wouldn't want to tarnish your record for being one of the most evil demons around?" An awkward smile tugged on my lips.

"You think I'm evil?" he asked playfully.

"Aren't all demons evil? That's what the Bible says, doesn't it?"

"Depends on which Bible you read. In the Christian Bible, we are fallen angels who chose to side with Lucifer in the war." He loosened his grip on the injury and began dressing it as he spoke. "In the Quran, we are merely whispers to persuade evildoing in an abstract sense. In Buddhism, there are different types of demons, and we are almost godlike in nature, ruling over aspects of human life and death."

He paused his story to spread ointment over my cut, the warmth of my finger melting it.

"In Hinduism, some believe we are like goblins. Mischievous creatures that shapeshift into animals or enticingly beautiful women to lure men into infidelity and war."

I huffed a laugh at this. I had hated growing up in a Christian home because of the misogyny and the contradictions. I'd never lost my faith in higher powers, but I couldn't imagine that women were created to only serve men.

"And which one is true?" I asked, watching him focus intently while he wrapped my finger in a new bandage.

He stilled, holding my hand in his palm gently. His eyes didn't leave the seam of our connection. "That isn't for me to dictate, now is it?"

"I always thought all religious texts were written by humans, which makes them fairly unreliable narrators." I pulled away gently from him.

"Now, that is something only recent humans have started to contemplate." He framed my legs with his arms, leaning his palms on either side of me.

"Not the most original realization, I suppose."

"In the end, they are only stories. Like all of history that was written by those who won battles and twisted the details to boast of their victories. Or by scholars who were disproven thousands of years after their deaths. Such is the simple mind of the human race." The amber of his irises searched my own with every philosophical statement.

The burn of embarrassment for existing as a human hit my neck then sank into my stomach. His waist pressed into my knees as he stood taller and brought his hands to rest on the tops of my thighs.

I swallowed against the knot in my throat and searched for some sort of snappy comeback or defense for my own race, but nothing came. In all honesty, humans sucked. Aside from chocolate, what had we created that was all that great?

"At some point, it won't matter anymore," he said, mercifully breaking the silence. "A blend of cultures and beliefs will eventually overtake the lines that you've drawn in the primordial sand."

"And I would wager, demons would still be seen as evil," I said, my words falling out of my mouth before I could catch them.

"If Father has anything to say about it, then yes." He smirked, a rebellious air in his tone.

I had a hard time believing him. He and Vepar had kidnapped me, after all. They'd shown up to my house as visions of death, taken me miles away from L.A., and had held me captive since. While they hadn't hurt me physically, their actions and reasoning about keeping me safe were tied up with their own interests in what I could be hiding and what power I could bring them. Even bandaging my injury was a clouded gesture of kindness.

"We have no reason to hate or be cruel to you, or any human. Our Fall was not due to our want to inflict evil on what our Father had created. We have no qualms with your kind."

"Then why collect souls for the Devil? Why exchange human favors for their eternity in Hell?"

He dipped his chin, a wolfish grin spreading over his handsome face. "You're not going to like the answer to that."

"I wasn't expecting to," I retorted.

"Spite." He shrugged. "Lucifer ordered us to turn as many of our Father's creations against him as often as possible. We are rewarded for our participation in their little numbers game, giving us an existence with a purpose, and I'd be lying if I said it wasn't entertaining."

I let loose another question without batting an eye. "Are the exchanges always through business deals and convoluted promises?"

"We've gotten creative over the years. Found new ways of tempting human hearts to hand over their souls. Human lust can be most effective."

"That's terrible. You sleep with humans just for their souls?"

He flicked his eyes back up to mine and leaned in close. His hands gripped my legs for balance as he lowered his face level with mine.

"We get bored easily." The dulcet tone muted the world around us. "And to stave off the infuriating boredom that is this existence, I indulge in the sound of blood racing through human veins when they're pushed to the edge of exhaustion from climaxing. The screaming of my name is as melodious as a symphony played at the Musikverein."

His voice dropped again, and I held my breath to better hear him.

"Then there is spiteful deviousness, like properly fucking a woman so that she is ruined for all other lovers after me. Savoring the madness I can drive someone to by inflicting pain and pleasure so intense that they wouldn't know if they were coming or dying."

Fire licked at my cheeks as his honey-coated words tipped from his mouth. His eyes dropped to my lips, and they parted on the palpable gaze.

"But you wouldn't be interested in any of that, would you, Mara?"

My heart skipped a beat at the sound of my name on his tongue. My eyes were stuck on the source of the most glorious sounds I've ever heard.

"I—" My tongue refused to let loose the plea. He had wedged his hips between my legs, his words hypnotizing me into allowing him closer than he'd been before.

"Yes?" He spoke slowly, dragging the sound through his teeth. "I can feel the adrenaline pumping through you, Mara. Right here."

He squeezed my thighs, his thumbs pressing into the soft creases at the top of my legs, and my arteries answered. Pounding against the pressure of his hands. He pulled me closer, my bottom slipping to the edge of the countertop.

"I can feel the heat between your legs practically begging for my attention. But you won't give in to those impulses, will you, Mara? You'll refuse to give yourself over to me and instead slip your fingers into your needy little cunt while whispering my name in your bed tonight."

My eyes closed on the sinful image he was painting, his hardened cock flush to my center. The fabric of our pants became the dam that held back the flood of need. His fingers laced through my hair and straightened my spine, pulling more of my body into his.

"Soft whimpers will escape your lips while you rub your clit, faster and harder, while wishing it were my tongue. You'll think about calling my name, knowing I'm only down the hall. Knowing I have no reservations about spreading your legs open to devour you for hours."

My heart pounded in my chest and my lungs ached from holding in my last breath. I didn't want to miss one word. Zepar's hand in my hair tightened possessively as his hips pushed deeper against me until I let out a small, wanton sound.

"Tell me I'm right, Mara," he said, his mouth hovering over mine and the heat from my name burning my tongue. "Tell me that you would never let a demon plunge his cock into you. That you wouldn't take every inch of me then beg for more."

I gasped, at last taking in fresh oxygen, and he caught my bottom lip between his teeth.

He held me there for only a second before his restraint crashed and his tongue swept in to explore. A gentle suck of his mouth to mine and my hips opened up wider, inviting him closer.

He pulled back and hovered again. "You would never fall for my tricks. Would you?"

The pressure of his body released all at once, and he backed away and out of the bathroom, leaving me to drown in an ocean of confusion. The lapping waves pulled my head under crushing questions. The warmth that had pleasantly brushed my cheeks was now stained with harsh embarrassment.

14

ZEPAR

LEAD ME
INTO
TEMPTATION

We didn't have many rules when it came to the collection of human souls, but there was no sense in squabbling over our claims. The demon to make first contact and seal the deal was the rightful owner of that soul and had to be persuaded to transfer its ownership to another demon. Simple as that. Vepar had insisted his only intent with Mara was to use her against Mikael, but I was toeing a line that had been drawn since The Fall.

She had been reluctant at first, but she'd leaned into me. Opened herself up for me to creep beneath her skin and into her nerves. The taste of her tongue still tainted my taste buds as I put too much distance between us. I'd never betrayed my Fallen brothers and sisters before, and this human wasn't anything more than any other before her.

Then why is my jaw clenched and my chest full of fire?

Every burning ember of my being was pulling for me to do the unspeakable. I could turn back and find her. The voice at the back of my mind nagging me to make her mine became a sucking vortex devoid of any other thought except for the dip of her hips, the need to bend her over the couch and fuck her until she couldn't breathe. To hear her scream my Father's name and wake the King of Hell.

Flashes of what I'd do to her body to make her face contort in pain and ecstasy made my cock swell again.

I needed to get away from her.

Get the stench of her off my clothing and skin before I did something I would regret.

The hall to my office was miles long, and I felt like I was wading in waist-deep sand. My feet sank into the unseen concrete that threatened to pull me under and suffocate me with every step I took to further the distance between my body and hers. By the time I made it to my office door, I had broken out in a sweat and was panting heavily.

At my desk, I pulled my phone out and called Vepar. He needed to find somewhere else to take Mara. Whatever this reaction was, it wasn't safe for either of us.

He answered without a greeting. "I'll be back in a couple hours."

"You need to get back here, now," I said between labored breaths.

"What's the matter, brother? A small human too much for you to handle?" he asked mockingly, but I felt no shame in admitting that the situation had become more than I had volunteered for.

"I kissed her," I blurted out, the words like broken glass up my throat.

Vepar was silent a moment. I checked the screen to see if he had hung up on me.

"You kissed her? And?" He sounded confused.

"I couldn't stop myself. Something is pulling me to her." I took my shirt off and tossed it to the sofa, but it did little to free me from the contrition of gravity making itself known on my every nerve.

"You've been around her for hours. Why are you being affected now?"

"I-I don't know. Her hand was hurt. I-I can't explain it fully, but it's too much to be contained by the two of us alone. We need to find somewhere else to stow her away." I stumbled over the words, searching for a reasonable explanation as to why I was having a panic attack after a simple and meaningless kiss.

"No," he simply said.

No?

"She stays with you. Whatever curse her soul has been endowed with has clearly gotten to you. If she were to go somewhere else, it could be too dangerous to leave unprotected. Until we find out what is happening to you, she is to be concealed within your walls."

He was right. This vise around my heart was due to hidden gifts she must possess deep under her human exterior. Maybe the release of her blood had infected me. I just needed to get her out of my system. One way or another.

"Right. Okay." I wiped the sweat from my brow with the back of my hand and took a long breath. The pressure from the interaction melted away with the realization that it was all an illusion.

"And, Zepar. It would be in your best interest to keep your hands off her." A reminder that though he may not have interest in fucking her, she was his.

I hung up, not needing to acknowledge his warning. I'd surely burst into flames if I allowed anything of the sort to happen again. Things would be clearer soon. I would stay in my office for a few hours and ignore any and all distractions that were walking around my house.

The beautiful and bewildering disturbance to my life would be gone soon. Another clench to my chest at the thought, further confusing and conflicting me.

Vepar would return with Eli, and the matter would be put to rest. He would see right through any veil that shrouded what Mara was unknowingly hiding. Until then, I couldn't show her the fear that was starting to replace the longing.

15

MARA

KNIGHT OF SERPENTS

The rest of the afternoon had been eaten up by the replay of the moment Zepar and I shared in the bathroom. He had retreated into his office and hadn't come out until Vepar barged into my room in the early evening with his arms laden with bags, boxes, and garment bags.

"I have someone I would like for you to meet. He's downstairs with Zepar."

I debated telling him about the kiss, but the moment had felt almost like a dream. I had almost convinced myself that it wasn't real.

Vepar seemed agitated. His demeanor and words were punchy, as if I were more of a chore to check off than his captive. After he was satisfied with the arrangement of clothing in my closet, he looked me over and waved his hand to the door, "Shall we?"

He led me down the dark hallway, staying several feet ahead until we

reached a break in the wall. The dull orange light was coming from an oversized fireplace in what I could only guess was a lounge or library, although there were very few books on the coupled shelves at the far wall. The wood paneling reminded me of a smoking lounge in old TV shows where men would drink scotch and smoke cigars, gossiping about women and the businesses they had overtaken recently. The set of three thick leather couches and an armchair faced each other, separated by a low table and a large, almost out of place potted plant.

Zepar stood from the chair and gave his twin a welcoming nod before coming to place his hand on my shoulder to bring me further into the room. I looked up to meet his eyes, the words of some sort of apology or recognition of our kiss lodged in my throat when he smiled warmly. The heated look in his gaze melted away the awkward knot in my chest. An unspoken agreement to gloss over the now-secret moment. It didn't feel right, but I nestled it in the back of my mind with the rest of the tattered and convoluted feelings I'd been collecting.

He broke our stare and took my attention with him to the other being in the sitting area. Vepar stepped around us to the closest leather loveseat and sunk down into the corner to lounge and watch from the sideline.

Standing next to the mouth of the lit fireplace was a tall and dark man, no demon. They were all demons here, weren't they? Either way, his features were just as striking as Zepar's were. Impossibly high cheekbones, full lips, a slender figure, but based on the width of his shoulders, he was fit beneath his fine navy suit. His umber skin was set aglow by the burning logs he was admiring, the licks of flames reflecting off his brown and gold flecked irises. He turned to Zepar and lipped his chin in acknowledgment before his eyes landed on me.

"Vepar," he greeted my escort with a quick glance then returned to me. "And who is this lovely creature you've brought along to our nightcap?"

He slid his hands into his pockets then looked me over from head to toe, tilting his head slightly as if he were admiring a piece of art, searching the strokes for hidden meaning or intention from an artist's fever dreams. A playful smile pulled a dimple from his cheek once he reached my face again, and a pleasant warmed rose to my neck.

"This is Mara," Zepar answered at my side. "She's a guest of Vepar's, and you will be nice to her, Eli."

Eli. His name was Eli. Oddly normal for a demon. Or at least the demons I had met so far. Were they all this handsome in human form, or were they changing their appearances to make me feel more comfortable? I didn't dare meet his eyes, but I looked over his features for signs of rot or decay like I had seen when I'd first met Zepar and Vepar.

Eli didn't blur or vibrate out of focus; every pore was in high definition.

"Hello, Mara." Eli addressed me, stepping a few paces closer.

I finally looked up into his eyes, and his pupils dilated after taking in the sight of me. I swallowed hard at the knot in my throat.

He was unbearably beautiful to witness, but I couldn't pull my gaze away. My head was as light as a feather due to the air in my lungs becoming too thin. A hunger to please him flooded me. I would do anything to hear his approval, including letting him use me as a doormat.

The hand at my shoulder squeezed gently, and a deep, sexy voice brushed the top of my ear. "You're drooling, darling."

Zepar wiped his thumb over my bottom lip, and the fire of embarrassment filled my cheeks. Shock at the intimate touch shook me enough to clear my mind of the images of Eli having his every whim met by my body. My eyes drifted from Eli to Zepar, who smiled down to me. Mischief and amusement danced on his crooked smirk. He returned his attention to Eli and spoke with a shift in his voice from his more casual tone. "Care for that nightcap then, brother?"

A warmth spread in my chest as he moved past me toward the liquor cart near a large mahogany desk. I brought my fingers up to my lips, and the phantom of his touch quickly faded.

Eli's concentration on me broke away, and he met Zepar's gaze as he crossed the room. "I'll take a whiskey."

They both turned away, leaving me in the middle of the ornate rug waiting awkwardly.

The clink of ice and glass pinged through the room, joined by the pop and sizzle of the firewood. Several moments later, Zepar returned to me with two glasses of amber liquid in his hands. His fingers brushed mine in the transfer, sending sparks up my arm. I looked up to find his eyes intent on me once again. They glinted with their own flecks of gold in the firelight. I could plant myself in their depths and feel perfectly at home for eternity.

It became all too real in that moment that I was drinking smoky liquor with three demons who looked like they had been created solely to tempt humans with lust.

"Thanks," I said rather quickly.

I needed to get a grip. I was making a fool of myself.

"You're welcome." Zepar smiled again. A sweltering summer smile that had my insides quivering like Jell-O.

He stepped around me and sat at the couch in front of the fireplace and crossed an ankle over his knee. His arm stretched across the back of the lush leather.

Eli joined his brother on the couch and raised his drink to me. "Come. Sit with us." He pointed to the solitary armchair across from them. "Tell me about yourself. It's been a very long time since I've had such interesting company."

He nudged Zepar and chuckled.

I looked down into my glass a moment, composing my thoughts. Eli wanted to hear about me? What at all would be so interesting to an ageless demon?

"You might be disappointed," I replied but obeyed the request and sat down. The chair cushion sank under me, making me feel even more like a child amongst gods.

Eli's brows raised as he took a sip of his drink. "You'd be surprised what we find entertaining. I once had a weekend snowed in with a monk in Tibet who had taken a vow of silence. He was a glorious dancer." Eli gave a broad, infectious smile.

I tucked my lips between my teeth but failed to hide my amusement. Zepar huffed a laugh into his drink, droplets of amber liquid smattering the tip of his nose. For demons, they were witty and easy to acclimate to. I thumbed the lip of my glass, at a loss for an anecdote to share and not finding anything to say that would be worth any of them hearing.

"Tell us about your family," Eli graciously probed. "How you got involved with that scum of a man…Curt, was it?"

I glanced at Vepar, wondering if he was the one who'd told Eli about our deal or if he just knew everything organically. I took a breath to steady myself and started with my boring backstory.

"My parents lived in a tiny town in the middle of nowhere Oklahoma. Curt and I met when I was nineteen and couldn't manage to get my life together enough to pick a direction. He promised me a life of excitement away from the Southwest. Told me that I would never have to step foot in my hometown again if I didn't want to. His charm faded to cruelty about six weeks after I cut ties with everyone I grew up knowing. That was about five years ago."

I'd confessed far too easily.

"Dreadful. And what merciful being drove you to call upon Vepar? A witch, I presume?" Eli's continued curiosity was filling me with bold and reckless abandon.

"Yeah. Abuelita Carmen. She took me under her wing a couple years ago. Curt used her apothecary as a drop site in exchange for protection." I was becoming more aware of how much of my guts I was spilling, but none of them looked in the least bit bored.

Eli looked from me to Zepar then back with a puzzled expression. "What type of protection could that cockroach of a human provide to a seasoned *bruja*?"

"A rival dealer had been harassing her business and extorting her to the point of going bankrupt. Curt took care of the asshole but kept her on the hook. A small retaliation was being kind to me and providing me with the means to get rid of him when the time came."

"Vepar being the means?" Zepar said more than asked.

I nodded, the obvious answer to the statement. I sat and sipped on my drink, on display to them. I realized how little I'd done with my life in comparison to them.

Eli cleared his throat and looked between Vepar and me. "What did you give to Vepar to clear up your problem with Curt?"

"He…" I hesitated a moment, unsure if I was expected to answer. I hadn't promised him anything I owned except— "My name."

Eli blinked in surprise and looked at Vepar, who eyed me over the rim of his glass. He took a long pull of his drink, ignoring his brother's loud expression.

"That, my dear, is quite the story." Eli rounded back to me. "It is very rare for our brother to take such pity on anyone."

"I guess my soul was too boring to take?" I tried to smile but felt more confused as to why Vepar hadn't seen my soul enticing enough to take as payment.

When I glanced at Vepar again, he remained stony. The lack of his participation in this conversation added to the squirming anxiety growing in my belly. Though I wasn't uncomfortable in the way they spoke to me, I questioned their intentions one by one.

Each demon held similar features as a whole: tall, fit, handsome, the rings or flecks of gold in their eyes, their easy humor. They were every desire for a man I'd ever had rolled into three dangerous beings.

"Can I ask a question?" I hoped I could redirect the spotlight from my pitiful existence and awkward silence. "Is this how you always look?"

Eli laughed a hearty and full sound. "She is bold, Zepar! I hope she sticks around a while." He downed the rest of his drink before standing to refill his glass.

"We chose a human form a long time ago," Zepar replied. "What you saw when Vepar and I came to collect you was our more…demonic forms. For special occasions." He winked.

The ghost of the smell of rotting flesh hit me in a wave. It had been overwhelming and had taken several washes of my hair to rinse it away.

Zepar glanced at me before addressing Eli again. "I will admit, there is a reason we have chosen these bodies. Vepar and I are among the Fallen who have a way of inflaming human desire. A little gift from our creation. You'll find that demons each have their own attributes that aid us in tempting your kind. Eligos is also a duke of Hell, but he has the ability of a seer. He sort of specializes in foreseeing outcomes and can bring answers to light when they are hard for us to uncover on our own. I've brought him here to meet you and help us see why it is the angels want to destroy you."

Zepar spoke casually, but his explanation flooded me with self doubt. Was I only feeling this attraction toward him and Eli because of their demon powers of seduction? I wasn't sure what to trust in myself anymore. I shook that thought away to hear Eli's smoky voice chiming in.

"For what it's worth, you must be very special to have Mikael go to such lengths to find you."

It was a reminder that I was seen as some sort of weapon, and the idea of being seen as dangerous blushed my cheeks and dug a pit in my stomach.

"How does it work?" I asked, taking in three sets of fiery eyes now on me.

Eli stood up and took several steps closer. The heat from his stare created a knot in my throat. The large gulps of bourbon I was downing were struggling to pass it.

"There is nothing to fear, Mara. I have assured Vepar and Zepar that I would leave you in one piece." He smiled again, and the nervous quaking of my torso calmed to a tremor.

He extended his hand to bring me to my feet before him.

Vepar and Zepar remained seated on the couches. Vepar picked at his nails but Zepar watched us carefully over the rim of his glass. His drink was all but gone in a few sips. I couldn't be sure, but I thought I caught his shoulders tightening at Eli's promise.

Eli gently pried my glass from my hands and passed it to Zepar who drained it before setting the vessel on the low table.

I looked up into Eli's eyes, their dark and gilded irises being eaten up by his expanding pupils. He raised a hand and placed it on my chest. The warmth of his touch spread over my skin through my thin shirt and seeped down to my fingers and toes. A wave of peace dulled my senses to the room around us. The fire died down, and in my peripheral, Zepar shadowed into nothing. My hands at my sides became heavy, and my head lulled back. At some point, I went from only seeing Eli's exquisite features to seeing nothing at all.

A cool and calming voice rang through me, hushed at first, but it grew louder in the passing moments. I strained my ears to make out the syllables. The timbre seemed familiar in some way, though I couldn't put my finger on who the disembodied voice belonged to. It was as if it were far off, like an early memory or a fleeting dream. There was a vision of a forest, then a flash of ocean water, another shift to snow-covered mountains, and dry, cracked desert earth.

The voice became louder and louder as my surroundings molded and shifted, until in one piercing scream, I heard the words clearly.

Maphteah.

With a crash, my body fell out of the suddenly chaotic air. A whirl of wind and a force of some unseen presence threw its mass out around me like an atom bomb's cloud.

I opened my eyes to see the coffee table, couch, and chair had been haphazardly flung out of the way. Vepar groaned as he sat up next to a splintered side table. Unmarked and only slightly ruffled, Eli stood over me with a look of concern and wonder. Zepar was nowhere to be seen.

The focus of the room came back to me after the strange journey my consciousness had just taken. The darkened ceiling above me danced in a dimmer glow from the fireplace, as if the once large logs were only nuggets of coal.

The dizzy spin of the framed pictures on the walls began to slow, and my equilibrium balanced once again. My hands groped at the floor to find Zepar's warm biceps. He had me slumped between his sprawled legs; the hard surface my head rested on was his thigh.

I shot upright and was met with a dance of white lights over my vision.

"Easy there, love," Eli's smooth voice warned. "That was no ordinary hallucination. I do believe we tapped into something much older and sacred than we should have."

Zepar's hand settled on my back to stabilize me. The pressure of his hand was hot against my damp shirt. I brought my hands to my face and felt the slick sweat that stung my eyes. I blinked away the salt, but it was no use.

The feel of a soft terry cloth met the back of my hands from above, and I gladly took it.

Vepar stood next to Eli, a stern look knitting his brow. Zepar moved behind me and hoisted me to my feet. His hands did not leave my body until he had settled me back into the leather armchair that Vepar had pulled right side up for me. Zepar strode over to his brothers, and the three watched me dab away the sweat from my neck and face.

Eli spoke first, breaking the silence. "*Maphteah*…Key."

"Mara is a Key?" Vepar's apprehensive voice came next. "Key to what?"

I shifted my sight to Zepar, whose jaw feathered but did not open to add to the speculation.

Eli turned to Zepar and Vepar, finally taking his attention away from me. "Your guess is as good as mine, but I suggest, like any key to a vast fortune, you do not speak of it to anyone outside of this room until you find out its port."

"I suppose you're right." Vepar scrubbed his hand over his chin, his features still lost in introspection.

Eli tipped the liquor cart back on its feet and then fanned his fingers through the air over it. A tall bottle of alcohol appeared; it would seem the others had all been broken by the blast that had come from…me?

He uncorked it then took a long swig before he walked to Vepar and passed the bottle off. Vepar pressed the glass to his lips in a mock kiss before taking several large gulps. He didn't shrink when our eyes connected. He smiled wickedly, a look that gave me the impression that he was more than impressed with what the encounter with Eli had brought forth.

My stomach tightened and groaned, threatening to purge itself. My body felt like it was containing a wildfire. The heat under my skin continued to drain my glands of every ounce of sweat while I took in sharp breaths. Zepar appeared at my side again and handed me a glass of ice water. I didn't bother to guess where he had gotten it from.

I choked down half the glass before the squelching burn subsided and I was able to put words together, albeit shaky and unsure. "There is something inside of me? A key to… something?"

"Keys," Eli started, "are subjective. You could be the tool or a way to decipher a riddle. The answers, I'm terrified to say, are not clear to even me."

If he was worried, then Zepar and Vepar were in a full panic. They looked between each other, unspoken words seeming to pass between them.

"You have decent wards around your home, Zep, but I suggest another line of defense if you're taking her to see Sitri. He will feel what we have just woken within her. Everyone will." Eli warned.

Zepar simply nodded and stalked out of the room. I watched after him, a call for him to wait caught in my chest. Vulnerability replaced his presence.

"I don't have to tell you what this will look like when the other Fallen get word that you have found something truly magnificent in a common human." Eli's voice brought me back to the two remaining demons.

"It's going to be a bloodbath." A sinister, crooked smile pulled at Vepar's lips.

16

ZEPAR

FORTUNE
OF THE
DUEL

I rummaged through my desk for the bottle of blood-red ink before going back to the study where Eli and Vepar were still keeping an eye on Mara. She was shaken from the vision she and Eli had shared, which was understandable. Most humans would have had a psychotic break upon finding out that something other than their own souls resided inside of them.

By the look on Eli's face when I walked through the door, he had seen more than had been revealed to Mara. But we'd all heard the echo from Mara's subconscious that came from somewhere in the universe.

I bent down in front of her and popped the cork of the old inkwell. It had been kicking around my desk drawers for ages, but I hadn't had any use for it in some time. The ink had been blessed by a brotherhood of priests in the fourteenth century. They had used it to pen wards

against demons on the walls of their village churches, but it didn't work the way they had intended. It didn't keep us away, though it did disable some of our abilities.

It would prevent other demons from penetrating Mara's mind and possessing her if they were so inclined. It wasn't an act we did these days because it made us more vulnerable to exorcisms and being banished back to Hell. Possession also took a great deal of strength and potency to keep the vessel from going mad or dying. This was a real possibility in Mara's case.

I dipped my forefinger into the pot, letting the liquid stain my skin and spread over my fingerprint.

"I'm going to mark you with this. It will protect you in ways Vepar's necklace won't," I explained, simplifying it for her.

She stayed quiet and watched my finger closely.

I lifted her T-shirt over her belly and past her navel. I looked up to her furrowed brow. Her eyes met mine, and a shot of electricity traveled through the dense air between us. The voice from within her had been tamped, but the ghost of its presence was still thickening the room. I dipped my chin and waited for her to give me permission to touch her with the mysterious red droplet hanging from my finger.

She took a breath and answered me with a slow nod.

I got to work. The sheen of the ink trailed behind my finger strokes and smeared over her soft stomach. An eye first, then a five-point star over it.

She looked from her new marking up to me then back down in time to see the ink seep into her skin and disappear completely.

"What was that?" She sat upright and rubbed her hand over the spot where the symbol had been.

"A mark of protection," Eli answered from behind me. "At least, protection from demons entering your body if unwanted."

I glanced over my shoulder at him. I half expected him to be smirking, but for once, my lighthearted brother was somber. He had tapped into something that none of us expected to be there. A darkness that went unnamed and unknown even by the human carrying it.

Vepar helped her to her feet and shot me a disappointed look before escorting her upstairs to rest before dinner. She didn't fight his instructions or look me in the eyes as she went. I wrangled the impulse to reach out to her, check that all her faculties were intact, but with Eli's and Vepar's concerned stances, I thought better of it.

I got to my feet and swatted the wrinkles from my slacks and jacket.

Eli took a seat and crossed his legs at his knees. His foot bobbed up and down to the rhythm of deep, absentminded thought. With his hand to his temple, he was the picture of contemplation.

I pushed the couch back to where it had been arranged before Mara had fallen and sat down. Eli examined me, but he didn't say a word.

Vepar returned a few moments later and began pacing the rug before the fireplace. His shadow passed through the fire's glow projected around the room. The metronomic movements became more aggravated until he stopped and looked between Eli and me.

"What the bloody hell just happened?"

"Your guess is as good as mine," Eli answered. "She could be the key to a great lost fortune or the convenience store in the middle of nowhere. Whatever it may be, it was lost to the world for thousands of years."

"Key or not, Mikael seems to think it's better if she stays lost," I reminded them.

"He can't get his hands on her." Vepar's words chorused through the aching hole that had been forming in my gut.

"And if he does?" Eli perked his brow to Vepar.

"Then I will hunt him down and kill him myself," I said too quickly.

The pugnacious threat to our brother's existence was far too excessive.

"At what point do we expect to see Lucifer become a factor in this unusual situation?" Eli shot off, and I choked back a new biting response.

"We don't," Vepar said. "Not until we find out to who and what she is so crucial. If then it seems to pertain to him, we will cross that burning bridge when it presents itself."

Eli rose from his chair and came to stand in front of me with his hand extended. "If that is the case, then I was never here."

I took his hand to give a firm but subtle squeeze, understanding his request to stay neutral and unburdened by the favor he had done by coming.

"Good luck to you, my brother," he said to me darkly. "She is an arresting find, for a human. But not worth losing everything you've built."

His hand faded away, leaving mine empty. I sighed, the unambiguous tension from more unanswered questions lifting slightly with one less mind racing for an explanation. Vepar sat across from me, finally halting his worried trek through the room.

We had inadvertently dragged ourselves into something bigger than our usual feud with the angels. Mikael had felt when Mara and Vepar had made their deal, but how could he have known that Mara had been something more than she appeared without any contact with her? She had been residing in the same walls as me for well over a day and I hadn't seen anything suspicious until now.

Questions whirled one after another until Vepar's voice pulled me from my crowded mind. "What do you think?"

"A great many things," I replied. "But overall, I think we are fucked."

"Can you feel it?" His eyes shot to the corners of the study, a slight rise of panic in his tone.

"Yes. But I can't explain the feeling it's giving off. Whatever the source of the energy is, it seems to be unbothered by us or being trapped within Mara. At least, for the time being." A sharp drop of my gut at my own words.

"And you clearly feel the separation of her soul and the presence?"

I narrowed my eyes at him. Of course there was separation. Mara was sweet, timid, kind, and most importantly, human. The residing creature in her soul was venom, coiled in defense but confident in its ability to destroy anyone who got in its path or threatened it. The power that had flowed through its voice had been a warning about the destruction it could cause if released. How could he not see that distinction?

"It's as if it is a black hole trapped within a star."

"That's a romantic sentiment," he said, scrubbing his hand over his chin. "But last I checked, the powers of stars and black holes were far greater than ours."

"Then we better hope that if she figures out how to harness it, she doesn't use it against us."

He huffed at my snide comment but didn't push the matter any further.

Mara would have been confused enough by the vision, and we had no time to explore the matter before having to present her to Sitri. Which was more of an advantage than a detriment. Having few answers would omit us from treason for the time being.

I thought up to Mara, who was now saddled with a new danger she had no control over. What she found upon further introspection or outside of these walls could bring the sky down on all of our heads.

"Tonight, she has to appear to be docile. Harmless. A puddle of lovesickness at my feet." Vepar stood and straightened the lapels of his suit. "The moments you've stolen never happened. She is nothing but mine."

"You don't have to—"

"I believe I do." His stern voice whipped out between us. "I couldn't care less that she favors you or that she would sooner peel her flesh from her bones before allowing me to touch her. But for this evening, you will play your part and I will play mine."

His face was strained, a plume of jealousy or something like it beneath his cool exterior. Mara was fascinating and infectious, but had my brother wished to be more intimate with her than he had previously let on?

"She is yours, Vepar. You answered her call. You made that deal. Her wandering eyes don't change that. Do with her what you wish." I choked back my rumbling disdain for my own words, cursing the allure of what was hiding inside of her for the discord it was causing between my twin and me.

"I know that," he snapped. "I know she is mine, but I'm not a monster. Taking what doesn't want to be mine is below me."

I rolled my eyes at his tantrum. It reminded me too much of Sitri. "You brought me into this. How was I to know that she was the capsule for…for…whatever it is. The hold it has over me will be gone the moment you take her somewhere else."

"And who would I trust to protect her? My own shadow has crossed the lines of demonic agreement." He threw his hands in the air and faced the fire, turning his back to me.

"I thought you said you couldn't care less, brother?" I perked my brow, but he didn't need to turn to hear my skepticism.

He shook his head then ran his fingers through his hair. The sag of his shoulders made him small and meek.

"When she had summoned me, there was…a moment. I had brushed it off, thinking that it was a product of having not made a personal deal in almost a hundred years. But now, I know it was this energy, or being, inside of her. The connection had snapped in place so strongly. And just now, it called to me as well," he admitted to my surprise. "This thing buried inside of her, I would wager it called to Eli, but he is more capable than we are to deny it."

"I will not fight over this human with you." I crossed the room to his side then clapped his shoulder. "I will play the supportive brother tonight. But I will also step aside if that is what you wish for me to do. You and Mara can stay here together, and I will keep my distance until you figure out where to take her."

He seemed to be wrestling with his own thoughts, the lines of his face pulling and the vein in his temple rising in his silence. We had been inseparable from the moment we were created in the Heavens. Molded from the same breath our Father had expelled into the universe. To never be alone in this existence, walking at each other's side for all eternity. No other angels had been given such a gift. But when a bond was shared so deeply, it could be tested and cause irreparable damage when strained.

"No," he finally said and met my eye. "I will hold the claim over her, brother. But she has chosen for herself who she trusts most and who she wishes to cling to. Her blood is on your name. And that is your burden to bear."

I swallowed against the dry notch in my throat.

He strode back to the liquor cart in shambles and pulled the stopper from the cracked and leaking crystal bourbon bottle. Forgoing a glass, he gripped its neck and brought the rim to his lips. He chugged down several gulps before putting it back. He would burn off the buzz within hours, but his desperation to escape the warring emotions told me more than his words. The pain my brother felt only slightly overpowered my guilt for winning over Mara's affections. His trips to bring her gifts made more sense now. In his own way, he wasn't only making her comfortable to keep her submissive to her confines and win over her loyalty; he'd wanted to show her his own brand of care.

He had never been the most understanding when it came to human emotions, often using them for his own pleasures and leading humans to an early grave. His tastes in companions had shifted in the many years we'd roamed this plane, but there were only so many different holes to fill or trinkets to collect. I loved my brother more than anything that had ever been, but he was perpetually and purposefully shallow, and it would seem that for the first time, he was being confronted with his own faults.

Mara was sure to be the end of me. I only hoped that she would not be the end of him as well.

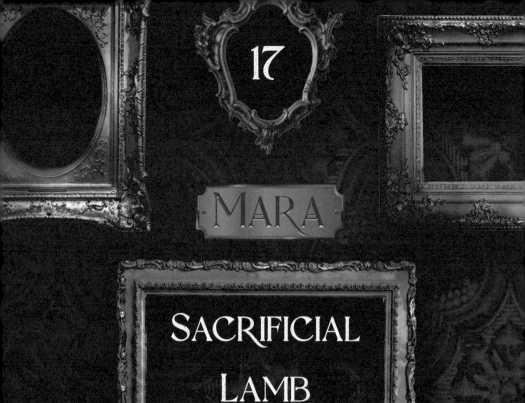

17

·MARA·

SACRIFICIAL LAMB

Eli was gone by the time I had showered and wandered back downstairs for dinner. I had scrubbed every inch of my flesh, but the prickling that had bubbled under my skin had only turned to a simmer in the hot water. The marking that Zepar had made was gone, but his tender touch had done more than the eye-shaped symbol. The short passes of his fingers over my stomach had dipped low in my pelvis. There had been some squirming from the tension we had shared, but now there was an added pressure within me that I didn't understand. Something about me that he wanted to protect. But did I really trust him or Vepar? Did I have a choice?

They hadn't thrown me out to the hellhounds in the yard yet, so for at least one last meal, I would be left to breathe. I was still wearing a robe from my bathroom, not wanting to get dressed too early and

spill something on the beautiful gown that Vepar had bought. The one Zepar had known I would love.

Zepar.

Everything about him was a whirl of half-hearted emotions and disjointed thoughts. The kiss we shared before he stormed off was intoxicating, and then he caught me before I could fall when I'd fainted. One moment he was flirtatious and his mood lighter than air. But there were dark and shadowy places where a harmless kiss or touch of my cheek could turn into a raging storm ready to consume me.

He and Vepar were already seated at the table when I arrived. The celebrity chef had been relieved and the dinner he had prepared had been set in a dining room I had seen briefly on my earlier tour. Zepar's style from the sitting room and the kitchen flowed into the intimate space.

The window on the far wall drew my eye first. The bare frame looked out onto a wall of pine trees. The strip of moonlight between the line of forest and the back of the house was eaten up only feet into the thick trunks. The ominous presence of the view acted almost like another dinner guest.

Vepar was seated at one end of the long table, his phone in hand and his thumb tapping leisurely. He had been dressed for our outing when he appeared earlier. The light-blue suit accented his dusky complexion and brought out the pop of gold around his otherwise dark eyes. He looked up briefly then continued his browsing, marking my movements into the room.

He cleared his throat as I reached my hand out to the closest chair. "I'd like for you to sit near me, if you please." The tone was oddly possessive.

I sidestepped and sat where he requested, unsure what the sudden change in mannerisms was about but not willing to ask.

"That's a good little lamb." A cocky side grin accompanied the sultry look in his eyes when they met mine.

I opened my mouth, but words escaped me.

Zepar was at the other end of the table, a stack of contracts in his lap. With his attention on his work and his lack of presence, it felt as if he were coming to a meeting of the minds and not an informal dinner in his own home. He was dressed in a maroon suit much like the one I had seen him in the first night I'd been brought here. The imprinted black florals at his lapels gave more dimension to his look.

Vepar leaned forward and grabbed up the serving platter of beef Wellington in front of him before laying a slab of it on his plate. After setting it down close enough for me to reach, he moved on to the bowl of roasted vegetables. He repeated the movements with a third dish before glancing up at me with his brows raised.

"You'll want to eat. You'll need your strength and a foundation for a night of drinking," he said with an encouraging nudge of his chin in my direction.

"Although, getting blackout drunk does sound like a convenient escape from what is sure to be a most odious evening," Zepar chimed in over his paperwork. His dry voice held none of the fire or flirtation it had earlier in the day.

I picked up a serving fork and stabbed a cut of meat for my plate then moved on to the others that had been passed down to me. I filled my plate then slid the remaining dishes down to Zepar. He didn't bother to thank me or acknowledge the stale tension as he dished out his meal.

They dug in without looking at each other or saying a word. Only the clinking of forks and knives over the fine china broke the uneasy silence. Anxiety rose in my chest as the minutes ticked by without a

I couldn't take it anymore. Whatever had happened with Eli was too much not to talk about, and the way Zepar was giving me the cold shoulder was jarring my last nerve.

I slammed my utensils down on the cream-colored tablecloth, and their eyes bolted to each other then to me between them.

"What is wrong with you two?" I said louder than I'd intended, but I didn't regret the outburst. I would have rather been run down by hellhounds or vengeful angels than spend one more second in their aggressively passive silence.

Zepar glanced at Vepar, cleared his throat, then looked back down to his food. "There is no need to have a tantrum. When we arrive at The Deacon later tonight, you will be a doting trophy on Vepar's arm."

"What does that even mean? And what does that have to do with the way you're acting here. Now?"

"I have been reminded that my place is to just sit idly by as the supporting figurehead," Zepar said.

"Your place isn't to speak to me? To explain to me what Eli saw and why we are still going to The Deacon after this bizarre meal?"

"To kiss you," Vepar answered, not taking his eyes off his brother across the table, a dangerous look in that gaze.

"What? Why would you care if he kissed me?" Heat rose to my cheeks, and a flutter of harsh embarrassment broke open in my chest to chorus with the frustrated anguish that had burrowed down deep.

They remained quiet.

I exhaled a ragged breath and put my hands on the table, bracketing my untouched dinner. They seemed to be having a separate conversation from the one I was having, and it was maddening. My shoulders sagged at the mental refereeing I was putting in at what should have been the meal of a lifetime, cooked by one of the world's most renowned chefs.

"I don't care," Vepar said, his haughty tone echoing his disinterest in ever touching me intimately.

An ember of a thought as to why I wasn't good enough for him to give me a second glance nagged at me, but it was quickly extinguished by common sense.

Vepar continued, "My brother could have his way with you in all of the ways he pleased on every square inch of this blessed rock, but tonight, little lamb, is a masquerade of appearances. However our relationship presents, you are mine by our laws. It's in our nature to push the bounds of human emotions, but if Zepar were to cross that line in front of any of the other Fallen, our protection of you and whatever purpose you so serve will be shredded."

"It meant nothing. It's not like he was intending for it to even happen." I looked between them, but Zepar didn't hold my gaze.

"We have all made vows to protect the very delicate balance of our society, which is why something as simple as a kiss cannot be seen as anything else but a betrayal of my trust." Vepar's eyes sparkled. "To everyone else, you are my new mortal instrument. A shiny plaything that caught my eye and will be used to your fullest until it comes time to throw you out."

The idea of him being the one to have touched or kissed me affronted me in an unexpected way. He was handsome, witty, and respectful. Not to mention he had impeccable taste in clothing and jewelry. But a cloudy veil of slight discomfort came with the thought of his mouth on mine. Or that he would at all look at me as more than just an object to enrage his angel brethren.

"There are many other boundaries we do not adhere to on this plane, but without those markings in the sand, we would be thrown into chaos." Vepar's noxious words sent a shiver over my skin. "We'd become the monsters every living being believes we are. The evil that lurks in the darkest of moments and influences others to do unspeakable things without rhyme or reason."

I didn't know their rules or what constituted betrayal amongst the agents of mortal sin, but Zepar's momentary lapse in judgment could have rippling consequences that would not only affect me but Vepar as well. The frail intricacy of the performance we had to put on would easily be seen through, and it brought forth a sternness in Vepar that I could feel lapping over my bare arms.

"Tonight, you will not be anything more than a work of art to be seen. An exornation that no one but me will be permitted to touch. Not Sitri. Not Zepar. If my fingers remotely increase in pressure on your skin, you will plaster yourself to my side and retreat to my body. You will take any and all cues as a call to affectionate action."

I cringed at the impression our deception would have to give, but I understood. If I was going to sell the idea that I was nothing more than a mass of holes for Vepar to wet his dick in, I had to behave as if I were grateful for every single glance he made in my direction.

Eli had pulled forth something from an endless cavern inside of me, and the quick glimpse had spooked all three demons into covert actions. They had felt—maybe even heard—the screaming of the ethereal being for themselves.

Eli certainly had. The look in his haunted eyes would be seared in my memory forever.

Zepar had held me more gingerly than he had before. He hadn't allowed his hands to wander over me when I'd lain between his legs on the floor. I couldn't describe the feel of the room in that moment. It was something akin to fear or panic, but also an ingrained respect for something so intangible. I'd wanted to rip the sensation from my being. The low hum of something too great to contain had made itself known, and it was now stalking me in the far reaches of my mind—or body. I couldn't tell the difference. Was the magic—if that was even what it was—lingering in my blood and bones? Or was this what connecting with your own soul felt like: discovering the detachment from your whole being and letting it manifest into something all its own and live within you as its own entity?

My head hurt, and an icy rush of dread plunged into my stomach. The subconscious need to stand up and walk around hit me. I needed to move. Touch some grass…feel like more than just a cage for something that didn't feel like it belonged to me anymore now that it had been disturbed.

"I'm going to get some air," I announced.

I stood and left the pair of them sitting at the table before they could protest my sudden departure.

I made it to the hall outside of my room before Zepar caught up to me.

"Mara, wait," he said, though my feet had already stopped. I was both surprised and comforted to see him. "I can only imagine how scared you must be—"

"I'm not scared. I'm broken," I cut in harshly. "The two of you came into my home uninvited. Stole me from my life and brought me here under the guise of protecting me. But all you've both done is poked and prodded, provoking the other demons around you into believing I'm something to be coveted when I am nothing."

An unexpected sob lurched from my chest, and tears flowed down my cheeks. I took a deep breath and fought through the impulse to collapse.

"I may not have had a comfortable life but I was ready to build one. I wanted a fresh start without the threat of Curt, but what I got was much worse. I'm too much of a coward to make a run for it because there may or may not be rabid wolves at the door waiting for a good chase. I am too weak to intimidate either of you to take me home. And I was stupid enough to think that you would somehow bring me a little comfort in this."

A look of mournful surprise flooded his expression as he listened intently to my rant.

I brought my hands up to my chest and clutched the terry cloth of my robe. "This powerless existence wasn't nearly as unbearable when you looked at me or touched me. But now that you know there is some kind of beast living inside of me, you haven't so much as looked me in the eye."

I blinked away my tears, my last words cracked and hoarse from my grief.

The distorted image of Zepar standing before me was cleared then by the sudden movement of his body plowing into mine. My lungs expelled all their air as he slammed my back against the wall and wrapped my legs around his waist. His mouth crashed into mine in a feverish storm of lips, tongue, and teeth.

The drapes of my robe opened, and his silky shirt rubbed against me. He pulled the fabric off my shoulders and peppered hot kisses over my chest and neck. The sound of his panting breath against my skin hollowed my lower stomach. A whimper crept from my tear-strained vocal cords, and he replied with a wanton groan.

"Fuck." He stilled with his face buried in the crook of my neck and let my body slip down his torso until his hard cock met my own pulsating need.

I looked into his face as he pulled away, but he didn't release my thighs from his grip. His cheeks flushed, and his expression smoothed from desire to realization.

I wished I could have heard what he was thinking. If he was already steeped in regret or if he was calculating all the repercussions that could come with another unexpected effusion of passion.

He lowered me to my feet and took several steps back.

I pulled my jumbled robe around myself and placed my hand over my mouth to hold on to the fleeting taste of him on my lips. The stubble of his chin had left a burning itch on my chest and neck that was intensified by the ebb of adrenaline in my veins.

He straightened his tie and cleared his throat before turning to the staircase and leaving me alone in my confusion once again.

"You'll get the life you want, Mara." He paused and looked over his shoulder. "You have my word."

The kindness in his voice almost made me believe him.

18

ZEPAR

THE

DEACON

Vepar had taken Mara's plate up to her room after scolding me for following her upstairs.

"She needs to have tougher skin if she is going to survive the night," he had said.

He was probably right. But when she'd looked at me with those big, brown eyes full of tears and her hot skin had touched mine, I'd wanted to rip apart anyone who had ever harmed her.

I had half a mind to find Curt's soul in Hell and shred it to pieces for mistreating her for so many years. Those ideas were proof I needed to calm myself before accompanying Mara and Vepar to The Deacon. I wasn't her protector. She hadn't asked me to be. But it seemed I was willing to accept the position any time I had the chance.

Vepar stood at the bottom of the stairs, tapping his foot and staring at

the time on his phone. He wanted us to arrive right at eleven to show we were not eager or intimidated, but his worry was evident on his brow.

"Come on down, little lamb," he hollered up through the house.

"We have plenty of time," I said, checking for myself.

Five till.

He and I had been dressed for hours and had been talking strategy while Mara had been sulking and dressing. Vepar wanted Sitri to believe that he and Mara were a couple. That he had fulfilled her wish, but when he'd gone to collect her soul, he'd decided to take more than that. Claiming such would accomplish the goal of the evening and not give Sitri the opportunity to ask Mara too many questions. He would feel the presence that Eli had woken within Mara. Even when she was on a separate floor with concrete, marble, and many panels of wood between us, I could feel the tang of the ancient magic curling through the air like the smoke of a cigar, slowly filling the corners and leaking out into the world, growing in its confines.

Whether she knew it or not, Mara was harboring a power in her essence. Her outburst at dinner was full of more confidence than I'd seen from her, her emotions elevating from the fumes gripping every cell of her body. A soul on fire. And we couldn't let Sitri see the smoke.

"Finally," Vepar sighed.

Mara appeared at the top of the landing and rolled her eyes at his impatience. The deep green dress I had suggested hugged the curves of her hips. She had curled her hair into soft waves and dusted her cheeks with blush. Her dramatic eyes were shadowed with gold and caged by thick lashes.

Exquisite.

My heart hammered in my chest as she took each step to meet us at the bottom of the staircase, her jaw held high. The vibrance of the unleashed potential had her glowing from the inside out.

"You look lovely. Now, what is your only instruction for this evening?" Vepar coached her.

"I am yours." The smolder in her voice drew a smile to my face but sparked something else in my chest.

"That's a good little lamb," Vepar cooed and adjusted her necklace.

The letter and Vepar's sigil coin fell into place between her breasts. She turned to me next and wordlessly asked for my opinion with a gesture of her arms and bare shoulders.

"You—" I cleared my cracking voice. "You look beautiful."

Her deep red lips pulled into her cheeks. "Thanks."

"When we get in, do not look to my brother for anything. He is there simply for decoration," Vepar interjected. "And isn't he a fine one at that?"

Mara nodded, already slipping into her position as Vepar's silent lover.

He placed a hand on her shoulder, and she looked down at the contact but didn't fight it. She leaned into him and looked up into his face with doe eyes. He smiled approvingly.

"We will be in and out as quickly as possible. Do your best to resist Sitri and his cohorts. It may prove to be more difficult than you think," Vepar warned, his feet taking up a circle around her.

"What do you mean?" Mara watched him and straightened the short hem of her dress as he passed behind her.

"Sitri has a way of attracting unsuspecting humans into his toxic proximity. But with Zepar and I there, you won't be sucked down into his undertow," he assured her as he tugged on one of her curls to check the hold and bounce. "You will bend to my hand and will. Be aware of any slight touch, and anticipate my every need."

He tested her with a nudge to her lower back, and she crossed to his other side where he draped his arm over her shoulder.

"Just follow our lead and everything will be fine." He finished his inspection and came to stand next to me. "Ready, brother?"

I nodded. My voice caught in my throat when Mara glanced at me one last time before stepping into Vepar's side, and we disappeared through time and distance to a busy downtown L.A. street.

The Deacon masqueraded as a nightclub in the heart of Los Angeles. It was seemingly placid and on the books, as one would say. The police had never been called for any disturbances or unruly patrons. But the bouncers, bartenders, and floor attendants were all demons under Sitri's legion. Lesser spirits that catered to his every whim and groveled at his feet for his crumbs. The humans who entered were swept up into the frenzy of music, flashing lights, alcohol, and lust. Secret rooms lined the back walls for those who had heard through the grapevine that The Deacon doubled as a pleasure club.

Unbeknownst to those lucky few, the rooms were monitored by cameras, and the footage taken was held for favors if they were ever needed. Politicians, CEOs, and humans of wealth were often caught with their pants down during orchestrated meetings between them and a demon masked as a lover for the evening.

Sitri had made himself the perfect flytrap filled with temptations and whispers.

Tonight, he was sitting at an oversized booth, caged in by a low table and a human woman on each arm. Their pupils were blown three times their natural state from intoxication or from Sitri's influence. He was blessed with beauty but could be deadly cruel. Next to him was Ezequiel, an unsurprising addition to the meeting Sitri had requested.

Ezequiel was ungodly charismatic, charming, and handsome. One of the Golden Six, he was a Watcher Angel living between the veil of demon and angelic divinity. He no longer resided in Heaven but was not welcome in Hell amongst the Fallen. He was the embodiment of lust and sinful pleasures of the flesh. Humans leaped at the chance to mop sweat from his brow like the droplets were coveted gems. It wasn't hard to find the reasons he and Sitri had become such a pair in the last several hundred years.

The human perched on his lap swayed his hips gently and off the beat of the music being pumped through the sound system, moving to a melody being emitted by the creature by whom they had been ensnared. It was a stroke of his own good luck that this meeting had been arranged; they may survive the evening with their minds intact.

Sitri's eyes locked on mine as we approached through the throngs of gyrating bodies. Ezequiel kept his attention pressed to the human who moved into the center of his lap. The human ground down onto Ezequiel as he bit his lip and rolled his eyes to the back of his head.

Mara's shy face lit up when Sitri's gaze shifted to her, and he didn't take his eyes off Mara when he leaned over to speak to one of the women at his side, then to the other.

Both humans' faces fell as they stood together and gave looks of disappointment at being ushered away. One tugged at the arm of the man Ezequiel had been entertaining. The three huffed and stalked away into the mass of drunken patrons. Sitri leaned forward to watch their asses bounce in their high heels, only momentarily relieving Mara from the weight of his eyes.

Vepar took the opportunity to place his hand on Mara's shoulder and hold her back from walking straight into Ezequiel's now vacant lap. She looked back at Vepar, her eyes caught in surprise and confusion. She wouldn't have had any idea why her body was drawn to the pair of beings sitting before her or why she was feeling compelled to straddle either of them.

Vepar reached his hand out to greet Sitri, but the prince did not move. When Vepar pulled his hand back, he turned to Mara. "Mara, this is one of the Princes of Hell. My prince, meet Mara."

There was a tense moment as we quietly waited for Sitri to engage.

Sitri leaned forward and quickly snatched Mara's hand to bring to his lips. "Welcome, Mara. You may call me Sitri," he said into the soft flesh and offered her his true name.

Vepar gently pulled at Mara's elbow, a silent request that she step back from Sitri's reach. Her hand fell back to her side as her back pressed against Vepar's chest. Sitri straightened with a cocky smile, the fresh bloom of challenge engaging him fully. His eyes became vipers stalking their next meal, egging Vepar on to overstep so he could strike.

I cleared my throat and spoke to both Ezequiel and Sitri. "Our sincerest apologies for interrupting your evening. You seemed to be pleasantly occupied."

I looked around for the humans who had been congregating at their booth, but they had melted into the surroundings, no longer fused to the interest that had been flowing through them moments ago.

"Plenty more from where they came," Ezequiel remarked, bored.

"But not like Mara," Sitri cut in. "Isn't that right, pet?"

Mara's attention snapped from where it had been lingering between the four of us. She blushed, and her jaw shut tight at the sound of her name from Sitri's lips. The low tone of deep magic coming from inside of Mara had been muffled by the markings I had drawn. But her increased stress was sending a pulse of power out around her. I watched Sitri and Ezequiel for a sign that they had felt it too. If they had, they were adept at hiding it.

"She has been a lovely guest." I interrupted another prolonged stare between Sitri and Mara.

Her eyes shot to me at her side with the realization that she was in more danger than we had prepared her for back at the house. She stepped back into Vepar, as he had instructed her to do if she felt uneasy. Ezequiel's eyes followed Vepar's arm as it raised and draped across Mara's shoulders, pulling her into a shielding embrace.

"There's no need to be shy, darling. We won't bite." Ezequiel huffed a laugh. "Unless you're into that sort of thing."

He smiled widely at his own wit, and Sitri chuckled along with him.

"Vepar?" Mara looked up to my brother, pleading for him to direct her in some way.

"The rules are simple, gentlemen," I chimed in, once again out of turn. "Vepar has staked his claim on this soul and this human already. She is out of your greedy grasps."

Sitri got to his feet and rounded the table to approach Mara. I stood my ground as his arm made contact with mine as he passed between her and me.

"I don't touch things owned by another, dear ones. But maybe Vepar would settle on a price for this tempting creature?" Sitri didn't take his eyes away from Mara as he spoke.

Ezequiel's gaze roved over the lot of us, seeming to be amused by the tension and the promise of an altercation if Sitri pressed the matter.

"I've only just taken her for myself. She isn't properly broken in," Vepar countered, pulling Mara behind him and into my side.

"All the more reason to discuss your terms. We like our human toys with a little fight left in them." Ezequiel's greedy hands wrung tightly before him. His patience was likely to run out soon.

Mara reached behind her back and gripped the side of my slacks, another silent request for safety. But as much as I would have loved to shred Ezequiel to pieces in the middle of the club, Sitri was calculating their next move and watching our interactions closely.

"She isn't for sale," I said out of turn again and took a step closer to Mara's back, her fist pressing into my thigh as a result.

I knew then that I had gone too far.

Sitri lashed out, grasped the back of my neck, and brought me to my knees. Mara's screech of terror muffled into Vepar's chest as he pulled her out of the away. Sitri wrapped both hands around my throat and held me tight, his strength crushing in on my windpipe. I struggled to breathe but didn't strain against him.

"Now, now, sweet Zepar. Let this be your one and only warning to remain the unbiased party in this exchange. You are not the owner of this human either and have no say in her price. Do we have an understanding of how the rest of this evening will unfold?" His dark voice vibrated through me, and I nodded in agreement.

He dragged me from my knees and threw me to the booth where he had been sitting.

Ezequiel laughed and slapped a hand on my chest. "Welcome to this end of the show, brother. Let's get you a drink to calm your nerves."

He raised his fingers and snapped. A human carrying a tray of clear shot glasses and a full bottle of vodka appeared instantaneously. Ezequiel passed me a pair of shots then took two for himself. Without hesitation, he downed the first then the second in two gulps. He eyed me, and I followed his lead before returning my attention to Vepar, Mara, and Sitri. The waitress moved toward them to offer the tray, and Sitri smiled at her as she beamed up at him.

"I think we are all a little on edge at the moment," Ezequiel proclaimed to the group, "Let's sit and discuss it further. With less hostility."

Relief did not come to me after the first two drinks. Or after the next four.

Mara was given three shots in a row then sat between Vepar and me. Sitri pulled up a loose chair from a table and sat in Mara's line of sight. She settled into the crook of Vepar's arm, holding on for dear life.

"Vepar, what will it take for you to transfer ownership of Mara to me?" Sitri slumped down into his chair, a renewed shot at the brim of his lips.

"I will have to think on it further. Mara is quite the commodity at the moment," Vepar responded, playing with the tips of Mara's curls.

"That is what I've heard." Sitri shot a glance to Ezequiel, who downed another shot of vodka. "And why do our brothers in light wish to whisk her out of your grasp?"

I watched the sloshed swing of Mara's head from being to being, each speaking of her as if she weren't there. Most humans would have shouted in outrage by that point. But somewhere between being kidnapped and the heated moment before we came here, it seemed she'd begun to trust Vepar and me. Enough to not let the mask slip from her beautiful face.

"She's the latest to call upon me," Vepar replied, a mask of boredom slipping into place. It was artificial and thin after the altercation. "It has been several years since the last and more still since I took a human as a companion. I imagine they believe I have ulterior motives in my affections."

"That is what has been passed through the grapevine." Ezequiel narrowed his eyes to Vepar. "Word for word, in fact."

He and Sitri exchanged a quick glance, a wordless conclusion passing between them that thickened the tension the liquor was failing to loosen.

"What did you call upon Vepar for, Mara?" Ezequiel addressed her, and Vepar looked down at her, giving her a nod of permission to speak.

"I-I asked him to take care of my ex. I owed him money and he had a price on my head." Her mousy voice shook.

Sitri considered her explanation, searching for deeper meaning to her call to Vepar. "That sounds trivial."

"Wrong place, wrong time. Isn't that right, little lamb?" Vepar cooed, planting a kiss on the top of her head.

Mara closed her eyes at the show of affection. She leaned into Vepar then looked up to him, her eyes sparkling. "You saved my life."

Her tone shifted from uneasy to grateful, her character sinking into place as self-preservation took over.

Vepar looked into her eyes and hooked her chin in his fingers, tilting her face up to him. He pressed his lips to hers, and the surprise of it brought a small squeak from her chest. Heat rose up my neck, and anger boiled through my veins. I took another shot to combat the urge to rip the illusion apart. The discussion of their connection hadn't elicited a visceral response, but seeing it performed before me was sickening.

"That is quite cloying, isn't it, Zepar," Sitri shot toward me.

Vepar and Mara parted, and the knot in my chest loosened.

"The most," I replied before another shot of liquor.

Ezequiel sneered, an unclean amusement dawning on his face as he focused on me. "What's the matter, darling duke? Is that the ugly head of jealousy rearing inside of you?"

"There's nothing to be jealous over. There are plenty of humans that I can spend my time with. The one you had earlier was quite handsome. Maybe I'll go and find them." I poured another shot of liquor into my glass and downed it while I peered around in a lazy attempt to see where his companion had scurried off to.

Ezequiel shook his head with a crooked smile, not allowing his cool to drop from my half-drunken threat. He cocked his head to Vepar and Mara. "Your shadow is bold tonight, Vep."

"I have been blessed with a loyal and protective brother," Vepar replied into his next shot.

Ezequiel chuckled and sat back against the booth, letting his head full of bouncy blond waves lull on the cushion. Even in the dim lighting of the club, his creamy, golden skin shone bright and otherworldly compared to the humans swarming around us.

A group of humans absentmindedly lingered at the edge of Sitri's orbit, each one more intoxicated than the next and lost in the music from the pounding speakers. Sitri stretched out his arm and hooked the nearest human and brought them to his lap. The young woman's smile didn't drop, and her jovial demeanor did not crack with the forced change of her company.

She turned at the waist and met Sitri's sultry expression. He whispered something into her ear while his hands and eyes wandered over her bulging breasts.

Mara squirmed next to me, still taking shelter under Vepar's arm.

Sitri's hand trailed up his new ornament's neck and took hold beneath her chin to bring her mouth to his.

I rolled my eyes and glanced around the crowded club and waited for his lascivious mannerisms to subside. He was always like this when he called a meeting. His boastful actions drove his every move. If he wasn't making a spectacle of himself, then he wasn't breathing.

Vepar dipped his chin down and spoke into Mara's ear too low for me to hear, but I didn't miss the action. I couldn't stop myself from fixating on every move he made or every touch they shared. My head pounded the longer I contained my incensed discontent for the ruse. I had agreed to come as a safeguard so that Sitri would know Vepar wasn't alone and to ensure Mara's safety. I had promised her that much. But sitting here now with her soft, exposed thigh pressed to the outer seam of my slacks and her head to my brother's chest, a storm of inexplicable and conflicting emotions filled me.

Ezequiel clapped his hands together loudly, crashing through every wall the rest of us had built. Sitri gave a hearty laugh and pushed the young woman from his lap and slapped her ass as if sending cattle back out to pasture after branding.

Mara practically jumped out of her skin and into Vepar's lap, bringing a boisterous laugh from Ezequiel, while the other woman gasped and giggled as she found her friends and rejoined the throng of folly.

Sitri shrugged coolly as he swung his attention back to the group and set his sights on Mara again. "What do you think, Mara? I could protect you from those blasted angels, and being here with me has to be more enjoyable than staying with Vepar or Zepar." His blue eyes sparkled at Mara as he sized her up.

Vepar's grip on Mara's shoulder tightened then released, allowing her to sit up on her own. She looked from him to Sitri then cleared her throat. Her hand wandered up from Vepar's knee to his belt, pausing briefly over the front of his slacks that seemed to be tighter than before. She lifted her leg and rested it over his knee, furthering the look of mutual claim she and Vepar shared. The hem of her dress slid up, revealing more skin to me and Ezequiel, who sat on my other side. I could feel his eyes over my shoulder, shooting toward the same landmark I had viewed myself. I wanted to rip his eyes from their sockets with the severed hand of my brother, who was now smoothing his hand over her ass as I simmered next to them.

"I'm very comfortable with the two of them at the moment, but I'll keep your offer in mind." She gave a simple smile.

"Very well." Sitri rolled his shoulders, not used to being denied whatever pleasure he set his sights on. "My door is always open. When you grow tired of being groomed for slaughter, little lamb—" His expression quickly melted into a low threat. "—call upon me."

He extended his arm over the middle of the low table between us and opened his fist to allow a delicate necklace to dangle from his fingertips. The large garnet gemstone pendant jerked against gravity when it came to the end of its chain. It glowed a dark, ominous blood red in the stage lights.

Mara looked to Vepar for permission before reaching out and allowing the gift to drop into her palm. She brought it to her lap and traced the edges of the fig-sized gem with her fingers.

"I believe our business is done here." Vepar stood and pulled Mara up by her arm, taking her from the trance of the object of manipulation.

"Ezequiel, always a pleasure." Vepar dipped his chin.

"I'm sure," Ezequiel responded with a disingenuous smile.

"Sitri." Vepar acknowledged him last and hooked his arm around Mara's waist.

Sitri got to his feet and stepped aside for the three of us to pass by him. Mara and Vepar headed to the door without looking back, but Sitri stopped me by the shoulder when I came to his side.

He leaned his head over and spoke into my ear but didn't meet my eye. "Best keep your wits about you, brother. Even the sweetest fruits are deadly, and that one will surely be your end if you get in my way again." The air of arrogance laced his every word, not unfamiliar, but the next threat had my spine snapping straight.

"I'd hate to have to bring Lucifer into the dispute if you continue to shroud your true intentions behind Vepar's claim. Mara will call, and when she does, I will answer swiftly. And if you so much as step between us, your last images of her will be my cock choking the life from her beautiful brown eyes."

He released me, and he and Ezequiel sauntered out onto the dance floor without a second glance.

19

MARA

TAKE ME TO CHURCH

I stumbled into the entryway of Zepar's house when we reappeared from the crushing, dark nothingness. Vepar let me drop to my knees as he let out a frustrated, booming shout that vibrated the walls and shook the door behind us.

On weak ankles, I got to my feet and leaned against the closest wall. Vepar paced the floor with his hands at his sides. I watched him closely, unsure if the haze I was seeing loom over his face and body was the liquor or the loss of his cool causing him to slip into a new form I hadn't seen before.

Moments later, Zepar appeared, his brow knitted together and his shoulders tense. He raised his hand and pinched the bridge of his nose, wrinkling his darkened features. They both looked haggard, as if the interactions at The Deacon had been a battle and not a pissing contest.

"That insolent bastard!" Vepar stomped off in the direction of the kitchen, leaving Zepar and me in his vengeful wake.

"Are you all right?" Zepar said in an unnaturally calm voice.

"Yeah. I'm fine."

I wrapped my arms around my body and waited for the uneasy quaking in my knees to stop. I eyed the staircase and thought about kicking my heels off and escaping up them. I looked down to my feet and remembered the massive precious stone I was clutching in my fist. I opened my hand and gazed down at it, gawking at the sheer size.

There had been a shot of fire up my arm when Sitri had kissed my hand. My stomach had done a full flip at the feel of his lips on my knuckle. More terrifying than that, I'd heard the misty, far off voice in my head whisper…something.

Princeps meus est.

It had been a low hum at first then grew to assault my ears when our skin touched. I couldn't explain it, but part of me knew he had heard it too.

The mass of Zepar's body loomed over me. I hadn't noticed him move across the room, but I felt like I'd lost myself each time I had looked into the garnet's depths. A thrum of something primal pulsed through my abdomen when it glinted in the light. Like something inside was waiting for me to invite it out into the world. The thought of something inherently evil staring back up at me sent a shock through my system.

Zepar's hand moved over the gem and brought my attention up to his face, a kind and pitiful look in his eyes. The moment we had shared before leaving flashed before me, his hands gripping my waist and his hard cock pinning me against the wall. The flames of his gaze in my memory set my cheeks on fire once again.

I shook my head and took a small step back. I placed a hand over his, sandwiching his hand in mine, then turned to transfer the necklace to his palm.

"I won't be needing that," I said, my voice strained from the sting of the vodka and having to shout over the loud music.

"You're sure?" he asked, but his playful tone didn't match his face. "Haniel outdid himself on this piece."

The edges of the stone caught the light from the chandelier overhead and gave it a viscous eddy in his open palm. With every slight pull of one of his digits, it vied for attention.

"Zepar." I stepped around him, sobering enough to finally carry myself up the first few steps. "I have never in my life been more terrified as I am when I look at that gift."

I took my feet out of the red heels and held them in my fingers. He came to stand at the base of the first step, meeting my eye.

"It is nothing in comparison to the ways Sitri would break you if he gets his way." His smoldering warning was unwarranted.

I had no intention of calling on Sitri or putting myself in the hands of another demon. I knew full well that I had lucked out. Every other demon I had met had the intent to either use me for their own gain or destroy my mind and body. Even sweet Eli had the potential to wreck me, though not maliciously; I could see how easy it could be to lose every last shred of myself in his possession.

A strange appreciation for Zepar bloomed in my chest. He had restrained himself at The Deacon when I'd reached for him, an instinct I hadn't been able to ignore. But he'd also put himself between Sitri and me and Vepar. I wanted to thank him, but I also wanted to go upstairs and go to bed. To erase the slimy feeling of Sitri's lips on my hand and his eyes boring into my chest.

"You did well tonight," he said with sincerity. "Vepar is too blinded by his hatred and frustration to see it, but your commitment and loyalty very well saved our hides in there."

"The only loyalty or commitment I have is to myself and the hopes that I will live long enough to find a way to clear my name with both angels and demons. It was self-preservation. You don't owe me any gratitude," I replied, more coldly than I'd intended.

Maybe I was drunker than I felt. Or maybe I was becoming too comfortable with Zepar.

I turned and took a step up, but he wrapped a hand around my wrist and tugged me off balance. I fell back, letting go of my shoes, and reached out to stop myself from falling to the ground. Instead, I landed with my arms pinned to his chest, his face only an inch away. His dark eyes were so close, I wondered if he could see right through me and down into my soul. When he spoke, it was a deadly whisper that gripped me in fear and sent butterflies loose behind my navel.

"I promised you once before that I wouldn't let anyone hurt you, but let me be very clear now. Not a single being on this plane or any other will touch a single hair on your head unless they slit my throat first. If that means that I have to tear down the Heavens, then so be it."

His intense gaze flashed, and I did the unthinkable. I reached up and tangled my fingers through the dark hair at the back of his head and met my lips with his. The string of quick movements caught him off guard, and he stilled a moment before leaning into the kiss and returning it. The hard lines of his lips relaxed into soft strokes against mine. His hand at my back trailed to opposite poles of my spine. He cradled my head in his palm and weaved his fingers into my starched brown curls. The other smoothed over the silky fabric of my dress and the curve of my ass.

I parted my lips and ran my tongue over his bottom lip, inviting him to deepen the kiss. With a gruff groan from his chest, he swept over the rim of my mouth and pulled me harder into his firm torso. The sinking flutter in my gut warned that I was treading a dangerous line, but the warmth of his body and the spice of his cologne replaced any good sense I had to stop myself.

His hand reached the slit at my hip, and he hooked his finger under the lace of my panties, following the curve of it over my skin and cupping my ass. He hoisted me further up his lean figure. At the new angle, he trailed a line of kisses over my chin and down my neck. He sank his teeth into the sensitive crook, pulling a whine from my throat and igniting fervor in every nerve he touched.

"Zepar," I breathed. I was unable to reel in my need, but I didn't pull away or loosen my grip at the base of his neck.

I wanted more. I wanted to feel his body sink mine into a soft mattress, and I wanted to give over to everything my conscience was screaming at me to run from.

He would let me go; I knew that much for certain. He had said it had to be my choice to break free of my restraints. That he would wait for me to release my inhibitions. The temptation grew heavier.

"Don't stop," I breathed. "Please."

The sucking abyss blacked out my vision for a moment, and we reappeared in my bedroom. The back of my knees hit the mattress followed by my ass then my torso. Zepar stood at the edge of the bed, his heated eyes pinning me in place. My leaded limbs were too timid to move in fear he would reconsider my pleading.

I pulled at the hem of my dress to bring the slit up to the top of my hips, then I hooked my thumbs into the lace waistband and pushed my panties down my thighs. His jaw fell, and his hands went to loosen the tie at his neck. Then he shrugged off his jacket and let it fall to the floor.

His hands went to the tops of my thighs and lifted the bunched lace off my legs, leaving me bare to him. Anticipation filled my chest as he got to his knees. His hands slipped up to my lower back and pulled me toward him.

His lips grazed the sensitive spot just inside of my knee. A dark hum of lust came from his chest while his mouth opened and closed in a trail up my thigh. With each inch he took, my shallow breath hitched in my lungs until he reached the apex. His warm breath fanned over my skin and the tip of his tongue made slow, intentional circles at the crease of my hip.

I bit down on my lip to stop myself from laughing at the tingling that shot into my gut. The pads of his fingers moved over my clit and began mimicking the movements of his tongue as it roved closer to my aching center. The tickle quickly turned to scorching pleasure as he dipped two fingers into me and found that deep spot.

His lips domed over my needy and pulsing nerves, and his tongue flicked and whirled as his fingers pumped. I'd never felt so much stimulation at once.

And with that, a rush of thoughts clouded me as the pressure began to build.

Curt hadn't been the most inventive lover, often using me for his own release then leaving me to take care of myself later. Eric hadn't been less selfish the night before my kidnapping.

God.

I had the head of one of my kidnappers between my legs. And what was worse, I'd practically begged him. Shame filled me, pushing me away from the edge of an orgasm. I pulled myself up, and Zepar immediately stopped. The desire in his eyes cooled to concern.

"Mara?" He rocked back onto his heels and looked at me fully.

I sat up and adjusted my dress. "I'm sorry. I—"

"It's okay. If you changed your mind, that's fine." He sighed, but not with aggravation or disappointment. Relief, maybe?

"No. I need this. Fuck, I need you so bad," I said with my cheeks warm at the admission.

A cocky expression pushed his brows up, and his fox-like grin set into place. He was so gorgeous with the gloss of my excitement still clinging to his lips.

"I don't have that much experience…" I sounded young and

immature but couldn't find the words for the mashing of emotions I was battling.

"With fucking demons? I figured as much." He came and sat next to me on the bed.

He sat back on the heels of his palms, and his black shirt stretched over his muscular torso. His hair was still mussed from my fingers, and the spicy scent of his cologne loomed around us. His cock was still hard against his slacks. I looked away but cursed myself for cutting off what was sure to have been the best sex of my life.

"Do you want me to leave?" he asked but didn't move.

I opened my mouth to protest, but words didn't find their way off the tip of my tongue. I didn't want him to go. I wanted to erase the last few moments and go back to kissing with his hands all over my ass.

"I don't want to, but I will," he clarified, and a pressure relieved in my chest.

"I'm going to change." I hopped to my feet.

I pulled the dress over my head and tossed it to the floor on my way to the dresser. Pulling my loosening curls into a bun on top of my head, I snuck a glance over my shoulder to see him taking in every bit of my backside. Vepar had filled my drawers with silk and lace, surely from the most expensive boutiques in L.A. My hands found a black silk slip and pulled it over my head and down my body.

I turned back to Zepar. The hungry look in his eyes was hardly restrained by his curiosity.

"Can I touch you first?" I prowled closer, allowing him time to think, but he answered without hesitation.

"Anywhere you'd like."

He sat up and began unbuttoning the cuffs of his shirt, and the tattoo on his forearm peeked out from the parting fabric. The dark lines on his brown skin didn't show any sign of fading over time. My palm wouldn't have covered the many prongs and the simple lines that connected them. It almost resembled a large vase with an inverted

I stepped between his knees and fingered the smooth circle through its hole at the hem of his shirt then moved on to the next to reveal another few inches of his chest with each one. His fingers met me halfway and finished the task.

The shirt joined the growing pile of clothing on the floor, and I allowed my eyes to take in the swell of his muscles at his arms, shoulders, and chest. I placed my hand on his warm skin and trekked up over the mound of his shoulder to the back of his neck.

My fingers spread up through his short hair, the black satin strands giving way easily. When our eyes met, it was brief but held a wonder that I wasn't used to seeing directed at me. He searched my face for a thought or direction; the ghost of concern still shadowed his lust. I brushed my lips against his, and he hesitantly reciprocated, keeping his hands gentle and giving me full license to make the next move.

His fingers feathered the backs of my legs and lingered below the hem of silk. My mouth was tentative on his, but with each sweep of my tongue, his hands rose higher. His chest pressed to me, warming the cool garment through to my budded nipples. The soft pressure of his palms over my backside pulled at my legs to mount his lap.

The clench of uncertainty loosened into brewing pressure behind my navel. His hands smoothed up my sides underneath the gown, one cupping my breast, the other pulling the neckline down to bare the other to him. He looked up to me, a kind request for permission, and I nodded without looking away as his head dipped to my chest. A sweet flutter grew in my stomach as his mouth moved down my breast and took in the peak. His tongue flicked and circled, edging me closer to the pinnacle of my desire and chasing away all other thoughts that didn't include his mouth, fingers, and cock.

A deep and carnal hum came from his throat as my hips began to grind down on him. The cool metal of his belt buckle in tandem with his warm belly dusted with hair brought a whine of need up through my lips. He cursed through a heavy breath then clamped his teeth down onto my nub. An orgasm sent my head spinning with the sudden release of pressure within me.

In a quick whirl of the room, my back sank into the sheets and Zepar hovered over me. The fever of his eyes threatened to overtake the leash he had on his restraint. My hands shot to his belt and the button of his slacks. The sound of shoes crashed to the floor below. He stood to let all his clothing except his briefs fall away. The mattress dented at his knees as he settled again between my legs and laid his body on top of mine. His arms bracketed my head, and the weight of him gave me comfort.

I brought my hand to his cheek and smoothed my thumb over his pillowy lips. The quickening in my lower stomach was making me braver than I had been.

He leaned in closer to brush his lips over mine softly. "I could wait an eternity, but once you are ready, I'm going to break down every insecurity you have. Free you from any hesitation that is holding you back. I am going to show you, darling, why lust is the most powerful sin."

His words set me on fire.

A fever swept me under a mix of ferocity and thirst. I pulled him to me, my hands grasping for any part of him all at once. Our mouths crashed in an attempt to consume each other. I needed him more than I needed oxygen in my lungs, and the ache of not having enough of either was going to kill me. His cock was rock hard against my clit, and the sleek cotton and silk between us burned as if caught on fire. My fingers worked the waistband of his designer briefs, revealing him.

I wasn't sure what to expect from a demon's cock. The times he had been hard against me had convinced me that he was bigger than anyone else I had ever had. By my own admission, that hadn't been very many.

He shimmied out of the remainder of his cloth restraints and pressed the head of his cock to my entrance. My pulse raced in my ears, and my heart thrashed in my chest. Air did not make it past my shallow lungs.

He stared down at me, waiting.

The fire in his gaze was my last warning that the claim he was about to make on my body would rip me to shreds inside and out. That the moment he pushed through and dove in, he would infect every thought I would have from that moment after.

In that one look, he held a promise and a threat: I was never going to be the same after allowing him to penetrate my mind and body.

He pulsed against me.

One.

Then he swallowed hard, his throat bobbing.

Two.

He took a deep breath and furrowed his brow. Then it happened. I nodded and pushed my hips up to meet him.

Three.

"Fuck!" he groaned into my neck as his hips shuddered on impact.

I couldn't breathe. I forgot how. The searing stretch of me around him was all-consuming.

He bit into my shoulder, and a gush of fresh air pushed its way into my lungs. The rapid rise and fall of my chest wasn't enough to catch up with my thoughts or the surge of adrenaline coursing through my veins. He pulled away to thrust again, and another shock traveled to my nerve endings.

He lifted off my chest enough for our eyes to meet, and a look of disbelief met mine. I wrapped my legs around his waist, and he dipped his hand under my ass. He hoisted us to the top of the bed and braced his feet against the footboard. I rocked my hips and chased release, but the angle wasn't right just yet. The frustration in my moan put him into action again, and he drove himself down into me deep. Then deeper still. I wasn't sure how much more I could take, but the ache was not sated yet.

I dug my fingers into his hip to pull him further inside, but he stilled.

A look in his eye reminded me of who was inside of me. "If you keep that up, I'm going to give you what you think you want so badly. But you're not ready. We are going to go slow this time so you can walk in the morning."

My throat dried, but my thighs quaked at the mix of power and kindness in his tone.

He was right. I wouldn't be able to handle him at his full force, and how much longer could I expect him to keep himself under control when I wasn't giving any indication that I wanted him to hold back.

"Slow?" I breathed.

"Very slow." He pushed then pulled out delicately. "Painfully."

The swaying movements of his hips brought me closer to the edge. I closed my eyes and let my other senses take in the moment: the fullness of him inside of me, the heat from his body mixed with the satin sheets below me, the tender curses that came from under his breath. Lost in him, I could feel myself slipping away from the fear and guilt that plagued me outside of this room.

I opened my eyes to find him watching me with a curious expression. He thrust once more then pulled completely out. I mewed in disappointment. My body was no longer complete without the feel of him inside of me. The emptiness screamed at the sudden loss of pressure.

"What's the matter?" My brows knitted together.

"I want to feel you free yourself on top of me."

He lay down and took hold of my wrist, guiding me to straddle him. Then he placed my hand over the head of his cock. It throbbed at my touch, and he kicked his head back against the pillow when I took a stronger grip and worked my way down to the base. My fingers wrapped around his shaft, the tips struggling to touch as I pulled up then pushed down. His chest rose and held his deep breaths until I made another full pass over the head.

The pool of heat between my legs ached with every sound of pleasure my hands dragged from him. I sat up on my knees as high as I could and brought his tip to my center, where I made deliberate circles over the head of his cock, and watched as his eyes darted from my face down to my cunt. His fingers dug into the tops of my thighs, and his stomach tensed. I slowly eased down onto him, taking him deeper than he had been before.

He hissed as I bounced the last inch of him inside of me. "Fuck, you feel so good, Mara." He took me by the waist and squeezed, pulling me over him slowly, and groaned. "Just like this."

The friction of him against my clit brought me right over the edge. I moaned through my orgasm and put my hands on his chest to keep myself from collapsing.

His arms didn't waver.

He dragged my hips over his cock while waves of pleasure swelled then crashed over my senses.

Through the spasms and electricity shooting to my fingers and toes, he slowed but didn't completely stop. Instead, he began subtle thrusts from underneath me. His fingers dimpled my flesh, and the pinch of his hold intensified the sensation between my legs.

"Look at me," he demanded, his face schooled on restraining his own needs. Our gazes connected. "Are you my good girl?"

I nodded for his approval, my eyes not leaving his as he had instructed.

"Do you want to come again, darling?"

"Uh-huh," I moaned. "Please."

His hips stilled, and his hands pulled me down harder but sped up their rhythm. I was climbing again, faster than before, hitting the epitome of pressure and release as his voice rang through the room in a harsh command.

"Come for me, Mara. Who does this tight pussy belong to now?"

"Fuck!" A burst of light flashed as I squeezed my eyelids together through my orgasm. "Zepar!"

My arms gave out, and I collapsed onto his chest. Without missing a moment, he wrapped his arms around me and began pounding thrusts into me. I gasped for breath, but each punishing blow forced air from my lungs. I turned my head to watch the lines around his eyes and mouth contort with pleasure. His husky voice in my ear was a slew of cursing, moaning, and hitched breathing. My thighs pressed into his sides as another orgasm gripped my lower belly. The slapping of our damp skin whirled through the room faster and faster as he got closer to his own release.

"You're mine, Zepar," I breathed into his ear, the words inflating the desire in my chest.

His eyes snapped open, and his head turned to me. "Oh, fuck," was all he said. Over and over again until his legs shook and his hips shuddered.

The pulsating release filled every deep nook of my pussy and spilled as he pulled out of me. He loosened his arms but held me in place gently as he caught his breath. Another curse stained his lips as a corner of his mouth pulled up into a content, cocky smile.

I slumped over to lie in the wedge between his sweat-slick body and his arm.

He pulled me toward him to plant a kiss on my brow then rolled away to the bathroom. He came back with a damp washcloth and a dry towel, a gesture I had never seen from any man before him.

He placed a knee onto the bed and pulled my legs open before dipping his mouth over my overstimulated clit. He gave it a slow and light brush of his lips then wiped away the mess with the warm cloth. There was another brush of his lips before he used the soft, dry towel. I hissed, the new texture rougher than he had intended.

He looked up to me and watched me as his tongue flattened over my clit then took it into his warm mouth. I gasped as he began to suck softly and moaned when a gruff sound from his chest sent vibrations through me. He huffed a sound of impatience, and I came as if on demand, a slow, agonizing orgasm that was almost painful to complete. I had never experienced anything like it before.

He licked his lips and discarded the rags off to the side of the bed before lying down next to me again.

He gathered me up into his arms, and our legs tangled together. I wanted to feel every inch of my body touched by this man. By this demon.

"Next time," he said into my brow, "I won't hold back."

20

ZEPAR

BURN
MY BONES

Mara had fallen asleep on my arm hours ago. The sun had already started to peek through the curtains in her room to shed light on the pivotal mistake I had made the night before. I'd shown Sitri that Vepar wasn't the only one who cared that Mara was kept safe. I didn't regret sleeping with Mara. In fact, I was having a hard time not waking her for another round. I wanted to take her to the game room and see what sort of bravery we had unlocked last night.

You're mine, Zepar.

Fuck, that had felt good.

She had felt good.

I'd spent many nights tangled up in humans' bodies. Often with several humans at once. But the way her words had sparked fire through my blood in that moment was once in a lifetime. She'd taken

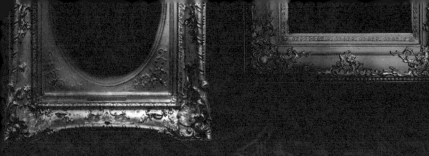

hold of her confidence and had held no fear that I would reject her. I'd never thought about a human taking possession of me. That wasn't how this all worked, after all.

I was made of power, fallen grace, and sin. All morality that had been left in me after the Fall had long since been molded into duty. But here I was, lying next to a human whom I had promised to keep safe as long as I could, basking in the lingering sweat that coated our skin with no other motive but to watch her sleep soundly with the marks my teeth had made still pink on her shoulder. I was ignoring the throbbing of my cock at the memory of the certainty in her voice in that pivotal moment.

Mine.

If I were hers and took her as my own, how could I make that clear to the angels and the other demons? The act would bring every eternal being to my doorstep, but I'd rip every last one of them to shreds just to hear those words come from her lips again.

The last echo of sanity told me that it wasn't really Mara that was pulling me down into these treacherous depths. It was that voice. That being lurking behind the shine of her eyes. The subtle thrum of power that subliminally said my name when she did. I'd heard it then as clearly as I had in the study so many hours before. It wasn't just Mara who was reaching out to me, claiming me. That mystical force had stretched out its vines to wrap around my being.

I reminded myself that it could have been any other demon. Told myself that if Vepar had been the one to shove his cock into Mara last night that he would have been the one obsessing over how to reach down into Mara again to hear that voice say his name. It was the siren's call for protection, and who better to man the front lines than a powerful demon entranced by the vessel's pussy. The perfect defense mechanism.

Mara had no malice toward me. I believed she did enjoy herself and took comfort in my attention, but the driving force behind her actions had been influenced, and I would never know if this infatuation we shared was real or manufactured for the sake of preserving the mysterious energy dwelling inside of her every molecule.

I sighed and kissed her temple before sliding away to dress and get some air. She stirred a moment but didn't wake fully.

"Zepar?" her sleepy voice whispered. Her hands groped around where my body had been.

I rounded the bed and got to my knees at her side. With her eyes closed, she rolled to her side to face me. Sleep still held on to her with its greedy possession, but a hint of satisfaction softened her features when she heard my voice.

"I have to get some work done." I kissed her red, smudged lips. "I'll be back soon."

She reached out and found my arm, and the hairs there bristled at the sensation, pulling into goosebumps to be closer to her.

"Stay with me."

I wanted to. I would have abandoned every last meeting or duty to be closer to her. Lying next to her for the night wasn't enough. My cock being buried inside of her wasn't close enough. The sudden madness of that emotion set fire to my insides.

"Dream of me," I whispered and pressed her palm to my lips, leaving her with one last kiss.

I pulled away to stand, and she didn't protest. I grabbed my clothes and left her room, only once looking back at the curve of her body under the sheet. I needed to get my head on straight and take a very cold shower.

After I showered and dressed for the office, I heard the front door downstairs shut and two voices muttering as they came up the stairs. Vepar entered my room first, followed by Andras.

"She is as quiet as a mouse. You won't even know she's here," Vepar said to Andras.

"What's this about?" I said, looping my tie in the mirror.

"Vepar has asked me to babysit his human while you're away." Andras' thick accent filled the room with its baritone.

"Is that so?" I eyed Vepar, who was perusing the colognes on my dresser.

"We both have meetings all day at the firm, and I can't have her wandering about your house unattended," Vepar replied coolly.

Andras was a lesser demon who was more of a utility to the dukes. Vepar called upon him when he needed his dirtier work to be taken care of more discreetly. Andras had been given little responsibility on this plane other than to slaughter legions of humans. He was a stocky and boorish man with thick, mousey-brown hair and tattoos covering him from head to toe—his attempt to blend in with those of us who carried our sigils branded onto our skin and soul. Today, he was dressed in all black, giving his skin a stark contrast. His only other defining feature past the ink was his crystal-blue eyes.

I narrowed my gaze to Vepar, who crossed the room to my side. "Don't worry, dear brother. Andras will not let anything befall our sweet Mara." He turned around to Andras, who was running his fingers over a painting on my wall. "Isn't that right, Andras?"

Andras grunted his response and eyed me. I'd not invited him into my home prior, and the discontent of the fact didn't go unnoticed. I could reschedule my later meetings until tomorrow, but I had three mergers and a stockholder meeting that I had to attend this morning. I took a deep breath to push down the impulse to burn my life to ash so I could watch over Mara's every move myself.

No. Andras would do just fine as long as he kept his distance. There was no telling how he would react if he realized the looming presence in my home was hiding inside Mara. It was obvious that there was a surge of old magic thrumming through my walls, but for all he knew, it was coming from any other item that I had collected over the years. It was no secret that Vepar and I were collectors of rare and mysterious things. Among that notion, Mara was in good company.

I slipped on my suit jacket and ran my hand through my hair one last time in front of the mirror. Sleeplessness was evident under my eyes, but I was energized by uncertainty.

As I passed Andras, I took hold of his arm and spoke my only warning. "Touch her and I will rip you to pieces and feed you to the hounds. She doesn't leave the house, and you do not go into her room."

His dark smirk stirred rage in my stomach, but before I could say another word, Vepar was dragging me through the void to the office in downtown L.A. He clapped my shoulder and gave me a reassuring nod before moving into the hustle of the work room beyond the elevator we had appeared in.

My receptionist caught sight of me and came barreling toward me with a stack of contracts and a wide smile on her simple face. No other human woman would be as beautiful as Mara. Their smile wouldn't be as radiant. Their hips wouldn't sway the same. The swell of their breasts under their shirts wouldn't draw my eyes the same way. I hadn't realized I was making the comparisons until Maddie spoke and her voice was dull and leaded against the crisp, bell-like way Mara had said my name.

"Mr. Zepar, I'm sorry to have to do this but you're needed in the conference room right away. There was an issue with this morning's scheduled meetings, and the group from Bakersfield is in a panic over the merger."

My lips pulled into my cheeks. This wasn't unplanned. When humans were made to feel they were losing everything they had been working for, they became desperate. This sort of calculated chaos was how I cultivated so many relationships in the business world but also how I raked in hundreds of souls a quarter for Lucifer. This was when I truly orchestrated my position as the best.

I spotted Vepar across the rows of desks. He was speaking to another human who was wiping sweat from their temple. Vepar gave me a wolfish grin, and I knew he was also off to collect a horde of souls. It would be a productive day, as long as I could keep my mind off Mara.

The boardroom Maddie had pointed me to was full of the worried faces of men who had spent their year-end bonuses on third or fourth houses and yachts. Each one of them reeked of fear and worry. The sweat stains under their arms and at the collars of their shirts were the marks of men teetering on the brink of losing it all. Their eyes shifted to me as I entered the room and took up my position at the head of the table.

Sour, gritty anticipation lay thick in the air. I would promise to ensure their company's survival, which was enough to make them come in their trousers. But what they were about to give to me was far more valuable. Each and every one would be signing away their soul to me in the next hour. Then I would move on to the next group of feeble minds to reap the spoils of hostile takeovers.

"Gentlemen." I plastered a smile on my face. "Who is ready to make a deal?"

Expecting a demon to be there in the morning after sleeping together was probably foolish, but the way he had looked at me, really saw me, made me think there was something more between us.

I went to the bathroom and looked at myself in the mirror. Aside from a few small marks from him on my neck and pinpoint bruises on my hips. I was intact, an accomplishment considering who had been gripping on to me in the night. The memory sank into my stomach as my fingertips smoothed over the dark spots. My pulse quickened at the heat brushing up my neck, and a deep longing for more filled my belly. No other man had made me feel so much, and I badly wanted to chase that high over and over again.

Nostrum. Eius sumus.

There was a ring of a bell beneath the echo of these words as

they filled my mind from somewhere within me. I wasn't sure what language it was, and yet I knew what the dark and silky voice was telling me. Zepar had a hold over me, and whatever, or whoever, was hiding under my skin wanted it that way.

I shivered at the thought but still hoped Zepar was thinking of me, craving me the way I was craving him. He'd given me a taste of what I had been missing from physical relationships, and now the thirst and hunger were making me manic.

I took a deep breath then splashed cold water over my face and chest. Droplets of water stained the silk slip I'd worn through the night. The smell of spice and lust was still woven into the delicate threads. I pulled the material over my head and scrunched it into a ball. I filled my lungs with the aroma until I was sure I had seared the scent into my memory.

There couldn't have been a more addicting smell than that of passionate obsession.

I finally tossed the dress into the hamper and put my hair up into a tangled bun on the top of my head. I wasn't ready to shower and rinse away the remnants of Zepar from my skin. I found my jeans and a T-shirt to slip into; I hadn't rummaged through the other clothing bags and boxes that Vepar had brought over yesterday. He had been so proud of the wardrobe he had handpicked that it was only fair that he would be around when I looked through it. He may not have thought much of me, but he had an affinity for dressing me up. And I would never say it out loud, but I didn't mind the attention.

I traveled down the stairs to the kitchen to make something to eat and was met by a large, brooding being sitting at the kitchen island. His eyes met mine over his mug of coffee.

"Um. Hi," I said, my eyes darting around the kitchen for a sign of familiarity. "Is Vepar or Zepar here?"

"They had work," he said in a gruff morning tone even though it was past noon.

With my feet frozen in place, I cleared my throat.

"I'm Mara. Who are you?" I cringed at my forwardness, but it didn't seem to be common courtesy for demons to politely introduce themselves.

He perked his brow and eyed me suspiciously. "Nice try, wee one."

"No. I—" I stammered. "Just, what would you like for me to call you?"

Would it ever not be awkward to ask a demon for their name or how they'd like to be addressed?

"That'll depend," he volleyed.

I pulled my arms across my chest, shrinking at the insinuating tone of his voice. "Depend on what?"

The corners of his lips pulled at his scruffy cheeks. He turned on the stool and stood fully. He was much taller than I thought he would be, at least six three and towering over my small five-foot-three frame. I looked up to him as he took two strides toward me and eyed me over. His brow furrowed as his gaze snagged on my breasts under the shirt, then an approving sneer formed when he reached my hips.

"Call me Dras, fer now." He looked away from me and went to sit back down at the kitchen island.

My lungs filled with relief. "Okay. Dras."

He smiled and sniggered before taking a long sip of his coffee. I watched his throat bob as he swallowed another gulp then put the mug down in front of him. He was hard to read.

I thought back to the way Eli and Zepar had greeted me. They'd had a warmth about them that had been laden with trustworthiness. But Dras was prickly, slimy, and mocking. I supposed that was more appealing than the way Sitri had behaved. Ezequiel had been passive and ignored me completely. Maybe that was what I would have preferred. Maybe this was truer to how other demons behaved and I'd had yet to encounter it.

It struck me then that I had no idea how many demons there were walking around the world. What did this one do with his time? He looked like a club bouncer or a bookie, but I wasn't going to ask. He also had the tough outward scruff of a hit man from a movie I'd seen ages ago. His hands wrapped around his mug were massive. I could see one punch from him would knock out any man I knew with the first blow. He could probably strangle someone one-handed. He was the most terrifying demon I had met thus far, including Zepar and Vepar in their demonic forms.

I shook myself to stop staring and went to the fridge to replace the anxiety in my stomach with food. Vepar kept a well-stocked fridge. Veggies and fruits were in the crisper, cheese and dried meats in another drawer. The thing he seemed to be missing was good junk food.

It wouldn't have been important for a demon to eat healthily or really at all if they were immortal and just about indestructible. Another swarm of questions about the anatomy and physiology of demons clouded my purpose for holding the fridge door open. I reached in and moved a glass bottle of expensive-looking orange juice to find a loaf of coffee cake that was wrapped in plastic next to a carton of free-range eggs.

When I turned around with the plate of coffee cake in hand, Dras was gone. His coffee mug sat half-full, but he was nowhere to be seen. I leaned into the hallway toward Zepar's office but saw no trace. If it weren't for the mug, I would have sworn I'd dreamed him up.

I decided it wasn't my place to question the movements of demons and sat down to pick at the slice of coffee cake and reflect on the night before.

I felt foolish for thinking I could have held myself together. That

Sitri, Ezequiel, Vepar, and Zepar were like other men. That being around them would have been any less intimidating than being around anyone else I hardly knew.

I had reached for Zepar though I'd been told not to. I had wanted to crawl into his arms when Sitri had turned his attention to me. Sitri had been very handsome, and there had been something screaming at me to touch him. The way his lustrous eyes flicked over my body had sent off a burst of butterflies in my gut. The way his hands had roamed over the human he had plucked out of the crowd gave me a flash of something akin to jealousy.

Jealousy. Envy. Lust. Perhaps he was one of the deadly sins in solid form.

And then the kiss Vepar and I had shared.

The hollow cavern in my chest filled with nervous energy. Zepar had tensed at my side when his twin kissed me and held me close. Vepar's lips had been just as soft and welcoming but not nearly as meaningful. Not to say he hadn't meant to kiss me for the benefit of our illusion, but the way his tongue had swept into my mouth had felt more foreign than another new lover's would have. It had felt timid. Restrained. Respectable, even.

He had gotten hard against the front of his slacks, and his hands had felt intimate parts of my body for Sitri's benefit.

In the heat of our return, Vepar and I hadn't talked before he'd stormed off to the other room, and I had been too preoccupied with Zepar to think about where Vepar had gone.

Zepar and I hadn't acknowledged all that had happened either. He had been furious under his cool exterior. The way he had grabbed me and kissed me on the stairs was surely a manifestation of relief that we'd made it out of the club alive, but also that he hadn't been comfortable with the way Vepar had touched or kissed me. The thought that he could have been jealous sent a skitter of ego over my skin and a smirk to my lips.

Who knew I could have such an effect over an ageless, almighty demon?

I pondered it too deeply as I shoved another corner of cake into my dry mouth. I looked around to the espresso machine on the counter and examined the buttons. It seemed pretty self-explanatory until I pressed what I thought was the coffee grinding button and steam shot from the wand all over the counter.

I shrieked and jumped back into Dras' solid chest. He had silently reappeared.

I fell to the floor and tried to scurry away from him and the loud espresso maker. Embarrassment flooded me as he looked down at me blankly. It felt like when I was a child and my father caught me rummaging through my mother's jewelry box.

I opened my mouth to defend myself against Dras' scathing presence but came up with nothing.

Dras leaned down, picked me up effortlessly, and planted me back on my feet before pushing me aside.

"Sit." He pointed to the other side of the kitchen island, and I did as I was told.

He calmed the steamer's tantrum and then began grinding beans for the pull. I watched him go to the fridge for the carton of milk then pour some into the steaming pitcher.

He turned back to me, his steely expression unchanged. "What do ya want? I'll make it before ya tan the thing."

Dras was surly and was having none of my incompetence. I couldn't blame him, I supposed. He had been talked into watching over me without any introduction.

"A latte would be great," I piped up. "Thank you."

I shoved a large piece of cake into my mouth to keep my foot from entering it while he expertly made my drink and set it down in front of me. A layer of foamed milk lay over the espresso with no finesse, but it tasted just as good as the last that had been made for me.

Dras lumbered back out of the kitchen and toward the stairs without another glance at me. It wasn't as if I needed someone to sit with me. I just needed someone more powerful than I was to defend me if an angel or demon came to kill me. Any loud scream would prompt Dras into action, I hoped.

I finished my coffee and headed up to my room. It was just about one in the afternoon, and my body was telling me it was time for a nap. I hadn't gotten nearly enough sleep in the last…

How long had I even been here? It all blended together. Days and nights crashed into a lifetime. Stress would do that. But it had only been a couple of days since Curt had died and I'd been kidnapped. I had learned I had more questions than answers about myself than I ever had before.

When I reached the second-floor landing, I noticed my door had been left open and the sounds of someone rummaging through my things met me several steps away from the threshold.

My feet planted to the floor.

Why would Dras be going through my room?

I took a step back and jumped out of my skin when I hit something solid in the middle of the hallway. My shoulders locked as I slowly turned my head to see the tall, gruff demon who was meant to protect me staring back down. A squeak of surprise only barely made it out of my throat when his hand clapped over my chin and my nose. His thick arm wrapped around me and lifted me from my feet. I fought for air through his oversized knuckles and thrashed about to get loose.

"Don't fight. It'll only make what's coming next more traumatic for ya." He grunted into my hair.

His words filled me with fear and fight.

I dug my nails into his hand and kicked at his knees and shins as hard as I could. But he just laughed darkly and held me tighter against his chest, unwavering against my attacks.

The last thing I saw before blacking out was the small, familiar figure of Focalor coming out of my bedroom.

When I came to, I was lying on my messed-up bed. My eyes cleared to see the ceiling and chandelier swaying over my head. I pinched my eyelids closed to focus my vision, and when I opened them again, I saw movement out of my peripheral.

"Oy," Dras called to his accomplice, who had been out of my line of sight. "She's awake."

Focalor came into view next to the bed and stared down at me with a nasty cringe. She'd had a similar look on her face the first time we'd met, and by the looks of my room, she had even less appreciation for my situation.

I tried to pull myself up to sit or scramble away but found my wrists had been bound along with my ankles. This was not the way I thought those clasps on the bed would be used.

"Let me out of here! Let me go!" I pulled against the restraints like a mouse in a trap. She had caught me, but what was she planning on doing with me?

"Andras," Focalor called back to Dras, "lock the door on your way out. Do not let them in."

My eyes darted to the cruel smirk on Dras' face as he obeyed her instructions. My pulse raced and my breathing became frantic as she took another step closer.

"Zepar!" I called out as she put her knee on the edge of the bed.

"He isn't here, little one," she said, unnaturally calm and sweet.

Her tone reminded me of when my mother had taken me to the doctor for a shot, knowing full well I was terrified of needles. The false sense of comfort only added to my distress.

Focalor came to straddle my stomach, holding me down to the bed and inhibiting any attempt to get loose from my shackles.

She leaned down, and her lips brushed my earlobe. "They were too weak to do what needed to be done to protect the rest of us. You cannot be."

Her voice was barely audible over my panting. She wasn't heavy—she was about my height—but it was like some kind of force was pushing me down with more strength than her legs alone.

Curre!

The voice screamed through me, and the sensation of something growing inside of me looking for a way out coupled with my terror of Focalor on top of me.

"Please stop!" I cried, tears falling to the sides of my temples.

She raised her face to meet mine, her eyes flaring with a golden backlight behind her blue irises. Her terribly beautiful features were all sharp edges and striking definition. Her blonde hair fell over her shoulder in one long braid.

"You will be welcomed into His Kingdom with open and loving arms. There is nothing to fear, little one. Only bliss and peace await you in the end."

The sound of a snap popped in my left ear. She straightened and slowly raised a long, silver dagger over her head. I screamed and bucked underneath her, but she did not budge. She looked up into the point of the blade and began to pray over me. "Oh, Father. Take this act of Your will as a promise that I am forever Your hand in good against evil. May Your righteousness be honored and Your judgment be just and true."

My throat went dry as she looked down at me with fiery determination.

My body clenched and my eyes closed, bracing for impact. One last thought raced through my mind.

"Vepar!" My scream echoed around the room.

A searing pain pierced my chest. I was going to die. The blade was making its way past my skin. The force that was tossing my body against my cuffed extremities had to have been my soul being expelled from me.

There was a crash on the floor next to me and a gush of wind. A yelp of pain that didn't come from my lungs filled the room. My eyes shot open to see Focalor no longer perched on top of me and the door to the room blown off its hinges. A groan of pain mixed with the settling of debris around the floor before a booming voice echoed through the chaos.

"You're dead, Focalor." Vepar stormed across the room and rounded the bed.

He reached down below my line of sight and pulled a bloodied Focalor from the ground by her arm. Oily, black streaks crossed her pale skin from gashes on her forehead, lip, and cheek. She grimaced at Vepar's hold as he pulled her out into the middle of the room. Dras was getting to his knees and used the back of his ripped sleeve to wipe the blood from his broken nose.

"Let her go, Vepar," Dras wheezed. "I wouldn't want to have to shred you to pieces in front of your human pet."

Vepar brought Focalor to her feet and held her by the scruff of her neck before Dras, who stumbled to his feet and pinched the bridge of his nose to tamp the drip.

I pulled on the cuffs at my wrists to get a better view of the three demons getting ready to tear each other apart, but there was no give. If they did start to kill each other, my only hope for survival was that the bed would be out of the direct line of fire.

"I will deal with you next, Andras. You lowly snake, I trusted you," Vepar scolded, but Dras chuckled then squealed in pain.

Dras fell to the ground with a thud, and the most glorious sight I had ever seen registered when I looked at the splintered doorframe.

Zepar.

The unmistakable look of dark enjoyment was drawn over his brow and crooked smirk. He scanned between me, Focalor, Vepar, and then down to Dras, who had made it back up to his knees. Zepar's presence in the room was electric, dangerous, and unpredictable. The buzz of his anger through the air was tart and exhilarating. With his crisp, black suit and blood-red dress shirt, he was the god of death.

"I warned you." Zepar grabbed the back of Dras' head in a tight fist and pulled.

Focalor, who had been silent, whimpered and reached her hand out to Dras. Vepar snatched up her blood-splattered T-shirt from the middle of her back and pulled her onto her ass.

"He was only doing it on my order," she pleaded to Vepar and Zepar. "It's me you want to punish, not Andras."

"Ever the martyr, dear sister," Zepar answered, not taking his eyes or hands off Dras.

Vepar leaned down to Focalor's ear but did not whisper his decree. "Mara is mine. You know the laws, Focalor. I have the right to destroy you both for your disloyalty."

"Disloyalty!" Focalor protested. "You should be the ones bloodied and battered for your disloyalty. You're choosing this human over your own family. Over our purpose. Over our Father."

My stomach caved in on itself. She was either deranged or devoted. And there had been plenty of times in my life when I'd known people who were both.

Zepar's eyes lifted to meet mine, and he parted his lips to speak down to Dras with a subtle tilt to his head. "Was the reward Focalor promised worth your betrayal, Andras?"

"She told me Mara was dangerous," Dras grunted out through clenched teeth. "She was right. Whatever that human is, it isn't right. I could feel the presence within her the moment I laid eyes on her."

Zepar's gaze did not leave mine while Dras spoke, but there was no look of surprise from him. I swallowed the knot in my throat, and the muscles in my neck ached from straining to see their exchange. Fear and the need to run had slipped into curiosity and confusion. The lurking darkness that had been crowding within me was speaking to other demons, or it was at least loud enough for them to hear it. Like some kind of demonic dog whistle.

"You are right." Zepar's voice was deep and venomous. "She is dangerous. She wields me."

Dras screamed and heaved as Zepar cut open Dras' throat. Oozing, blackened blood drained from the long slice. He gurgled and choked on it until his eyes rolled to the back of his head. Zepar released the body to fall to the floor. A small engraved brass dagger had been the weapon of choice and dripped with the sludgy rust in Zepar's hand.

Focalor let out a mournful wail. I tore my eyes away from Dras' lifeless body to see her thrashing against Vepar's hold and tears streaming down her face. If she hadn't just tried to kill me, I would have felt sad for her loss, felt her pain more deeply than my own shock that Zepar just murdered one of his own for being part of her plot.

"Now for you." Zepar pointed the dirty edge of his dagger in Focalor's direction, and she bucked back against her captor.

"No. Zepar, don't do this. You have to see what this human is doing to us," she said between panting grief and panic. "What her every breath is bringing our kind closer and closer to. She will be the end of us all."

Zepar laid the dagger against her jaw, the tip jutting into her tender flesh, and raised her gaze to meet his. "You are not my problem to contend with, my once most-adored sister. Vepar will see to your fate."

He lifted his gaze to Vepar, who dipped his chin behind Focalor's ear. "Let's go have some fun at my house, Focalor. I've just redone the dungeon. I think you'll find it quite cozy for the next several hundred years."

The eerie timbre of his voice sent ice through my veins but butterflies into my stomach. The roiling inside of me loosened when Vepar and Focalor disappeared into thin air. I let the tension in my muscles go, and my head fell back onto the bed. Zepar came to stand

at the edge of the mattress and looked down at me. The deadly gleam
had gone from his eyes and had been replaced by worry.

. He waved a hand over me, and my hands and feet were released
from the cuffs. I pulled my arms and legs into my torso and sat up in
the middle of the crumpled sheets.

He looked down at the mess of Dras' body then pinched the bridge
of his nose. "I don't typically ask this of my guests, but would you like
to sleep in my room tonight?"

My heart leaped into my throat. I hadn't seen his room, and that felt
somehow like a much bigger gesture than he was probably intending.
I couldn't find the words that said "only if you really want me to" or
"yes, please hold me and never let go."

Both feelings felt weak, but at what point in this entire fiasco had I
not been vulnerable. Vepar wanted me to behave as if I had an army
at my back, but at every turn, I was being bombarded with crushing
blows to my confidence that I would live another day.

I nodded and scooted toward Zepar and dangled my feet over the
edge. The floor was coated in slick fluid from Dras' wound, and rivers
of blood snaked over the grooves of the wood floor planks. I stared
down into the sheen of its abyss. Dras had gotten off easy for betraying
Zepar and Vepar. I shuddered to think what was in store for Focalor at
Vepar's home in Purgatory.

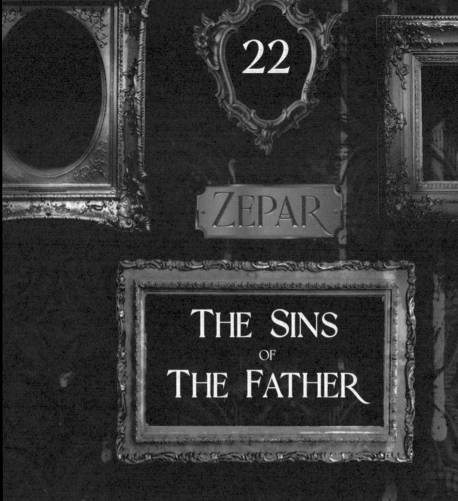

22

ZEPAR

THE SINS
OF
THE FATHER

Mara's attention was glued to what remained of Andras. The enflamed rage that had taken over my senses was dissipating, and in its wake, the regret was setting in.

Andras had been a good soldier to many of the princes and dukes of Hell. He had always sided with what was fair and equal, and in doing so had become one of the most trusted weapons among us. Many of which would say that he didn't deserve what I had dealt him, but the betrayal was greater than any I would have expected of him.

His trust in Focalor had been more than that of most other demons because Andras had also believed we didn't deserve to be cast from Heaven all those eons ago. He'd been waiting for the hand of our Father to return us to our rightful place in His kingdom.

A notion that had clearly gone from delirium to danger.

I bent down and scooped Mara off the bed, careful to avoid having even the smallest drop of blood touch her. She jolted at my touch but settled into my arms when her eyes met mine.

I looked down over her body. From what I could tell, she was unharmed physically except for an irritated mark on her chest from the necklace's charms.

Vepar and I had been in the middle of a joint meeting when his chest began to irritate him. It had been a sign that Mara was in distress. He'd excused himself from the boardroom, and only seconds later, he was ripped through the void to her aid. It had taken a few moments for me to untangle myself from the rest of the board and join him. It had felt like an eternity.

Now that she was safely in my arms, I could breathe easier. But I knew that at any moment she could be attacked again by angel or demon. One failed attempt wouldn't stave off the rest. If anything, Focalor's near success would challenge many more to try what she couldn't accomplish. I needed to find a way to keep Mara safe but also keep her from a life of fear. That was what she had always wanted. That was what I had promised her.

She was silent during the long walk to my room. My halls had never felt so foreign and thin. Focalor had sunk her talons into Andras and together they had made my home a trap. I could never forgive her for that.

I pushed the door to my room open with my knee and didn't sense any other dangers. My room had the heaviest wards in the house, against angel and demon alike. I had only trusted a few enough to invite them into the room before, but I wouldn't make that mistake again.

Upon crossing the threshold, I pulled Mara into my chest as tightly as I could before speaking the words out into the room in booming Aramaic.

"None shall enter here."

The tongue of my Father's most devout followers had been adopted by the Fallen in rebellion, but it had also become so sparsely used in modern days that it was our safest method of communication and protection.

The air in the room swelled then relaxed against the newly warded walls. I lowered Mara to her feet then turned to shut the door. When I turned back around, Mara was holding her necklace in her hands. The chain had broken when she called upon Vepar. I wondered if she had noticed the mark it had left on her skin. Shock was still holding on tight to her senses from the far-off look in her brown eyes.

The dull hum of her hiding resident was quieting now that it was no longer in danger. When I had appeared, its high-pitched whining had been like nails on a chalkboard. It had made incapacitating Andras easier but hadn't distracted Focalor from her mission.

"Mara?" I took a step closer but waited for her to respond.

"It's broken," she said coolly, not looking away from the snapped clasp and charred charms in her palms.

"Vepar can get you a new one tomorrow." I tried to sound reassuring; it had saved her life after all.

Her eyes slowly panned up to mine. "A new one?"

"To keep you safe."

"Safe?" she repeated.

I was lost for what that meant. I had told her she was safe in her room, in my house. As we stood looking into each other's eyes, I assumed we would be safe for at least another night, but the word and concept were losing their meanings. Safety would always be a goal for the human race, but the meaning was different for each of them. Mara had experienced real horrors since meeting Vepar; I wouldn't know what safety meant for her any longer.

I pulled myself away from her gaze and shrugged off my jacket. My phone in my pocket hadn't stopped buzzing since Vepar had been called away. The entire firm was up in arms over our sudden departure. I rejected an incoming call from Maddie then dialed Vepar's number.

He answered on the third ring.

"Is our sister set in her new domain?"

"She is secure for now. I am going back to the office to salvage our jobs. If anyone asks, you have food poisoning."

I smiled into the phone. No one would believe him, but he was about to flush their pockets with cash, so they would smile and take it.

"I'm going to stay here with Mara. It's not worth the risk of us both leaving her again."

He sighed, his guilt heavy in his breath.

"She's fine, but she'll need a new beacon. The necklace's magic snapped it in two."

"Cheap trinket." He cursed. "I'll get one on my way after I close these contracts. Give me a few hours and we'll figure something else out."

"Maddie has my files. She'll advise you if you need anything."

"See you later, brother."

His line cut out, and I turned my phone off completely. Even with him back in the office, my receptionist would want confirmation that I hadn't died of some mysterious ailment.

I turned around to find Mara coming out of her stupor and investigating my room. My large bed, which sat in the center of the spacious room, didn't have the same equipment hers had, but she circled to the headboard to inspect it anyway. A pang of guilt sank into my stomach at the reminder that what should have been meant for pleasure had been used to almost take her life.

"Zepar. Could you hear me?" she asked in a daze.

I crossed to the opposite side of the bed to give her space and to take off my tie. I let the ends fall to my chest and started to unbutton my shirt before I answered.

"No. But I knew I shouldn't have left."

Her eyes tracked my hands as they trailed down my chest. She pulled her bottom lip in between her teeth and wrapped her arms around herself.

"Mara, what can I do for you?" I dipped my chin to meet her gaze over my bared skin peeking through my shirt.

"I-I don't know." She shook her head, and I walked around the bed to her side.

I took her chin in my fingers and tilted her face up to mine to lay a kiss on her forehead.

"Let's take a shower," I suggested, and she nodded.

I led her into the bathroom and turned on the water to let it warm. Then I gripped the hem of her shirt and lifted it over her head. The marks from my teeth still were pink on her soft skin. My fingers glided down her sides and met at the button on her jeans. Her eyes didn't leave my face as I hooked my thumbs into her waistband and pushed the pants down to her ankles. Warmth brimmed in my chest at the way she took comfort in my touch. That she allowed me, after all that had happened, to take care of her.

She removed her underwear and the tie in her hair that had barely kept her hair in its ragged knot from all her thrashing about during the attack. After I undressed myself, we stepped into the free-standing shower together. She stared at me for a long while, wordlessly. The night before had been such a frenzy that our nudity had been secondary to the needs that had been met. Standing under the hot water together now was a new experience.

The pink mark where the necklace had been between her full breasts was starting to clear. Her curvy hips and soft waist reminded me of works of marble in the Louvre. The dimples at her hips begged for my fingers to grip. My nerves screamed to touch her and feel her wet skin against mine. But I kept my distance.

She leaned her head back into the water and let it soak her hair, sending streams down her body. Her hands scrubbed over her face and remnants of last night's makeup streaked over her cheeks. The longer I watched her, the more I lost myself. Without thinking, I wiped away a loose eyelash from under her eye. A small smile tugged at the corners of her mouth, and tension released between my shoulders.

I took a step into her and reached over her head to the bottles of soap on the rack hanging from the stone wall. The smell of eucalyptus filled the shower as I poured some shampoo into my hand then set the bottle back down.

"May I?" I jutted my chin to her, and she cocked her head.

"You want to wash my hair?"

"Not if you don't want me to." I smiled at the scrunch of her nose, but she turned around nonetheless.

I massaged the suds into her scalp then worked the bubbles to the ends of her hair before taking the showerhead off its mount to rinse the soap down her back.

The splashing of water at our feet distracted me from the reality that would meet us soon, either this evening or in the coming morning. But for a small window of time, all that mattered was that I'd awkwardly asked to bathe her and she'd obliged.

She took down the bottle of bodywash and my loofa before she turned around to me. "My turn."

I raised my brows at her demanding tone, but I didn't hide the grin it brought to my face. I returned the showerhead to its hook and allowed her unencumbered access to my body.

She wet the sponge and dumped a good amount of soap onto it before lathering it up. She started with my chest. One of her hands gripped my arm as the other scrubbed over my already clean skin. I had showered earlier in the morning, but I didn't tell her that.

She reached my stomach and made swirling patterns with the hair trailing down to my groin. Then over my hips and up my sides to my arms then shoulders, thoroughly covering my torso with the thick, white soap.

When she was satisfied with the job she'd done, she wrung out the loofa and held it out for me to take. As I reached up to grab the bottle of conditioner, her fingers whirled the bubbles at my chest in circles. She flattened her hand and rubbed my slick skin then explored lower. Her smile fell from her lips, but curiosity mounted her brow as her hands hesitantly roved over the crest of my hips then down to the thicker hair at the apex of my thighs. The rush of blood to my cock betrayed me almost immediately.

She rolled her eyes up to mine, and her hand took a firm hold of my shaft. Her lips parted, and her deep breaths brushed over me, setting my flesh on fire. I pulsed in her hand as she worked her wrist up and down. My chest shuddered at the pull in my stomach and at my restraint to not pin her to the wall and fuck her right then and there.

I reached my hand up to the back of her neck and crashed my lips over hers. The need to taste her on my tongue in any way I could took hold of me. She whimpered my name into my open mouth and added another crack to the dam of my fetter. Her hold on my cock stiffened, and she pumped faster between rubbing her hand over the head. Every nerve ending responded to her rhythm.

Our brows met. I looked down between us. My hips tensed as I climbed to the peak, and I looked into her determined eyes as she relished what she was doing to me.

"Do you like it when I touch you, Zepar?" she breathed, and I cursed my answer. "Tell me," she continued. "Say my name, and tell me how I make you feel."

That voice under hers had filled her with a confidence that had me losing all control over my thoughts.

"Mara, fuck," I panted out. "You feel so damn good."

"Am I going to make you come?"

My head and eyes rolled back. The sultry demand of her voice was too much. "Yes."

"Are you going to come for me?"

The sound that roughed out past my lips was more animal than demon. Her hands brought me crashing, shattering, breaking over the edge of an orgasm. My hot, spilled pleasure covered the back of her hand, and when my gaze found her face, she was wearing a devious grin at her prowess. I throbbed as she released me and rinsed her hand off in the stream of water.

She pulled the showerhead off the mount, sprayed my torso clean, then turned the water off. I watched her step out of the shower and wrap a towel around her body. My knees felt weak from pleasure but also the surprise that this woman had possessed me once again. The creature residing inside of her was wild and wicked.

I wrapped a towel around my waist, but when I stepped out of the shower, I scooped her up into my arms.

"I'm not done with you yet," I said into her lips then kissed her deeply.

Her legs circled my hips and her arms hooked around my neck as I walked us out to my bed. I laid her down and pulled at her towel. Her legs fell open to me. Waiting for me to reciprocate, luring me to what would surely be my undoing.

I dropped to my knees on the floor and domed my mouth over her engorged clit. Her warm pussy was slick for me already. I slipped two fingers inside as I swirled my tongue around her. Her sweet excitement coated my tastebuds, and I hummed my contentment. Her peaked breasts bounced as she panted through every new direction my mouth took.

I sucked her clit between my teeth and gently rolled it, flicking my tongue over and over the nerve. She screamed my name, and I drove my fingers into her harder. With every stroke she was getting closer to climax, and I desperately wanted to give it to her. I rotated between sucking and whirling until her inner walls clenched around my fingers and her legs jolted and struggled to come together around me.

Withdrawing my fingers, I broadened my tongue over her and licked long, fanned swipes while she came down from the high. Her thighs relaxed, and I rose to move her farther onto the bed. I wasn't done with her yet.

My cock was hard again, and I was welcomed inside of her warmly. She gasped and wrapped her legs around me. I drove my hips down into her, hitting her deepest spots.

"Is this what you wanted, Mara?" I thrust hard and deep.

She opened her mouth wide but didn't speak or breathe. I pulled out to my tip then crashed into her again, this time eliciting a scream of pleasure.

I relieved the pressure again. "Close your mouth, love, before I fuck it."

She slapped her hand over her mouth and moaned through the creases of her fingers. I smirked and eased into her slowly, bringing my name over her muffled sounds of desire. My hips stalled, and she bucked under me, searching for the right angle for her release.

"You haven't answered me," I said, kissing the back of her hand between my words.

"I need you, please." She pulled her hand away and whined, her cunt still begging for me to move.

"Where has that demanding woman gone? Don't be shy, darling," I teased with a pulsating thrust.

"Fuck me, Zepar," she demanded, her cheeks stained red. "Don't hold back. "

She would regret that, but I plunged down into her harder and faster. Her fingernails dug into my back as I delivered blow after blow. When I was sure that I had found a rhythm that pleased her, I hovered above her and pulled her arms up above her head. When she was pinned to the bed and unable to hold on to me, I lowered my lips to her then kissed down to her neck, chest, then a tip of her breast.

I cupped it with my free hand and sucked the peak a moment then bit down, causing her to shutter and call out. The wicked pleasure at the way her breath quickened and her body responded to me clouded my resolve. I slowed my pace but deepened my length with each rock of my pelvis. My tongue slid to her other breast over the valley of her chest. I wanted to experience every inch of her body. Taste the sweet and salt of her skin.

Her pleading hums mimicked the cadence of my cock slipping in and out of her. Every breath was laced with need as she edged the orgasm I had coaxed for her. Her wrists wiggled in the cuff of my fingers and I allowed her to break free to brace herself for what I was going to deliver next.

Her heavy breathing at my shoulder as I plowed into her became harder as we reached climax together. My cock twitched inside of her until she rode out the tail end of her orgasm.

I pulled out of her and lay next to her, both of us trying to catch our breath. She squeezed her legs together and shuddered with a full sigh. My hand found one of our towels, and I sat up to clean her thighs.

"I can do that." She reached down, but the smooth swipe of the fluffy fabric stopped her.

"I like to see the mess I've made." I smirked and pulled one of her legs to the side.

She watched me over the mounds of her breasts until I tossed the soiled towel to the floor. I got up and pulled the blanket back as she slipped off the side of the bed. While she dried her hair with the unused towel, I went to my dresser for a pair of boxer briefs.

"Can I borrow a shirt?"

I opened my dresser for a black T-shirt, which she shimmied over her head and down her body. The hem hardly covered her ass, but she looked good wearing my clothes.

The bounce of her steps tempted the length of the shirt as she walked over to the bed and got under the covers. I followed her steps, and she scooted over to my side. Her leg crossed over my bare thigh, and she settled into the seam of my body. Her fingers traced over the muscles at my stomach, zigging lower then zagging up to my chest.

She started to doze off moments later. Her breathing deepened and her hands flattened to my lower stomach.

I adjusted, but she held me closer. "No, stay. Please." She looked up to me with hooded eyes and full, pillowy lips.

"I'm not going anywhere for now."

Her eyes closed without much persuasion, and her hand slipped down over my boxers. My body responded to her even through fabric.

Lucifer, help me. I could fuck her for hours and still want more.

I was finally able to slip behind the door without disturbing a sleeping Mara when a crisp white envelope with gold lettering appeared in a puff of bright light. It gently landed in my open palm. A pale pink feather was tucked inside the note, the hallmark of who had sent it.

Z-

My place. As soon as it is the most convenient. Bring Vepar.
Regards,

R

I rolled my eyes and stuffed the note and feather back into the envelope. I trekked downstairs to find Vepar in the kitchen, pouring himself a cup of coffee. A bottle of aspirin sat next to his mug.

"Have a little too much fun today, brother?" I sat across from him on a stool, slapped the note down, and sent it skidding toward him with a flick of my fingers.

"For fuck's sake. Is that from who I think it is?" He rolled his neck, popping the cartilage with each pull of his muscles.

" You knew this was coming next. After that display at The Deacon, it was only a matter of time before he called upon us."

"Let's get this over with."

I closed my eyes and let the void between the folds of time and space take me into it. There was a rush of wind to my ears and a blast of chilled air to my face before my body came to a halt. Vepar sighed as he appeared next to me on the evening-damp lawn. The modern architecture of the white home looked like a set of child's building blocks stacked and teetering on their edges. The view beyond was of the Los Angeles valley lit by the orange, pink, and sapphire sunset. A circuit board of a city that rarely slept was coming to life in the early evening.

Vepar took the lead and headed toward the glass-paneled door and rang the bell. We waited a moment as the echo of footsteps from within approached and a figure came into focus through the glass.

Raphael swung the door open, and a wide smile cut his dark features. "Welcome, brothers. Come, come." He stepped to the side and ushered us through the door.

The moment my feet crossed the threshold, they were cemented in place. A force held me there, making it impossible to retreat or move farther inside. Vepar struggled as his knees gave out, and he landed on his ass next to me.

A burst of laughter came from Raphael several steps in front of us.

"We didn't come here to play games with you, Raph," Vepar shouted from the floor.

"You're right," Raphael said between his snickering and waved his hand to release the ward. "I am sorry. It was only a bit of fun. To lighten the mood."

His jovial tone bounced around the entryway into the high-ceilinged living room. He waved us over to the sitting area. A set of white leather couches sank into the floor and surrounded an open gas fireplace. The purple and blue flames licked the mix of clear and white stones piled in its center.

"Please, sit with me. It's time we hashed this nonsense out." Raphael encouraged us to sit before he reclined in his own seat.

"There is nothing to work out, Raphael. The rules apply to you as well. I have claimed the human, so her soul belongs to me," Vepar postulated. "By the guidelines of our Father, she is tainted and irredeemable. Unworthy of your grace."

Raphael grinned. "Special circumstances, my wayward brother."

Though we operated out of the same city, I hadn't seen Raphael in several years. By no coincidence, at that. I avoided him like the ten plagues. He resided on Earth and enjoyed the luxuries of humans. He'd presented himself as a faith healer several hundred years ago and had invested in snake oil, self-help gurus, and self-operated vacuums, all of which had built a human wealth that surpassed that of most. He sat comfortably amongst the millionaires of Los Angeles and didn't bring attention to himself.

He used the excuse of charity to explain why he spent more time down here than in Heaven. Several years back, his cover was almost blown due to too many miraculous healings at a local hospital he owned and operated as Dr. Grace. Humans who came in for inoperable brain tumors would wake up from surgery without a cell of cancer left behind. Who knew being too good would put a target on your back?

Since then, he had enjoyed the rewards of his investments, putting on lavish parties, charity balls, and marathons for entertainment and the good of mankind.

"You're right, Vepar. We do abide by the same constraints passed down to us by the Almighty, but there is something you are forgetting." He admired the fire lazily, not concerned for the laws the rest of us followed out of fear of being destroyed.

"That you are an archangel." Vepar rolled his eyes to our brother, who smiled broadly.

"Exactly. I can forgive her if she were only to ask." His arrogance peeked through his angelic tone.

"And why would you bestow such a gift on a human you know nothing about?" I chimed in, the ache in my chest opening up at the thought of him putting his hands on Mara to cleanse her.

"Honest?" He perked his brow and shrugged. "Mikael has been in my ear day and night over the situation and I like my sleep."

"What if she refuses?" Vepar asked what I was thinking, but this play wasn't as solid as Vepar thought.

"You believe she would be so consumed by evil that she would shy away from the Light and grace? She would choose to throw her soul to the snakes over the relief that my purification could give? Is she so lost?"

Neither Vepar nor I could speak for Mara and what she would want. But the trap he would lay for her wouldn't give her solace. The purification he spoke of likely meant her death and her soul being taken to Heaven as quickly as possible to disarm both sides.

I considered this offer for a moment. It would mean my life going back to the way it was only days before. It would mean that she would no longer be suffering the terror of being hunted. But she would lose her mortal life and forever the potential to fulfill her dreams and aspirations: to live and be free of Curt or any other who had hurt her. The life she had been building for herself and planning to lay brick by brick after freeing herself from Curt and the rest of us would be dashed away. The flame of her existence would be snuffed for the sake of the comfort of angels and demons who didn't care about her or know of her name before last week.

No.

She deserved to love. She deserved to live out her days safely and comfortably until her final judgment came naturally like all other humans.

I took a breath and calmed my nerves. Any hint of desperation in my tone would set off an alarm for Raphael and he would know he had me cornered.

"There is an alternative." I hummed into my glass.

"What would that be, little shadow?"

The nickname grated against my nerves.

"Call off your disciples and we will call off ours. She will go forth and not look back to either side until her dying day."

He cocked his head and gave me a sideways glance. My solution held no weight, and he knew that. He squinted, then a predatory, crooked grin spread over his previously curious face.

Shit.

"Do you recall the story of King Solomon and the harlot mothers?"

He rose from his seat and walked around the fire's edge to the window. The floor-to-ceiling glass overlooked the ornamental reflecting pool rippling in the wind.

"I don't believe my suggestion compares—"

"The threat is all the same and you have shown your hand, brother. And we both know she would not walk away from you." His silky tone was laced with knowing but was too cryptic to tell how much.

Vepar stood with his fists clenched. "She has no ties to us, but she doesn't deserve to die because she called upon me to fix a problem. If anyone should feel your wrath, it is Mikael for causing such a stir in the first place."

Vepar and I together could fight our way out of Raphael's home, but if we survived him, it would mean a legion of angels being sent to my door.

"No ties, you say?" Raphael deigned to Vepar, the cunning grin turning more malicious by the moment. "Do you believe me to be so blinded by my time living among the humans? I can see the stain of her on your lips, Zepar. The scent of her skin clings to your clothing like tar. You cannot conceal the marks of intimacy so easily with only a shower or spritz of cologne."

I internally cursed myself beneath my mask of indifference. I had let it slip momentarily, and as expected, Raphael had gleaned all he needed to by the flash.

Vepar vibrated with fury. "Who I allow to play with my pretty things is not your concern," he shot back. "I deny your proposal and will not give up my claim to Mara. You may forgive her when I have seen fit to let her shrivel and die away."

"You're insufferable. Always have been. The both of you." Raphael had lost all patience for the conversation. "I am offering you a chance to rid your lives of the inconvenience and you turn your nose up at it."

"What you are doing is finding a solution for your own peace," I chimed in, standing and ready to leave.

Raphael faced me, his skin igniting from within as we agitated the holy light of his being. It was like looking through a sheer lampshade into a bright bulb.

I clenched my fists and readied for the blow he was priming himself to land.

"Why would Mikael, and ultimately you, be this invested?" I asked, knowing he wouldn't answer truthfully. "If you are sick of Mikael's chirping, then why not quiet your own house and leave ours be?"

"That is none of your concern, and if you are unwilling to abide by my gentle request to relinquish her, then you are bringing what's coming to your door by your own hand."

"How very prophetic," Vepar chortled, dragging Raphael's attention to him.

The most-loved archangels would never reveal their intentions for any of their actions. They hid behind their relationship with our Father and His will to manipulate demons and humans alike.

Raphael's face darkened into an inauspicious grimace. "You have been warned. I suggest you ready yourselves for the pox that comes on swift wings."

I glanced to Vepar and then back to Raphael. His angelic brawn billowed up around the lines of his body. It was time to go so we could live to fight the battle he was insisting upon. I reached over to the sleeve of Vepar's jacket and tugged us both into the void back to my house.

We reappeared in the study moments later, and Vepar slumped down into the nearest chair, his face in his hands. He reminded me again of when we were much younger and more foolish. When we would breach the guiding lines that demons were told to follow. When famine, war, and illness were the only fathomable ways of collecting souls and angering our holy brethren into action. When we were constantly looking to scratch the itch of rebellion, long before we were given jurisdiction over certain parts of this place.

He sighed heavily and looked up at me. "His Great and Illustrious Eminence has now spoken. We are righteously and wholly fucked."

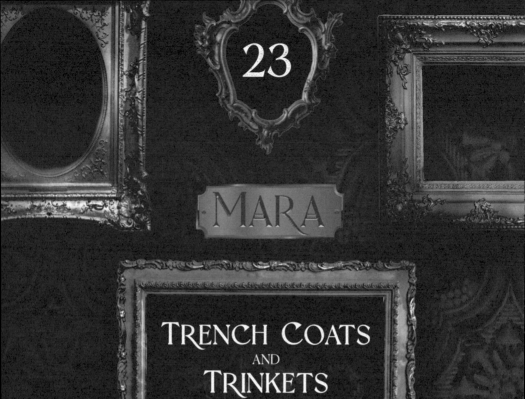

23

MARA

TRENCH COATS
AND
TRINKETS

The lack of Zepar's breathing woke me. It was dark out the window, but I didn't know how long I had been sleeping. I got up to go to the bathroom and decided to snoop around Zepar's medicine cabinet.

He had enough moisturizers, hair cream, aftershave, and expensive hygiene products to fill a beauty store. The drawers had extra toothbrushes and toothpaste, washcloths, and cotton swabs. I took a toothbrush out of one of the packages and set it out on the counter to use after I grabbed something to eat. I needed to get something in my stomach if I was going to go back to sleep while he was gone.

I walked out to the main space of his room and the door was still closed. Whatever he said when we walked in after the attack had felt like a security blanket had wrapped around me. Like when he had smeared that ink over my stomach. I wondered if that mark of

protection had worn off like the necklace, but there wasn't a demon around to check.

I reached for the doorknob and took a deep breath. Whatever monsters lurked on the other side of the door would be less terrifying than Focalor's blade over my chest.

Nothing greeted me when I swung the door open and padded down the hall to the stairs. The slight sticking of my bare feet against the wood floors was the only sound throughout the house until I reached the kitchen. I heard the reverb of voices as I looked for something to help me sleep. He must have needed to make a call or something.

I grabbed a banana and peeled it while I looked for something with protein or more sugar.

I pulled out a tub of cottage cheese and decided it would do. In the morning I would look around for ingredients for pancakes. A few stacks of warm and fluffy pillows covered in maple syrup sounded better than the watery cheese curds I was pushing around with my spoon, but I was sore from pulling at my restraints. Tired even after so much sleep. I finished off the tub and rinsed it and left it in the sink.

I stretched my arms over my head and made my way back toward the staircase to Zepar's room to wait for him when the voices floated out from the office.

"Raphael was clear. Unless we do something, he will come for Mara and kill us both to get to her."

Zepar sounded angry and defensive.

I didn't know who Raphael was, but I assumed they were talking about the archangel since it sounded as if they wouldn't be able to stop him from taking me away.

"What do you want to do, then?" Vepar replied, his tone much more simmered. "You have been the one to warm her bed. How do you see this playing out?"

I held my hand over my mouth to slow my breathing and pressed as close to the wall as I could to hear the plans they were concocting without my input.

"We ask Sitri to hang on to her, then we go to see Ipos," Zepar said, sending terror through me.

"Ipos? You want to go to that tin can in the desert to call on Ipos? Why would you think that nutty fool is going to help?" Vepar's voice traveled through the room and back again. He must have taken up pacing.

"Ipos may be crazy, but it's for good reason," Zepar said. "When you have been the omniscient seer for thousands of years, you would have lost your mind as well to keep yourself from jumping into the deepest pit of Hell."

What would this Ipos know about me that no one else would? More than Eli had found?

"And Sitri? You trust him not to turn her over to those who would do anything for Raphael just for the chance to suck his cock?"

"Sitri has more power than the both of us combined, though it pains me to admit it. She will be out of angel hands until we get back." Zepar's shadow was visible on the far wall. His shoulders slumped as he spoke, mimicking the fatigue in his voice.

"You are assuming Sitri will relinquish his hold over Mara when we go to get her back," Vepar countered.

They were both silent for a long moment before Zepar said, "What would you do?"

"I'm at a loss. Focalor has made it clear through her lashings that she has tainted many demons we have previously trusted. Eli has expressed again that, though he is fond of Mara, he doesn't want anything to do with this mess. So, it would seem that Sitri would be our last option. We know he will keep her alive long enough to figure out why we have all been so drawn to her."

The way Sitri's eyes had wandered over my body and how he had treated Zepar and Vepar made my skin crawl. Being given over to Sitri for safekeeping sent my stomach into cramping knots, but being left alone in this house also terrified me. Maybe Eli had the right idea to stay away.

Through the crack in the door, I could see their shadows but leaned forward and caught a glimpse of Zepar's back. He was leaning over the fireplace with his hand on the wall to brace himself. He looked tired, exhausted by the constant juggling of defense and offense. The tips of my fingers flexed and itched to touch him.

Sweat seeped from my pores, and Zepar's shirt clung to my back. That feeling of needing to run rang out through me. I didn't want to be the reason for any of this anymore. Zepar and Vepar couldn't keep me from being killed forever, and I needed to get out of the state of panic at every turn.

I crept back from the door and bolted up the stairs to my room. I just needed shoes and pants. If I left without them knowing or having any sort of trace on me and kept going, maybe we could all just forget I'd existed in this strange reality. The rush of fear pounded in my ears as I pulled on a pair of joggers from one of the drawers.

With a pair of shoes and a leather jacket I'd found hanging in the closet, I crept back down the stairs. Zepar was nowhere to be seen, not that this scenario hadn't played out before: me making my way to the door to face the hellhounds, angels, and demons who all wanted to see me dead. But now, it wasn't just me. Those same forces, save the hounds, were plotting to kill Zepar and Vepar to get to me.

I opened the deadbolt and then the door. The crisp night air met my face as I took a step onto the long driveway, the crunch of the stones under my feet quickening.

I was halfway down the drive when the sound of another set of footsteps came barreling up behind me. Expecting to see Zepar, I turned and dropped my shoulders but was met with the face of a large black dog with glowing red eyes and razor-sharp teeth. The hellhound was real, and it was chasing after me. I didn't have time to scream or think before my feet were carrying me to the tree line at the edge of the property.

The snapping of the giant's jaws at my heels ushered me farther into the woods and had me leaping over fallen trees and ducking under low branches. The trunks thickened and closed in on each other as I slithered through the underbrush. Over my own panting, I strained to listen for the terrible beast, but it was gone.

I reached up and pulled myself onto a branch of an evergreen then scurried up several more feet before daring to look. Both Vepar and Zepar had said the hounds would chase me down if I left. I hadn't fully believed them, and I was regretting it as sap and needles coated my knees and hands. I waited for several long minutes for any sound of paws or teeth, but there was no sign it was still following me. I didn't expect that it would have given up so easily. It had to be a trap. The vile thing was out there somewhere stalking me, and it was doing it too well.

I looked up over a bundle of trees and saw a broken trail. It could have been a road or a stream. Either way, it wasn't sitting in a tree waiting to become dinner. I slowly climbed down and scanned the foot of the forest. I saw neither hide nor tail of the devil Doberman.

It was now or never.

I shot toward the clearing and sprinted over more downed trunks and boulders. The trees began to thin, and a river of black concrete came into view. My feet hit the blacktop at breakneck speed, putting as much distance between me and Zepar's house as possible.

An arctic flood filled my belly when a set of red eyes blinked at me several yards down the road. It had known where I was going and had been waiting for me to catch up with it. I planted my feet out of fear. The woods on either side of me were well-known to this creature. No matter which way I ran, it would find me and tear me to pieces.

I pushed oxygen into my lungs and readied to scream when a bright, white light flashed before my eyes, followed by a yelp of pain. I shielded my eyes with my arm and watched the bright beam wither away. The outline of a man approached me. My heart stilled as a bronzed, warm smile greeted me.

"Hello, Mara." The stranger knew my name. That wasn't a good sign. "I'm not here to hurt you."

He held his hands up in defense, and I took a step back onto a twig. The snap of it shot up my spine and feathered over my back. The sensation sent an itch to my muscles. My calves and tendons coiled and readied to bound away if he took another step closer. The hellhound was dead or at least knocked out. One less obstacle for me to outrun.

"You're far from the clutches of Vepar," the tall, handsome man remarked. His eyes wandered over me then regrouped on my face with a too-sweet smirk. "It looks like you are no longer bound to him. How clever you must be."

Was that true? Had the necklace breaking actually severed the tie Vepar and I had?

I decided this stranger wasn't the one to ask to clarify. So I did what felt the most natural.

I lied.

"No, he is still my owner." My voice wavered. "We made a deal."

"I could help you be rid of that." His brows popped at the end of his statement.

"I'm fine, thanks. Having backup when meeting strange men that mysteriously appear in the woods is the best practice these days," I said, gaining another few steps back.

He straightened his posture and squared his shoulders. "How rude I have been. I am the angel Mikael, and I have come to help you."

"An angel?" I cringed at his admission. "Shouldn't you be wearing a trench coat or something?"

He was dressed simply in jeans, a T-shirt, and a black jacket with the short collar flipped up to the night air. He looked more like a movie star than a hand of God.

"A trench coat? In Southern California?"

I shrugged, and he deflated his chest.

"Mara, I have come to save you from perdition and bring you into eternal love and salvation."

I took another step back. Only several feet separated us, but it felt like he was all over my skin, making it crawl.

"You mean, you're here to kill me."

"I am here to deliver you from evil and bring you—"

"Into the arms of the Father? Yeah, I've heard this speech before. Zepar beheaded one of the demons who tried to deliver me earlier today."

He sneered at my cheek. "The dark and deceitful have convinced you that they could match my might. I assure you the demon he killed was low on the chain of power compared to me."

"But you aren't the top of the chain either, are you?"

His faux-humble exterior dropped. The insult hadn't missed the mark. He looked me up and down, surely searching for where I was hiding my audacity. I'd been running for my life for as long as I could remember. I'd had enough of men coming to save me.

"I am one of the most powerful beings to have ever been. The embodiment of purity and light."

"And you're here to kill me in the middle of the woods while I am defenseless. If you are so powerful, why have you waited until I was far away from Vepar to come?" I prattled on, my mind racing for an escape while my mouth sassed him further.

My fingers brushed up over my chest where the necklace had sat and had been replaced with a healing rash. Vepar had said he would still be able to hear and sense me, but that wasn't a comforting guarantee if our bond was truly cut as Mikael had said.

Mikael closed the distance between us, his face coming far too close to mine in a blink of my eyes.

"Be not afraid, my child. For I am going to liberate you of your soul and the heavy weight of your burdens."

I screamed as loud as I could as his hand wrapped around my throat. The vibration of my vocal cords echoed around the trees into the night. I kicked my knee up into his groin, but he hardly budged and snaked his other hand around the back of my neck.

"No!" I pushed and thrashed against his chest, beating my fists into him with all my strength.

"This nightmare will all be over soon," he breathed into my ear.

His hands squeezed, crushing my windpipe and cutting off all sound out and air in. My knees gave out, and he guided my body to the ground. The cold concrete bit into my back. I pounded my fists against his arms until white lights began to flash over my eyes and my arms dropped. My hand landed on the pavement over something large and cold. I groped at it, and with my last bit of will, I gripped it.

A rush of wind lifted Mikael off of me and tossed him away.

I coughed and choked down air past my bruising cartilage. I sat straight up and looked around for Zepar. It had to have been him who'd found me. But I didn't see him. The two shadowed beings shouting at each other several feet away weren't Zepar or Vepar.

I looked down into my hand to see the necklace Sitri had given me at The Deacon.

Then the realization hit me.

Sitri had saved me. That was his voice berating Mikael.

But how had it found me when I had given it to Zepar?

The large garnet beamed up at me and warmed my hand, almost as if it were happy to have been of service and fulfill its purpose.

A wet thud drew my attention to the scuffling in the middle of the street. Mikael's nose was bleeding bright red, unlike the sludgy liquid that had come from Dras.

"You shouldn't have come, little brother." Sitri's cynical voice sounded through the air, followed by another powerful blow of his fist to the side of Mikael's face.

"I have to take her, Sitri. You don't know what will happen if she is permitted to live." Mikael braced himself for another blow.

"I don't care about what I do not know of the work of angels," Sitri fired back, tossing Mikael to the ground. "I suggest you leave now, before I call upon our brothers. Vepar will be particularly interested in the fact that you touched something that was not yours."

"Why would you care about Vepar's claim over this human?" Mikael spat blood to the ground, gingerly getting to his feet.

"I don't. But I'd love to see you being put in your place by one of the Fallen. Down here with the lowly dogs, little sunbeam, you wouldn't last a day."

"I will never have to," Mikael volleyed then looked up the road to me. "This is not over, Mara. Raphael will come for you and his power is far greater than the snakes you have made friends with."

"We will be waiting." Sitri smirked at me then started walking toward me as Mikael faded away into the darkness of the sky.

Sitri extended his hand to help me to my feet, but when I was firmly standing, my body was being pulled through a darkness that opened into the entryway of Zepar's house. The garnet pendant was still firmly clutched in my other hand when Zepar and Vepar opened the front door, anger and shock on their faces.

Zepar looked between Sitri and me then down to the fisted necklace.

"Fuck." He sighed.

"What were you thinking? You were as good as dead the moment you stepped out of this house," Zepar scolded.

Sitri was lounging in the wingback chair by the fireplace in Zepar's office. When we appeared, Zepar had been dressed to come after me. He had on a hoodie and a pair of running shoes. Vepar was still in his suit from earlier in the day but had taken off his jacket and tie. Vepar had taken my wrist and dragged me into the office with Sitri and Zepar at our heels.

The three of them carried a different mood to the situation.

Zepar was fuming that I'd left and hadn't looked me in the eye. Vepar was more concerned that Sitri's amulet had been my savior. And Sitri was smugly lounging, watching the other two battle their internal rage.

"How did you find that necklace?" Zepar looked down into my lap where the thing sat. "I locked it in my safe."

My eyes dropped to it too. The garnet was now cracked on a diagonal, I assumed from use or from hitting the concrete. My jaw hung open. I didn't know how it had gotten into my hand or how I had been able to use it with Mikael strangling me.

"That was my doing, actually." Sitri smirked and raised his brows to me. "I had Haniel make that piece special for me. Once I had given it to my intended victim, it would find its way to them when they need it the most. The second it touched her skin at The Deacon, it was tracking her every move. She was safe with Vepar's necklace around her neck, until it was used. I imagine my gift has been closer to her than she realized for much longer than the last twenty minutes."

"It's broken now?" I chirped, my voice hoarse from Mikael's attack and the dry air out in the woods.

Though the stone was fractured, the darkness was still present. Each section vibrated in its setting, and the surface glinted in the firelight. I looked up to Zepar as he crossed the room and stared into the dancing flames. His arms crossed at this chest sent a brooding shadow across the large center rug. His cold anger sent a shiver over my skin.

Look at me. Please. You would understand why I left if you would just look at me.

"I'll get you a new one." Sitri winked at me with a fox-like grin.

I shot a look to Vepar, pleading for him to remind Sitri of his claim over me. He gave me a constrained nod then turned to speak to Zepar's back.

"As we discussed earlier, we need to go before the next wave of attack."

Their code was not needed.

Zepar stared into the fireplace. His back inflated before he sighed heavily then turned to Sitri.

"We need you to take Mara somewhere safe." Zepar slid his hands into his pockets before glancing back at Vepar. "There is an errand we have to run, and it wouldn't be safe to take her with us."

"I heard what happened to the last caretaker you trusted," Sitri said, holding up his hand to inspect his fingernails. "Why should I take on the risk?"

"Don't then," Vepar interjected. "She will be left here unprotected."

Sitri surveyed them. He knew it was a bluff, but he wasn't going to get the groveling he wanted. The look on his face was a mix of disappointment and boredom, but when he panned back to me, he shifted in his seat and cocked his head.

"All right then. The sweet dove can come with me, if she promises to behave herself." Sitri twisted up his lips, and his eyes darkened. My stomach sank at this arrangement and at the look of triumph on Sitri's face. "No more walks in dark forests alone."

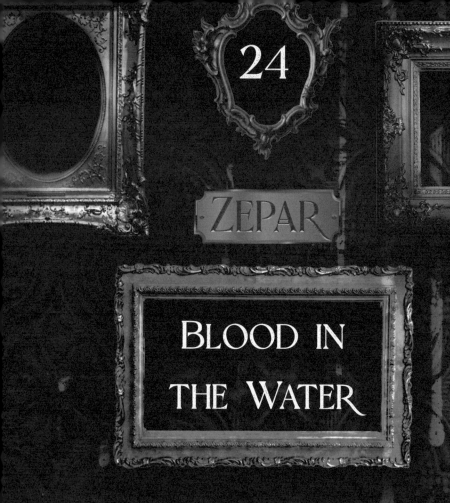

24

ZEPAR

BLOOD IN THE WATER

Sitri stood to walk the length of the room and stopped in front of Mara, his hand outstretched for her to take. She hesitantly laid her fingers into his palm and looked between Vepar and me. Her wide eyes searched for one of us to save her from the new monster that had her in its snare. The low pulse of anger in my chest bubbled up my neck.

She'd left.

She'd walked out the door without saying a word, and she'd left me.

No.

She'd finally gotten the courage to run from all of this. I couldn't blame her for that, but I blamed myself for getting too attached to someone who hadn't wanted to be here in the first place. I'd let her sink her teeth into me, and I'd believed that she wanted me. I'd believed her when she said that I had brought her comfort. My mind

was so clouded by the feeling of being wanted or needed that I didn't see what she had been planning: to wait until my back was turned so she could run.

I understood why she would want to leave, but I couldn't push down the rage I felt for the stupidity of her actions. To leave in the middle of the night unprotected. Had we not stressed enough the severity of her situation?

And now she was being passed into the hands of one of the demons I trusted the least. How had Sitri become our last resort, the safe haven?

I hated this.

I hated her hand being cupped in his, and I hated the greedy look on his face. That was the face of a man who would not part easily with his prize.

"Sitri," I warned.

"Don't worry, my illustrious duke, I won't do anything you wouldn't do," he replied with a defiant smirk.

Mara eyed him up and down. A look of terror hit her as she turned to face me, but before her eyes met mine, Sitri tore them through the void without allowing Vepar or me a chance to give her any reassurance that we would be back for her.

It was then that it hit me. Even if we made it back without Ipos turning on us, we had no other solution for her refuge when we returned. She may end up staying with Sitri for much longer than several hours. The thought churned my stomach.

"Get dressed. It isn't too late to call upon Ipos," Vepar said, bringing me out of my vicious thought spiral.

"No. We go in the morning when we have rested and have our strength. She will be safe with Sitri, after all."

Vepar clenched his jaw. His reservations were different than my own. He and Sitri had a past deeper than playing keep-away with their toys. The few run-ins that I'd had with Sitri were mild and abrupt. Years of having him watching over my shoulder was enough to make me go mad. But his sleazy treatment of the legions beneath him was cruel to say the least. He also had a way of manipulating situations in his favor by greasing the palms of humans, lower-level demons, and lesser angels. One in particular was the Watcher Angel, Ezequiel. Their bond was unusual and they often used their combined abilities to skirt around the rules of the Soul Armistice.

Staying out of each other's atmosphere and not mingling in the same circles was easy for me to do. But Vepar and Sitri had clashed over the years since we'd all settled into Southern California and Sitri had been awarded the West Coast as his territory, a position that Vepar had vied for on countless occasions to King Lucifer but lost to Sitri in the end.

I sat in the chair next to the fire and watched the flames float and sway above the logs, listening to them speak to me through pops and sizzles of the wood. I had felt Mara leave the house when something in my head had stopped humming. The distant drawing of strings from her inner voice had been pulled taut and then snapped when she had gotten too far. Then came the scream from outside. I'd felt as if I were being plunged into a dark, frozen lake. I couldn't feel her or sense which direction she had gone, but I had been prepared to scour every inch of the county to find her. I hadn't needed to.

The look on Sitri's face when I'd opened the door would be imprinted into my memory for the rest of this lifetime, or longer. He'd had blood splattered over his face and hands. He had told me, as we'd walked down the hall to this office, that he had found Mara with Mikael out in the woods about two miles from the house. How she'd managed to survive the encounter was beyond what I was capable of imagining.

Mikael's hand indentations around Mara's neck were all the explanation I'd needed. He would certainly pay for that someday, but not tonight.

Tonight, I needed to clear my head, be without Mara's siren song ringing in my ears and through my house, manipulating me at every turn.

That's what this was, after all.

Without her here, I could cleanse myself from the constant exposure and think rationally. Without her here, I could stop myself from thinking of all the ways I wanted to dismember Mikael or how desperately I wanted to feel her skin on mine, to lay my head on her chest just to hear her heart beating. All I would need was time to let this fever for her run its course.

Vepar slumped down in the couch across from me. "Waiting is a mistake. And we have made plenty of those as of late."

"Don't talk to me about mistakes."

Vepar sat forward, leaning his forearms on his knees. He cupped a fist in his other hand and ran his tongue along his teeth, rightfully judging me for my hypocrisy.

"You didn't have to fuck her." He wasn't aggravated, or the least bit stern in his tone, but his snark told me that he was not willing to take the blame I was attempting to lay at his feet. "You shouldn't have for several reasons, but the spell her cunt must have put on you is beginning to get on my last nerve."

A spell.

I wished that were all it was. I could shake a spell with a simple wave of my hand.

This hold she had on me was deeper, more confusing, and it was consuming me from the inside out. I was being torn to pieces.

"You're right," I said, scrubbing my hand down my face. "All the more reason to take the distance we have made and put it to good use. You can stay here tonight. We'll travel to New Mexico in the morning."

I stood and headed to the door when his last words caught me. "Let's hope that Sitri leaves something of Mara left to save."

25

MARA

DELIVER ME

I swallowed down the darkness as we passed through it once again. The transition was rougher somehow with Sitri at the helm. When the black abyss pressed in on me and Zepar's form had melted away into nothing, my chest ached and my heart tore open. There were things I'd needed to say, but in less than a blink of my eyes, I was somewhere new, and the sense of dread seeped deep into my bones.

Sitri let go of my hand, and my balance shifted at the sudden loss of a stable being. We were in a living room high above downtown L.A. by the view out of the floor-to-ceiling windows that lined the two walls I was facing.

"Come along, my little dove." Sitri's voice trailed away into the penthouse.

The plush rug under my feet gave way to hardwood floors and a

brightly lit hallway as I followed him. The long art canvases on the wall had a simple theme about them; they looked to be from the same artist. A mixture of thick and smooth black lines with gold-leaf patches made haphazardly through the brushstrokes of paintings.

I came to a break in the wall and paused in the frame.

Sitri was standing inside the room, taking off his leather jacket and his T-shirt. He was all dangerous, cut angles. His lean muscles stretched and bulged with the movements of his arms and shoulders.

I dragged my eyes away when he turned around.

"Don't be shy, little dove." He swaggered to a dresser and pulled out a shirt. "I will find you something more suitable to wear in the morning, but for tonight, you can wear this."

He tossed it into my waiting hands but didn't take his eyes off me. He had said not to be shy. But did he expect me to undress right in front of him?

"Where is your bathroom? I should freshen up." I hung the shirt over my arm and waited for him to point me in a direction.

My eyes caught on the tattoo on his right pectoral. It was similar to Vepar's: the hollow belly of a ship with thin masts coming from the deck. Sitri's was much simpler than Vepar's, the one thing about him that seemed to be muted and clashed with his large persona. The tattoo above it, the one draped across his collarbones, fit the atmosphere he created around himself. Thin loops were scrawled tightly together to give the illusion of a necklace, but I couldn't make out the words from this distance.

I knew I had been trying to work it out for too long when he cleared his throat. My cheeks heated and I pulled my eyes away to search the room once again for the bathroom.

His lips perked. "Right over there."

He waved his hand and a door that had been tucked behind the bedroom door opened. I looked inside then turned to peer behind me into the hall and realized there were no other rooms for me to escape to for the night.

"I will sleep on the couch."

He came to stand directly in front of me. "I can't allow that. Zepar and Vepar were very clear that it would be my head if something happened to you. I'm not letting you out of my sight."

I took in a breath and with it, the fresh scent of his cologne. He didn't have the same feel as Zepar when he stood close to me. The malaise he inspired in me made my insides quiver. If I had to share a bed with him, I was surely going to ruin his sheets with vomit if he touched me.

"There is an interesting mystique about you, Mara." His eyes wandered over me from head to toe then back again. "I felt it the night we met at The Deacon. I could sense you were no ordinary human. But you knew that already, didn't you?"

He smiled down at me, taking in the sight of my face like he was searching for this unseen obscurity everyone was so keen to discover, only to fear it once they'd found it. Maybe that wouldn't be terrible. If Eli had run for the hills, maybe Sitri was smart enough to do the same.

I pushed down my discomfort and squared my shoulders. "I could show you."

"In all my years on this plane, it has been a rare occasion that a human could show me anything spectacular." His face crept closer with each word. His eyes never left mine.

"I'm not spectacular, Sitri. From what I'm told, I am feared more than a demon in the eyes of the angels."

"My name from your lips is worth the risk." His gaze dropped to my mouth. "It's there behind your voice. The wrath is building inside of you somewhere deep."

"You hear it in my voice?" I leaned back to better see him.

"I can. Like a bell ringing just under the resonance." His lids lowered slowly. "Say my name."

I did as he asked. "Sitri?"

He bent his ear to catch the last syllables passing over my lips. The sound pulled the edges of his mouth into an elated grin.

"Again."

"Sitri," I repeated, this time lower and slower.

He smoothed his hands up the sides of my arms and held me still. I stiffened at the touch but didn't fight it.

"Again." The whimsy behind the request grew with each turn.

I swallowed down an eagerness in my belly that had begun to bloom.

"Sitri," I said slower than the last time. "Sitri."

He rolled his head back, and his whole frame vibrated.

"Fuck, Mara." He brought his eyes back to mine, satisfaction brightening him. "That is enrapturing. I can see why the dukes would want to keep you all to themselves."

I pulled my bottom lip in between my teeth to stop myself from smiling, but the blush on my cheeks gave me away. This kind of attention was still new to me, and the gnawing excitement welling in my chest was hard to ignore.

"I'm going to go change," I said, stepping easily from his hands.

"I'll be waiting." He watched me slip into the bathroom and shut the door.

I pressed my back to the door and caught my breath. In the mirror on the opposite wall, I looked small. And tired. More tired than I'd ever felt. The events of the evening started to press in on me as I pulled my jacket, shirt, and pants off. I turned on the faucet to warm the water. A set of cupboards edged the left side of the bathroom, and to my right was a massive bathtub, shower stall, and toilet. I was tempted to shower, but there was something vulnerable about getting completely undressed with Sitri waiting for me in the other room.

Instead, I found washcloths and a bottle of lavender and lemon soap. I washed my face with water before lathering and washing my underarms, chest, and neck. The grime of my sweat still clung to my skin, but a part of me hoped that the scent of Zepar would deter Sitri from getting carried away with his interest.

I slipped his T-shirt on over my head and let it fall down my body. It was smaller than Zepar's. He and Sitri were both rather fit, but Zepar had more mass and broader shoulders. Sitri was leaner and a couple inches shorter which made his shirt short on me. The hem hit the bottom curve of my ass and left very little to the imagination. I debated sleeping in the bathtub for several moments before taking a deep breath and opening the bathroom door.

Sitri had dimmed the lights in the room and was sitting up in the large bed with the blankets over his lap. I tugged at the bottom of the shirt as I walked to the other side and slid my legs between the sheets. Sitri watched every action with hunger and restraint.

"I'm not going to hurt you, Mara," he said, rolling over onto his side to face me. "I'm not that sort of monster."

Again, my eyes were drawn to the ink on his skin. Being closer to him, I could make out the words in intricate black and white lines.

Audax Princeps Sanguinis et Pulveris.

"Bold Prince of Blood and Dust," he said, dragging my sight to his.

An amused smile welcomed my curiosity once again. It wasn't hard to see that he would take any attention I would give him. I guessed it was Latin but wouldn't have been able to make heads or tails about what it meant without him telling me. He didn't elaborate any further, and I didn't ask. That felt too intimate, and sharing a bed was already encroaching on tempting a future regret.

I pulled the blanket up to my chest and lay back on the pillow under my head. I had no reason to trust him, but Vepar and Zepar had warned me about Sitri and had insinuated that if Sitri desired, he would use his power over human lust to use me in whatever fashion he pleased. But if that were true, he hadn't bothered using his abilities. And he'd had plenty of chances already.

This wasn't at all how I'd thought this situation would play out. Going from sleeping in one demon's bed to another was a rapid turn of events. The regret of leaving Zepar's room came crashing in on me, and with it swept in the festering fear that I didn't know when I would be able to talk to him again. Unease teemed through me, driving sleep farther from my eyes.

"How did they draw it out into the open?" Sitri's voice stirred me from thought.

"You know what it is?" I furrowed my brows at him and his odd question.

I knew how they'd brought forth the beast within me to come out of its hiding, but I had no idea what it was or where it had come from, if it had been there my whole life, or if it had come to inhabit me recently. I didn't have an answer for him, the same as I didn't have any answer for Zepar or Vepar.

"I don't. But I would imagine it's old. Possibly older than me."

"How could that be? How would it have gotten inside of me?"

"Things that go bump in the night need places to hide." His eyes drooped closed as he adjusted his pillow. "The best way to do that would be to go dormant inside of an unsuspecting human lineage for thousands of years. It's risky. That type of blood magic could be cut off with a plague or mass-casualty disaster."

"This happens often, then?"

"Not anymore. It's not unheard of these days, but as my intuition is usually right, I would say that this dark passenger would have been in your family line for hundreds of years, maybe even longer."

"Can you get it out?"

He yawned. "I may be foolish enough to sleep next to it, but I would be a damned idiot to try and pull it from you. Not to mention, it could kill you if I were to try. What a waste that would be."

K. ELLE MORRISON | 243

"Thanks, I guess."

He shifted next to me, bringing his body to the middle of the mattress. "The door is locked and we are a hundred floors up. Don't do anything stupid."

I looked up to the door he had closed while I was in the bathroom. The doorknob would need a key to get out if it was locked. I didn't bother to check once his breathing deepened. I had nowhere to go, and Mikael had found me too quickly the last time I ran from my demon watchers.

Sleep caught up with me eventually. It pulled me into a whirl of memories and dreams: flashes of Zepar's body over mine, then of the hellhound chasing me through the woods, bright lights, and screams through the dark. Then a pair of arms wrapped around me to soothe me into a calming rest.

"Shh, little dove."

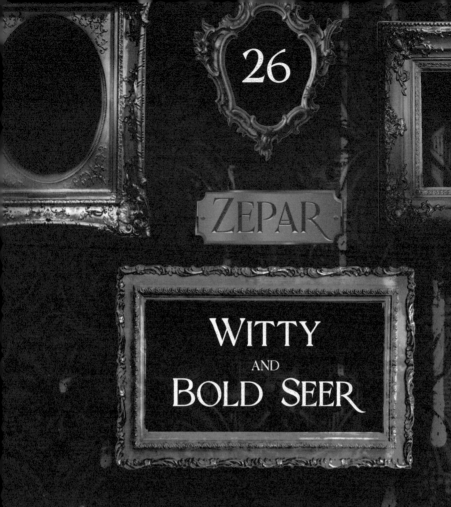

26

ZEPAR

WITTY
AND
BOLD SEER

The night had dragged on, but the dawn came too quickly. I had a pounding headache from tossing and turning all night. Every couple of hours, I irrationally got out of bed with the intention of going to Sitri's and retrieving Mara. I would get to my bedroom door before I convinced myself to turn back and chase sleep again.

When the sun rose and crept through my window, I dressed quickly and headed downstairs to the kitchen for coffee. I needed it if I was going to get through the rest of this next task. Ipos was bound to welcome Vepar and me, but who was to know if he already knew of our reason for seeking him out.

Vepar was already in the kitchen when I came in. He had a cup of coffee in his hand as he scrolled through emails on his phone. "I've called us both in. There will be hell to pay when we get back to the

office, but it's all par for the course."

"Maddie will handle the rearrangements."

"Bless her." He smirked around the rim of his mug.

The New Mexican terrain was vast but mostly empty besides cattle and Joshua trees. Ipos had acquired hundreds of acres of land about fifty years ago and moved into a rusting travel trailer in the middle of it. He had warded it from lesser spirits who came looking for their futures to be revealed to them. They would ask for lottery numbers, bank codes, or simply if they would ever ascend into the higher ranks of the demon world. Though Ipos was the seer, his predictions often were morphed or changed by circumstance.

The future was fickle and easily manipulated, which was why he'd removed himself from the rest of us so long ago. He had been blamed for soured outcomes and failed endeavors. No one heeded Ipos' warnings if they thought luck was in their favor.

I knocked on the metal door of Ipos' trailer as the sun came up over the dusty mountains. The whole trailer shook as he made his way to open it.

"Well. Come on in. I was wondering when you'd be along."

Ipos' rusty mane toppled over his bare shoulders. He'd been living out in the middle of the Chihuahuan Desert for so many years and he looked the part. His dirty and ripped sweatpants hung low on his hips, and his skin was dry, freckled, and burned from the dry air.

The door clanged behind us as he led us to the built-in bench at the small table. He dipped his hand to one, inviting us to sit. His sigil tattoo flashed on his forearm. He'd been amongst our Father's favorites once, long before the seeds of conflict had been planted among us.

"You boys like tequila? My own distillery's just over the border." He took a clear bottle from his freezer and gave it a subtle shake, the liquid sloshing its pitchy tune against its confines.

"My favorite brand," Vepar answered.

Ipos brought over three red plastic cups and poured a generous glug into each. He held his own up and we joined in a cheers before taking our first sips. It was smooth and burned my tongue on the way down. It clashed with the quick cup of coffee in my stomach.

"Now that we have the niceties out of the way, let's cut to what brings you here?" Ipos raised his brow to us knowingly. "Or should I say who?"

"Isn't that your whole gift?" Vepar snarked back. "You already know what we have come to ask."

"Amusement is all I have when every waking second is predicted for me."

Vepar gave me a side-eyed glance, an amused glint in his eye. "Ipos, what is Mara, and why is Mikael so intent on killing her?"

Vepar had chosen his words carefully. Like many gifts given to the Fallen, the narrower the direction when invoked, the more accurate the outcome.

"Mara is much more than she appears. As far as she knows..." He smiled, watching how intent his audience was on him, "...she's only human."

"And what exactly is she?" I asked.

Ipos looked from Vepar to me then down into his cup. A white sheen shone over his eyes before he closed them. Light leaked through his heavy lids. "She is a Key."

"A Key to what, exactly?" I asked another question that awaited another cryptic answer.

"The Daughters of the First Daughter shall roam the Earth until the time comes to raise the Fallen to reign in Heaven," he started, and his eyes shifted to their original state. "An exchange. A payment to the Dark One. Her soul pure of mortal sin…clean of the original sin."

"She's a descendant of Lilith?" Vepar gawked at Ipos, the legend resurfacing in our memories.

Ipos stood once more and began pacing the length of the trailer's tight quarters.

Legends and prophecies often started as rumors made by man, but if they were spoken enough, with time and enough conviction, they came to pass as truth. With enough belief from the mouths of humans, nothing was impossible.

Ipos took a deep breath and began the story we thought we had known so well.

"Muddled by thousands of years of human lives, the prophecy spoke of Lilith, the supposed mother of monsters, depending on who you ask. In the days of the Garden, Lilith came before Eve. Adam's first wife was equally made from the earth and defied Adam at every turn. She was a wild and willful woman who fled the Garden and the cruel nature of her husband. Lucifer found her wandering the desert close to death and took pity on her, offering her a place to rest her head and an oasis of her own to live out the rest of her days, hidden from the Father."

He took a break to fill his cup again and downed its contents.

"She graciously accepted, but Lucifer quickly fell madly…no, not just madly—desperately, insanely, obsessively in love with Lilith," Ipos said pointedly. "When Adam grew lonely and shameful for his treatment of his wife, the Father sent three foolish angels to coerce Lilith to return to Adam. She refused, but Lucifer convinced her to agree and gave her an apple suffused with poison for her to take back to the Garden. Repayment for the abuse Adam had inflicted on Lucifer's beloved."

I watched as Ipos' shoulders sagged in his tale. Remembering back to the days before he isolated himself away from the other princes, he had been glorious. A force of flame and fury when his territory had been challenged by Sitri or Stolas in their avaricious power struggles. He'd given his throne to Orobas, the Prince of Gluttony, before becoming the hermit of the Southwest.

"Lilith did not give the apple to Adam in the end. She instead placed the apple in the ground, which grew into the Tree of Knowledge. This was the start of the chain reaction of man being cast out of Eden and into the cold world beyond to live and die as mortal beings." Ipos finished.

"Why wouldn't Lucifer have used one of Lilith's descendants before now?" Vepar asked, another question that came straight from my own thoughts. "If they're truly the Keys to his release from Hell and would allow him to take back our home, why has he allowed them to live so long?"

Ipos shrugged and gave a knowing perk of his brow.

Realization dawned on me. "He couldn't, could he? He deals in sins and corrupt souls. He wouldn't know how to see the pure-of-sin bloodline. There would have been no way to track them or hunt them down. He had to wait for one of them to find him, or by an extension of his hand."

I wasn't sure if what I was saying was fact, but it made sense when many things likely never would. Vepar and I shared a moment of silence. Half of the prophecy had been fulfilled when Vepar answered her call, but what of the other half?

Ipos sat down next to me and stared at the top of the table. "Lucifer put his own protection onto Lilith when he took her in from destitution, shielding her from the Almighty with his own power. But the mark of Lucifer's protection and the cleanliness of Mara's soul would be a ferocious combination. It's why you were so drawn to her. Why Sitri has found himself enthralled by her presence and would do anything to keep her for himself."

Jealousy bubbled within my chest. I cursed myself for giving in to that allure so easily and for wanting to rip Sitri's throat out for even looking at her.

"Like the head of her line, Mara is not marked with the sins of Adam. No matter what arbitrary rules have befallen the humans after Eve was created, she is as pure as Heaven itself." The bitter tone in Ipos' voice brought the raging boil of my blood back to a simmer.

"Lilith escaped Lucifer and the Garden. Where did she go?" I finally asked, testing a theory I'd had since Ipos began his story.

"She ran with a most precious gift," Ipos answered. "The spawn of the King of Hell, the most hated of the Fallen, grew in her swollen womb. Her children would have been slaughtered upon their first breath if our angelic brothers had their way."

He paused again as if the confession were wearing him thin. And perhaps it was. This was no ordinary Bible story. This was the start of Lucifer's game of souls, the collection of humans who didn't obey our Father or committed crimes too great to be forgiven. These were the souls to be brought into our fold and populate Hell.

"Those children were born untainted, without the sin of Eve or the betrayal Lucifer had plotted against the Father."

Ipos surveyed us for a moment, letting the stories we had known longer than most come to life before us.

"But unlike the stories told in that damned book, there were many people on Earth outside of the Garden. Adam, Eve, and Lilith had a simpler version of divine power. Once Adam and Eve had defied His will, they lost it. But Lilith still retained her watered-down magic. Lilith fled to Africa to live out the remainder of her mortal life. She and her children went on to age and die surrounded by their friends and family. Though Lilith did not have more than two children, she had many grandchildren, and they had grandchildren and so on. Ghosts amongst the heavens and heathens alike."

I traced the line of his story in my mind, tying loose ends of our history together to make a cohesive image. The mystery came together with more answers, but more questions arose with the passing seconds. It was a harsh reality that I'd mistaken the illusion of attraction for Mara as anything more than the draw of an ancient being hiding away inside of her. It had not been of my own volition, and possibly not hers either.

"Lilith refused to enter the gates and fled from Lucifer's obsession by locking herself away in the blood of her daughter. Then her granddaughter and so on. Lilith's line extended decade after decade, escaping extinction by near misses. Plagues. Floods. Famine. All the way down to Mara. The last of her blood." Ipos looked at Vepar, then his eyes settled on mine. "She passed down from generation to generation, hiding in plain sight."

He pulled the lids of his right eye wide open for effect. His piercing blue eyes were almost clear even in the darkened trailer.

The voice inside of Mara was Lilith's soul.

My stomach churned and flipped at the thought that I was not only fucking a descendant of Lilith, but she'd had a front-row seat to the show within Mara the entire time.

"These feelings. This draw I have for Mara. It's been Lilith's power, then?" My chest clenched at the thought. I had to know.

"Are you asking for clarity or for your own relief?" Ipos' mischievous nature came through once again in a cocky smile.

"Tell me." My jaw clenched, preparing for the hit to my ego.

"She has claimed you, Zepar. Her soul has been bound to yours, much like her lineage's matron was bound to Lucifer once she claimed him as her own. There is no prophecy or witch magic that could create such a bond."

I swallowed hard and took a drink from my cup to mask my grief and anger. I had feared the answer on both sides of the coin. To allow myself to believe that Mara's intentions hadn't been her own would have made it easier to walk away and give Sitri the duty of keeping her safe. But to know that we shared an unfabricated bond meant she wasn't a fever I could sweat out. Fucking her wouldn't get her out of my system.

Every moment I had walked this plane had brought me closer to her: my brother answering her call, Eli digging through her mind and pulling forth the voice of Lilith through her soul, and now Sitri had his filthy hands all over her as we sat here in this God-forsaken desert.

"How did Mikael know about her before we did?" Vepar's mind, sharper than my own, was still at work on the puzzle.

"I doubt he did. Like you, Mikael felt the moment you made a deal with her and the demon half of the prophecy was activated, as he is your keeper." Ipos didn't seem sure about this answer.

"And when Eli stirred Lilith from her slumber?" Vepar lowered his voice, his last question our reason for coming.

"The contact with a creature of His creation had already disturbed her dormancy, but yes. Eli pulled Lilith's consciousness to the forefront and he made Mara aware of the force she was containing, an unforeseen complication to the angels who seek to destroy her before Hell rises and tears down the walls of Heaven to unite us once more." Ipos rubbed at his oily, sunburned temples with his forefingers, his voice becoming more exhausted with every new explanation.

"Thank you, Ipos. What can we do for you as payment?" I laid my hand on his shoulder and felt the cool sweat collecting on his clammy skin.

"Tell no one that you came to see me. You were never here." He looked up at us. "But tell Gaap that he owes me for the last time he came to disturb me."

"I can do that." I gave him a gracious smile and held up my cup to him.

I wondered when Gaap had last been to see Ipos but imagined it had been ages. Gaap had been wandering the globe in pursuit of new adventures for the last fifty years.

"I have to rest," Ipos said as he stood and began walking to the back of the trailer to the sleeping cot. "I suggest you boys figure out a plan of attack before rushing in like fools. Lilith's presence won't protect Mara from death. And she's escaped it too many times already."

"Ipos." Vepar stood and followed Ipos back to the foot of the bed. "How does this end?"

"I cannot answer that, brother. But Zepar," he said over his shoulder to me, "this doesn't need to end with blood on your name."

Vepar and I climbed out of the trailer and walked several yards from Ipos' home before Vepar rounded on me.

"Was it Mara who claimed you? Or Lilith?" What he was insinuating added to the tangle of theories I had.

"Ipos seems to think it was a combination of the two, but I can't see beyond what you do. This is…complicated. Messy."

I had no defense for allowing what had transpired between Mara and me to happen the way it did. There had been a change in her and in me when she told me I was hers. What was meant to be a flirtatious show of domination during sex had defied the Soul Armistice.

But there were still uncertain factors at work. Mara's body housed two souls, both present. The nature of which could have produced many outcomes. Vepar's protection had been around her neck when she or Lilith made their proclamation and the bond had still held strong enough to call to him when Mara was in danger. Without Vepar and Sitri's beacons, she would have been killed by Focalor and Mikael. Haniel's magic was simple and protected the intended victims as long as it touched their skin.

Once again, I was torn between hating Sitri and acknowledging that his morbid interest in Mara was the reason she was still alive. He had cursed her the moment he had placed that necklace in her hand at The Deacon, but it had been a failsafe. He had said as much back in my office.

The way Mara's hand had clutched his had jealousy rearing through me. Her new savior. The constriction around my chest was making my skin crawl and my entrails itch. The burrowing of anxiety and betrayal consumed me from the inside out.

"Are you too weak to fight for what I know you want more than anything? Or are you ready to perish right here?" Vepar reprimanded. "I should leave you to be eaten by wild pigs and your corpse to rot in the scorching sun."

"Then do so. The curse of her existence will be the death of us both at any moment. Raphael will make sure of that."

Frustration and rash decisions were catching up with the both of us. If what Ipos said was right, then Mara and Lilith were predestined to collide to bring Heaven to its knees. Vepar and I were the instigators of what would surely be the next war of angels and demons.

He scoffed. "You want to wait for Raphael to come to collect her then kill us both for good measure?"

"Of course not, but going on a rampage and gutting any demon or angel that comes near her is reckless and would have the same end. We don't have the strength or resources to protect her, even with our legions of lesser spirits. What would you have us do to protect her from Raphael and every other archangel who will be at his back?"

That was putting my bloodlust lightly. I didn't just want to defend Mara; I wanted to place her on a throne made from the ash of every angel that resided in Heaven and every demon who would dare look at her. The feral beast that had occupied my consciousness during my most brutal moments through history was preparing to burn this world to the ground. No flood, fire, or earthquake would match my destruction if my rage was set loose.

He turned to me, the sound of unabashed hope lacing his words. "We find an angel to grant her favor, finish out the ritual, and bring the prophecy to light."

"Then what? Dear Ol' Dad will bring us into his bosom with open arms for playing the fates? If you believe that, you're as mad as Focalor."

He let out a frustrated bellow that echoed over the hard desert floor. The shiver of dry grass and pebbles over cracked earth answered him. We had worked our way into a corner with no way of coming out on the other side without catastrophic casualties for both angels and demons.

"Lucifer," Vepar said with caution. "We could—"

"He would have our heads right then and there."

"He was an archangel once. His favor could be seen as a loophole."

"I don't think we have any of those left. And even if by some chance that were to work, the war it would spark would end all of existence."

The wrath of Lucifer and Our Father would tear at the delicate threads of the universe and reality. The balance would finally tip in our favor, but at what cost? We would lose everything.

"There are no options left. As it stands, we are caught between killing her ourselves and ending this entire issue or protecting her until it causes a more volatile reaction." He had reached the end of his patience. He was metaphorically throwing his hands up and waving his white flag.

I didn't blame him. The exhaustion had been eating away at me for days, and the last bit of sanity I was clinging to told me to let Mara go. Let Sitri keep her and receive the consequences when they finally caught up to him. Raphael wouldn't smite Sitri; that would be too quick of a punishment. Instead, he would destroy everything Sitri had built then banish him to Hell for thousands of years to be dealt with by Lucifer. Sitri's legions would fight off the angels' attacks for as long as they could, but even his power would fail him. My heart tore to pieces at the thought of Mara dying wrapped in Sitri's arms, but what choice did I have now?

My phone buzzed in my pocket; it was my secretary letting me know that my daily meetings were starting in twenty minutes and she had the files for each ready for my approval. The collection of souls would have to be the only triumph that came from this disaster of a morning. For now, the crumbling of this plane was stalled until Raphael found Sitri.

Though I hated it, Sitri would be the one to have to take on the responsibility of caring for Mara. If she were going to have a chance at a life outside the clutches of angels and demons, it would have to be without my involvement.

"I'm going to work," I finally said, my shoulders slumping at my own defeat.

"Fine. Then she stays where she's at until her life comes to an end. We wash our hands of this?" Vepar clarified.

"I see no other option." I put my phone back in my pocket. "See you at the office?"

"No, I think I need to work out some frustration on a more deserving individual." His dark eyes glinted with his devilishness.

I opened my mouth to respond, but he faded into the warm wind, and I followed soon after but reappeared in the garage of our office building. I had a spare suit in the back seat of the car I kept at the office to keep up appearances. The sweat stains under my arms would raise too many eyebrows, and I needed to use spite and rage to steal away as many human souls as I could, a small victory in what was sure to be the end of days.

27

·MARA·

HORNS

It took me a moment to remember where I was and whose arms were wrapped around me. Sitri's foreign skin warmed my back and caged me to the soft white sheets. If he was awake, he hadn't moved from his position behind me. The arm that coiled around my waist was tucked tight between my hip and the mattress. The other cradled my neck and stuck out over to the edge of the bed. The relaxed ebb and flow of his torso, filling then shrinking with each of his slow and deep breaths, was flush to my back. The T-shirt was all at once too thin and too thick of a barrier to his bare chest.

The way my body curved into his didn't feel right, but it didn't fill me with dread either. I knew the moment he woke up the small bit of calm in the way he hummed into my hair would end. Or because for the first time in a long time, I wasn't running. Mikael had been

wounded both physically and emotionally by Sitri when he saved my life. I would imagine he wouldn't try again right away. Focalor was somewhere caged at Vepar's home, and the guilt of it somehow being my fault wasn't plaguing me.

What would Zepar think if he saw Sitri and me lying like this?

I told myself he would be enraged. But the gnawing voice in the back of my mind twisted my gut with doubt. He had been furious when he opened the door last night and saw Sitri holding my hand on the front step. But I had run, and I hadn't told him why. I hadn't trusted him enough to protect me and keep himself alive. And Vepar had handed me over with little hesitation. He had made up his mind long before I had taken to the forest and was chased by that terrifying beast.

Then my thoughts turned to Mikael: the first real proof that angels were after me for reasons I still didn't understand. I had something they were scared to have unleashed. It didn't feel evil or wrong inside of me, and demons seemed to be divided on what it was and if I should be killed or protected.

"I can hear your head buzzing with worry, little dove." Sitri's sleep-heavy voice came brushing over the crest of my ear.

My spine went rigid, and I wiggled out of his grasp. "It's been a weird…life. I think I've earned the right to have a buzzing brain."

He rolled onto his back and stretched his arms over his head as I got up to go to the bathroom. "I could fix that for you."

"Do angels and demons have the same script somewhere? You all have the same deceitful way of saying 'I can cure you with death.' It's becoming redundant," I said before closing the door behind me, but when I turned around, he was standing in front of the sink basin.

I jumped back and gasped, though I was long past being scared of him.

He closed the distance between us in an instant, pinning me to the door with the looming mass of his body. The wolfish grin on his face was becoming more familiar but sent my stomach plunging all the same.

"I don't hold my title for nothing. I'm a prince of Hell, commander of sixty legions, and ward of the west because I am one of the most powerful beings to walk this plane."

The sigil marked on his chest brightened, the dark outline of the ship and three masts bold against his pale skin as if to draw my eye to its meaning. He brought his fingers up my arm, over my shoulder, and caressed his thumb across my neck. The muscles there tightened and squirmed to pull away, but I had nowhere to go.

"When I said I could fix the worry weighing on your head, I didn't mean I would remove it. I meant that I could be your solution. Make a deal with me. Speak it, and I'll make it true."

"But Vepar—"

"Your deal with Vepar has been absolved. The constraints of your agreement no longer tether you to him."

"How?" I squeaked out over the tension in my chest.

"Claim any other demons lately?" A corner of his mouth twitched upward into a telling smirk.

The pull in my belly dipped. Had Vepar felt the bond of our agreement sever? Were he and Zepar even aware of the act having this sort of omission?

They had to know if Sitri did, right?

There were too many questions with too little oxygen getting past the knot in my throat.

Sitri stared down through me, waiting for an answer he already knew and visibly enjoying my distressed state.

"I'm willing to make a deal with you, Mara. No human alive can say they've had the pleasure of doing so."

That didn't bring me any comfort. The sinking feeling of being a fly caught in the web of a black widow pressed in on me. But if the spider was willing to free me, shouldn't I take it?

"What would you want in return?" I dared to ask and surprised the both of us.

A cold and cunning grin cut his face. He was practically drooling. I knew it would be a mistake to accept his offer, but once again, I was turning to demons for my salvation. He removed his hand from my throat and pressed his hands to the door on either side of my head, his face lowering to meet my eyes, his lashes lowering as he watched my mouth.

"You," he whispered over my lips.

Sitri had coaxed me out of his bedroom with a cup of tea. I wasn't fond of tea, but it was hot and sweet. There was comfort in holding a warm mug that even the trembling foreign being in me calmed to as I followed Sitri down the hall.

I shouldn't have been surprised to see the fully furnished spare bedroom on the other side of the penthouse. It had a lot of the same design themes as the rest of his home: clean, white, high-tech. The walk-in closet held clothing for who he called his most esteemed guests.

He stood leaning against the doorframe, holding my cup and keeping a watchful eye on me. He had already dressed in a light-blue suit, a white dress shirt that was unbuttoned casually, and tan loafers. With his light-blond hair and tanned skin, he looked like he was ready to board a grand yacht in the Mediterranean. It was hard not to stare at the script tattoo that hung at his neck; the stark-white shirt made it pop more than it had when he was half-naked. My hand twitched at my side, wanting to trace the dark lines framed by the collar and buttons.

I shook myself from the traitorous thought and turned back to the thickly laden closet. I ran my fingers across the line of dresses and let the fabrics tickle my fingertips as I made my way through the black, red, and gold garments.

"That one." Sitri's voice halted my hand over a small black dress.

I pulled the hanger out and held the short hem between my fingers. It would be a miracle if it covered my ass and chest at the same time.

"You're not serious?" I furrowed my brow at him. "This thing looks like a top more than a dress."

"Come now, little dove, I want to show you off." He grinned and his eyes panned my body, taking a too-long look at my ass.

I was still wearing the shirt he lent me the night before at his insistence. His excuse was that my other clothes were being cleaned, though I hadn't seen anyone come or go with my jeans, T-shirt, and jacket.

"When all this is over, I will take you shopping, but for now, the safety of this closet will have to do." He pushed away from the frame and came to stand next to me.

He took a sip from my tea then plucked the hanger from my hand and held it up to my torso, measuring it with his eyes, then he took it away to scan me. Though he didn't say it, he looked displeased. He handed my mug back into my frigid fingers and put the dress back. After placing the discarded dress with the rest, he shuffled through a few more. The next one he held up had a bit more coverage in the bust but was just as short. It wasn't only black; it was absent of all color like a void in space, too thick for light to pass.

I reached out and thumbed the lightweight threads, which slipped over my fingertips and escaped my nerves like a down feather. It would be like wearing nothing at all, and the thought sent a flutter to my core.

"By the expression on your face, I'd say this is the one," he said flirtatiously. "I'll trust you will be capable of finding a pair of shoes to match."

His chin gestured toward the wall behind me where rows and rows of shoeboxes were lined neatly. Every box had a luxury logo printed on the side—not surprising—but the sudden thought that just one pair would pay my rent for three months came to mind. Would that ever matter again?

I was either going to die at the hand of an angel or demon before seeing my apartment once more. Or I was going to be a caged pet to be put on display. The evidence of my internal turmoil must have been on my face because Sitri's hand cupped my chin and pulled it up for me to meet his eyes.

"Your power lies in your strength, little dove." He leaned forward to brush his lips over the crown of my head, and my breath caught in my chest.

This was not what I imagined being alone with Sitri would be like. He had been cunning and conniving the first time I had met him, but since rescuing me in the woods, he had been charming, witty, and easy to be around. But the hunger in his eyes when he'd offered me a deal earlier was still tugging at emotional strings.

"I have some calls to return downstairs. Being one of the richest and most powerful beings in L.A. keeps me busy. I'll bring you lunch in a couple hours." He laid the dress over my arm and took one last heated glance down my body before leaving me.

"Make yourself at home," he called through the void.

I let out a breath, one that I very well may have been holding since unlocking Zepar's door the night before. The penthouse was hollow and cold. It didn't feel lived in as Zepar's house had. There were no photos on the walls, only abstract art pieces that elicited feelings and thought. The art, like the home, was faceless. Anyone with millions of dollars could have lived here.

The kitchen, to my dismay, did not have a coffeemaker of any type.

K. ELLE MORRISON | 263

Sitri preferred tea, another defining contrast to my last demon warden. I went to the fridge and found that as well as being a tea drinker, Sitri was a vegetarian. Fruits and vegetables filled the drawers, and different plant-based milks and condiments lined the fridge door. The only familiarity was a carton of eggs set next to a block of cheddar cheese.

My heart and stomach leaped at the sight. I took them out and searched the cupboards for a frying pan. I decided on a cheese and veggie omelet with a refill of English Breakfast tea.

I ate then explored the rest of the penthouse. Somehow, Sitri had made it so I couldn't unlock or open the front door. I pushed away the panic that welled inside of me with the explanation that no one would be able to get in if I couldn't get out. The lie was enough to tear me away from fear and make my way through the other rooms.

The first was an office, but instead of a desk, there was a retro vinyl player and a wall of records. The room seemed out of place with the rest of Sitri's style but further built the realization that I didn't know anything about Sitri or what his existence looked like.

The last door in the hall led to a bathroom that was large enough for several people to stand inside of at once. Three vanities were lit by bright white bulbs, and the tub was round and more of a Jacuzzi than a bath.

Instead of books or religious texts, Sitri had an assortment of fashion magazines and catalogs. They were better than nothing. I browsed through a stack on his dining room table and took them back to the bathroom to flip through to pass time in the large tub after I washed away the residual terror of the night before and the lingering smell of Sitri's cologne from my hair.

I had been left alone at Zepar's house before, but not truly alone within the house. There was a sense of freedom in being alone, but Sitri could pop in at any moment no matter what door I was behind.

When Sitri did finally come back, it was afternoon, and he came through the front door, to my surprise. He dropped two large bags of takeout on the table. "Miss me?"

"Terribly," I said with a roll of my eyes.

The smile that my comment had brought to his face was amused and warm. "Hope you like Thai food."

I did. I loved it, actually. I had been sitting on the couch in a cotton robe while I watched TV. I hadn't bothered getting dressed; the designer closet didn't have anything comfortable to lounge in.

He held up his hand when I sat up. "You look perfect where you are. I'll bring lunch to you."

I wasn't sure how to feel about this type of doting. The way that he spoke to me was a mix of seeing me as a possession or toy and something he seemed to cherish. What even was that?

A moment later, he came in holding a takeout container on a plate and a couple bottles of water. He had taken off his jacket and rolled up his sleeves, and I noticed a thin scar on the inside of his arm that I hadn't seen earlier. He sat down next to me and propped his foot up on the edge of his marble-topped coffee table that sat before us. The act was domestically smooth.

"Thanks," I said as I dug into my yellow chicken curry.

I peeked over to his plate—a veggie pad Thai.

"I didn't think demons would be vegetarians." I shoveled a chunk of piping-hot potato into my mouth and he smiled.

"I only eat what I kill."

My eyes flew to his face, and he cracked a wide grin over his food.

I swallowed hard, burning my throat. "You what?"

He laughed and twisted his fork on his plate. "I like to hunt. It reminds me of the days before city skyscrapers crowded the coasts and the dull sound of car engines was a constant soundtrack to my life."

He met my gaze. "I don't eat humans," he clarified, and I melted back into the couch cushions and redirected my attention to my own plate.

"At least not in that way."

That comment sent me choking and coughing on a spoonful of jasmine rice. I sat up and pounded my palm over my chest to swallow the remaining grains before shooting him an exasperated look.

"You asked." He smiled around a forkful of sprouts and sauce-coated noodles. "Here. Water. You look dehydrated."

His kindness and care was not what I expected. I didn't respond but watched him as he took the plastic lid off the bottle then handed it to me.

Our eyes met and I searched his blue irises for a clue to what his intentions were but found nothing. I opened my mouth to finally ask when there was a knock at the door.

His features darkened at the surprise visitor before getting up to answer. He peeked through the door crevice then dropped his chin to his chest before opening it. A tall, tanned, and hairy man stood in the doorway. He wore his golden, sandy hair in a knot at the top of his head but his bushy beard was thick and unruly.

"Sitri." The stranger greeted with a nod and walked into the entryway.

Sitri shut the door behind the guest and ran his fingers through his hair that suddenly looked brighter and more tamed in comparison.

"The world must be coming to an end if you're here," Sitri said, annoyance more than fear lacing his statement.

"I had an interesting conversation with two of your dukes, Sitri. You shouldn't be so surprised that I would speak to you next."

I watched the two men look each other over in silence. My belly squirmed, and there was a very present tension coming from their stalemate.

"Say what you must, then I suggest you run back to that rusted out barrel in the middle of nowhere that you call sanctuary." Sitri's gruff tone sounded more familiar to how I had perceived him before he saved my life, the sadistic jerk from the nightclub returning to defend his territory.

"My vision does not only concern you." The stranger turned his face toward me. "What I have to say will clear up many questions you have, Mara."

He took a step but Sitri grabbed his arm, the fire in his eyes a warning and a promise.

"Finally picking on someone your own size, Sitri? Let's not forget that I could bring this entire building down with a snap of my fingers, same as you."

My stomach dropped. I felt that energy when he entered, but his words confirmed that this being was just as powerful as the prince I was being kept by. Sitri released and recoiled at the reminder and then our eyes met. The calm and kindness that had been there moments before was replaced with annoyance, and possibly worry.

I stood and placed my plate on the table before crossing the room to stand by Sitri's side and waited for whatever news that had transpired between Vepar, Zepar, and this demon.

"You may call me Ipos. My visions have told me a great deal about you, Mara. In particular, that you are in great danger." Ipos' sun-blistered lips cracked and bled as he spoke to me, his eyes intent on my face.

"That is no secret, brother. Every angel and demon in the west knows that by now. Let's skip the grandeur and get to the point." Sitri shifted next to me impatiently.

Ipos narrowed his eyes to Sitri then went on, "*Maphteah*, the Key. The being within you is one of our Father's creations. A holy and pure being. She is the Key to unlock the gates of Heaven and Hell and reunite the Children of Light, a prophecy passed down from man but made true with enough belief."

His words sounded more like riddles than an explanation, but I didn't dare interrupt him.

"Lilith. The first wife of Adam was the obsession of Lucifer as you have become for Sitri." He glanced at Sitri, who cleared his throat and

"But she knew, as you do, that true love is much deeper than infatuation and lust. Something our demon king, Lucifer, and the Prince of Lust do not possess."

"You're wearing my patience, Ipos." Sitri stated, anger glooming his brow.

"You have offered her a deal, and she should know the fine print," Ipos snapped at Sitri.

"What's he talking about?" I took a step back and looked up to Sitri.

"He's been driven mad by too much sun and loneliness," Sitri answered but didn't meet my eyes.

"You haven't been able to stop craving her since you laid eyes on her. At first, you had simple curiosity when Mikael came to you about Vepar's deal with Mara. But eventually, you saw what had been awakened and you knew you had to have her. It's why you gave her your most powerful beacon. I have seen it, brother, the mad pacing you've done on this very floor scheming and waiting for her to call upon you." The whites of Ipos' eyes began to brighten, like a light behind them had been sparked.

"And what of it? I have her now and she is safe. I can provide her with the means to the end. Ezequiel will help me make it so."

"I have seen what she will become." Ipos' hushed voice cut at the thick tension that had grown among us. "You will suffer greatly, *Princeps Sanguinis et Pulveris*."

"But she will not," Sitri finished.

Ipos gave a heavy sigh. He and Sitri stared at one another for a long moment in silence.

"So be it. I've come and delivered my warning, so I will wash my hands of it."

A loud thunderous pop sounded around us and Ipos was gone, and I rounded on Sitri.

"What the fuck was he talking about?"

Sitri scrubbed his hand down his face and walked back toward the couch. He stopped with his hands on his hips before turning back to face me.

"You asked for a way to protect yourself and free you from relying on demons. I have found a way to hold up my end of our bargain to keep you safe. Forever. Not just a few more days as Vepar or Zepar could." he said, his more stern tone still lingering.

"How?"

"I have made an arrangement with Ezequiel. He and I together can manipulate the fates and release you from your human form. It would bind the being, Lilith, inside of your demon exterior."

He watched as I took in what he was saying.

"You want to turn me into a demon?"

"Yes," he said, "I would sire you with my dark divinity, then Ezequiel would cleanse you of your mortal tarnishments…To complete the ritual, you will have to extinguish one of His most adored lights, replacing it with the dark."

The stirring being within me had a name. A name I had learned about in Sunday school. The magnitude of that realization sent a chill over my body.

"Mara." Sitri's voice brought me back from my panic. "This is the only way."

"Is it?" Tears had begun to well behind my eyes, and my throat was tight. "Or is it the way you thought you could keep me?"

"I could give you anything and everything you've ever wanted. Zepar could never—"

"I love him, Sitri." My voice cracked and tears trickled down my cheeks.

I had accepted Sitri's bargain. The moment the words had left my tongue, I had regretted it, but the need to protect Zepar was bigger than myself.

"Perhaps that will change," he said, "but for now, we don't have time to consider what the aftermath will look like. I'll call Ezequiel."

He turned and began walking down the hall toward his bedroom but stopped before reaching his door.

"He doesn't see what I do, Mara."

"I know," I answered. "He just sees me."

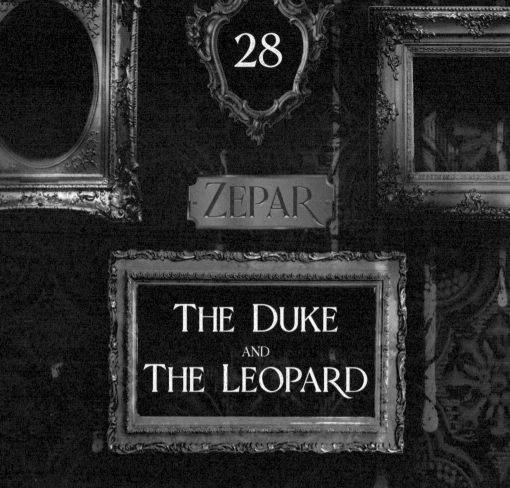

28

ZEPAR

THE DUKE
AND
THE LEOPARD

Ipos' words still buzzed through my mind as I paced the floor in my downtown L.A. office. My secretary had gone home about an hour ago, warning me to take care of myself tonight and reminding me of the several mergers I had on the docket for the next week. The distraction that had been put toward keeping Mara alive had derailed the last, and any further lapse in my judgment would reflect poorly on my business as a whole. I couldn't risk having to retreat to Hell for fifty years and starting over again.

The amber liquid clung to the edge of the glass, leaving a subtle wake with each sway of my wrist.

Through all of this, Mara had been strong and powerful in ways I hadn't seen another human act when they realized they were marked for death by the most holy and unholy of creatures. She had looked

her mortality in the face and embraced the opportunities that were presented to her.

The prophecy was merely a story, like all the rest. Ipos' predictions could turn at the slightest agitation. He had run to that forsaken desert many years ago to escape the constant harassment about the futures and fortunes but also to escape the blame for prophecies gone astray and unfavorable outcomes.

For the prophecy he'd spoken of, Mara would have to gain the favor of an angel to fulfill it, but the likelihood of an angel coming to her aid was very low with Raphael and Mikael bent on killing her.

Mara's fate had been sealed the moment she'd called upon Vepar, but every step we had taken since had pushed her further to the edge of this cliff. She would be seen as a weapon or sought after for the slumbering magic that writhed in her blood. Aside from her wit, she had no real power to destroy the Holy Ones herself, but her every breath would threaten their comfortable existence and the favor they held with the Father. For any angel to team with a demon to reunite Heaven and Hell would go against every order they had ever been given.

Word that Mara was with Sitri would spread to the far reaches within the next few hours. The ice-cold pit in my chest ached at the thought of Sitri's hands all over her, and the burn of something rebellious rose up in me once again. Vepar didn't have a hold on Mara's soul any longer, and if Sitri had figured it out, he would have no reason to allow Mara to walk away from him. But risking everything to see her again and hold her close, being her barrier to every monster at her back, those desires were becoming harder to ignore. I'd have no choice but to drink myself numb and live with any regret that came next. Because if I allowed those emotions to get the best of me, there was nowhere we could run where we wouldn't be found.

I refilled my glass to the rim and drank down half of it before I felt the gentle breeze. Kami appeared when I turned around and sent a flood of new bruises to my already raw emotions. She was draped in an impossibly white robe that hugged her waist and hung off her shoulders, the picture of pure, a vision of an angel appearing to a desperate sinner in his most despairing hour. She had a knack for catching me when my strength was at its lowest. It had always been her badge of honor: somehow knowing when I was close to leaping off the deep end of my own self-hatred.

She placed her hand on my chest, the familiar warmth spreading over my skin. The smell of fresh air and linen was in her hair but there was something new in her face—a brush of rain over heat-blistered earth. She turned her eyes up to meet mine, and my heart beat faster against my ribs at the sight of her golden-brown face so close to me.

Salvation. For the briefest of moments, I was released from my guilt.

"What have I done to deserve your presence twice in one century?" I asked, the pressure in my chest releasing at the sound of her breathing.

"Zep, I'm here for the human woman. Give me Mara and come home with me," she pleaded.

The tone in her voice perked my brow. She had never once mentioned my return to Heaven to be with her. In all the Earthly time we had danced our dance, the prospect of my returning to Heaven with her hadn't been possible.

"What?" I held her at arm's length, and her hand fell to her side.

"I've arranged for you to come home. But just you, if you can produce the human."

She wrapped her arms around my torso and laid her head against me. My hands drifted to her bare back, warmth crawling up my biceps and chest. Sunshine and summer rain filled my being the longer our bodies touched. I wanted badly to hold her like this for the rest of time and allow her to wash away my guilt and the cracked, broken heart that was hardly beating in my chest. To follow her back home and never leave her side and forget that for a brief moment in my existence, someone else had held my infatuation.

But the striking reality of her offer shunted the light that she had been pouring into me.

"Why only me? Vepar was the one to find Mara. Why would I be granted such a gift?" I stepped out of her embrace and looked her over.

There was a pitiful mourning on her face where happiness or joy or the anticipation of spending the rest of eternity together should have been.

No.

She didn't want this. She never had and never would. The truth of what we really were at our cores came rushing through the veil she had draped between us. I was a demon. No matter if I were permitted to go home with her or not, I would always be seen as one of the Fallen and she would always be my handler, taking responsibility for any actions I had done in the past and any I would do in the future. She would be at my side out of duty to the Father, not out of the love I desperately needed or wanted.

Vepar had been right. We could never go home. I just hadn't realized why until now. Hell was our home for better or worse, and Mara wasn't only the Key, she was the only way to end the constant tug-of-war between angels and demons.

Kami had been sent to persuade me before a heavier hand was applied.

She was here to take and dispose of Mara so demons wouldn't be able to use her either.

Mikael wouldn't have only sent Kami to me; he was smarter than to put all his faith in swaying me. He would have arranged for other angels to visit their wards in an attempt to corner Sitri and send him into a panic.

The goal was to get rid of Mara by the hands of an angel or not.

Sitri didn't have enough protection to ward off every demon within L.A., let alone the surrounding area that would love nothing more than to cash in on whatever promises were being made in the betrayal.

I had to get to Mara. I had to find Sitri and where he was holing up from the downpour of turncoats. He would go down fighting, but he would be slain by sheer force and numbers.

I looked to Kami, who was watching me intently, waiting for my undying fealty for her and for me to take the opportunity she had presented. But as she searched my face, the light behind her eyes dimmed. She'd seen that my loyalty had shifted, that I not only questioned her position but was finally breaking the hold her convoluted affections had held over me for all this time.

I needed Mara more than I ever thought I needed Kami. The artificial spark that once kept me within Kami's orbit had gone out in her attempt to keep me on my leash.

Mara was where my heart truly lay. Somewhere between offering my home as a safe haven and watching her leave with Sitri, I had lied to myself more deeply than I ever had before.

Again, the words Ipos spoke rang through me and drowned out the crushing weight of my next choice. Mara's soul and mine were intertwined, but it was more than that now. She was what my existence had been missing for thousands of years.

I stepped around Kami and made to walk out of the door when she snatched my hand and pulled me back around. A rush of warmth and longing pulled at me from her touch, though nothing like I had felt from her before. She was desperate to keep me tangled in her reluctant web.

"Don't do this, Zep," she pleaded. "This human is not worth you being blinked out of existence."

"Hakamiah, I know my place. For longer than I care to admit, you were one reason I chose to stay on Earth. I haunted this world for the quick glances of you I stole over the years. I starved for any bit of you for thousands of years, sustained by the crumbs. The temptation of you held me to the arbitrary rules bestowed upon the Fallen by Michael, Raphael, and Gabriel." I paused and cupped her face in my palms one last time.

Her eyes welled, tears threatening to break free of her lashes and stain her cheeks. She placed her hands over mine and took a deep breath.

"Please. I am begging you." Her voice cracked.

"What I thought was love was nothing compared to what I feel for Mara, and I will not allow anyone to take her from me. For whatever we shared for all these years, I'm warning you now. Stay out of my way because I will protect her with my last breath, and I will not hesitate to take you or anyone else with me."

I pulled my hand away, and her shoulders heaved with a sob.

"I'll miss you." Her voice faded as she dissipated from my office.

I received her message clearly; she wasn't choosing this fight, and though she likely would miss me if I were to be killed in the battle, she would not mourn. Her freedom from me was far greater a reward than a sacrifice.

I didn't linger on this thought as I pressed the elevator button to summon it to my floor and rode it down to the parking garage. When I got into my car, I pulled out my phone and dialed Vepar. Wherever he was, he would know where Mara had been taken.

"Brother Dearest," he answered smugly. "What can I do for you this fine evening?"

"Where are they, Vepar." My tone was harsher than I had intended.

"I don't know who you mean. Be more specific," he taunted.

"Mara. Sitri. Where are they?" I turned out onto the boulevard and headed in the most likely direction.

"Now why would you need to know where the meaningless mange would be?"

I glowered with impatience. "I'll tell you while I break your jaw."

The sound of wind and a small pop and he was sitting beside me in the car, a devoutly arrogant look about him. He knew me all too well and had been ready for my call by the look of his attire. He dripped with wealth and class in his designer suit and his long hair slicked back.

I knew what his answer was going to be if he was dressed this way and not for a casual battle.

"The Deacon," he answered, clearly enjoying my sudden madness.

The valet rushed over, but Vepar and I were already stalking past him before he reached the curb. I tossed my keys up, uncaring if he caught them or not. The doorman looked us over, shaking his head and holding up a hand to stop us.

"I didn't ask for permission." Vepar flourished his hand in a swiping motion and the demon went flying to the side, landing on his back.

Inside, Sitri and Mara were nowhere to be seen. The booth he had occupied the last time we had come was full of Hollywood starlets drinking Champagne and hooting loudly along with the music. I looked at Vepar through the flashing lights then around to the bar. A row of more humans than usual lined it, several with a glass in each hand. Vepar clapped my shoulder and pointed to the dance floor where more humans were jostling about, dry humping each other's body parts and screaming with glee.

A small group of demons descended the staircase from the upper VIP area, all of them dressed more casually than typically done at The Deacon. I nudged Vepar's arm and nodded to where the group had come from. He returned the gesture and followed me across the room. Hands of human women grabbed at our cuffs as we passed, and one of them placed herself in front of me. Her hips whirled and her arms hooked mine, attempting to dance with me, restrain me, or both.

I shouted through the music, but my voice was lost in the pounding bass. With my hands on her shoulders, I turned her around to pass her off to a human man sitting in a chair. He hollered approval, and his hands began to travel over the woman's large rear end.

I realized then that they both had a glazed-over expression. Neither seemed to be fully aware of their surroundings. Only the drink and music seemed to be driving their behavior. This wasn't out of character for most humans in nightclubs, but the odd expression was plastered on every human I saw.

Vepar pulled at my shoulder, bringing his mouth close to my ear. "Sitri has fucked with their minds. They've all lost it."

"This looks like Ezequiel's work," I shouted.

I moved deeper into the fray with Vepar at my back. A large lesser demon stood at the bottom of the staircase when we made it through the dance floor. His hand extended to stop us, but his frame took up the width of the entryway. He looked from me to Vepar then brought a cigar to his lips. He took a long puff before blowing smoke in our faces.

"The prince isn't seeing anyone tonight. He is indisposed." The demon's brow quirked, and a sleazy grin spread over his yellowed teeth.

Vepar shouldered me aside and came to stand in front of our blockade. Vepar leaned into the demon's ear, and almost instantly the fellow sank into desperate fear. The bodyguard's face paled as Vepar pulled back, a look of triumph on his face. With a flick of his finger, Vepar encouraged our free passage and began walking up the stairs. I followed behind him. The demon sank to the floor and curled himself up into a ball.

I watched my brother as he climbed the stairs ahead of me, and we met at the landing. The music dulled; the glass panes and a warding around the doorframe provided a muffling barrier. Deals were made often in his club. Of course Sitri would need a quiet place to make them.

Vepar peered down to the sea of bodies below, the sweat-drenched humans emitting a visible heat. Whatever spell Sitri or Ezequiel had placed on their patrons was likely to result in a few casualties by the end of the night—alcohol poisoning, dehydration, or trampling injuries by the look of the crowd around the bar.

Vepar cleared his throat and nudged my shoulder. "After you."

29

MARA

MOUTH FULL OF RAZORS

The door flung open and Zepar stepped inside, his eyes fixed on Sitri. I stood from where I had been sitting at the corner of the desk and took one step before Ezequiel grabbed my wrist and pulled me back against his frame.

"To what do I owe this unannounced, and rather rude, intrusion?" Sitri scoffed.

Zepar's eyes darkened as they snagged on Ezequiel's hand still wrapped around my arm.

"Vepar has no claim over her any longer." Sitri stood and rounded his desk to stand as a shield to me. "We both know that to be true."

"If she is free from Vepar, that means she can choose where she would like to go and who with." Zepar's eyes met mine for the first time, and the silent plea in his gaze sent a tightening to my chest.

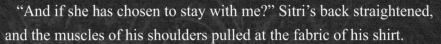

"And if she has chosen to stay with me?" Sitri's back straightened, and the muscles of his shoulders pulled at the fabric of his shirt.

"It will mean nothing unless we figure out a way to keep her alive," Vepar chimed in from the doorway, where he was leaning and watching the spectacle.

Ezequiel's hand squeezed but not painfully. My eyes flicked between Zepar and Vepar then to the back of Sitri's head. The two sides marked the other's movements and waited for the air between them to erupt in chaos. Anticipation took on its own presence among us.

Zepar's jaw feathered, and his chest filled. "Sitri—"

A sonic boom and the floor quaking under our feet cut off Zepar's words. The bass from the club stopped, and the sound of muffled screams hammered against the windows and walls. When the ground stopped threatening to open up beneath us, all four celestial beings bolted to the door.

Sitri shouted over his shoulder, "Stay here, Mara."

He was out of his mind if he thought I was going to listen. I followed all four of them out onto the landing and watched them file down the stairs as fast as they could without toppling into a pile at the bottom. I stopped a few steps above where they stood, giving me the advantage of seeing over the heads of the crowd.

The floor of the club was riddled with broken bodies and blood. The ones still standing were barricading the entry of the office and yelling at the source of the disturbance. One large being stood at the center of the dance floor. A shower of golden sparks and bright white light emitted from somewhere behind or above them, blinding me to their face.

Ezequiel pushed through the blockade of possessed humans, and his skin took on a glow as if he had been set aflame from the inside out. The yelps of pain and anguish immediately halted, and the human puppets stilled. The sudden silence assaulted my ears. I almost wondered if I had gone deaf.

"You shouldn't be here, brother," Ezequiel pronounced, and the being's accosting light dimmed. Both angels' beams ceased.

White and pale-pink toned feathered wings parted to reveal the tall, beautiful man who had been alone at the center of the attack. His wide smile didn't meet his eyes as he sized up the three demons standing before me then shifted his gaze back to Ezequiel.

"Neither should you, Watcher." He practically hissed Ezequiel's title. "But we are here for the same reason, aren't we?"

His eyes flitted to me. "You have become a festering thorn in my side, *Maphteah*."

My mouth went dry at the sound of the label from this stranger. There was an eerie calm in his tone that sent a shiver down my spine. I stepped down directly behind Sitri. His arm slid back, and his hand met my hip as he pushed himself in front of me.

Zepar moved through the wall of humans to Ezequiel's side, bringing the attention away once again. "I know you didn't come alone, Raphael. Where is Mikael? The horde of demons you've manipulated into action with the promise of going home?"

Raphael. The archangel that he and Vepar had spoken to before I'd made a run for it.

Raphael was here to kill me. The well in my stomach deepened. Mikael had said that Raphael was more powerful than demons or himself.

Ezequiel's light dulled, but he spoke for Raphael. "They are outside waiting for his signal. I can hear them."

"I see Hakamiah has failed in her mission to sway you, Zepar. How tragic. But then again, she never was a good actress." Raphael's snide tone had sounded harsh, even to me. Whoever Hakamiah was, it would seem she was part of the betrayal that was evident on Zepar's face.

I strained my ears to hear what Ezequiel had but could only hear the sound of my pulse and the low hum of Lilith's voice. I couldn't make out the syllables, but the queasy feeling in my gut told me she wanted me to get out of here as fast as I could. But for once, I couldn't run.

"A Watcher on your side has put a damper on my initial party invitation." Raphael rolled his shoulders. "Angel blood is too precious to spill, even if it is tainted."

His wings fluttered behind him, and he adjusted his shoulders to accommodate their weight.

Raphael's lip tightened into a disgusted grimace as he panned from Ezequiel to Zepar. "But he is right. Mikael has assembled enough spirits on both sides to tear this building down to the studs if necessary."

"They'll have a hard time getting in. And when they do, we will be long gone but not without leaving a volatile gift waiting for them when they pass through the threshold," Sitri called, divulging a layer of the defense he and Ezequiel had laid for lesser angels who may have been brave enough to come retrieve me. He and Ezequiel had thought they would be able to convince any demon to their side or kill them if they refused.

"It doesn't have to come to detonative threats, *Princeps Sanguinis*. I have all the might needed to dispatch you and your band of dogs to get what I want if an agreement cannot be met." Raphael's voice easily reached Sitri and me at the stairs, but Raphael's eyes never left the two beings before him. He watched as something brass and sharp appeared in Zepar's palm, the movement not missed by any of us.

"Time to end this little game you've been playing, Zepar. Allow me to do what I came here to do, and I will spare you and your brother. Only one has to die tonight."

"You're right, Raphael. Only one here has to die for this madness to end," Zepar answered and threw the blade that had killed Dras through

It missed Raphael's torso and head but it buried itself into one of his wings, causing him to hiss in pain as a shimmery gold and white substance leaked from the wound and dripped down the heavenly feathers.

Raphael ripped the dagger out then and pulled his wings in tight to his body. "That was hostile, Zepar." He seethed through clenched teeth, regaining his composure, and threw the weapon to the ground. "You are no match for me, even at your brightest."

"I have been to see Ipos," Zepar said. "I know the threat Mara poses to the balance, what lives are intertwined with her mortal soul. But she can continue to live without fulfilling the prophecy he had foreseen."

"That old sun-cat couldn't prognosticate his way out of a public park," Raphael chortled. "You truly believe the delusions of a madman?"

"You wouldn't be here if he were wrong," Vepar said as he stepped through the line of defense next and stood between Zepar and Ezequiel.

Raphael narrowed his eyes to Vepar, anger wrinkling his brow. "You should hold your tongue, Vepar. I have half a mind to remove you along with your pet for good measure."

Vepar and Zepar held their hands out in front of them, and a rush of electricity and a smoky substance whirled at their fingertips. Vepar balled his fist, and it disappeared under the cloud he had created and wound his arm back. When he let loose the blast, Raphael blocked it easily with his uninjured wing and a wave of his hand.

Zepar brought his palms together before him where the buildup of power shot bolts of lightning in all directions and grew as he widened his stance. The boulder-sized sphere sucked at the air in the club. It was as if he had taken a raging thunderstorm and condensed it between his hands. Raphael's eyes zeroed in and his own hands began to burn brightly with pure sunlight.

With a forceful shout, Zepar propelled his missile, but it was met by a blast from Raphael. The wave of power broke into all corners of the room. Sitri's body shielded me, but spots flashed over my vision.

I blinked and rubbed my face until I could see the fuzzy outlines and shadows of the men battling in the middle of the room. Ezequiel shouted out something that sounded like a command or plea for them to stop, but it was drowned out by a high-pitched siren that Raphael's attack had brought from Lilith within me.

In a split second, Vepar and Zepar were on their knees doubled over in pain with their hands pressed to the sides of their heads. Ezequiel rushed to Vepar, who had been standing closest to him, but whatever effect Raphael was having on the two demons, Ezequiel could not stop it.

"Enough!" Ezequiel shouted, ceasing the ringing in my ear and the battle.

Vepar and Zepar fell to the floor, the immense pain they had been experiencing seemingly halted for the time being. Raphael crossed his arms over his chest and laughed as Ezequiel helped Vepar to his feet.

"Admit defeat and I will kill her quickly. And because I'm feeling generous, I will leave her body here for you to bury."

"You will have to kill me first," Zepar choked out from his place on the floor, still too weak to stand.

I placed my hand on Sitri's shoulder, and he tensed against my chest. His hand at my hip tightened with the hostility of the conversation. I leaned into him and brought my cheek to rest just behind his ear. "Let me go."

His jaw twitched, but he removed his hand and allowed me to pass him. My stomach hollowed but not from my own fear. From Sitri. From Lilith. The connection between Sitri and I now that we had set our deal in motion was getting stronger by the minute.

The humans inhabited by spirits were unmoving, Ezequiel abandoning the control over them as he pulled Zepar to his feet.

Raphael watched me intently as I came closer with Sitri at my back. I squared my shoulders and swallowed down the tears tightening the back of my throat.

"If you promise not to hurt them, I won't fight you," I said, my voice weakened with fear.

Zepar grunted. "Mara, no."

I didn't answer him. I didn't look at him. If I did, I wouldn't be able to do what had to be done. I wouldn't have the strength to save his life because I knew the pain in his voice wasn't there because of Raphael's attack.

Raphael's face split into a triumphant smile then a jolly chuckle. "I will not be making a deal with you, *Maphteah*." He cocked his head and furrowed his brow. "Did you believe that your act of bravery would be enough to make me forget my senses?"

"I don't know what to believe anymore, but I will come quietly if it means Zepar and the others will be spared."

The angel's face held no pity. I was nothing but a speck of dust to him. But even the smallest grain of sand could cause a great disturbance to the inner workings of fine-tuned machines.

That was what I had become. My entire existence had shifted from one of the Father's creations to a thing of inconvenience for life to continue as it always had. The weight of a feather to an already stressed dam that had been holding back the flood of demons banging on the walls beyond. To remove me from the issue would solve his, and every other angel's, problems.

There was no way out or around this fate, but I forced myself to believe that my brief life would save Zepar. That the love that I had for him would withstand the terror of dying at the hands of an angel.

In my peripheral vision, I saw Zepar lunge forward, but with a quick wave of his hand, Raphael's powerful energy threw all three demons to the floor around me. Sitri called out my name and struggled against an unseen force keeping him pinned to the floor. Vepar cursed and dragged his torso toward my ankle but was thrown back once again before the tips of his fingers could graze my skin. The barrier Raphael had built around us was the last nail in my coffin.

Raphael outstretched his hand and a sword's hilt materialized in his fist. The blade shone brightly in the dim room. He held it over his head.

"Have no fear, for I am the healer of the Earth from all that the demons have defiled," he proclaimed and brought down his mighty blade.

I closed my eyes tight.

A flash of hot light filled my vision through my lids. Then came the whirl of wind and the spray of something cool and wet to my cheeks. Sun and rain showered over me like a summer storm. A crack of thunder sounded in the hollow chamber I'd been plunged into. The high-pitched ringing in my ears grew louder and louder until it became the only sensation I could feel. It vibrated my bones, muscles, and nerves. Then I was plunged into ice water, and the pitchy whine was replaced by my lungs gasping for air and millions of needles piercing every inch of my skin.

If this was dying, I didn't want to know what the pits of Hell were. The agony tore at my flesh and consciousness. How was I still feeling anything?

I pried my eyelids open to find myself and Raphael surrounded by nothing but white light. The searing pain cooled and pressure in my chest broke open to a serene nothingness.

No floor, no ceiling. Just the achromatic space that separated Raphael's body and mine. Zepar, Vepar, and Sitri were gone, but I could hear their muffled shouts from somewhere far away.

The blur of my vision subsided to reveal the look of horror and shock in Raphael's eyes. His sword was no longer gripped in his fingers. I let out a deep breath and focused on the angel before me, and his dumbfounded confusion quickly turned to anger. He drew back his fist and lunged to land his blow, but he was stopped by another unseen barrier and dropped to his knees.

I felt a warm hand on my shoulder as the light extinguished and the broken and battered backdrop of The Deacon came back into view. To my right, Sitri watched us from behind the invisible wall, his face contorted into pain. On the other side of me were the frantic faces of Vepar and Zepar. All three demons had oily blood coming from their noses and ears.

I turned to see Ezequiel who had penetrated the shield and now stood at my back. He took my hand in his, pressing the hilt of the dropped sword into my palm and forcing my fingers to stretch and tighten around it. I parted my lips, wetting their rough and dry surfaces with my tongue. Tears fell from my eyes and splashed at my chest as I squeezed my eyelids shut.

I looked back up to Ezequiel, and he gave me a subtle nod before his gaze fell to the archangel at my feet. I followed his line of sight to Raphael, who was stretching his fingers over the floor, searching for his weapon, not realizing that it had found its way into my hands.

I raised my arms, allowing the point of the blade to settle between the wings on the back of the angel I was about to murder. I took a breath, a long and contemplated inhale to steady my weak wrists.

"Now." Ezequiel's voice came crystal clear behind me.

The breath from Ezequiel's lips passed just over the crest of my ear. But his words smoothed over the tops of my shoulders, then my arms, the pressure giving me stability and guiding my strength down into the flesh and bone of one of the purest beings this world had known.

A blaze caught at the base of the blade and traveled down into the gasping and screaming archangel, who burst into flames himself within seconds. The body of a once all-powerful being turned to dust and spilled over the floor and my feet, leaving only the hilt behind.

My insides quaked at the sight. What monster had I been born from those ashes?

Zepar stumbled forward and cupped my face in his blackened hands. Like the force of life from Raphael's body, the protection that had encapsulated us had been snuffed out. The fire in Zepar's eyes screamed for me to speak. The leaking blood from his nose had made a trail around his mouth and dipped over the curve of his chin. The dark stain on his skin sent a flash of anger through me. Even though the being that caused him pain was dead and gone, I had a fury building in my chest.

"Mara?" Zepar looked deep into my eyes, and his features softened when I answered.

"I'm okay. I'm not hurt."

He wrapped his arms around my shoulders and breathed a heavy sigh into my sweat-damp hair. He pulled away enough to meet my eyes once again. My vision blurred from tears, but more than ever before, I saw him: the man who had been willing to give his life for mine.

"I've never been more terrified to lose someone," he said, bringing his hand back to my cheek. "What was that?"

He scanned the men standing around us before he narrowed in on Ezequiel, who had gotten Sitri to his feet.

"I…I made a deal," I said, my chest clenching at the admission. "I made a deal with Sitri."

Zepar shot Sitri a lethal glare.

"Tell them what I gave you, little dove," he said cynically, holding Zepar's venomous stare.

"Sitri granted me the ability to protect myself against angels and demons," I said, stepping out of Zepar's reach and standing between the two demons who were ready to tear each other apart at any moment.

I placed my hands on Zepar's chest, but hate still darkened his face. Vepar came to stand next to us and he held a similar ire, but it was directed to both Sitri and me. I had betrayed him as well in my deal. I hadn't belonged to him for longer than we both had realized but now the remnants of our cold and severed connection felt tumultuous.

"And what is it you gave to him, lamb?" Vepar furrowed his brow.

"Me," I croaked.

Zepar and Vepar froze in shock, their faces collectively dropping from anger to confusion and then back to fury.

"You snake. I'll kill you." Zepar stepped around me to get to Sitri.

Fists and faces collided until Vepar and Ezequiel pulled them apart.

"Stop!" I held my hands out between them, and Sitri laughed behind me.

"She gave me herself in whatever form I felt fit," Sitri said, further adding to the agitation in the air.

"What the fuck is that supposed to mean?" Vepar grunted as he held Zepar's arms back.

Ezequiel stepped to my side. It was his turn to be the bearer of bad news. "Sitri came to me this morning and explained that your little lamb needed protection. I couldn't give her that, but I could help in a transformation that would solve the problem. The deal she made with Sitri made it so I could cleanse her of her mortal sins, then she would have to willingly sacrifice herself before killing one of the most holy of our Father's sons," he said, a lilt of pride in his tone. "And she did so without hesitation."

I swallowed hard at my dry throat. "I knew you would put yourself in front of me, and I couldn't see you hurt or worse."

Zepar ripped off his jacket and dropped it to the floor next to him then went for his tie before rolling up his sleeves. He was waiting for the catch. The one I had been so careful to agree to on several conditions.

"Sitri offered to help me in exchange for my soul that had been entwined with Lilith's. He didn't want just mine, he wanted everything, but we couldn't pull her out without killing me."

"Defeated the purpose, didn't it, little dove?" Sitri cooed from behind me.

He slid his hand up my arm and pulled my loose hair over my shoulder. His warm breath fanned over my neck before he planted a gentle but possessive kiss on my cheek. My skin burned at the touch, but the pain tearing at my heart was worse.

Zepar's nostrils flared and his eyes widened as rage bubbled up into his features once again. I'd known this conversation was going to be painful if we ever had a chance to have it. The words to make him understand why I had made this deal were far from my tongue, and with every second that passed, they edged farther away.

"Instead, I asked for him to make me into a weapon to protect you. He made me into a demon."

"You don't have that kind of power," Zepar snapped to Sitri.

"You're right, dear duke. But combined with Ezequiel's power, it could be done." Sitri wove his fingers through mine then brought our joined hands up to eye level.

A sphere of stormy clouds bloomed from our bond, and our hands disappeared within it. The warming sensation at my fingers from Sitri's touch met the icy chill of the mist surrounding our connection. Sitri pulled his hand away, and the formed ball of energy hovered over my palm. I held it out for Zepar and Vepar to see.

They stood silent for a moment, the new situation sinking into their racing minds.

"I take it Ipos had a hand in your plot?" Vepar asked the three of us.

I glanced at Sitri, waiting for him to answer, but it was Ezequiel who spoke up first.

"The arrangement would halt the prophecy and lock Lilith safely away within Mara for all eternity. She was able to kill Raphael because of the protection Lilith had been given so long ago combined with mine and Sitri's help. No demon prince or duke could say that. Only Lucifer himself has had the ability to destroy an archangel unassisted but he has always refused to kill his own brothers. That won't be an issue with *Maphteah*."

A tangle of emotions squirmed in my belly at Ezequiel's words.

"Who else knows of this deal?" Zepar's voice drew me back from the edge of despair.

"No one but Ipos. And as long as Mara keeps to our arrangement, no one ever will. For all anyone will hear, Raphael fell upon his own sword during the scuffle," Sitri answered, the tip of his finger tracing the line of my jaw.

"What arrangement?" Zepar growled through gritted teeth.

Sitri's head rose, and he moved to my side, his hand on my shoulder. "Mara has made her choice, but she owes me her life and yours."

My stomach tumbled at the mischievous gleam in his eye. When he had offered to make this deal, we'd felt the immediate connection between his soul and mine, but it was different than what I had felt with Vepar. Duller. Artificial. I was a product of Sitri, but I had somehow retained the need and want I'd had for Zepar before the transformation. Ezequiel had no explanation, but we hadn't had time to come up with any theories. The test was coming and we had to work fast.

"He made me into a demon, but after one thousand years of freedom, I default back to his side," I said, knowing that it didn't matter how much time would pass, Zepar would want to kill Sitri.

"If Ezequiel also made an agreement with you, then that would've activated the prophecy. How have the walls of Heaven and Hell remained standing?" Vepar asked.

"He didn't make the deal with Mara. He made it with me." Sitri shrugged. "Missed opportunities, I suppose."

"She is still the great love of your life. Only now, she doesn't have an expiration date." Ezequiel smiled, attempting to lift the mood. But this didn't make the clamp around my heart loosen.

"Why make her such a generous offer?" Zepar said, his tone becoming more impatient.

The obsession that Sitri had over what I could be to him was still a secret between him and me, and a ripple of understanding passed through our strange new connection.

"Mara has the free will to go with whom she chooses. But that will also mean that the moment she pleases, she can return to my side and live as my princess. I suggest you treat her as such," Sitri said, the pressure from his hand guiding me toward Zepar. Then he took a step back with Ezequiel.

Vepar folded his arms over his chest as he worked the last of the details out. "But she'll be connected to you, drawn to you as her creator. Such a proud moment for you, Sitri."

I glanced at Sitri over my shoulder. His lips curled at his own cleverness. Vepar was right. I had a feeling of owing Sitri. There was a debt I would have every day to him. His infatuation with me had driven him to act, but he had said he would wait several hundred years for me if he had to. He wanted me to come to him of my own volition.

"I can't say that I am disappointed by my current position in Mara's existence," Sitri replied.

Zepar glowered at him but had nothing more to say.

"Now that this is settled, I better let our other guests know their invitations have been rescinded and to vacate the surrounding street before they trigger the warding and blow us all up." Ezequiel scooped up a handful of ash and long, white discarded feathers from the floor and headed toward the door.

Sitri stepped over the pile of ash and grabbed a feather for himself, turning it over and admiring the opalescent color as light shifted over it. He held it up to Vepar as an offer of pacification, which Vepar took reluctantly. Vepar passed it into Zepar's hands. A doleful twitch of his lips was his only response to the gesture before he slipped it into his back pocket.

Sitri cleared his throat and drew our attention to him. "I'm ready for a drink. Anyone else?"

Vepar turned, and Sitri draped his arm over his shoulder and started them toward the bar.

Ezequiel returned and joined the two demons.

I stayed with Zepar and waited for him to either leave out of rage or yell at me for all the destruction I had caused.

"I would have killed and died for you," he said after several silent moments.

My heart sank at his words, at the notion that he had those feelings but I had found solace in someone else. I had done what I felt I needed to do to protect what was mine, and whether he felt it in that moment of passion, Zepar was mine. I'd had so little in my human life to call my own, and when I made that claim over him, I knew I would have done anything to keep him.

"Now you'll never have to," I said, swallowing past the painful strain in my throat.

"I suppose not," he answered, his eyes wandering over me.

Perhaps he was looking for the signs of my new power or the parts of me that were demonic. I had been looking for them myself. The low hum within me had silenced. Lilith was still within me, but she had gone quiet again. There were many questions I had about my new self. The choices Sitri and I made had happened so quickly and without careful consideration. A thousand years was unfathomable to my human brain, but as a demon I imagined it would feel too short when the time came to pay my debt.

Being a princess of Hell was my new form of mortal end. The dread of the unknown still hung over my head, but the sense of freedom that the next one thousand years would bring was more than I could comprehend. It would mean nothing if Zepar didn't stop looking at me like I was a bomb primed to explode.

"Zepar?" So many more questions laced my words as I watched him.

"Mara." He closed the distance between us and cupped my cheek then drew my face closer to his. "For the next thousand years, and then for the eternity after, I am yours."

He kissed me deeply, and the spark I felt the first time he touched me set my insides ablaze. For the first time, I knew what I had been made for. I had found a reason to be stronger than I had ever been. With every failure I had seen, I had found myself one step closer to where my heart would be safe.

Where I was safe.

He felt like home.

30

ZEPAR

ABANDON GRACE

Mara kissed my bare shoulder, her breast pressed to my back as we watched the sunrise over the clear, blue ocean. We hadn't left the hotel in two days, but I had promised her that we would go sightseeing after breakfast. We'd find a waterfall to make love under or a hidden beach where we could strip down so I could devour her in the warm sun. But I was having a hard time convincing myself to allow anyone else on Earth to lay their eyes on her. On what was mine.

"I love you," she whispered against my ear in that breathy tone that went straight to my cock.

"I love you, my darling." I brought her hand to my lips.

Word had made it to Heaven and Hell that there was a newly formed

demon and one less archangel. As Sitri had promised, no one knew the circumstances of her creation, but the rumors were that the demise of an angel and my willingness to sacrifice myself for her had created a chain reaction.

I had taken a leave of absence at work to show Mara how to use her new abilities, but I had also wanted to make every single day we had together count. We both could feel her connection to Sitri in ways we hadn't expected. They could feel one another's emotions even hundreds of miles away. Fits of Sitri's anger or pleasure affected her severely. His anguish when he found that we had hopped on a jet to Maui without his knowledge had sent Mara into convulsing pain.

He had called the morning after I brought her home and gloated about the orgasms they had shared while she and I had been together. His infiltration of our private moments would be a trial to overcome, but the way her face lit up when she was able to harness her new power or the bliss one kiss could bring made dealing with the bratty prince worth the intrusions.

She held the love I hadn't known I needed. The loneliness that had been a part of me until she claimed me felt like a distant memory. The hunger that had plagued my existence had been sated, and she was my feast for the rest of time. She would not bring unity between Heaven and Hell, but she was my peace.

In her hands and heart, I was whole.

THE END

BONUS SHORT STORY

Please enjoy this short story that is meant to connect *Blood On My Name* to *Prince Of Lust*.

The Princes of Sins series is an interconnected series which follows each Prince of Sin through their own story. These novellas will be released in quick succession.

Follow our Prince of Lust in his new story on May 23rd!

Pre-order available now

31

SITRI

HERE
KITTY KITTY

The second bottle of vodka finally got the room spinning.

The two women I had brought upstairs were tasting each other on the couch across the living room, oblivious to me but gratefully lapping at the other's lips. I wondered if they realized where they were or if they had forgotten about the serpent monitoring them from its own island in the same sea.

It didn't matter.

Neither had stirred my cock into action down in the club, but their eagerness to undress had prospects. Their heady arousal and willingness for a night free of inhibitions were enough to draw forth my interest. I could watch, touch myself, see someone who wasn't there dip their fingers into one of their cunts. I could pretend long enough to get off. Long enough for the influence of my power to bring them both to climax higher and harder than either had ever experienced before.

I could.

If the shots of liquor cleared my head instead of driving me to bed alone—once again.

Every night since I'd watched her walk away in the arms of another, I attempted to quell my hunger with any being that would participate. But it was only the image of her face and my own touch that would scratch the itch gnawing at my spine.

I slipped my hand down the front of my pants to the appendage struggling to stiffen.

It had once moved mountains. Pleased kings and queens. The conquests of my lengthy history dredged up memories of orgies that brought empires to their knees.

I had been a god to the humans who had given everything they'd owned for a taste of me.

Now, the part of me that had been blessed to shatter every being it had entered lay limp in my palm.

My frustration and starved sigh perked one of the women's brows. She tilted her head in my direction from between the legs that were straddling her face.

"Aren't you going to join us?" She spread the legs over her wide open to entice me, but there were now two of her and several whirling legs haloing around her.

"Ladies first." I waved my hand as an invitation to ignore me further.

Without hesitation, she resumed sucking at the clit above her face, bringing the owner to moans of pleasure.

I strained my eyes to focus, but a whisper from the back of my mind slinked its way to my drunken ears.

What's the matter, Prince of Sin? No kitty good enough for your cock?

None present, I answered the smoky inner voice.

"None?"

The sh▓▓ bell of her words snapped my attention to the soft blush of her cheek only a breath away from my face.

"Missing me still?" Her legs slid down the couch, and the curves of her hips, then breasts filled the spot on the cushion next to me.

A weight of relief sat on my chest. "More than you could know, little dove."

Her lips twisted into a knowing smirk. She could feel my desperation. I knew she did, but I also knew that nothing I said or felt would bring her any closer. The deal we made was on a ticking clock, but I made the agreement before she had metamorphosed into the ravishing hellcat perched on her knees next to me. The thread between us that formed when her human soul was bound into her demon body had set me ablaze. It had taken every ounce of restraint to not rip Zepar to shreds and take her for my own right then and there.

But then I felt the joy, love, and the slew of other emotions she had when he touched her. Our connection would be the death of my sanity. To feel her being pleased by one of my brothers or the butterflies in her belly when she saw him smile was a knife to my chest. But she felt something for me too. It was there in the rubble of the fortress Lilith had made inside of her, in the way she sent me glimpses of herself enjoying her new life that I had granted her.

A thankful, warm ghost of a hand at my shoulder when I was at my loneliest surrounded by thrashing bodies on The Deacon's dance floor. Small flashes of the sun, ocean, or lively markets while she and Zepar traipsed around Western Europe, then along the Mediterranean on what could only be described as their honeymoon.

"He's not here with you?" I threw a wary glance around the room.

I hadn't felt either of them appear, but the drink had dulled my senses thoroughly at that point.

Mara's eyes flicked toward the jumble of legs and breasts and pleasurable humming, then they came back to me. There was heat in her gaze. I'd have done anything for that blush of fire to have been caused by my hands or cock.

"He's not my keeper, Sitri." The warmth of her sultry breath brushed the crest of my ear again. "Remember?"

My head lolled back onto the ridge of the couch, and I looked up into her face. She'd cut her hair, and her already brown skin had tanned to a bronze in the Moroccan sun.

"You have no keeper, princess." My fingers brushed a wavy lock of hair from her cheek, the only warmth from her skin I would feel for the night.

"I think I prefer little dove."

I raised a brow to that, and her lips pulled to her cheeks.

My heart sank with that subtle grin. The smoke and drink mixed with the respite of her being within arm's reach for the first time in weeks was like a lungful of air after being trapped in a coffin in a rotting mausoleum. The burden and punishment for creating such a powerful being without the blessings of the Father or Lucifer was that I would constantly be torn apart from the inside out every second I couldn't touch her.

I should have let Raphael kill us all.

I would have been better off snuffed from existence than waiting a thousand years for her to be chained to my side. But what brought me the most agony also brought me the most hope to cling to.

In 999 years, 7 months, and 2 days, she would be only mine.

Forever.

I just had to survive until then.

"What brings you to the after-party this evening?" I asked her. "Taking pity on me for the night, I hope?"

She rolled her eyes. Her playful confidence shot straight to my previously lifeless cock.

"You brought me here." She raked her hair from one side to the other, then she propped her chin on the arm angled on the back cushion.

Her brown eyes watched for my confession, but I didn't summon her. Not on purpose. I didn't know I was capable. Another urge I would have to learn to suppress for a millennium.

"I hope you weren't . . . busy," I teased.

"You've felt more dark and broody lately." She wrinkled her nose but paused for her eyes to roam over my face, then down my slumped torso. "You've felt so far away."

"I'm not the one who left the continent for a holiday." I attempted to mask my disdain with a smile but failed.

The comment earned me a look of pathos.

"Don't worry about me, little dove. I will do better to relieve you of my thoughts. As much as it pains me to be on the outside of it, I want to see you happy. Free."

She smiled weakly.

"For now." I winked.

She leaned over me and pressed her lips to my brow, then she pulled away, ready to fade back into the night and leave me wondering if I had imagined her. I hadn't. The scalding spot where her lips had been a moment ago was proof enough that she had been real.

Her gaze traveled slowly over to the two women who were panting through another shared orgasm. I didn't join her in the intrusion, but a breeze of jealousy for her attention being stolen away stalled my lungs.

"They're very beautiful, Sitri." Her voice dipped into a husky whisper. "Couldn't you just see yourself entwined with them? That one looks to be very good with her tongue."

I swallowed. My cock throbbed in my palm as she spoke. She shifted on her knees, the tingle between her thighs mimicked my own.

"She could take you into her throat as the other rode your face. Look." She nudged her chin in their direction, but I didn't move my eyes from the hunger on her face. "She's already wet for you."

One of the women dropped to her knees between my legs. Her hands smoothed up my thighs and over my opened pants. I dragged my gaze away from Mara to meet the grungy green eyes of the blonde who looked up at me longingly.

"Give her what she wants, Sitri," Mara whispered in my ear, her voice becoming faint as it sank back into my subconscious and left me to my own devices.

"What's your name, pet?" I laced my fingers through her hair with one hand; the other was still occupied by my erection.

"Mandy," she answered, pulling at the waistband of my jeans.

"Are you going to take care of me, Mandy?" I pulled my cock out of my underwear and let her take the shaft in both hands.

She didn't speak again, only nodded eagerly.

The other woman came to sit beside me, her large breasts at my eye level. Her lips met mine. The taste of Mandy hung from her tongue while Mandy began sucking at my tip.

The mercy Mara had given me didn't go unnoticed.

However this complicated existence would play out going forward was put on the back burner for the night as I worked weeks of frustration out on their cunts, mouths, and asses.

32

MARA

HONEYMOONERS

I slipped through the void back to the bedroom that Zepar and I now shared. His leave from work ended a week ago, and though Vepar, his twin and partner at the law firm, had kept up with their schemes while we were gone, Zepar had been working double time to catch up. The finance world had been flung into a panic over a midterm stock crash, and the number of deals his very powerful firm was making meant it was raking in hundreds of souls a day.

Or at least that was what he said after he stumbled into bed at 2 in the morning before going back to the office at six.

I missed Italy. I missed Greece.

I missed the man who showed me what it meant to be free from what a human life had been.

I knew he needed to keep up appearances so there wasn't a reason

for Lucifer to ask too many questions. Or worse, order Zepar back to Hell for hundreds of years for slacking off.

We had no clue what Hell would do when word spread that Sitri had sired me. So far, Lucifer hadn't demanded to see me or have my creation investigated, which had been one of Zepar's biggest worries.

I had just settled between the sheets when the door to the bedroom opened and Zepar's exhausted frame lumbered in. He yawned and came over to my side of the bed for a quick peck on the cheek before he headed to the bathroom for a shower.

He left the door open as he undressed and turned the water on to warm. I knew it would be brief, but it was likely the only time I would get to speak with him that didn't include short texts between hours of waiting for a reply.

He was just stepping into the stream of steamy water when I leaned against the doorframe.

"I missed you," he said through his hands while he scrubbed soap over his face. "I promise it isn't always like this."

"I know. Sometimes you're free to stop the world from ending due to ancient prophecies that you helped awaken."

He chuckled and moved on to washing the gel from his dark, wavy hair. The suds trailed down the coiled muscles of his shoulders, chest, stomach, and, finally, his thighs. I was gawking, but he was mine to stare at. Every thick inch of him was only mine, and I would spend the rest of time learning every cell in his body. That sent heat to my core.

I pulled my nightgown over my head and left it on the floor. Then I stepped into the shower in front of him. The chill of my fingers against the warmed skin of his stomach caused him to clench. He looked at me, and water from his hair and nose cascaded down my breasts.

"How badly did you miss me?" I asked, rising to the tips of my toes for our lips to meet.

He groaned into my mouth when my hands circled his erect shaft and slowly worked up and down. His hands traveled over my arms then back down to my ass. He bent down, his lips trailing kisses over my neck and shoulder, then cupped the backs of my thighs and hoisted me up. My legs wrapped around his waist, and his mouth opened to suck on the tip of my nipple. The heat of his tongue circling my stiffened nub drew a moan from my chest.

"Were you a good girl while I was gone? Didn't lure any poor souls to their demise?" he asked, moving to the valley between my breasts.

I had no reason to lie, but a twinge of hesitation caused me to pause long enough for him to look up at me between kisses.

"I mostly finished unpacking my things," I said.

He dipped his face back between my breasts again.

He shifted his hips and pushed my back into the cool shower wall and worked his way back up to my lips. His tongue swept into my eager mouth and explored deeper. The ache between my thighs grew as he coaxed another moan from me with only his mouth on mine. He pulled away and dragged his tongue over the line of my jaw.

"All I thought about today was seeing you with your hands and feet bound together with my ropes." His husky voice echoed in my ear. "I could practically hear you begging for all of me."

I mewed my approval and circled my hips against his belly, enticing him to get to what we both needed.

"Is that what you want too, darling?" His fingers dug into the flesh of my ass. "Do you want me to tie you to the ceiling and have my way with you?"

"Uh-huh." I breathed through my desperation. "I want you to take all of me."

"You look so pretty when you beg for my cock." He lined his swollen head to my needy pussy and pulsed against me.

"Zepar, please." I bucked against him.

"Please, what?" He smiled that wicked smile that could send me over the edge all on its own.

He pinned me to the wall, slowly slipped an inch inside, then stopped. I groaned in frustration. The ache to be filled fully consumed me.

"Do you need me?" he teased.

"Yes." My heavy breathing muted my words.

"Louder, Mara," he almost sang with an amused timbre.

He pulsed again then started to pull away. My body reacted to the loss of pressure with a whine and me clawing at his back.

"Please, Zepar. Oh, fuck. Please." My voice was ragged.

He thrust hard and deep. And delivered blow after blow of his hips. My lungs ached with my sharp inhales.

The mounting pressure in my belly was coming to a peak when he stalled deep inside of me. I squeezed his hips with my thighs, but he didn't budge.

I let out a frustrated but eager moan.

"Do you want me to make you come, darling?" His gravelly words hit the hollow between my neck and shoulder.

The sound that escaped me was a mix between a demand and a plea.

He pushed deeper but stopped.

"Use your words, Mara."

I opened my eyes and looked into his gold ones. The fire behind them was wicked with his demand.

"Fuck, Zepar. I need to come."

I did. The pinnacle of my pleasure was stretched and tearing through me, but I needed the full release. I needed to hit the heights of what he could bring to my body.

I hiccupped as his cock throbbed against every surface surrounding him. I was so close to the edge that the smallest movement could shatter me. His lips over my chest left soft, sweet blazes as he moved down to suck my nipple between his teeth then tugged on the stiff nub.

I bit into my lower lip to restrain my crazed hunger. I pushed my chest into him, silently begging for more. More of his mouth on my skin, more of his tongue, more of his cock.

His gruff, amused groan vibrated over my breast as he broadened his tongue and stroked over my peaked nipple.

"You need it?"

Another lap. The pull behind my navel followed his rhythm.

"You need me?"

Agonizing anticipation pulsed through my nerves.

"I want to give it to you."

A slow trail from the sensitive underside of my breast to the flat of my chest.

"I want to feel you come around my cock. Hear you scream my name. Watch you gasp for air as I fuck you hard and deep." He squeezed and widened his grip on my ass, preparing himself for the infliction of his promises.

"Please." I nodded along with his words. "Fuck me, Zepar."

He searched my face with hooded eyes, giving me one last moment to breathe through my need before he unleashed himself on me.

The first swift thrust sent a jolt of electricity to my toes.

The second deepened his position.

He pulled my lower back away from the wall before he crashed into me over and over through my first, then second orgasm.

As I came down from my high, his hips shuddered and he spilled over. He cursed out my name through gritted teeth then slumped against my chest. My legs unraveled from around him, and we shared a breath as the rest of the world filled our previously lust-fueled vision.

33

SITRI

RITUALS
AND
RINGS

Last night was a new ring of Hell.

Mara had been close enough to touch. Close enough to hold in my arms and never let go.

After Mara left, I thought about going after her. A brief moment of jealousy and need had me thinking of flexing my authority. But she would never be mine that way, not truly.

If I wanted Mara to come to me willingly, I had to find a way to drive a wedge between her and Zepar. And what better way to add pressure to the faults in their relationship than to introduce Mara to the one being in all the planes who'd had Zepar's heart the longest?

I felt the air shift.

The curtains were drawn, but the last bit of the dusk peeked through the bottom edge, casting a golden glow across the floor in the shunted rectangle. Then a body pushed against the gauzy fabric and rippled down. The distorted spill of light lapped at the tips of my toes, followed by a solid fist to my jaw.

I cursed in surprise more than pain. "Nice right hook, Hakamiah."

"What do you want, Sitri?" She folded her arms over her chest, but there was a bit of amusement behind her scowl.

I righted myself and rubbed the point of impact. I didn't hide the grin her outburst brought to my face.

"I can't call upon an old friend? We used to have so much fun torturing our mutual duke." A small dribble of blood slid from my mouth as I spoke from where my tooth punctured my inner cheek.

Zepar may have been a good soldier, but he had never had as much freedom as he thought. Answering to me or our Father through Kami, Zepar's leash had been fairly short. She had been his tethered heavenly half, and I was his prince.

"Is this some kind of booty call?" She watched me carefully, marking each of my steps to the bed.

"Is that what the young ones are calling it these days?" I replied, sitting down on the edge of the bed. I leaned back onto my palms. "No. I have had my fair share of Zepar's sloppy seconds."

A flash of anger crossed her face before she could restrain herself. The muscle in her arm flinched, as she was probably itching to strike me again. She released a short, angry breath, and I knew I had sparked the fuse attached to a fiery bomb.

"Have you spoken to him recently?" I narrowed my eyes at her and watched as her anger gave way to annoyance and maybe a slight bit of pain.

Zepar had betrayed her, broken free of her hold over him to save Mara, his one true love.

"I have better things to do with my existence than answer the call of the Fallen," she said, turning her shoulder and ready to take flight.

"You haven't met his new paramour then? She's quite the being. Demon now, you know? Pure and untrained darkness."

She whipped back around at that. "From the rumors that have made it to Heaven, it would seem she has you to thank for that."

I strained against the pull in my cheek, but the edges of my lips twisted nonetheless. "You flatter me. I couldn't possibly have that much power."

Her eyes traveled down to my body and back up to my cocky grin. The wrinkles at her brow gave the impression of someone who had more information than they would allow to be seen. She was beautiful in the way Ezequiel was: pure sunlight and holy devotion. But what Kami lacked was depth, which Ezequiel had gained during his torturous time on Earth. She never knew loss like the Fallen had, and that naivety was emblazoned in the nearly poreless glow of her perfect skin.

"What do you want, Sitri? Speak quickly, my patience is thin."

"Ah, but your curiosity is as thick as honey, isn't it?"

She didn't voice her response. She didn't have to. The crestfallen look on her face said it all. Those who had stayed and fought for our Father had their own inner battles to wage. They'd been used as weapons against their own in countless shows of holy justice against the beings they were sworn to protect. Being the instruments of His will came with scars that marred them in unspeakable ways.

"I want to right a wrong. Mara was created and I let her walk out of my door into the world. She should be—"

"With you? At your side?" Kami's words sliced through my lie. "You have your strengths, Sitri, but bluffing isn't one of them. You're in love with her, too."

She put it so simply.

Love.

I wasn't in love with Mara. It was more than the concepts of poets or artists. Deeper. Down to the very fragments of our beings. She was a missing piece of my soul that had been torn away and refused to return. I craved Mara in the way the damned craved salvation.

"You've wasted my time and yours. I'm not going to help you win her heart." She wrinkled her nose at the disgusting thought and waited for me to get to my knees and beg for her help, but I wasn't as foolish as I may have sounded.

I knew a lost cause when I saw it. I didn't side with Lucifer in the Fall out of spite or vanity; I had done it for a cause I knew was right: freedom for the Fallen. Kami and the rest of the angels believed they had made the righteous and just choice to protect their hierarchy. Now, they resided in Heaven, watching as mankind advanced and rejected a Father they had slain their own brothers and sisters to honor.

"I suppose you're right," I said, waving my hand in dismissal. "Until we meet again, sister."

With one last disdainful scowl, she dissipated into the ray of light between the curtains. She had been more indifferent to Zepar's new circumstance than I'd thought, but she was right about one thing: bluffing wasn't my attribute. That was another prince's virtue, and even he would see that the odds weren't in my favor.

Stolas, the Prince of Greed, never invested in matters of the heart unless the payout was in the form of power or wealth.

I needed to get dressed. I couldn't traipse down to the club late once again. Ezequiel had been furious at me for missing half our staff meeting last night, and rightly so. In the many decades we had been partners, I'd never let him down, and with as much power as I held over the lesser beings in Los Angeles, I couldn't be seen losing my grip over a woman. Even if I did hold the honor of being the one to have sired her.

It wasn't until I was grabbing my keys off the counter that I felt the unwelcome presence. But by then, her voice was already affronting me like metal in a wood chipper.

"You could have called on me, old friend."

Fuck.

It was the voice that made my eyes roll and my stomach plunge in one fell swoop.

Hahajah, my constraining angel.

"What do you want, Haja?"

"Is that any way to speak to your favorite guardian angel?"

She loved to tease me. I'd made the mistake of taking her to bed several centuries ago, and she loved to remind me that she had worn me down. I was convinced the only reason she hadn't Fallen with the rest of us was cowardice until we slept together.

She relished the power she held in her position among the angels. She was seen as a guiding light to humans and a savior of those who searched for glory and luck. When her blessings weren't bestowed, she wasn't cursed or blamed. The poor fools who prayed to her thanked her for the consideration and hoped they'd be worthy of her gifts next time they needed her.

They were better off selling their souls to me. A pact with a demon, if done skillfully, would result in more than just luck or good fortune.

"You haven't dropped in for half a millennium, Haja. Why are you loitering in my living room now?"

She stood from the corner of the couch where she had been perched and swayed her feline hips toward me. "Your new and vast power has reached all the ears in heaven. Not a single angel isn't talking about the new demon you sired. Playing with the fate of the human race is against the Soul Armistice, my sultry prince."

Her finger followed the buttons of my shirt down to my belt, then outlined the buckle. The threat of her skin on mine created an itch that the claws of a wild animal couldn't scratch.

"I don't take kindly to threats. If you have some holy punishment to bestow, do so or leave."

If there were to be consequences, Lucifer would have administered them weeks ago. Whatever Haja wanted, she was here to get it through blackmail. Plain and simple.

"I could put a stop to the rumors," she started, her doe eyes masking the predator lurking below. "For a favor."

What sort of favor would an angel need from me?

My insides curled in on themselves. I knew full well this one agreement could land me in Hell for eternity. But then there was Mara to consider. If my creation were seen as too dangerous, she could be destroyed and I would be forced to watch—restrained as she was ripped to pieces then wiped from existence.

"Fine," I said through gritted teeth.

Haja jumped back on the balls of her bare feet and clamped her hands. The giggle and toothy grin reminded me of a teenage human who'd just gotten asked on their first date

"Oh, Bitru, you are way more fun when you're backed into a corner."

That name. I hated that name.

The mistranslation from her tongue grated on the nerve in my temple. Not only had it been a butchering of my true name, but she rolled the *r* like a tourist in Spain.

I wanted to heave her out the door.

"You have two minutes before I change my mind and opt to have my head removed from my body." I crossed my arms and leaned my hip on the countertop's edge.

She might have had me in a corner, but I could still retain my dignity, even as she stripped me of my virility.

"Well, about three millennia ago, Lucifer borrowed something from me and I'd like it back."

"You're using the one chip you have against me to settle a sibling dispute?" I cocked my head. This seemed far too easy, which meant she was sending me into a trap.

"You know he's never taken a call from a lesser angel since the Fall, and I need it for a lovely little witch friend of mine."

And there it was. Hahaja was planning on consorting with a witch and using the item as a way to intensify whatever power this witch possessed.

"What is it?"

"A ring of copper. He likely holds it close but it would be too small for him to wear on his hand." She flourished her dainty fingers for effect.

"Consider the task done, and you're now welcome to vacate my kitchen."

My sass elicited a wink before she was gone in the blink of an eye.

Stealing from the King of Hell.

I didn't suspect he would lend the ring to me if Haja thought he would still have it after all this time. He wore jewels and rings of gold often, but I'd never noticed one made of copper. Wherever he kept it, I would have to buy myself time to find it. And I knew who I was going to take with me to make that happen.

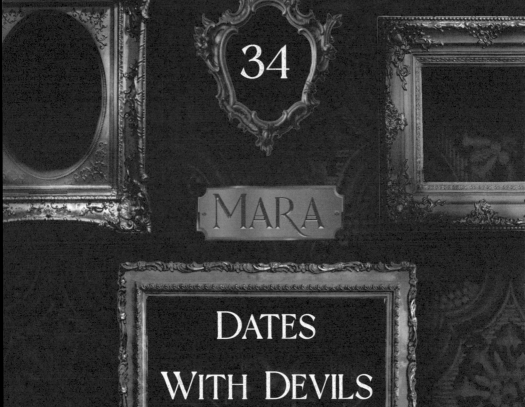

34

· MARA ·

DATES
WITH DEVILS

Zepar's side of the bed was a cold, jumbled mess when I woke up in the morning. I didn't hear him get ready or leave but did have a text from him waiting:

Zepar
Good morning, beautiful. I left a gift for you in the kitchen.

I stretched and opened up the camera app on my phone then took a quick shot of my bare back and chest and sent it as my response. In my head, he was in the middle of a boring meeting and took a quick glance down at his phone and blushed brightly for everyone to see.

It would be a long wait for the actual response, so I pulled on one of his T-shirts and walked downstairs to find what he'd left for me. On the counter was a small black box wrapped in a bright red ribbon. A note card was propped up against it. Not bothering to read the note first, I tore off the ribbon and opened the box.

Inside was a gorgeous diamond-and-ruby bra chain.

I was not expecting this type of jewelry at all. A necklace, earrings, or even a bracelet, sure. But this thing looked like it had been made to frame the curves of my breasts and the large ruby center stone would sit between.

What would I wear this with? It was clearly meant to be seen.

The card glared up at me, unread.

As I ran my fingertips along the cool metal and gems, I read the note:

Darling,

This is part one of your gift. Part two is in our closet.

Be ready for part three. Tonight, 8 pm.

—Zepar

"How sweet. He leaves you love notes."

I jumped out of my skin and spun to see Sitri leaning against the doorframe of the kitchen.

"What in the Hell are you doing here?" I snapped more fiercely than I intended, but sneaking up on me was crossing all of my boundaries.

He smirked his signature crooked, pearly toothed smile. His blue eyes shined with their golden rings in the warm afternoon sun coming through the kitchen windows. It wasn't hard to believe that he was once an angel with a face like that. His white shirt was unbuttoned, and the slight dip of the tattooed script from one collarbone to the other peeked through and made my stomach tumble.

A feeling he basked in, judging by how long it took him to answer.

"I've come to take you on a field trip. An old . . . acquaintance dropped in on me this morning."

He pushed away from the frame and prowled closer until our chests met. His long fingers intertwined with mine, our palms flush together.

A calming warmth washed over me. The connection between us flowed freely. Dangerously.

There was no question that Zepar had my whole heart, but Sitri had a part of my soul—or rather, I had a part of his. It was hard to ignore when we were in the same space and he knew it well. I'd put oceans between us for months to adjust and get the effusive emotions under control.

He hadn't made it easy. There were endless nights of fucking whatever hole he could just to send my heart racing and my body reacting. It wasn't a coincidence that he would be in bed with someone while Zepar and I were making love. The texts to my phone the next morning had praised how he'd never come so hard in all his years than when we were coming together, further confusing and torturing me.

Zepar was patient, but there was only so much he could take. After a few threatening phone calls, Sitri backed off and allowed me time to settle the spate of chaos inside of me.

Last night was the first time we had seen each other in the flesh, and I thought it would be a long time before we saw each other again. The struggle of seeing him in sorrow had hurt me, but the power over him at times shot to my head and filled me with an odd sense of pride in my own potency.

"Where are we going?" I said, my voice small and distracted by the fresh, familiar scent of his cologne.

"Hell, my little dove," he whispered into my cheek. "Time to meet the King of Hell."

The full spectrum of terror and anxiety rolled through my stomach as I ran upstairs to get dressed, Sitri at my heels.

"Why does he want to see me? I thought he didn't care about me?" I said while I looked through my clothes hanging on one side of the massive walk-in closet. Zepar's many suits and loafers lined the opposite wall, the majority of which were a shade of red, maroon, or crimson.

I ran a hand down the one he'd been wearing the night I met him. The memory ran down my spine and nestled low in my belly.

"That isn't the reason we're going. He borrowed something that I am meant to return," he replied lazily. I assumed he was snooping around while I dressed. "Come on, little dove. Perdition awaits."

"What do I wear to meet the Devil? I haven't tried to slip between planes on my own. I won't know how to find my way out of Hell if your mouth gets us into trouble and we have to run for our lives." I pulled a black dress down my body as I sassed him.

"You're meant to be the distraction. Wearing nothing at all would be more helpful than that dress." His unruffled voice came from where he had opened the door just enough to peek inside.

I threw a scowl over my shoulder and slipped some shoes on my feet. It didn't matter what I wore. Lucifer would be more enticed by his past lover locked away in the recesses of my soul. Lilith was snuggly slumbering. She hadn't so much as whispered to me in the dead of night since Sitri's ritual to sire me had been completed. It wasn't the same unawareness of her like when I was human. Our existence was redolent of being on one floor of a house and knowing that someone else lingered on another. But I questioned if that would be the case if Lucifer were knocking on the front door.

I gave myself one last look in the mirror. The garment bag hanging on the back of the door sent a pang of guilt through my chest. The dress Zepar left for me was stunning. It was blood-red and almost transparent with a waist-high slit on one side, and the plunging neckline would reveal the bra chain.

Wherever he planned to take me, he wanted to show me off. I just hoped I would make it back from Sitri's fool's errand in one piece to see Zepar's face when he came home to find me wearing it.

"You have four hours to get me back. Not a minute later," I warned Sitri when he opened the closet door fully.

He answered with a tilt of his head and a playful grin. "Two dates in one day? You're scandalous, Mara."

I rolled my eyes, held out my hand to him, and waited for him to take me to meet the most feared being that had ever existed.

35

SITRI

THE BELLY
OF
THE BEAST

The way Mara trusted me without explanation both broke and mended a piece of me.

How quickly I had gone from wanting to use Hakamiah to tear her from Zepar to using her as a distraction to keep her breathing was baffling even to me.

How had Haja so easily manipulated me into this game of fetch?

Looking at Mara's bewildered face as she took in where we were was the obvious reason for my eager canine behavior. She was worth the humiliation and possible death if our intentions were found out.

The entrance of Lucifer's castle in Hell was daunting. Every wing of the mighty fortress led to unspeakable horrors. With our hands linked, I held her arm close under mine as we entered and walked the long passage that would lead us to Lucifer's office. He would be taking counsel with his kings. He was the supreme ruler, but titles were a way to give those he valued the most more agency over lesser spirits and demons. Paimon would likely be in his presence. His nose rarely exited Lucifer's ass these days.

Our feet clapped in a rhythmic cadence over the polished black stone floor until we reached another large carved-obsidian door. The depiction of Lucifer in dragon form being driven down to Hell by Michael was embedded with gold, precious stones, and obsidian from the deepest pits of Hell. A memorial to the day he'd become an equal to our Father and raised the empire of the Fallen.

Mara's wide eyes roved over the gargantuan mural, the irony not lost on her judging by the expression on her face. She lifted her hand and traced the edge of the hellfire that swallowed up the angels falling from thick, supernal clouds.

"We lost many but gained more than we could have imagined," I said, bringing her gaze to mine.

She didn't speak, but the look in her eyes was something I hadn't seen before.

Empathy? Pity?

I couldn't pin it but didn't have time to decipher it. The door quaked open at the hair-thin seam down the middle of the mural. The flaming sword in Michael's hand separated from the fiery dragon's belly and opened up into the vast chamber beyond.

Lucifer sat on his throne that lorded above a long slab of ancient stone that had been faceted into a table. The seats that lined either side were made of human bone that had been twisted, molded, and sculpted into individual thrones for the other princes, kings, and dukes. All seventy-one were inscribed with our true names and sigils and arranged in order of status.

Mara marked every one we passed with a slight nod of her head, either counting them or looking for familiar names.

Finally, we reached the end of the row of seats. Lucifer watched and waited stoically. He had been silent, and Mara hadn't noticed his presence because once she did, she clutched my arm and pulled me close.

Standing to his right was King Paimon, who cleared his throat to uselessly announce us. "Your Highness, the Prince of Lust and his sired, Mara."

"Mara," Lucifer purred and got to his feet.

Lucifer took Mara in for a long, breathless moment. His tall, soft appearance had been seen as a curse. Our Father's most beautiful son was captured by his own pride and vanity. With a heart full of rage, pain, and jealousy, Lucifer had been cast out, but not before convincing so many of us to follow. How could we have said no to a face like his?

When Mara managed to tear her eyes away from the Devil himself, she looked for guidance from me. The urge to ride in and be her savior once again took hold of me in its iron grasp.

I was a fool for bringing her to see him.

I took a shallow breath and patched together what scraps of myself I had left to lubricate the meeting. Ten minutes was all I needed to find the ring and take Mara far from Hell for good.

"My almighty king. This meeting has been long overdue." I dropped my hand to the small of Mara's back and gave her a light nudge to take a step closer. "Within this new demon is the immortal soul of Lilith. Mara was the last of her bloodline."

Lucifer stepped down from his dais and drew nearer, his hands clasped behind his back as if he were inspecting a work of art for impurities.

"Lilith," Lucifer finally whispered, like he was greeting a long-lost friend.

Lilith would not answer him. Not only had she been running from him for centuries and hiding within the blood of her daughters, she was now locked away deep inside the demonic shell that I had built around Mara. Yet he waited for a response all the same.

It was when he bent down farther to get a better look into Mara's eyes that the thin gold chain around his neck slipped from beneath his shirt and dangled in the air. Hanging from it was a small ring. Blue tarnish crusted its battered surface just as Hahajah had said it would.

"What makes you believe that this creature is welcome here after the atrocities she caused?" Paimon hissed from his place next to a throne he would never sit upon.

"Creature?" Mara snapped to no one in particular, but all eyes locked on her at once.

"The chaos that woman caused was—" Paimon shouted.

"Was not her own." Lucifer bit out every word in a harsh warning to his loyal king. Then he straightened and offered a hand to Mara. "Ignore him. He doesn't like to share my affections with others."

A fiery glint behind Lucifer's soft, blue eyes sent a chill up my spine. Paimon wasn't used to seeing anyone retain our king's interest like Mara had in a matter of moments. He would surely pay for his bold tongue after we departed. Maybe Lucifer would be too tired from punishing Paimon to notice the ring had left in one of our pockets.

The trinket sat on Lucifer's pressed tie, standing out against the black silk like a smudge of filth. It was now or never, and I wasn't going to walk out of Hell knowing that I would never see Mara again once Haja sang to all the wrong angels.

"My king," I said, wrapping my arm across his shoulder and turning him to face Mara again, away from Paimon's prying eyes. "I brought Mara here to show you that your once beloved is safe and well cared for."

Mara's eyes bulged. She couldn't reach Lilith now that she was a demon, but Lucifer didn't have to know that. I gave her a raise of my brow and hoped to all formerly holy men in this realm that she understood the word I was screaming inside of my head.

Lie.

"Mara, will you allow our king to speak through you to Lilith?" I was laying it on thicker than I should have, but several minutes had passed and each one that ticked by was too suspicious.

"Of course," Mara said with that airy, confident voice she had used on me just last night, and it sent a jolt to my core.

She closed her eyes and raised her chin up as if she were summoning a prayer from deep within her. Lucifer and I waited for what would happen next.

"Speak," she said, a lower timbre to her usual supple tone.

"My darling," Lucifer said in relief.

I pressed my hand over his chest. My palm warmed over the ring on the chain—and the one I had slipped off my own finger. A quick fusion of energy and the rings would be switched, but it had to be the right moment. When he was at his most distracted.

"Lucifer."

There was a bell-like chime under Mara's breath, but I knew it couldn't have been Lilith. How was Mara imitating her?

In less than a second, I snapped the necklace holding Haja's ring and zapped mine in its place with the skill of fingers that had strummed over lovers for far too many years. I'd slipped the copper ring onto my pinky just in time for Lucifer to lunge for Mara, his hands cupping her cheeks, and take possession of her lips with his.

Paimon gasped. "Your Highness!"

Mara melted into Lucifer's arms for a moment before pushing him away.

"I'm so sorry." She panted. "She's gone. I'm sorry."

Lucifer stepped back, a broken expression on his face that I hadn't seen in many centuries. He shook it off as quickly as it had come upon him and straightened himself.

"My apologies." He gave her a cocky smile. "She always was hard to hold onto."

A joke at his own expense, but I stayed silent.

It was time to get us out of Hell as quickly as I could.

"Thank you for taking our appointment on such short notice, my

332 | BLOOD ON MY NAME

king. I hope you are sufficiently convinced that Lilith and Mara are safe and will be an asset to your kingdom of Hell." I stepped in close to Mara's side.

"Yes." Lucifer smiled a lethal but gentle smile, not taking his eyes off Mara's face.

"Thank you. I promise not to be any trouble." Her mousy words were tipping the scales.

He wanted her to make trouble. But that would be a conversation for a less dangerous day.

"We must be going." I took the crook of Mara's arm and pulled her back a step to indicate we were, in fact, leaving. "I have several appointments to see at The Deacon."

"Paimon." Lucifer summoned his lap dog without looking back at him. "Be a dear and retrieve your favorite form of torture. Time to remind you of your manners when we are in the presence of esteemed guests."

I watched Paimon's face fall then nodded to Lucifer. "Until our next meeting, my king."

36

MARA

STRAINING
AGAINST
THE THREAD

Sitri pulled me through the dark and empty pocket between time and space. His hands gripped the sensitive flesh at my waist, and the burn of his flesh on mine sent an itch over every inch of my skin.

When my feet hit the ground, I threw myself from him and landed hard on his apartment floor.

"Are you all right?" He tried to haul me back to my feet, only to have me scurry away again.

"Fuck you!"

I turned to storm out of the room only to slam into his chest. My eyes followed the trail of buttons on his shirt to the bare skin and dark ink peeking out beneath.

My gaze met his stormy, dilated pupils. The strength of his deep voice dried my throat, and my stomach sank with a lead-dense force.

"I *am* the Prince of Fuck." He took a loaded pause to relish the fact that he had stunned me speechless. "I know ways to fuck you that would leave you questioning your entire existence beyond spreading your legs for my cock. One night in bed with me, Mara, and I would ruin you."

I couldn't breathe.

One moment, I was furious with him, ready to tear him apart with my bare hands for putting Zepar at risk when I had given up everything to save him. Then he turned that fire into molten glass that filled my core and scorched every foul word I could have called him.

He cocked his head then lowered his face so that we were at eye level. The floor under me fell away as I watched his tongue wet his lip.

My back pressed into something hard and solid; I hoped it was the door and not a wall in his bedroom. The weight of his lean, muscular frame boxed me in, and his hips ground against mine. His hand flattened on my lower back, and it took all my remaining strength to keep myself from allowing him to wedge his leg between mine.

I was still waiting for some sort of rebuttal or refusal to come out of my mouth.

"One word and you'd come until your body was drenched in sweat and shaking and you were seeing Heaven," he whispered, the husky promises going straight to my head. "And once you came back to earth, I'd fuck every single hole on every surface of Zepar's house while you begged me not to stop."

My heart pounded, and I ached in places I knew I shouldn't. I knew his abilities to seduce and spark lust were potent, but he hadn't turned those powers of persuasion onto me.

Were his words amplified or deadened by our connection?

I chose to believe that if I weren't a demon he'd sired, I would've been able to walk away by now. The thought that a human would endure his full puissance and not combust shot chills down my spine. But I'd been human once. All I had to do was hold out and keep the word he was coaxing out of me off my tongue a little longer, then I could walk away.

That was what I wanted, right?

Every scenario ran through my head at once: visions of shared, gasping breaths, his hands cupping my ass as he pounded me into the wall. My flesh broke out in a cold sweat. Images of his fingers trailing up my skirt and pumping in and out of me while I rode his hand to climax.

My thighs were slick and my panties were drenched with each new fantasy that rolled through my consciousness.

"No," I gritted out. My legs squeezed together, searching for relief from the pulse pounding in my pussy. "Please, stop."

"I love the way you beg." He sounded disheartened. Let down that I was still refusing him when I was so obviously begging for him in every other way.

He pulled away and turned his back on me, then stormed out of the living room and disappeared into the hallway. I panted through the painful feeling of loss within my body, as if we'd been merged then ripped apart without warning. His pride may have been bruised, but I was sure I was going to die from the intense buildup and sudden drop.

I didn't wait for my being to adjust. The proximity to his brooding was too much to bear in my vulnerable state. I stepped through the void into my and Zepar's entryway, only to collapse on the cool tiles with a whimper.

The first wave of grief breached my cheeks.

The footsteps thundering down the stairs were too outside of myself to acknowledge.

I shut my eyes tightly and saw fireworks exploding in the dark.

Zepar's muffled voice echoed through the house—or my head. Either way, he sounded more distant than the hands hoisting me into the air felt. With an arm under my knees and another behind my head, Zepar pulled me into his body while I weaned myself off the lust-fueled high Sitri had poisoned me with.

37

SITRI

BROKEN CROWNS

Haja materialized moments after Mara left, somehow sensing the treasure she wanted back had exited Hell and was now within her reach. She pinched it between two fingers and inspected it with the care of a priceless gem. For all intents and purposes, it very well could have been the key to the universe. I didn't ask what the ring would be used for or why Lucifer had felt it was important enough to keep it around his neck. That blindness could bite me in the ass at any time. But for one peaceful moment, I had Haja's silence.

"Good luck to the witch you curse with it," I said into a full glass of whiskey.

"She will do great things thanks to you." Haja glanced up from the ring to give me an appreciative look that felt like ice in my veins.

"I'll keep your obreption if you keep mine."

The pull of the corner of her mouth and darkened eyes told me far more than I needed to know.

She was the wrong kind of pure.

Haja dwelled on the side of our Father's might that drowned millions and spilled the blood of newborns.

Whatever she had planned for her little witch, it would not end well, and if I were not dodging fire of my own, I would pity the witch's soul for ever gaining the attention of my angelic counterpart.

Haja slipped the ring onto one of her dainty fingers and admired it for a moment before bounding on the balls of her bare feet. "Well, I'm off. Don't get into any more trouble, my dark little prince. I have run out of favors to give or ask for."

She left a kiss on my temple. Then she was gone before I could wipe the dot of her saliva away with the back of my hand.

It wouldn't take long to hear whether Lucifer had discovered the ring was missing. Maybe then I would be told why the damned thing was so important. But I wouldn't be volunteering myself as the culprit by any means. I may have been the thief, but I refused to lose my hand for Haja.

There was a knock on the door, probably Ezequiel coming to scold me for missing the staff meeting without telling him. I opened the door and fist bashed into the bridge of my nose.

Blinding pain.

"Fuck!"

"I didn't think you would be this stupid, Sitri," Zepar roared and shoved me on my ass. "You're going to wish Lucifer had banished you to the seventh circle of Hell when I'm done with you."

I staggered to my knees, only to have my breath knocked out of me by Zepar's fist to my stomach.

"Zepar . . . ," I wheezed. The slow trickle of warm fluid from my nose reached my lips and soured my tastebuds.

My body was lifted off the ground by my shirt, and the fabric ripped from my dead weight.

"You have one last shot," I hissed. "Make it count."

He was owed a pound of my flesh for much longer than Mara had been in our lives, and he was cashing in on the only moment I would permit it.

Mara was worth the week of healing from shattered ribs and blackened eyes.

"One last shot?" His breath rushed over my bruised and battered face, the heat of his anger radiating from his entire body. "Mara is meeting with Haniel and binding her powers to cut you off from her until the time comes that she is forced to stand at your side."

My stomach bottomed out as my body hit the floor.

Mara binding her power meant more than just our connection being cut off.

I'd lost her.

I'd pushed too far and underestimated the lengths she would go to keep me out of her orbit for the next thousand years.

"You have to stop her," I pleaded, knowing it was too late.

"*You* could have stopped her. You chose yourself." His voice held no pity or remorse for my situation.

Mara being bound would mean they could live together without the threat of my influence over her.

"I need her, Zepar."

It was the truth, not just the desperation building in my chest.

My eyes were already swollen shut, the black space swirling with pain, and sorrow. The loss of Mara's thread to my soul dwindled with every passing second.

Zepar's footsteps deadened as he moved toward the door. "I could have learned to live with your selfish invasions. To be honest, I'd assumed you were going to weasel your way into her heart and we would end up sharing her. I hated the idea, but it felt inevitable."

The ache in my chest became a sharp pain. The stabbing sensation from his words was his final hit, and he landed it with grace. If it had been any other demon on the opposite end of his wrath, I would have been impressed, maybe even proud.

"I won't thank you for what you did, but I will celebrate your foolishness by loving Mara every single day for the rest of time and never worrying that you'll be in the back of her mind, complicating her thoughts."

With a slam of the door, the last thread of Mara's connection to my soul was snapped.

She was gone.

And I was ruined.

Acknowledgments

Thank you to every reader who has reached out just to say they enjoyed my work. You make every struggle worth it.

A special thanks goes to Booktok for being there when I need to doom-scroll instead of editing.

I'd like to also thank my writing community which has grown since my first book was released. I am thankful for each new friend.

Thank you to my husband for always supporting everything I do, no matter how crazy or time consuming.

Bonus Chapters

Subscribe to K. Elle Morrison's FREE newsletter to receive bonus spicy chapter exploring a **special room in Zepar's home (IYKYK).**

Get an exclusive peek into Sitri's mind with a bonus chapter in his point of view. Get an advanced introduction of his brain to prepare for _Prince Of Lust: The Princes Of Sin_ series coming in May 2023. Available for pre-order now.

Kellemorrison.com

Other titles by K. Elle Morrison

Available now:

Prince Of Lust

Prince Of Greed

Prince Of Sloth

Prince Of Pride
Prince Of Gluttony
Prince Of Envy
Prince Of Wrath

The Black Banners Series:

Under The Black Banners

Dagger Of Ash & Gold

Audiobook:

Blood On My Name

To stay up-to-date on upcoming titles, bonus material, advanced reader opportunities, and so much more visit Kellemorrison.com to join the newsletter!

Bonus Material

For a bonus scene of Mara and Zepar using the playroom, subscribe to K. Elle Morrison's FREE Newsletter!

Kellemorrison.com

Made in United States
Cleveland, OH
01 June 2025

17418981R00190